Clive Egleton brings years of experience in the Intelligence and Counter Espionage fields to his enthralling novels of suspense. Widely regarded as one of Britain's leading thriller writers, he is the author of thirty highly acclaimed novels, most recently CRY HAVOC. He lives in the Isle of Wight.

ASSASSINATION DAY

Ross Frazer. Ex-Intelligence. Ex-Assassin. And dead — or is he? SIS officer Will Landon assumes he has a simple case ahead of him when asked to investigate the sensational autobiography by the mysterious Ross Frazer. It gets complicated when two people associated with the book are murdered. With only silence from his superiors and two bogus intelligence officers on his tail, one girl's recollection of the original document is all Landon has to go on. With time running out, he needs to start making some connections — and fast . . .

Books by Clive Egleton
Published by The House of Ulverscroft:

CLIVE EGLETON

ASSASSINATION DAY

Complete and Unabridged

CHARNWOOD
Leicester

First published in Great Britain in 2004 by
Hodder and Stoughton
a division of Hodder Headline
London

First Charnwood Edition
published 2004
by arrangement with
Hodder and Stoughton
a division of Hodder Headline
London

The moral right of the author has been asserted

British Library CIP Data

Egleton, Clive, 1927 –
    Assassination day.—Large print ed.—
    Charnwood library series
    1. Intelligence officers—Fiction
    2. Suspense fiction 3. Large type books
    I. Title
    823.9'14 [F]

    ISBN 1–84395–332–3

Published by
F. A. Thorpe (Publishing)
Anstey, Leicestershire

Set by Words & Graphics Ltd.
Anstey, Leicestershire
Printed and bound in Great Britain by
T. J. International Ltd., Padstow, Cornwall

This book is printed on acid-free paper

This book is dedicated to the memory of Kenneth Royce Ganley, good friend and fellow author.

1

Despite obtaining a First in Media Studies from Essex, Nancy Wilkins had scarcely been overwhelmed with job offers when she left university. In fact only Horizon, a small commercial radio station in Buckinghamshire, had been willing to take her on. She had spent a year on the front desk answering the phone, making cups of coffee for visiting dignitaries and generally making herself useful. In her spare time, Nancy had learned shorthand and had improved her touch-typing, all in the hope of furthering her career. She had also learned that, as far as the station manager was concerned, she was always going to be the airhead on reception.

She had decided to look for a job in London because her parents owned a semi-detached in Burnt Oak, and it was cheaper to live at home than rent a bedsit, especially when you were short of money. Responding to an advert in the Appointments Section of the *Daily Telegraph*, Nancy had applied for a clerical post in what she believed was the civil service. Her curriculum vitae had led to an interview, along with a considerable number of other hopefuls, at Welbury House, home of British Waterways. At twenty-three she had been the youngest applicant and had looked it. In those days she had been going through her free spirit phase and her taste had been somewhat unconventional for a

1

prospective civil servant. It said a lot for the selection board that her appearance hadn't put them off.

No mention of the Secret Intelligence Service had been made in the advertisement, which had merely stated that the civil service was recruiting clerical support for various government ministries. However, the application forms Nancy Wilkins had been invited to complete before attending the selection board had left her in no doubt that she would be handling classified material and would require the necessary security clearance. It therefore hadn't come as a total surprise to her when she had been requested to sign the Official Secrets Act before reporting to the chief archivist at Vauxhall Cross.

On her first day at the office, she had turned up in trainers, jeans, and a denim jacket over a dark blue cotton shirt. The betting among her fellow clerks had been that she wouldn't last three months. Contrary to expectation, three years later she was still going strong and had advanced from clerical assistant through clerical officer to acting executive officer on the Armed Forces Desk.

It was not a demanding appointment, nor a very exciting one. If somebody at Vauxhall Cross needed to see the security file of a particular serviceman it was Nancy's job to obtain it from the appropriate desk officer at the Ministry of Defence. Like the Security Vetting and Technical Services Division, the Pay Branch, Motor Transport and General Stores Sections, the Armed Forces Desk was part of Roy Kelso's administrative empire. In the nine weeks she had been on the desk Nancy Wilkins had never had reason to seek his advice. There was, of course, a first time for everything, and that morning she had been asked a question she didn't have the authority to answer even if she had been in possession of the facts.

Roy Kelso was a pain; in the opinion of many there was no other word to describe him. He was fifty-seven, tired, disappointed, embittered and small-minded, qualities that were not calculated to endear him to his subordinates. However, Nancy Wilkins could only judge Roy Kelso the way she found him and he had always been pleasant with her.

'So what's the problem, Nancy?' Kelso asked cheerfully when she walked into his office moments after phoning him to ask if he could spare her a few minutes.

'It concerns a conversation I had with Bob Marlow this morning.'

'Who's he?'

'Bob is the desk officer I deal with at the army's Directorate of Security. Anyway, he's a writer in his spare time, and Hodder Headline have published four of his novels. Bob's literary agent is a man called George Ventris.'

'Could you please get to the point, Nancy?' Kelso said, then softened his stricture with a hasty smile.

'The point is, Ventris rang Bob earlier this morning to ask if he knew anybody in 'The Firm' who would be prepared to say whether or not Ross Frazer was an SIS officer.'

3

'What's Ventris after? Some free publicity for his client?'

'Not according to what he said to Bob Marlow. Fact or fiction, Ventris is confident the book will be a runaway bestseller. But should Frazer have been one of ours, he will send us a copy of the typescript so that we can vet it. This will happen before he attempts to interest a publisher.'

'In other words, Ventris will allow us to censor the typescript?'

'Yes.'

'Not good enough, Nancy. We need to see the uncorrected proofs as well. You know why?'

Nancy was about to tell him, then sensed it was a purely rhetorical question and stilled her tongue.

'Because we need to be sure that any material we objected to hadn't been reinstated before the typescript went to the setters,' Kelso added triumphantly.

'Mr Ventris was already planning to do that,' Nancy told him, and watched the smile disappear from his mouth.

'Tell me about this Bob Marlow,' Kelso said tersely. 'Is he sound?'

Sound, meaning loyal, reliable, trustworthy, incorruptible: Nancy wondered how anyone could seriously expect her to make a judgement when Bob Marlow was just a voice on the telephone. Oh, it was Bob and Nancy, which was all very friendly, but they could pass one another in the street without either of them knowing it. There was nothing unusual about that; Rona, the section head who had been running the Armed Forces Desk for the past four years, had never met Bob Marlow either. It was no use trying to phone Rona for advice. She was currently on holiday somewhere in the South of France and her deputy, Elizabeth, had phoned in sick that morning, having tripped over an uneven paving stone and sprained her ankle badly. Both women, however, had spoken highly of Marlow and that was good enough for Nancy.

'I've no reason to doubt Bob's integrity, Mr Kelso.'

'Roy,' he said, and beamed at her. 'I don't believe in standing on my dignity. We're a team, Nancy.'

For the first time she could see why many of her peer group disliked the Assistant Director in charge of the Admin Wing.

'Now what can you tell me about Ross Frazer? Do you have his date and place of birth, for instance?'

Nancy glanced at the memo slip she was holding, then said, 'He was born in Inverness on the twenty-fourth of June 1928. Father, Keith Frazer, who was a regular officer in the Argyll and Sutherland Highlanders, was killed in action in Normandy on the tenth of July 1944. Ross followed his father into the regiment, passing out of Sandhurst with Intake 1 in June 1948. Subsequently he fought with the battalion in Korea, served in Hong Kong, Germany, and then Egypt, where he became the Grade III intelligence staff officer at Headquarters 3 Infantry Division. In March 1955 he joined the

5

Political Office, Middle East Forces and resigned his commission two years later. His service number was 370992.'

'Thank you, Nancy.' Kelso held out his left hand. 'Now, if you give me that slip of paper you're holding, I'll have a word with the Director General and we'll take it from there.'

'If it's any help, The Firm did have a Ross Frazer at one time. There's nothing to show he served in the army before joining us but the date and place of birth are the same.'

'Who told you that?'

'Brian Thomas, Head of the Security Vetting and Technical Services Division. There's no security file for Frazer but his personal details are recorded on the computer data base, plus the word 'Extinct'.'

'Frazer will be seventy in three weeks' time, Nancy; his security file would have been destroyed ages ago. That's what the word 'Extinct' indicates. I'm surprised Brian Thomas didn't tell you.'

'That's funny. He told me Ross Frazer was dead.'

★   ★   ★

In 1990 Victor Hazelwood had been the Grade I intelligence officer in charge of the Russian Desk and without exception his colleagues had believed he had reached his ceiling and would go no further. Then one September morning that year the Assistant Director, Eastern Bloc had collapsed and died in his office and Hazelwood

6

had taken over the department. A mere eighteen months later he had become Deputy Director General on the same day that Sir Stuart Dunglass had assumed the appointment of DG. This had been no coincidence. Behind his back, Dunglass had enjoyed the nickname of 'Jungle Jim', in recognition of the fact that he had spent the greater part of his service in the Far East. Since he had never conducted an intelligence operation in East Europe, he had persuaded a reluctant Foreign and Commonwealth Office that Hazelwood was easily the most experienced officer in that particular field and should be his deputy. The onset of cancer of the prostate had forced Dunglass into early retirement and Hazelwood, who had been keeping the chair warm for him on and off while he had been recovering from the effects of chemotherapy, had eventually been confirmed in post by an extremely reluctant Foreign Secretary.

His meteoric rise had not gone down well with the Admin King. Kelso could not forget that when he had been promoted to assistant director shortly after his thirty-ninth birthday, Hazelwood had merely been a senior intelligence officer in charge of the Russian Desk. Kelso had deluded himself into believing he was destined to go right to the top; ten years later it had dawned on him the selection board had determined he had reached his ceiling and would not be promoted. Consequently Kelso had become a tired, small-minded and deeply embittered man. He had let it been known to all and sundry that he couldn't wait for his fifty-fifth birthday to arrive, when he would be eligible for early retirement.

Kelso had even gone so far as to notify Hazelwood officially of his intention to retire. Then, with severance less than nine months away, the thought of leaving the SIS before he had to had so dismayed him that he had written a letter to Hazelwood expressing the hope that he would be allowed to withdraw his application. That Hazelwood had told him the job was his for as long as he wanted it had only made him feel even more hard done by.

He had sought to restore his injured pride in the pettiest way. Where every other assistant director had to go through the PA if they wished to see the Director General, Kelso would wait until he could see the door into the corridor was open, when he would walk into Hazelwood's office unannounced. This was a situation Dilys Crowther was not prepared to tolerate. When Hazelwood had been knighted in the New Year Honours List of 1997, he wasn't sure who had been the most thrilled, his wife, Alice, or his PA, who addressed him as 'Sir Victor' at every opportunity. That Kelso should regularly deprive her of this pleasure was something Dilys Crowther was determined to put a stop to. In furtherance of this decision she had persuaded Hazelwood to keep the door into the corridor permanently locked, a simple but highly effective solution.

Whenever the communicating door started to open inwards while Dilys Crowther was still announcing his visitor, Hazelwood knew it had to be Roy Kelso.

'Come in, Roy,' he said ironically.

'This will only take a minute,' Kelso informed him, and promptly sat down in one of the armchairs the Property Services Agency issued for the use of visiting dignitaries. 'Have you heard of a Mr Ross Frazer who was born in Inverness on the twenty-fourth of June 1928?'

'Yes, he died some eight or nine years ago from injuries received in a traffic accident.'

'Was he a serving officer in the army before he came to us?'

'I think you had better tell me what this is all about, Roy.'

Kelso had come prepared for just such an invitation. He had all the facts at his fingertips and for once was succinct in relating what Nancy Wilkins had told him.

'Have you spoken to Marlow yet?' Hazelwood asked when he had finished.

Kelso shook his head. 'I thought I ought to have a word with you first. I can't help wondering how long this typescript has been lying around and why it has suddenly come to light. That's assuming the book was written by Ross Frazer, which I don't believe for a moment.'

'Neither do I,' Hazelwood said quietly. 'But that's only a guess until we see the typescript.'

'Are you saying that I should inform Marlow that Frazer was indeed one of ours?' Kelso said in a voice that was patently incredulous.

'I am, and while you're at it, get the address of the literary agency.'

'You obviously know something I don't.'

9

'You're right again, Roy,' Hazelwood said unperturbed. 'I've heard of Ross Frazer; you haven't.'

It was standard procedure to destroy an officer's security file after he or she had reached the age of sixty-six. Even if death occurred prior to that, the document was retained until the deceased's age was deemed to be sixty-six. There were, however, exceptions to every rule. The file on 370992 Captain Ross Frazer, Argyll and Sutherland Highlanders, was one of the seven documents that would be retained for all time because of its content. The seven files retained in perpetuity were held in a twin combination safe positioned in the strongroom next to the office occupied by Roger Benton, Head of the Pacific Basin and Rest of the World department. Both combinations were routinely changed every six months by the DG and his deputy. A slip of paper bearing the combination sequence was then sealed in an envelope with a red star label across the flap. A signature from the appropriate officer covering both the label and the flap was a further security measure. The same procedure applied to the second combination. In the fourteen months that had elapsed since Winston Reid had been appointed Deputy DG, the combinations had been changed three times. Five minutes after Kelso had departed, Hazelwood opened the safe in his office, removed the small brown envelope containing the combination and then went next door but one to see Reid.

'Sorry about this, Winston,' he said, 'but we

10

need to look at the safe in the strongroom.'

'May one ask why?'

'A Captain Ross Frazer, late of the Argyll and Sutherland Highlanders and the SIS, has just written a book.'

'But he died a long time ago.'

'Precisely. While you get your brown envelope out I'll see Roger Benton and sign for the key to the strongroom.'

Benton was the third man in the trinity; Hazelwood knew the first combination, Reid the second, Benton wasn't aware of either sequence of numbers. The beauty of the arrangement lay in the fact that neither the DG nor his deputy could make use of their knowledge without obtaining the key from the Head of the Pacific Basin and Rest of the World. This entailed signing for the key and recording why they needed to get into the strongroom. The record book showed that the key had been signed out eleven times in the last four years for the sole purpose of changing the combination on each occasion.

★   ★   ★

At Corpus Christi, Oxford, George Ventris had studied English under S. L. Masefield and had taken a Double First. After university he had decided to take a couple of years off to see something of the world and had ended up in South Vietnam as a stringer for the *Daily Mail*. He had been in Hue with the US Marines when the massive Tet offensive by the Viet Cong

11

started on 30 January 1968. On the fourth day of the battle Ventris had been in an observation post with a sergeant and two marines in the canal district of Hue when it had been hit by an RPG7 antitank missile. The grenade had passed through the observation slit, narrowly missing the sentry, and had struck the back wall of the bunker. The munition was designed to penetrate thirteen inches of armour and the shaped charge ensured all the explosive energy was directed forward from the point of impact. The sergeant was killed, Ventris and the other two marines suffered from varying degrees of concussion.

Ventris had returned home in May of that year and, arming himself with a number of introductions from S. L. Masefield, had managed to land himself a job as an editorial assistant at Hodder and Stoughton in Warwick Lane. Within two years he had been slotted in as an editor, which proved to be a smart move by the literary director. Ventris was an ultrafast reader and could devour a hundred-thousand-word novel in under five hours while still spotting any flaw there might be in the plot. He was also a creative editor, who knew where the narrative or dialogue needed to be tightened and how this could be done. Frequently he did this himself and then sent his suggestions to the author for approval. Prepublication, he could judge within fifty how many copies a novel would sell, and would fight his corner to ensure his authors were allocated a fair share of the publicity budget. Extremely good at talent spotting, he had discovered and nurtured three writers who had gone on to become bestselling authors.

By 1975 Ventris had earned himself the reputation of being by far and away the best editor in London. He was equally admired by every literary agent who'd ever sold a script to him. His greatest fan was Stephen Warwick, head of Warwick Thompson Associates, who had eventually persuaded him to join the agency in 1976. There was no Thompson: a veteran of the First World War, he had been killed during the Blitz when his house in Wembley, along with seven others, had been demolished by a thousand-pound bomb. Consequently, when Stephen Warwick retired in 1988, Ventris had taken on the agency. However, long before then he had become one of Britain's leading literary agents with a large stable of big-name authors. He also enjoyed a considerable reputation with agents and publishers in New York, which he visited once a year on business.

There had always been a close relationship between Warwick Thompson and the Julian H. Shubert Agency in New York. In fact it had been the agency's Ensley Holsinger who had brought Ventris the Ross Frazer book. Ventris frowned. Correction: she had given him the first fifteen chapters and a résumé of the next twenty-one. Admittedly the second half of the book promised to be even better, but considering Frazer had never appeared in print before, his audacity in seeking a substantial advance before completing the novel was breathtaking. Except there was a good chance it wasn't a novel. When Ventris had

13

read the script last night it had been evident to him that the author had a very detailed knowledge of the SIS, which could only have been acquired as a member of the intelligence community. Now, thanks to Bob Marlow, he knew this to be a fact.

Ventris was beginning to wish it was only a novel; if only half the content were true the book was an explosive mixture and there was no telling how certain people might react if it were published. He also questioned why Frazer had entrusted his typescript to Ensley Holsinger, the most junior associate of the Julian H. Shubert Agency. This was her first trip to London and she was really just showing her face around town. Nobody expected her to make a ground-breaking deal; Julian Shubert had made that clear weeks ago when he'd told Ventris he was sending her over for the experience. And the way the typescript had come into Ensley's possession was freakish. A few hours before Ensley was due to catch American Airlines flight 298 departing JFK at 21.30 hours, a girl she knew who lived in the same apartment building on the same floor had knocked on the door and handed the typescript to her in a neat folder.

The phone rang and Ventris knew the caller was Ensley even before he lifted the receiver and said hello.

'I'm sorry, George,' she said. 'I know I promised I would be no later than six but I've been running behind all afternoon — '

'Where are you now?' he asked, interrupting her.

14

'Transworld in the Uxbridge Road. I'm about to get a cab. They tell me it's only twenty minutes to Red Lion Square.'

'Don't worry, I'll wait for you.' He almost added, 'no matter how long it takes', and cringed at the thought. Ensley was a very attractive young woman but he was more than twice her age and he didn't want it said of him that there was no fool like an old fool.

'Thanks, George.'

'Think nothing of it,' he said, and put the phone down.

Ventris leaned back in the chair, stretched both arms above his head, then got to his feet, walked round the desk and went over to the window. Warwick Thompson occupied the top floor of the terraced house at 21 Red Lion Square, which was almost directly opposite Cassells, the publisher. The view from his office was undoubtedly the best, though ordinarily he didn't have time to admire it. This evening, however, was one of those rare exceptions.

The focal point was the private garden with its neatly manicured lawn, shrubs and trees in the centre of the square. Surrounded by tall iron railings, it was strictly for residents only and you needed a key to unlock the gate. Ventris didn't recognise the couple on the bench seat but then he knew very few people who actually lived in the square. All the same, they didn't look as though they belonged there.

As he watched, the couple stood up and walked along the asphalt path towards the gate where they were momentarily hidden from view by the tall shrubs. When Ventris next saw them they were striding purposefully towards 21 Red Lion Square. All his associates and the office staff had left, so too had the accountants on the second floor, as had the commissioner for oaths on the ground floor. For reasons he couldn't explain, Ventris felt he was being stalked.

2

Ventris stepped back from the window and looked round for some sort of weapon he could use to defend himself should the necessity arise. The only thing to hand was the brass paperknife on the desk, which was roughly eight inches in length. The blade was blunt, so too was the point, but it was strong enough to inflict a nasty wound without snapping in two. Maybe he was letting his imagination run riot but his instinct told him the couple in the park had been watching 21 Red Lion Square and had waited until they were satisfied everybody else had left the building before making their move.

The assumption that they were after him defied all logic. How could the couple be sure everybody had left the premises? Did they know how many people worked in the building? What if he hadn't bothered to wait for Ensley — would they have recognised him if he had departed with the others? Ventris ignored the questions; he hadn't got to where he was today on sound judgement alone. Half his success was down to a willingness to back a hunch. Slipping the paperknife into the waistband of his trousers, Ventris opened the door to his office and went out on to the landing.

The terraced house was unnaturally silent, then a floor-board creaked and he knew they were in the hall. He listened for the sound of their footstep on the staircase but it was soon evident that the intruders were testing each step before putting their full weight on it. Their stealth reinforced a growing conviction that they intended to harm him in some way.

Ventris heard the double click of a lock as one of them tried the door to the firm of accountants on the floor below. Not much longer now, he thought, and stepped away from the banisters to press his back against the inside wall.

'Can I help you?' he said in a loud voice.

'Mr Ventris?' a woman asked.

'That's me.'

'I'm Detective Sergeant Nicholson, Special Branch,' the woman told him as she came into view. 'And this is Detective Constable Leach,' she added, jerking a thumb over her shoulder.

The detective sergeant was wearing a navy-blue blazer with large gilt buttons over a knee-length coffee-coloured silk dress patterned with circular white orbs about the size of golf balls. She had dark brown hair drawn back in a ponytail, which made her face look hard. Ventris thought she was in her mid-thirties. Her companion was thickset with broad shoulders tapering to a narrow waist. The sports jacket he was wearing was tight across the chest.

'Do you have some means of identification, Sergeant?' Ventris asked politely.

'I certainly do.' Nicholson opened her shoulder bag, took out a wallet and flipped it open to show him what appeared to be a warrant card.

'So what can I do for you?' Ventris enquired.

'It's a confidential matter, sir. Perhaps we can go into your office where it's more private.'

'Everybody else has gone home, as I'm sure you know, Sergeant.'

'Nevertheless I don't think we should discuss our business on the landing.'

'Neither do I,' Leach said. Reaching behind Nicholson he opened the door to the office and ushered her inside.

'Where the hell do you think you're going?' Ventris demanded angrily.

'This is your office, isn't it, squire?'

His hostile attitude and sneering tone of voice enraged Ventris. Leach and his kind might be able to get away with murder policing a crime-ridden- run-down housing estate in North London, but not in this neighbourhood. Ventris followed Sergeant Nicholson into his own office and almost stumbled into her when Leach gave him a none-too-gentle shove. Nothing would have given Ventris greater pleasure than to spin round and lash out. Two things held him back: the presentiment that this was just what the detective constable hoped he would do; and the fact that at fifty-four he would be pitting himself against a man who was his junior by at least twenty years and was far heavier and much stronger.

Ventris sat down at the desk. 'Tell me, Sergeant Nicholson,' he said, his voice betraying a certain nervousness, 'do you always allow your DC to harass law-abiding citizens?'

'I'm not with you, sir,' Nicholson said politely.

'Constable Leach pushed me in the back.'

19

'I'm afraid I didn't see him do that.'

'He's lying,' Leach told her.

'You see what I mean?' Ventris said, and spread his hands. The Sony he used to dictate letters for the audio typist was by the telephone and he managed surreptitiously to set the tape running.

'You have just made a very serious allegation against my colleague, Mr Ventris, without, I may say, a shred of proof. If I were Detective Constable Leach, I'd be pretty angry too.'

'So that's how it is.'

'Not quite. We have reason to believe you are in possession of classified information, the property of Her Majesty's Government.'

'I'm a literary agent, what would I want with secret papers? They would be of no use to me; no publisher would touch such stuff with a barge pole.'

'The information is contained in what is said to be a novel written by Ross Frazer.'

'I'm afraid you have been given a bum steer. Ross Frazer is not one of my clients.'

When it came to getting the most favourable terms he could for one of his authors there was nobody better at poker than Ventris when he played his cards close to his chest.

Leach perched one buttock on the edge of the desk and leaned over Ventris, 'Frazer isn't anybody's client. He got himself stiffed nine years ago.'

'Stiffed?' Ventris repeated blankly.

'He lay down in the middle of the road and, surprise, surprise, a truck ran over him.' Leach

20

grinned. 'It was a dark night,' he added, and sniggered.

'You make it sound as though it wasn't an accident, Mr Leach.'

'It wasn't and I'm a detective constable.'

'Whatever. The fact is I'm not representing an author called Ross Frazer.'

'We know you are,' Nicholson said firmly. 'The typescript was delivered to you yesterday afternoon by a courier from New York.'

'I can assure you all we received from New York yesterday were contracts from Doubleday and St Martin's Press forwarded by our associates, Julian H. Shubert.'

'The script was delivered by a young woman.'

'Well, I'm sorry, Sergeant Nicholson, but you've been misinformed.'

'Then you won't mind if we look inside that safe you have behind your desk?'

'Not a bit. I assume you have a search warrant, Sergeant?'

'I can always get one, sir.'

He wondered why the Special Branch officers had tried to pull a fast one when their information was so accurate. If he could discover through Bob Marlow that Frazer had been a SIS agent he was damned sure Nicholson had been apprised of the fact. Although no expert, he couldn't believe a magistrate would refuse them a search warrant.

'Did you hear what I said, Mr Ventris?'

'Yes, indeed. Come back when you have a warrant signed by a magistrate.'

Ventris pushed his chair back and stood up.

21

He had had enough of the two Special Branch officers, especially Leach, and it was time he sent them packing.

'I'd like you to leave now,' he said.

'Hark at him,' Leach sneered. 'Who does he think he is?'

'Get your arse off my desk.'

Leach stood up, turned to face Ventris and swept the filing tray, Sony recorder, telephone and glass ashtray on to the floor. Before Ventris knew what was happening, the Special Branch officer grabbed hold of his shirt front and punched him twice in the face, drawing blood from his nose and mouth. Dazed by the blows, he staggered back, cannoned into the chair and, tipping it over, landed face down on the carpet. He was still trying to come to terms with the fact that he had been attacked by a police officer when Nicholson told her subordinate to lash his wrists behind him with plastic tape. As they rolled him over on to his back, he kicked out and caught Nicholson just below the kneecap.

'You bastard,' she yelled in pain. 'You fucking bastard.'

Leach clenched a fist and used it like a hammer to smash blow after blow into the pit of Ventris' stomach. Ventris gasped for air, swallowed a lot of blood in the process and choked on it. Barely conscious, he was physically unable to kick Nicholson off when she pinioned both legs under her body while she lashed his ankles together with plastic binding tape, which she had produced from her shoulder bag.

Leach was going through the pockets of

Ventris' single-breasted jacket, turning them inside out, looking for the key to the safe. Ventris would have told him where to find it but he no longer had the power of speech because Nicholson was busy stuffing his mouth with a wad of Kleenex tissues. Leach was now burrowing into the agent's trouser pockets, helping himself to the loose change and the car keys to the BMW 5 Series. Inevitably he found the makeshift weapon Ventris had tucked into the waistband of his trousers.

'Now, there's a funny place to keep a paperknife,' he said, and showed it to Nicholson.

'What about the key to the safe?'

'It's not on him.'

'Try the desk and put the phone back where it belongs, while you're at it.'

Leach replaced the transceiver, then stood up and put the phone down on the desk before nudging Ventris in the ribs with his foot.

'Is that where you keep the key, arsehole. In the desk? Nod your head if you do.'

Ventris did so. It was pointless to stretch things out because sooner or later they would find the key without any help from him. Right now all he wanted was to see the back of them as soon as possible.

From her shoulder bag Nicholson produced a reel of adhesive brown paper roughly two inches wide. Taping the free end behind his right ear she wound the adhesive round and round his head, sealing his mouth under three layers. It wasn't enough for Nicholson merely to gag him, she continued to unwind the adhesive paper and

23

methodically wrapped it over his nose and ears. The last thing Ventris saw before she masked his eyes was the lascivious smile on her lips. He had never felt so frightened in his life as he did at that moment.

Leach went through the drawers in the desk one by one, emptying the contents on to the floor until he found the key.

'Got it,' he announced triumphantly, then stepped over Ventris and unlocked the safe.

'What's in there?' Nicholson asked.

'One file cover inscribed with eight possible titles. The typescript inside comprises fifteen chapters and a synopsis of the remainder. The author is Ross Frazer.'

'OK. Find a Jiffy bag for the typescript and close up the safe.'

'Thanks for teaching me to suck eggs,' Leach said acidly. 'I was going to do that anyway.'

'Good. I think I know who brought the typescript over from New York. According to his appointments diary, Mr Ventris had a meeting with a Ms Ensley Holsinger of the Julian H. Shubert Agency at three o'clock yesterday afternoon.'

'And?'

'She's staying at the Dorchester.'

'I think we should look her up,' Leach said.

'So do I. Let's go.'

Ventris lay still and didn't make a move until he was sure they had both left his office. Nicholson and Leach had talked a lot too freely and that boded ill for him because he knew too much. The woman who claimed to be Detective

Sergeant Nicholson had taken measures to ensure he would eventually suffocate. With two layers of tape over his nose, breathing would have been impossible had he not managed to create a small air hole by distorting his facial muscles as she mummified him. What he had to do was free his wrists without overexerting himself and becoming breathless as a result. At the back of his mind was the fear that if he started fighting to get his breath he might seal the air vent.

There was nothing to betray the presence of another person but suddenly Ventris knew he was no longer alone. He was conscious of somebody crouching over him, then a pointed instrument probed the right eardrum.

Leach said, 'You're a sneaky bastard,' and hammered the paperknife upwards through the ear into the brain.

⋆　⋆　⋆

Ensley Holsinger checked her wristwatch for the umpteenth time. The editor at Transworld who had told her it was only twenty minutes to Red Lion Square had either been wildly optimistic or downright deceitful. She figured it was the latter on the grounds of the inordinate amount of time he had spent trying to make a date with her. She might have arranged something had he looked her in the eye once in a while instead of concentrating on her legs from the minute she had walked into his office to the moment she had got up to leave.

25

Five to seven. Ensley opened her handbag, took out the mobile and tried to contact George Ventris. The number rang out but he didn't answer the phone and she began to wonder if he had given up on her and gone home. On reflection Ensley decided he wouldn't do a thing like that because George was too much of a gentleman. Besides, when she had delivered the typescript to him yesterday afternoon she had noticed he had an answerphone, and she knew, having missed him once or twice when ringing from New York, that this always switched on after office hours.

As if endowed with extrasensory perception the cab driver told her they were approaching High Holborn and would be outside 21 Red Lion Square inside a couple of minutes. Ensley didn't believe him until she spotted the Underground station and recalled taking the next but one turning on the left yesterday afternoon.

The square was an oasis of calm; the noise of the traffic on Theobald's Road, High Holborn and Southampton Row to the north, south and west was no more than a distant hum. Nobody was out and about; furthermore, every front door within sight was closed.

'Doesn't look as if anybody is at home,' the cab driver observed. 'Do you want me to wait while you find out?'

'If you wouldn't mind.'

Ensley crossed the pavement, tried the front door and found it wasn't locked. She turned about, waved the cab driver goodbye and

26

stepped into the hall as he drove off.

Ensley closed the street door behind her. The building was unnaturally still; there were no settlement noises, no inexplicable creaks and groans. Unnerved by the brooding silence, she walked on tiptoe up the first two flights and on past the firm of accountants. A step, creaking underfoot, made her flinch and she called out to Ventris in a voice that sounded cracked. There was no answer but on reaching the top landing she could see the door to his office was slightly ajar. She pushed it open and walked inside, then suddenly froze.

The body was lying on the floor, its feet pointing in the direction of the office safe, its head surrounded by a filing tray, a Sony recorder, a glass ashtray, several cigar stubs and the contents of every drawer in the desk. Even though the features were masked by yards and yards of adhesive brown paper, she knew it had to be George Ventris. His legs had been lashed together about the ankles and his wrists had obviously been pinioned behind his back. It wasn't until Ensley moved nearer the body that she noticed there was a metal shaft protruding from his right ear. Some kind of liquid had seeped through the brown paper, trickled down the neck and stained the shirt collar. Then it dawned on her that the greyish matter she was looking at had stemmed from the brain.

Completely unnerved, Ensley backed away from the dead man, bumped into the wall behind her and sank down on to her haunches.

Like a robot programmed to carry out a simple task, she unzipped her bag, took out a packet of Marlboro and with some difficulty managed to light a cigarette. It was a good five minutes before her hand stopped shaking. Even then she was still in a daze and couldn't remember how to get in touch with the emergency services. The information was there in her guidebook but she had left that in her hotel room.

Her eyes fell on the phone book, which had ended up on the floor when the killer had emptied the drawers. She pushed herself forward on to hands and knees, retrieved the phone book and, righting the upturned ashtray, stubbed out the cigarette. The first page of the directory told her exactly what to do. Once connected to the police operator, the rest was child's play. Less than five minutes after making the 999 call, two uniformed police constables in a prowl car arrived at 21 Red Lion Square. They were shortly followed by scene of crime officers, the duty pathologist and detectives from E District.

★   ★   ★

From Red Lion Square, Nicholson and Leach had walked to Holborn Underground station where they had caught a Central Line train to Marble Arch, four stops down the westbound track. Emerging on to Oxford Street, they then made their way down Park Lane to the Dorchester. Long before they moved purposefully through the hotel lobby towards Reception they had agreed that Nicholson should do the talking.

'I'm Detective Sergeant Nicholson,' she informed the first available desk clerk, and produced her warrant card for inspection. 'My colleague is Detective Constable Leach. We believe you have a Miss Ensley Holsinger staying at the hotel. She would have arrived yesterday morning from New York.'

The desk clerk gazed at the warrant card, clearly puzzled. 'We are very conscious of our guests' right to privacy,' he began, then cleared his throat. 'I think I need to seek advice.'

'Perhaps it would be best if I asked the house manager?' Nicholson suggested tactfully.

'Yes, I believe Mr Jacklin can help us. If you wouldn't mind waiting a minute, I'll go and fetch him.'

'Thank you.' Nicholson smiled. 'By the way, what is your name?'

'Lawrence, madam.' The desk clerk dipped his head before moving away.

'You're going up in the world,' Leach observed when Lawrence was safely out of earshot. 'Madam instead of sergeant — that's classy.'

'He was just being polite.'

'Or maybe your warrant card didn't impress him like it should have done.'

'What are you implying?'

'I think this Lawrence knows a fake when he sees one.'

'For a man who is reputed to be a hard nose, you're awful short of balls, Leach.'

'You're wrong, lady. I can sense danger. I

mean, who is this guy Jacklin? For all we know he could be the house detective, head of security or whatever fancy name the Dorchester has for him.'

'Keep your voice down,' Nicholson hissed.

'You just want to shut me up. But you hear this, if the desk clerk doesn't return with his friend Jacklin in the next two minutes, I'm out of here. And if you've any sense, you'll come with me. In case you have forgotten, this Jiffy bag I'm holding contains a hundred and twenty-six pages of highly classified material. We would have a hard time explaining that away to the boys in blue.'

'You can stop worrying, here they come.'

From an office behind the reception counter Lawrence reappeared with a slightly built, round-shouldered man who had thinning blond hair. Once more, Nicholson produced her warrant card and introduced them both. The only difference this time was that she let it be known they were with Special Branch.

'And you wish to know if Miss Ensley Holsinger from New York is staying at the hotel?' Jacklin said, cutting in.

'Yes.'

'May one ask why?'

'I'm afraid we are restricted by the Official Secrets Act. However, I can tell you the FBI believe Miss Holsinger is in possession of Top Secret information which she may try to sell in this country under the guise of a novel. She is, in fact, a literary agent.'

'Really. That is interesting,' Jacklin said,

making it obvious he expected further enlighten-
ment before he deigned to tell her what she
wanted to know.

'The Bureau regards her as an innocent at
large,' Nicholson continued. 'The author Miss
Holsinger is presumably representing went to
great lengths to ensure his anonymity and it is
more than likely she has no idea that she is being
used as a courier.'

'And I believe you told Lawrence she arrived
yesterday morning?'

'Yes. The FBI was slow to alert us.'

'They told you Miss Holsinger was staying at
the Dorchester?'

'No, they gave us a list of the most popular
hotels with Americans visiting London. The
Dorchester is the first hotel we've visited. Like I
said, the FBI was anything but quick off the
mark. We don't intend to follow their example.'

'Miss Holsinger is staying here, her room
number is 408,' Jacklin said abruptly.

'And she is staying until when?' Nicholson
asked.

'Friday morning.'

'Thank you.'

'Is there anything we should be doing between
now and then?'

The apparent eagerness to co-operate with the
police was largely nullified by Jacklin's tone of
voice. To Nicholson it was evident he hoped she
wouldn't involve the hotel in whatever action was
deemed necessary.

'You're not required to do anything,' she
assured Jacklin. 'If we are ordered to detain Miss

Holsinger, her arrest will not be effected inside the hotel. We shall, of course, be keeping her under surveillance but I guarantee none of the guests or any of the staff will be aware of our presence in the lobby. We hope all your staff will be equally discreet.'

'You may depend on it,' Jacklin said.

Nicholson thanked him again, signalled Leach to follow her and, moving away from the counter, crossed the lobby and sat down in one of the easy chairs spaced around a small low table. There was nothing haphazard about her choice. From where she sat it was possible to watch both the hotel forecourt and the reception counter.

'What happens now?' Leach asked, joining her.

'We wait.'

Barely ten minutes later a police car pulled up outside the hotel entrance and a young woman wearing a short linen skirt with a matching dark green blazer alighted from the vehicle and walked into the lobby. Glossy dark brown hair, around five feet eight in low heels, 36-inch bust, trim waist, mouthwatering legs: Leach followed her lasciviously with his eyes as she moved towards the lifts.

'Did you ever see such a great-looking arse,' he breathed.

Nicholson ignored the comment. In all probability the girl was Ensley Holsinger and it figured she must have gone to Warwick Thompson Associates and had found Ventris lying dead on the floor of his office. Why else

32

would she have returned to the Dorchester in a police car?

'That's got to be Holsinger,' Leach murmured as if reading her thoughts.

'We need to be sure.' Nicholson stood up. 'If I'm not back inside four minutes get up and go.'

'Where are you off to then?'

'I told you, we need to be sure she is the one.'

Without appearing to be in a hurry, Nicholson moved purposefully towards the lifts and managed to squeeze into the same car as her quarry a second or two before the doors closed. When several people alighted at the third floor, she eased herself into a corner to ensure the American girl left the car before she did.

No two ways about it, the girl was unnaturally pale and looked shaken, which was another reason for believing she had to be Ensley Holsinger. Nevertheless, Nicholson still followed her when she got out at the next floor. Presumption became an established fact when the quarry let herself into room 408. With a murmured 'good evening' to her, Nicholson coolly walked on to the end of the corridor, turned the corner and used the staircase to reach the floor below. She then took the lift down to the lobby. As she moved towards the forecourt, Leach hurried to meet her and caught the unwelcome attention of Lawrence, the desk clerk. Although a minor hiccup, it was enough to worry Nicholson.

3

Before she was transferred to the Armed Forces Desk, Nancy Wilkins had worked for Will Landon, a Grade II intelligence officer in the East European Department, who also happened to be the SIS representative on the Combined Anti-Terrorist Organisation, better known as CATO. Landon was nearer her age than any other middle-ranking officer; at thirty-one he was just five years older than herself. He was six foot three and built like a heavyweight minus the scar tissue round the eyes normally associated with prizefighters. He had light brown hair with an auburn tinge and plain features that could be described as homely, but not by Nancy Wilkins. 'Strong' was her preferred adjective, meaning he was the sort of man who would never let you down or betray a confidence. And right now she needed to confide in someone she could trust implicitly.

Absenting herself from the Armed Forces Desk, Nancy took the first available lift up to the fourth floor and walked along the corridor to Will Landon's office. The room offered a commanding view of the railtracks from Vauxhall to Queenstown Road, Battersea, which was not the most enthralling vista in the world. Landon, however, was not in a position to pass judgement one way or the other thanks to IDAS, the Intelligence Data Access System, which the previous Deputy DG but one had introduced three years ago. Since it was a stand-alone system, all the terminals were located within Vauxhall Cross and were crypto-protected, which meant the system could not be accessed by an outsider. As a further safeguard, all visual display units had to be positioned out of sight of any window. Consequently Landon's unit was tucked away on a desk in the near corner of the room where it was screened by the door.

Nancy tapped on the open door and walked into the office to ask Landon if she could have a word with him. 'I'm badly in need of some advice,' she added.

'To do with your present appointment?' Landon asked.

'Yes.'

'You ought to consult Roy Kelso; after all, the Armed Forces Desk is part of his empire.'

'I'm afraid he wouldn't want to know.'

'In that case perhaps you'd better tell me what's troubling you. But close the door first.'

'Yes, of course.'

'So what is it, Nancy? Do you want to be moved to another job?'

'Not just yet,' Nancy said, then told him about the phone call she'd received from Bob Marlow yesterday morning concerning a Mr Ross Frazer and how the SIS came to be involved in what amounted to a literary enterprise. She tried to be as concise as possible but there was no way of truncating the information she needed to impart. 'I had another phone call from Bob Marlow ten minutes ago,' Nancy continued. 'He asked me if

I had heard about the murder in Red Lion Square yesterday evening. When I told Bob I hadn't paid much attention to the headlines on Kiss before I left for the office, he got very uptight and accused me of playing mind games with him. After he finally calmed down I learned the victim was George Ventris, head of Warwick Thompson Associates, the literary agency. Their office is in Red Lion Square but I didn't know that at the time.'

'And you think this murder is in some way connected with the book written by Ross Frazer?'

'Yes. What distresses me is that after I had briefed Mr Kelso he rang Bob Marlow to confirm that Ross Frazer had been one of ours. He also asked him for the business address of Warwick Thompson Associates.'

'That rather puts us in the spotlight,' Landon mused.

'It certainly doesn't look good and I don't know what I should do.'

'The answer is absolutely nothing,' Landon told her. 'Until this morning you didn't know the business address of Warwick Thompson Associates but Roy Kelso did, and you can bet he caught the news headlines and made the connection. It's up to him how he follows through, Nancy. OK?'

'Yes. Thanks for the advice.'

'Don't mention it.'

She opened the door and had one foot in the corridor when Landon told her how much he liked the outfit she was wearing. She could feel the colour suffusing her face and was thankful he couldn't see it.

* * *

The officer leading the Ventris murder investigation was Detective Chief Inspector Bernard Ogden from the Holborn divisional station on Theobald's Road. There were more senior detectives in E District but he had acted on the initial report from the uniformed officers who had responded to the 999 call, and his superintendent had left him in charge of the investigation.

The Ventris case would be his third murder inquiry. As a young, up-and-coming detective sergeant in Z District, he had run the crime index on what became known as the commuter-belt killer because the bodies of all four of his female victims had been found within a mile of the railway stations at Epsom, Sutton, Mitcham and South Croydon. Seven years later, as a newly promoted inspector serving in C District, he had been a member of the team that had investigated the raid on the Fargo Deposit Box Company in Knightsbridge, during which two security guards had been shot dead after they had been bound and gagged.

Ventris too had been murdered when he had been helpless to defend himself but there the similarity with the Fargo robbery ended. The latter crime had been an inside job and the two guards had been executed because one of them had recognised the voice of a former employee of

37

the security firm — at least that had been the supposition. Apart from a lot of typescripts from hopeful would-be authors and a small amount of petty cash, there had been nothing worth stealing at Warwick Thompson Associates. According to Ensley Holsinger, she had spoken on the phone to George Ventris at ten past six and had arrived at his office at three minutes to seven. Her 999 call from 21 Red Lion Square had been timed at four minutes past seven. The earlier phone call was also verifiable because she had been delayed by a Mr Hugh Dalton, an editor at Transworld, and she had used his telephone to ring Ventris. Even without the post-mortem they could fix the time of death within fifty-four minutes and you couldn't ask for better than that.

Ensley Holsinger had told Ogden she hadn't been greatly surprised to find the street door wasn't locked when she arrived to keep her appointment with Ventris because he had said he would wait for her. She had gone to the agency to hear what Ventris thought of the first fifteen chapters of a potential bestseller, which he had read the previous evening. However, Ms Holsinger had no idea what he had done with the typescript, which she had left with him on Tuesday afternoon. It certainly hadn't been on his desk when she had arrived.

Last night the chief inspector had taken her story on trust; this morning he had sent a detective to interview Hugh Dalton at Transworld in order to verify her statement and learn the purpose of her visit. The rest of the murder

38

team had been tasked to interview the other literary agents at Warwick Thompson Associates and cover all the people who lived or worked in Red Lion Square whom they had missed last night. Ogden hoped the other literary agents might be able to supply a motive for the killing or disclose the names of any enemies Ventris may have had. The detectives had also been briefed to ask office workers and residents alike if they had observed anybody behaving suspiciously in the neighbourhood.

Although Ogden was in charge of the investigation, he was still required to keep his superintendent fully informed concerning the action he was taking. On this, the first morning of the investigation, he had precious little to tell his superintendent and what he did have was disappointing. The paperknife had yielded nothing; the only prints found on the hilt had belonged to the deceased.

After briefing the superintendent, he checked with the civilian clerk manning the incident room to see if there had been any messages and learned that a Mr Pearson, Head of Special Services at the Forensic Science Laboratory wanted to have a word with him.

'It's about the Sony recorder SOCO retrieved from 21 Lion Square,' Pearson said.

'Sounds interesting.'

'It is. There were several letters on the tape dictated by the deceased, then suddenly there is this three-way conversation between Ventris, Detective Constable Leach and Sergeant Nicholson, a woman police officer. Sergeant Nicholson accused Ventris of possessing classified material. According to her the information is contained in a novel written by Ross Frazer. Ventris claimed Frazer was not one of his clients and Leach said he wasn't anybody's client because he had been killed nine years ago. In fact Leach implied he had been murdered. Thereafter the situation gets nastier and nastier. Towards the end, Leach sweeps everything off the desk and lays into Ventris.'

'I'd like to hear the tape,' Ogden said.

'You can. An enhanced copy is on the way to you now.'

'What do you mean, enhanced? Are you saying you have doctored the tape, Mr Pearson?'

'The quality became degraded after the Sony recorder was swept on to the floor. At times their conversation is almost inaudible, that's why we had to buff it up. Even now the quality is poor, so I had the conversation transcribed as a guide.'

'Thanks.'

'That's OK, it's all part of the job.' Pearson cleared his throat. 'I can't believe Nicholson and Leach are police officers,' he added, and put the phone down.

The enhanced tape and transcript was delivered by special dispatch service fifteen minutes later. As soon as Ogden heard the first exchange he knew there could be no question of him joining the rest of the team in Red Lion Square. He had been looking for a possible motive; now, incredible as it seemed, a man had been brutally done to death for the sake of an incomplete novel containing highly classified

40

information. To have seized the typescript hadn't been enough for Nicholson and Leach; they wanted the courier who had brought it to Ventris. The recording was definitely substandard at that point but according to the transcript they had discovered where Ensley Holsinger was staying and had decided to look her up.

Judging by what Leach had done to Ventris, the American girl was in grave danger. Ogden picked up the phone, rang the Dorchester and asked the hotel operator to put him through to room 408. There was no reply but it was twenty-five after eleven and he told himself that if Ensley Holsinger had come to any harm, the hotel would have informed the police. He tried Warwick Thompson Associates but nobody there knew what her programme was for today.

Suddenly he began to feel out of his depth. They had to contact Ensley Holsinger and instruct her to stay put until the police arrived. At the same time, with Special Branch, MI5 and maybe one or more government ministries involved, it was essential somebody at assistant commissioner level was fully briefed. Ogden got hold of two civilian clerks assigned to the investigation and told them to ring every publisher in town and find out which one was expecting to see Ensley Holsinger, then went to see his superintendent.

* * *

Roy Kelso was not the only person who had been promoted to assistant director shortly after

41

his thirty-ninth birthday. That Peter Ashton should have emulated this feat was, for most people, nothing short of a miracle. His detractors in the SIS and a good many officials in the Foreign and Commonwealth Office, plus a number of senior civil servants in the Ministry of Defence regarded him as a loose cannon. His admirers saw him as a brilliant field agent who had pulled off more coups than any other intelligence officer in the last fifty years. All of them had been delighted when Ashton had joined the top table. Nobody, however, expected him to last more than nine months before requesting permission to revert to his former role or resigning from The Firm.

So far Ashton had confounded them all. As of that afternoon he had been in post for one year, five months and four days. The reasons for his uncharacteristic behaviour were not hard to find. Thanks to Victor Hazelwood, who had put him in harm's way far too often, he had lost all anonymity. In the last ten years he had spent seventy-eight days in solitary confinement in Moscow's Lefortovo Prison and had survived three separate attempts to assassinate him in Russia, the United States and more recently in Lincoln. In addition he had taken a 6.35mm bullet from a Walther PPK semiautomatic pistol in the left shoulder immediately below the collarbone, which still occasionally troubled him on a cold winter's day. But the principal reason why he had buckled down to his new appointment had been the knowledge that in the not-too-distant past he had put his wife and family in danger. It had happened only the once but that had been once too often.

However, when push came to shove Ashton wasn't all that far removed from the sharp end. With the twofold purpose of justifying the re-establishment of the East European Department, and to bamboozle the Treasury, the SIS element of Military Operations (Special Projects) at the MoD was assigned to Ashton. His department was also required to provide the SIS representative at the weekly meeting of the Combined Anti-Terrorist Organisation. Tentative as these links were, Hazelwood had already used them once to involve Ashton's department in a quasi anti-terrorist role.

When Dilys Crowther, PA to the Director General, rang to say that Sir Victor wished to see him, Ashton suspected he was about to do so again.

The hunch was based on the fact that there had been no fresh developments in his bailiwick since the résumé he had given during the daily briefing. Commonly known as morning prayers, the meeting was chaired by the DG and attended by the Deputy DG and all heads of departments at 08.30 hours.

Hazelwood had made his reputation as a thruster, a man who made things happen. He did not like it when he was unable to influence events and the number of half-smoked Burma cheroots in the cut-down brass shellcase, which served as an ashtray, suggested he was having a bad day. The only surprise was the indirect way Hazelwood approached the problem.

43

'What time did you leave home this morning, Peter?' he asked out of the blue.

Sensing this was likely to be a long session, Ashton sat down in one of the two leather armchairs provided for visitors. 'Six o'clock, same as usual,' he told him.

'Did you listen to the radio?'

'Only while I was driving to the station.' Ashton lived on the coast at Bosham near Chichester and drove to Havant where he caught the six eighteen fast train to Waterloo, then doubled back one stop to Vauxhall.

'Then you will have heard of George Ventris?'

'Who's he?'

'The literary agent who was murdered yesterday evening,' Hazelwood said irritably.

'He wasn't named in the newscast I heard.'

'It doesn't matter. The point is a young American woman called Ensley Holsinger offered him a book allegedly written by Ross Frazer, who was one of ours.'

'Was?'

'He died almost nine years ago.'

'You mean this book has been kicking around that long?' Ashton said.

'The raw material certainly has.'

Hazelwood paused as if to collect his thoughts, then related how it had all started yesterday morning with Nancy Wilkins receiving a phone call from a desk officer she frequently spoke to at the army's Directorate of Security. The Firm had been asked to say whether or not Ross Frazer had been in the SIS. If the answer was yes, George Ventris was prepared to let them vet the

44

incomplete typescript.

'Since he already knew a great deal about Frazer's personal life, there was no point in pretending we had never heard of him.' Hazelwood opened the ornate hand-carved cigar box, one of a pair he'd purchased on a field trip to India a lifetime ago. Helping himself to another cheroot, he struck a match and lit it. 'Didn't want to ban the book,' he said between puffs. 'Quickest way I know of making it a bestseller on both sides of the pond. As things stood we would have two bites at the cherry, at the halfway stage and again on completion. What Ventris was offering was control of the book.'

'Could he have delivered that?' Ashton asked.

'It hardly matters now. The people who murdered Ventris took it, a man and a woman passing themselves off as Detective Constable Leach and Detective Sergeant Nicholson.'

'How do the police know this?'

'Ventris managed to switch on his Sony tape recorder without them noticing. I think he believed he was dealing with genuine officers and he wanted some hard evidence to back his complaint when he made it. What was on the tape also highlighted our possible involvement. Naturally the DCI in charge of the investigation reported this to his immediate superior in E District and so it went rapidly on up the chain of command to the Home Secretary, then across to the Foreign and Commonwealth Office whose Permanent Under Secretary of State and Head of the Diplomatic Service wasted no time in alerting the Secretary to the Cabinet. Thereafter

45

the world and his wife were on to me.'

'So?' Ashton said. It was a euphemistic way of asking why he was telling him all this and it worked.

'We have to assume Ms Ensley Holsinger has read the script. After all, she could scarcely do a hard sell on an experienced literary agent like George Ventris without knowing what the book is about.'

'I've no quarrel with that assumption.'

'I'm glad we agree,' Hazelwood said acidly, 'because I want Landon to have a word with this Ensley Holsinger. He is to find out exactly what the hell she does know. Make sure you tell him he is to be very discreet.'

In Hazelwood's dictionary being discreet meant you admitted nothing.

'He can't pretend he's not in the SIS, Victor.'

'I don't expect him to but he doesn't have to volunteer information.'

'What else?'

'Ms Holsinger is staying at the Dorchester; the police have warned her to expect Will Landon at six thirty p.m.'

'I mean what else is Will allowed to tell her?'

'Nothing. His job is to extract information, not to provide her with more.'

'With due respect, Director,' Ashton said coldly, 'that's not good enough. We will be sending Will in there blind. At the very least he has to know the name of the police officer in charge of the investigation.'

'Detective Chief Inspector Bernard Ogden of E District,' Hazelwood said abruptly.

'Well, that's a start. What about Frazer? I mean, supposing Ensley Holsinger knows something of his life history? Won't Landon look pretty stupid if he doesn't?'

Hazelwood opened the top right-hand drawer, took out a plain postcard and pushed it across the desk at Ashton.

'There you are then,' Hazelwood said. 'You wouldn't get anything more detailed or more concise out of *Who's Who*.'

Ashton scanned the card and looked up. 'Doesn't say where he died.'

'Paris, Tuesday the twenty-second of August 1989.' Hazelwood crushed the Burma cheroot in the brass ashtray. 'He was murdered — probably by the CIA.'

4

Landon glanced at his wristwatch and knew he was going to be late for his appointment with Ensley Holsinger. By the time Ashton had finished briefing him and he had drawn a fake Metropolitan Police warrant card from the Security Vetting and Technical Services Division, it was seven minutes to six. This had given him just over half an hour to get across town and arrive on time at the Dorchester. If he hadn't bothered with the warrant card he could have made it easily but he'd figured the stage prop would come in handy. Trouble was ex-Detective Chief Superintendent Brian Thomas, who ran the Security Vetting and Technical Services Division, wanted to know who had authorised the issue and hadn't been entirely convinced when informed Ashton had sanctioned it. He should have told Brian Thomas to forget the request but sheer obstinacy had made him hang on until the former police officer managed to contact Ashton, whom, it transpired, had been waylaid by the Deputy DG.

Landon had run all the way to the station and caught the Victoria Line train to Oxford Circus, where he had then boarded a westbound Central Line train going to Ealing Broadway. The weather had been unusually hot for early June and since his office caught the sun from first thing in the morning to late in the evening,

Landon couldn't have felt more washed out had he spent the whole working day locked inside a heated greenhouse. The last thing he had needed was to be stuck in a tunnel midway between Bond Street and Marble Arch, jam-packed into an overcrowded compartment. Twenty-five minutes after coming to a grinding halt the train started moving again. At no more than a walking pace it eventually pulled into Marble Arch.

As soon as the doors opened Landon spilled out on to the platform and made his way up to the street level. Crossing Oxford Street he went down Park Lane, doing up the collar button on his shirt and straightening the tie he had loosened in a fruitless attempt to cool down. For all that Landon had done the best he could to spruce himself up, the doorman still looked askance at him when he walked past and entered the Dorchester.

Landon approached the nearest desk clerk and produced the fake warrant card.

'The name is Landon,' he said. 'Miss Holsinger is expecting me. Do you happen to know if she is in her room?'

'I'm afraid I don't know, sir; like all our guests, Miss Holsinger has an electronic key. For what it's worth, I haven't seen her cross the lobby since I came on duty.'

The desk clerk pointed towards the lifts. 'May I suggest you use one of the house phones over there to call her, sir?'

'Thanks. Her room number is 408. Right?'

The desk clerk gazed at him quizzically. 'Are you asking me, sir?' he enquired.

Landon hadn't sought confirmation; it had simply been a throwaway line, the kind of remark he sometimes used to finish a conversation. If it hadn't been for the slight inflection in the clerk's voice Landon wouldn't have picked him up on it.

'You seem surprised,' Landon said, and paused long enough for the clerk to take the hint and inform him his name was Lawrence.

'As a matter of fact I was a little nonplussed,' Lawrence admitted, smiling. 'I thought your colleagues in Special Branch would have told you Miss Holsinger's room number.'

'My colleagues in Special Branch,' Landon repeated.

'Yes, sir. They were here yesterday evening, Detective Sergeant Nicholson and Detective Constable Leach.'

'OK. I'm going to call Miss Holsinger right now and when she comes down to the lobby I'm going to send her over to the reception desk and I want you to tell her exactly what you've told me.'

Landon walked over to the nearest house phone, lifted the transceiver from the cradle and got through to extension 408. The phone went unanswered for a good two minutes and he was about to hang up when the American girl finally came on the line.

'Miss Holsinger?' he said politely. 'My name is Landon. I believe you are expecting me?'

'I was at six thirty.'

'Yes. I'm sorry to be so late but there was some kind of hold-up on the Central Line — '

50

'I hear that happens all the time,' she said, interrupting him.

He let her bluntness pass unchallenged. A little discretion was called for when you showed up half an hour late for an appointment with a woman you've never met, never even spoken to before.

'I'll wait for you in the lobby, shall I?'

'We don't know each other well enough to meet anywhere else, Mr Landon. Now if you don't mind I'm going to finish showering.'

Landon was about to ask how he would recognise her when she hung up on him. The only description Ashton had been given by the DG could apply to any number of women: five feet eight in low heels, glossy dark brown hair, slim build, attractive-looking. No doubt DCI Ogden had given his immediate superior a more comprehensive description of the lady but as it was passed around Whitehall by word of mouth a number of pertinent details had obviously fallen by the wayside. Although they had tried to get in touch with Ogden, merely ascertaining the number of his mobile had been a time-consuming business. And when Ashton finally did contact the DCI, his transmissions kept breaking up and they were none the wiser.

Wasting no further time, Landon put the phone down, went over to the lifts and took the first available car up to the fourth floor.

If he was in a hurry, Landon could shower, scrape a razor over his beard, and get dressed inside ten minutes. While he didn't expect Ensley

Holsinger to emulate the feat he had hoped she wouldn't take for ever. As he soon discovered, it was impossible to loiter in the corridor without arousing suspicion; barely ten minutes into his self-appointed vigil, he was accosted by the hotel's chief of security and one of his assistants. The warrant card took most of the wind out of their sails but they were still too damned inquisitive for his liking and he was on the point of losing his temper when the American girl opened the door to her room and stepped into the corridor.

'Miss Ensley Holsinger?' he said, tight-lipped.

'Mr Will Landon, I presume?' she said coolly, and he could have sworn there was a faint smile at the corner of her mouth.

'Yes, I'm pleased to meet you. Shall we go down to the lobby?'

'By all means.'

Landon waved her to go ahead as though she were royalty.

Except, of course, it had nothing to do with deference. Maybe the two security men thought they were only doing their job but they had rubbed him up the wrong way and it wouldn't take much to make him blow his top. Above all, he didn't want Ms Holsinger to see the angry glint in his eyes because, even though they had only just met, he instinctively knew she would make some wisecrack and he would end up jumping down her throat.

He pressed the call button to go down, ushered Ensley Holsinger into the car when it arrived, then joined her. So did the hotel security

52

men. Exiting from the lift, Landon steered her towards reception.

'You see that youngish-looking man with the dark curly hair behind the counter?' Landon said, taking hold of her left elbow and gently drawing her to a halt.

'What about him?'

'His name is Lawrence. I'd like you to go over there and ask him to repeat everything he said to me a few minutes ago.'

'What is this, some kind of practical joke?'

'No, this is deadly serious — I mean that literally.'

'You'd better.'

She crossed the lobby, said something to Lawrence, then half turned about and pointed an accusing finger in Landon's direction before facing the desk clerk again. Their subsequent conversation lasted longer than Landon had thought likely. When Ensley Holsinger returned to him she looked preoccupied.

'Well?' Landon said, prompting her. 'Let's hear it.'

'Lawrence told me two Special Branch officers, called Leach and Nicholson, had visited the Dorchester yesterday evening looking for me. They told Lawrence I was in possession of classified material, though it was likely I didn't realise the script I was carrying contained Top Secret information. Apparently, they both left the hotel shortly after I returned from Red Lion Square. I asked Lawrence what they looked like and the woman he described bore a striking resemblance to the person who got out of the lift at the fourth floor and followed me along the corridor to my room. Nicholson murmured a good evening as she walked past.'

'Were there other people about?'

'Yes.'

'Then you were lucky,' Landon told her. 'Leach and Nicholson are bogus police officers. They murdered George Ventris shortly before you arrived at the agency.'

'How could you possibly know that?'

'George Ventris was a very brave man. He managed to switch on the Sony recorder he used for dictating letters. It picked up the conversation between Nicholson and Leach without them being aware of it. I'm surprised Chief Inspector Ogden made no mention of this when he caught up with you this afternoon.'

'It wasn't Ogden's fault. I'm afraid I did most of the talking after I learned he proposed to assign two plainclothes officers for my protection. They were going to live in my shadow until I flew home tomorrow. We reached a compromise. I promised to cancel a dinner date with family friends tonight and stay in; Ogden agreed to withdraw his close-protection officers soon as I returned to the Dorchester. I'm beginning to think I made the wrong decision.'

She had. The Sony had also picked up the last words spoken to Ventris by Leach, who'd called him a sneaky bastard. There had followed one muffled scream of agony and the methodical thump, thump, thump as the paperknife was driven into his brain. According to Ashton the police believed Leach had used one of his shoes as a makeshift hammer. But Landon said nothing of this to Ensley Holsinger. She was already on edge, nerves stretched tighter than a snare drum, and the last thing he wanted was for her to go to pieces on him.

'We should go,' Landon said quietly.

'Where to?'

'Some place where we can protect you.' He led her unprotesting to the lifts and pressed the nearest call button. 'First thing you have to do is pack everything.'

'The typescript must have been in the Jiffy bag he was carrying,' she said in a dull voice. 'Mr Jacklin saw it too.'

'Who's he?'

'The night manager.'

'Don't worry about it. I'll inform the police.'

'You know something, Mr Landon? This is my first visit to London and I'm not likely to forget it in a hurry.'

Despite the sardonic smile Landon reckoned she was still as brittle as eggshell china. Her hand shook when she opened the elegant Gucci handbag, took out the electronic card and inserted it in the lock. It was only after her third attempt to open the door that Ensley realised she had been inserting the card upside down.

'Thanks,' she muttered.

'What for?'

'For not plucking the key from my grasp and doing it yourself.'

'Well, that would have been a mite presumptuous.'

'So is following me into my room,' she said tartly.

'Please pack your things so that we can get out of here a.s.a.p.'

'What about my hotel bill?'

'Where's the problem? You let the desk clerk take an impression of your credit card, didn't you?'

'I'd forgotten that.'

Landon moved to the window, dug out his mobile and made a 999 call. When connected with the police operator, he gave his name, mobile phone number and told her where he was calling from. Landon said he had certain information concerning the Ventris murder that should be passed to DCI Ogden of E. District. He strongly urged that the police interview Mr Jacklin and Mr Lawrence of the Dorchester Hotel, both of whom could describe the bogus Special Branch officers the DCI was looking for.

'Tell him I've taken Miss Holsinger into protective custody,' Landon said, winding up. 'And make sure you give him my mobile number.'

'What's all this about protective custody?' Ensley demanded.

'It's just an expression; the police operator wouldn't have known what I'd meant if I'd said safe house.'

'Whose safe house?'

'One down on the south coast owned by a colleague and his wife. Now, are we ready to leave?'

'As I ever will be.'

'Good.'

Landon suggested it would look better if she rang the front desk and informed the receptionist that she had to recast her plans for personal reasons and would be checking out forthwith. He also thought Ensley should be the one to ring the concierge and ask for her bags to be collected. Both suggestions irritated her.

'How old do you think I am, Mr Landon?'

'What has your age got to do with it?'

'I'm not a child.'

'I can see that,' Landon told her.

'Then stop treating me like one. I know how to check myself out of a hotel.'

'Sorry. It won't happen again.'

'So you say.'

Landon glanced at his wristwatch. It wasn't the most accurate timepiece in the world and it regularly gained three or four minutes every twenty-four hours. As of that moment it was showing seven forty-three and he wondered if Ashton was still on his way home or had actually arrived in Bosham. It all depended on the DG. Hazelwood never left the office much before seven and, at a time when most people were thinking of going home, there was nothing he liked more than to mull things over with one of the heads of departments. Nine times out of ten the unlucky man was Ashton. The fact that they had known each other since the days when Hazelwood had been in charge of the Russian Desk had a lot to do with it.

Ashton had told Landon that if he believed Ensley Holsinger to be at risk, he should get her out of London and into a safe house, by which he had meant his place down at Bosham. Since it would only be for one night, Ashton was sure his wife wouldn't mind. Landon wondered if Harriet knew what her husband had let her in for. Reluctant to be the one who broke the news to Harriet, Landon decided he would wait a little longer before he phoned the Ashtons. He would take Ensley Holsinger back to his flat at 62 Stanhope Gardens and call Ashton when he collected his car from the lock-up garage in Gloucester Road.

'That will be the bellboy,' Ensley said.

Deep in thought Landon was slow to react. Before he could stop her she had answered the door and admitted the bellboy. Although the odds against it being Leach, Nicholson or some unknown hit man who'd rapped on the door were astronomical, he vowed never to be caught off guard again. Experience had taught him that nothing was impossible.

★ ★ ★

Light years ago OXO had run an advertising commercial featuring a housewife called Katie whose oaf of a husband was forever lumbering her with dinner parties for his boss or half a dozen clients at the last minute. Katie, of course, took it all in her stride and, with the help of some leftovers that had taken up residence in the fridge and a cube of OXO, always whipped up a fabulous meal with a cheery smile. In the real world, as Ashton could testify, wives like Harriet

58

were apt to look pretty boot-faced when confronted with such a situation. In this instance a cold front had suddenly moved in when Harriet had learned she might have to give Will Landon and Ensley Holsinger a bed each for the night.

It was Ashton's practice to shower and change into casual gear soon after arriving home. That evening he stood under the shower for a good fifteen minutes and took far longer to change than usual in the confident knowledge that Harriet would be more kindly disposed towards him when he reappeared. The great thing about Harriet was that it took a lot to provoke her and when roused, she never stayed angry for long. Tonight was no exception; when he walked into the kitchen Harriet was in a mood to tease him.

'I've just seen an old flame of yours,' Harriet said, and waved the spatula she was holding in the general direction of the Samsung on the breakfast bar. 'She was on TV.'

'Who do you mean?'

'Jill Sheridan — how many old flames have you got?'

Jill Sheridan; now there was a name to conjure with. They had been engaged once but Jill had been regarded as a high flier by the Secret Intelligence Service and she had broken it off in October '89, wanting to achieve her full potential. Jill's father had been an executive director with the Qatar General Petroleum Corporation and she had spent much of her childhood and early adolescence in the Persian Gulf. Arabic had been her second language,

Persian was an additional qualification she had acquired at the School of Oriental and African Studies. To the then Assistant Director of the Mid-East Department Jill Sheridan had been the ideal choice to run the intelligence setup in the United Arab Emirates from Bahrain. Despite the odd hiccup, she had made it all the way to Deputy Director General and the betting had been that she would be the first woman to head the SIS. However, throughout her career Jill Sheridan had had a reputation for skating on thin ice and in April 1997 it had suddenly given way under her and she'd had to resign.

'What did she have to say for herself?' Ashton enquired.

'Nothing. It was one of those holiday programmes which cover three or four package deals in half an hour. This one covered the Silk Route, ten days in Indonesia, a biking tour of North Wales and a long weekend in New York. Jill came in camera as she was leaving Saks.'

Saks, Bergdorf Goodman, Gucci; that was Jill all right. Give her a credit card good for forty grand and she would have the time of her life on Fifth Avenue. Ashton frowned. But what the hell was she doing in New York in the first place?

'You look sceptical,' Harriet observed. 'Jill may only have been in view for a mere two or three seconds but that's all I ever needed to make a positive identification.'

Harriet wasn't boasting: she had marvellous eyesight and a photographic memory for faces. She had been the brightest MI5 officer of her intake and had passed out top of the induction

60

course. She had been weaned on the Armed Forces Desk doing exactly the same job as Nancy Wilkins before being assigned to K2, the section responsible for monitoring the activities of subversives. Opportunities to serve outside the UK were few and far between, and Harriet had been delighted when she had been selected for a job with the British Services Security Organisation in Germany.

The break-up of the Warsaw Pact coupled with the phased withdrawal of the Red Army from East Germany had led to the disbandment of the BSSO, and her posting had been changed at virtually the last moment. Instead of going to Berlin, she had been seconded to the Security Vetting and Technical Services Division of the SIS, which in those days had been located at Benbow House, south of the river in Southwark. At first Harriet had been less than thrilled to find that her immediate superior was Peter Ashton. Given his propensity to cut corners and take risks, she could understand why he had been put out to grass in the Admin Wing. With the arrival of Harriet, Ashton knew that the temporary banishment from the Russian Desk was the best thing that had ever happened to him.

'You've got that perplexed expression on your face again,' Harriet told him. 'Are you by any chance thinking about Jill Sheridan?'

'Absolutely not.'

'Good. Whatever the lady was doing in New York is no longer any concern of yours. Jill ceased to be a threat the day she left The Firm.' Harriet crouched in front of the Creda and opened the oven door. 'The casserole is about ready,' she announced. 'If Will and this American girl don't show, we'll be eating it for the next three nights. You should have told him to let us know whether or not he would be coming down.'

'I think Will has just heard you,' Ashton said, and went into the study to answer the phone.

The good news was that after tonight beef casserole was off the menu; the bad news was that at eleven minutes past eight, Landon had only just collected his car from the lock-up garage and was on his way back to 62 Stanhope Gardens to pick up Ensley Holsinger. Nevertheless, with any luck, he expected to arrive at Roseland Cottage in a little over an hour's time. The proviso was certainly justified. Landon owned an eleven-year-old Aston Martin V8 vintage model, which he had lovingly restored to mint condition. In the process he had also souped up the engine so that it could easily do 175 miles an hour. Although Will had never driven the car flat out, he regularly clocked over a hundred on the motorways with the inevitable result that he had amassed a number of penalty points.

'Watch yourself,' Ashton had told him. 'A few more penalty points for speeding and you'll lose your licence.'

'I hear what you are saying, Peter.'

'Good.' Ashton paused, then asked if he'd had a chance to question Ms Holsinger yet.

'Not really. My number-one priority was to get her to a safe place soon as I learned Nicholson and Leach had been to the Dorchester looking for her shortly after killing Ventris. So far as I could tell she wasn't under close protection. Anyway, I contacted the emergency services and gave the police operator a message for DCI Ogden, informing him of the action I'd taken.'

'You did the right thing, Will.'

'Thanks. Incidentally does the name Amelia Cazelet mean anything to you?'

'I can't say it does. Who is she?'

'A friend of Ensley Holsinger, lives in the same apartment building on East 71st Street and owns a discount bookshop on 7th Avenue. Cazelet is the one who gave Ensley Ross Frazer's autobiography a few hours before she was due to catch her flight to London. I don't know how you would go about it but I believe we should put Amelia Cazelet under a microscope to see if she is for real.'

'Do you have a reason, Will?'

'Yeah, I have a funny feeling Ensley Holsinger is a bit of a liar.'

'That's good enough for me,' Ashton said, and put the phone down.

5

Twenty-one minutes past eight. In New York it was three twenty-one in the afternoon. Ashton reckoned he had over ninety minutes to play with before the British Consul in New York closed the shop and went home. Immediately after talking to Will Landon he had telephoned Hazelwood at his house in Willow Walk to let him know what he intended to do. From the SAS watchdog who was permanently in residence, he had learned that the DG was conferring with the Minister of State for Foreign and Commonwealth affairs. The corporal had also informed him that Hazelwood had given instructions that on no account were they to be interrupted unless it was literally a matter of life and death. The same stricture applied to Winston Reid, the Deputy DG, who it transpired was present at the request of the Minister of State. With ninety plus minutes in hand he could afford to wait an hour on the off chance that the meeting would break up earlier than the watchdog had led him to believe. But to Ashton that was the Micawber approach to life and he had never been in favour of waiting for something to turn up.

There were two ways of launching an investigation into Amelia Cazelet's background: he could ask Miles Delacombe, Head of Station, Washington, to initiate the necessary action, or go direct to The Firm's representative at the British Consulate in New York City and tell him to get on with it. On paper, Head of Station was the natural choice. He was the senior SIS officer in the US, had the necessary resources and was provided with secure transatlantic communications. Intelligence gathering was not the primary concern of the passport control officer at the British Consulate even though Jack Boothroyd was a Grade III SIS officer. His foremost duty was the interception of Indian and Pakistani nationals travelling on false papers, attempting to enter the UK by the back door using New York as their final departure point.

Although Jack Boothroyd didn't have anything like the resources Miles Delacombe was able to call on, he would be a whole lot easier to get on with. There was no love lost between Ashton and the Head of Station, Washington. Delacombe regarded him as a loose cannon and would take no action until he received a formal request from Hazelwood. He would also want to know why Landon was interested in the owner of an obscure discount bookshop in New York, and Hazelwood had made it pretty clear that anything to do with Ross Frazer was on a strictly need-to-know basis. Unlike the man in Washington, Jack Boothroyd would do as he was asked without wanting to know the reason why. After weighing the various pros and cons, Ashton did what he'd always intended to do and rang Jack Boothroyd.

'Hello, Jack,' he said. 'It's Peter Ashton. How are you and the family?'

'Things couldn't be better for us,' Boothroyd told him warily. 'And yours?'

'If you had asked me that question a week ago I would have given you the same answer. However, the fact is the old family business is going to be sued for breach of copyright by an American subagent.'

'I see,' Boothroyd murmured, 'leastways, I think I do.'

The British Consulate in New York didn't have a crypto-protected satellite link with the UK. Hence Ashton was obliged to conduct their conversation in veiled speech and he was beginning to wonder how much more he would have to divulge before Boothroyd caught on.

'I don't want to go into too many details over the phone, Jack, but we feel the lady in question is playing a minor role in some kind of scam. It could be the author himself has put her up to it,' Ashton continued.

'How can I help?' Boothroyd finally asked.

'Well, the lady's name is Amelia Cazelet. We understand that in addition to being a part-time literary agent, she owns a discount bookshop on 7th Avenue and has an apartment somewhere on East 71st Street. We'd like you to take a look at Ms Cazelet and tell us what you make of her. It would also be very helpful if you could find out who she is playing piggy in the middle for.'

There was a momentary silence, then Boothroyd said he had to look something up and would Ashton mind hanging on for a minute or two. While he waited, Harriet put her head round the study door to ask if he had managed

66

to contact Will Landon yet and thanked him sarcastically for letting her know she was required to make up two extra beds.

'Sorry to have kept you,' Boothroyd said presently, 'but I needed to be sure there weren't two women with the same name.'

'And?'

'There was only the one Amelia Cazelet and she is dead. Her body was fished out of the East River midway between Top Cove and the Triborough Bridge on Monday afternoon. She was a floater and had been in the water for two, possibly three days.'

'What are we talking about — accidental death, suicide — '

'Murder,' Boothroyd said, cutting in. 'Her wrists and ankles had been tied with baling wire.'

'Any idea of the motive?'

'The police are saying it's drug-related but I think they are guessing. There was no evidence to show she was a user, which leaves trafficking. There is speculation in the newspapers that her bookshop was a distribution point for crack. Admittedly the police have searched the store but if they had found something, you can bet they would have briefed the press. Incidentally Cazelet was the manager of Peel's Discount Bookshop, not the owner.'

'Was she a part-time literary agent?'

'Not as far as I know. Do you want me to find out?'

'No, it's not important. What I would like you to do is send me cuttings of every report that appears in the newspapers.'

'No problem.'

'You haven't heard the rest of it yet,' Ashton told him. 'This is not something you can delegate to one of the local staff. You will have to do it yourself.'

'It still isn't a problem.'

'This is private business, Jack, so don't send it through the usual channels. Dispatch the stuff through the US mail.'

The usual channel meant the communication was doubled enveloped. The inner one was addressed to the intended recipient while the outer was labelled for 'The Secretary, Box 800, London', the coded description for the SIS, which was known to every postman in the Lambeth area.

'Send the stuff to me at Roseland Cottage, Church Lane, Bosham, West Sussex. PO18 8HQ. OK?'

'Yes.'

To make absolutely sure, Ashton got him to read the address and postcode back, then thanked Boothroyd in advance and put the phone down.

Ensley Holsinger had established a unique record as a literary agent. She had acquired the autobiography of a man who had been dead for almost nine years, which had been delivered by a woman around the time her body had been fished out of the East River. Will Landon was right: the lady was one hell of a liar.

* * *

68

Before being elected to Parliament the Minister of State for Foreign and Commonwealth Affairs had been head of the English department at the largest comprehensive in Leicestershire with over a thousand pupils whose mixed abilities and varied ethnic backgrounds had, he maintained, equipped him for his present job. He would also have Hazelwood believe that the years spent as a backbencher on the Foreign Affairs Committee, coupled with an open and enquiring mind, were the other attributes that had led to his ministerial appointment. After twelve months in the appointment Hazelwood was sure the minister had been thoroughly brainwashed by the FCO. If proof of this contention were needed, the informal briefing arranged at the request of the minister for that evening provided it.

The agenda had covered the worsening situation in Kosovo, the likelihood of Macedonia being drawn into the conflict and, mindful of what had happened in Bosnia Herzegovina, how many Muslim volunteers from the Middle East might offer their services to the Kosovo Liberation Army. The man best qualified to answer these questions was the Head of the East European and Balkan Department, but clearly the FCO had been determined that their minister should not be indoctrinated by Messrs Ashton and Hazelwood. It was possible to justify their inclusion of Winston Reid because he was undeniably an expert on the political situation in the Middle East from the Balfour Declaration in November 1917 to yesterday's headlines in the broadsheets. However, Winston Reid had barely completed two years with the SIS and was still a Foreign Office man at heart. Privately, Hazelwood believed his Deputy DG was present to ensure the minister received what the mandarins in Whitehall called a balanced viewpoint.

Hazelwood also harboured darker thoughts. In June 1997 he had turned sixty, the mandatory age for retirement. He had already been extended in post for one year and was hoping he would be kept on for another twelve months. His present short-term contract expired on Friday, 26 June, three weeks to the day from tomorrow. To put it mildly, the Cabinet Secretary was cutting things a bit fine. It was hard to shake off the feeling that he had only been extended in 1997 because the incoming Labour government had no desire to play musical chairs while they were engaged in forming a new administration. But twelve months on, the government would undoubtedly feel confident enough to make whatever changes they deemed necessary and what could be simpler than to nominate Winston Reid as his successor? He would only have to move his personal things next door but one.

In a disconsolate mood, Hazelwood showed the two men out of the house and accompanied them as far as the wrought-iron gate set in the tall hedgerow, which was contrary to the security drill devised by his live-in bodyguard. The risk, however, was minimal; before Hazelwood could open the front door, the SAS corporal had switched off the hall light and the powerful sodium arc lamps that illuminated the garden and footpath.

'Did you see that?' Hazelwood muttered as the minister and Winston Reid drove off together into the gathering darkness, the official limousine following on behind.

'See what, sir?'

'Nothing, Corporal, I was just talking to myself.'

'Mr Ashton phoned while you were conferring with the two gentlemen, sir.'

'Do you know what he wanted?'

The SAS NCO shook his head. 'I told him you had left instructions that you weren't to be disturbed unless it was a matter of life and death. He didn't seem fussed so I guess it couldn't have been all that important . . . '

Hazelwood doubted if that was so. Ashton was not the sort of man to indulge in social chit-chat on the telephone. Furthermore, in all the years they had known one another, he could count the number of times Ashton had rung him at home on the fingers of both hands. Bidding the SAS corporal good night, Hazelwood went into the study, the one room in the house where he was free to smoke like a chimney if he had a mind to. He sat down at the desk, opened the ornate cigar box, the duplicate of the one at the office, and helped himself to a Burma cheroot before calling Ashton on the Mozart.

'I'm told you wanted to have a word with me,' he said when Ashton answered the phone. 'I assume it has something to do with Ensley Holsinger?'

'And the miraculous Amelia Cazelet,' Ashton told him.

71

'Who's she?'

'The woman who delivered Frazer's memoirs to Ms Holsinger several hours after her body had been fished out of the East River.'

'Makes you wonder how much of what she tells us we can actually believe.'

'She hasn't told Landon anything yet,' Ashton said, 'other than to name Amelia Cazelet.'

'You'll have to work on her then.'

'We'll do the best we can in the time that's available, which may not be much. She has a reservation on American Airlines Flight 215 departing London Heathrow at 14.05 hours tomorrow.'

'Is that what she told Landon?'

'No, I rang Terry Hicks and asked him to do a little hacking.'

To all intents and purposes Terry Hicks *was* the Technical Services Division. Widely regarded as the king of electronic warfare and counter-measures, he had, at the height of the Cold War, helped to build the plastic dome inside the British Embassy, Moscow, which at the time had been located on the Maurice Thorez Embankment, south of the river and directly opposite the Kremlin. The dome, shaped like an igloo, was completely soundproof and therefore ideal for Top Secret briefings. Unfortunately, after thirty minutes in the cocoon, people tended to emerge looking like wet dishcloths.

Part of his job was to make sure no outsider could hack into the Multi-Information Data Access System, commonly known as MIDAS. To do that successfully you had to be something of a hacker yourself and Hazelwood had heard it said that the loft in the Hicks household at 62 Sunleigh Road, Alperton was a computer nerd's paradise.

'Will anyone at American Airlines realise somebody has been looking at their flight manifests?'

'Not a chance,' Ashton assured him. 'The thing is, Ms Holsinger has another reservation for the same flight departing on Monday.'

'I see,' Hazelwood said, even though he had no idea where Ashton was going with the information. 'Exactly what do you have in mind?' he asked.

'I want Hicks to go into American Airlines data base again, wipe out tomorrow's reservation and confirm the one for Monday instead.'

'And then what, Peter?'

'We move the lady to Amberley Lodge and interrogate her in depth over the weekend.'

'Out of the question,' Hazelwood growled.

'I don't see why. The next course doesn't assemble at the Training School until Monday, June the fifteenth.'

'Somebody's been doing their homework.'

'Does that mean you are vetoing the proposal?'

'No it doesn't,' Hazelwood said irritably. 'I just want to be satisfied that the American girl is not going to scream blue murder when she does return to the US of A. Can you guarantee she won't raise a stink?'

'Right now she's frightened; that's something we should take advantage of.'

Hazelwood was tempted to remind Ashton that he hadn't answered the question but on reflection saw no point in pursuing it. Nobody could give such a guarantee when there were so many imponderables. The question that had to be addressed was whether he was willing to take a risk and see highly damaging extracts from the Ross Frazer file get into the public domain. It was a gamble Hazelwood was not prepared to contemplate.

'Do you have a shopping list handy?' he asked.

'Yes. I want three watchdogs, a brace of rooms overlooking the inner courtyard, two extra prowler guards — '

'Don't tell me,' Hazelwood said interrupting him. 'Save it for the commandant of the Training School. Soon as I put the phone down, I'm going to ring Amberley Lodge and tell him he is to provide everything you require.'

'Right.'

'He will then call you,' Hazelwood said, and hung up.

★   ★   ★

From Stanhope Gardens Landon made his way to the M4 and headed west to pick up the orbital motorway. Thereafter he looped round London in a southerly direction, leaving the motorway at Junction 10 for the A3 trunk road to Portsmouth. Although Ensley Holsinger wasn't the most uncommunicative woman he'd ever encountered, she was extremely reluctant to tell him much about herself. However, even though

74

he'd had little occasion to use the skills taught at the Training School, he was still a better-than-average interrogator. An easy manner, infinite patience and the ability to inspire trust were some of the tools Landon used to get close to the person he was questioning and to some extent they had worked with the American girl.

Ensley Holsinger, he learned, had been born in New Milton, Connecticut, would be twenty-five on 31 July and had majored in English at Boston University, where she had been a cheerleader. Her parents had split up prior to the degree ceremony and Daddy, who was a hot-shot attorney, had moved to Chicago, leaving the family home to Lauren, his wife. Ensley had taken herself off to New York and made the rounds of all the major publishing houses until she had eventually found a niche with Barnes and Wallace, part of the HarperCollins empire. Seventeen months ago she had caught the eye of someone called Evan at Julian H. Shubert, and had been invited to join the literary agency. While Landon hardly knew a damned thing about the publishing world, it seemed to him that Ensley's career to date had been nothing short of phenomenal.

'You got where you are now in what — three years after leaving Boston University?' Landon shook his head. 'How did you do it?' he asked.

'Networking,' she told him, 'meeting the right people at the right time and making a favourable impression.'

Landon glanced at her out of the corner of his

eye. To call Ensley attractive failed to do her justice; arresting was a more apposite description. In that respect she was another Harriet Ashton and he could imagine just what sort of impression Ensley must have made on the man she called Evan.

'Did you phone Evan to let him know what you thought of the script?' Landon asked casually.

'How could I? Amelia only gave it to me a few hours before I left for London.'

'That was Monday night. Presumably you read the script before delivering it to George Ventris the following afternoon?'

'Of course I did, but I wanted to hear what a really experienced literary agent made of it before phoning Evan.'

'So he knows nothing about the bestseller Frazer has written?'

'Who said it was a bestseller?' Ensley demanded.

'One of Ventris' authors, who is a desk officer at the Ministry of Defence. Ventris didn't think it was a work of fiction and asked him if he could find out whether Frazer had been in the SIS at one time.'

'The SIS,' she said blankly. 'What's that?'

Landon couldn't believe Ensley didn't know. 'The equivalent of your CIA,' he said tersely.

'OK. Are you telling me Ross Frazer has been a spook?'

'He was at one time.' Landon raised his eyes and looked into the rear-view mirror. He had first seen the Seat Toledo on the outskirts of

Guildford; seventeen minutes later and twenty-one miles further on it was still there, hanging back to keep one vehicle between them. Last time he had looked it had been a VW Polo; this time it was a white Transit van. 'Now let's stop pretending you didn't know,' Landon added. 'At the very least you must have guessed Frazer was connected with an intelligence service when you read the script. And there can't have been any doubt in your mind after Ventris was murdered and the typescript taken from his safe.'

'OK, you're right. What is it you want from me?'

'As much as you can recall from the typescript,' Landon told her. 'You never know, it might just save your life.'

'What are you trying to do,' she said, trying to sound jocular, 'scare the living daylights out of me?'

It was very clear to Landon that she didn't appreciate his deadpan black humour and had taken him literally.

'I'm sorry, it was a throwaway line and it wasn't very good. So can we start again?'

'Why not? The story is told first person and you don't get to know the name of the narrator.'

'Let's call him Ross Frazer.'

'As you wish. Anyway, the whole of the first fifteen chapters concerns a vendetta Frazer pursued against an American called Anthony Grimaldi.'

It had begun in 1955 at Buraimi, an inland oasis comprising nine villages on the frontiers of the sheikdom of Abu Dhabi and the sultanate of

Oman. The oasis had been the subject of a bitter dispute between Saudi Arabia and the states of Abu Dhabi and Oman, most of whose territory lay within the concession area of the Iraq Petroleum Company. Rich oilfields were thought to be situated near the oasis and the area had been of great interest to Aramco, the Arabian American Oil Company, which held the Saudi concession.

'In those days it seems that Ross Frazer was attached in some capacity to the Trucial Oman Scouts in Sharjah.' Ensley smiled. 'He said it was real Beau Geste country.'

'And Grimaldi?' Landon said, prompting her.

'He was a surveyor with Aramco who was endeavouring to establish the frontiers of all three states. According to Frazer, he was CIA.'

In 1952, three years before Frazer had joined the Trucial Oman Scouts, a Saudi armed force had passed through Abu Dhabi, occupied part of the Muscat position and distributed gold as an inducement . . . Skirmishing and accusations of bribery had followed for the next three years until the British and Saudi Governments agreed to arbitrate the correct frontier between Saudi Arabia and Abu Dhabi.

'The proceedings broke down in the October of 1955, when the British arbitrator resigned.' Ensley paused briefly, then said, 'This was after he had learned the Saudi representative had been in touch with his government during the hearing. The Trucial Oman Scouts then moved in, a few shots were fired and one Saudi trooper was killed before the garrison surrendered. They were sent home via Aden.'

'And where was Grimaldi when this was happening?'

'He had forewarning and got out twenty-four hours before the garrison was attacked.'

'There has to be more to it than that,' Landon said.

'Of course there is. The Suez invasion happened in 1956 and British influence throughout the Middle East began to unravel fast.'

Landon couldn't be sure the Seat Toledo was still tagging him. The light was going fast and he could no longer make out the configuration of the next but one vehicle in rear. The Ford Transit had turned off the dual carriageway on to the minor road to Liss and there was now a Jaguar closing on him fast as they bypassed Petersfield. Ensley Holsinger didn't say anything when Landon put his foot down and began to draw away from the Jaguar. She was too preoccupied holding forth.

'There was rioting in Bahrain, which was then under British protection,' she told him. 'The locals had decided they didn't like the cosy relationship the ruling family had with the UK government and wanted the link severed. The Brits said the trouble had been whipped up by agents acting for Gamal Abdel Nasser, the Egyptian leader. Frazer blamed it on Anthony Grimaldi.'

'Why?'

'No good reason except he happened to be in Bahrain on rest and recuperation when the

79

rioting took place. But he was no different from all the other oilmen who liked to get away from Saudi Arabia for a few days every other month. Some of them made straight for the bar of the RAF officers' mess when they got off the plane and didn't reappear until it was time to fly back.'

Ensley Holsinger appeared to have a photographic memory. She had skim-read the script between taking off from JFK and landing at Heathrow. Yet her résumé of the first fifteen chapters was brilliant. Landon couldn't think how she had put it together in the time available.

'There were very few fatalities as a result of the rioting but Frazer says that one of the victims really got to him. She was a Bahraini nurse who had been trained in England and had ceased to wear the veil. She was on her way to the hospital when she was caught by a mob, stripped naked and beaten to death.'

'And he blames Grimaldi for that?'

'Yeah. Frazer ended up killing him in Oman, but that's another — '

Ensley glanced at the speedometer, saw that it was topping a hundred and went rigid. 'For God's sake, slow down,' she yelled.

'Brace yourself,' Landon told her and floored the accelerator.

He pushed the Aston Martin as he'd never pushed her before, the needle moving up until it was quivering on a hundred and fifty. It was the start of the summer season and there was a fair amount of traffic on the road to the south coast considering it was almost nine o'clock. Engine snarling, he overtook everything, coaches, camper vans, towed caravans and one police Range Rover proceeding sedately at sixty miles an hour in the slow lane. The minor road to Rowland's Castle was coming up and it was vital to move into the line of traffic at speed and leave the motorway before the Seat Toledo got within visual distance of him. It was also desirable to vanish before the Range Rover put in an appearance.

Four hundred yards from the slip road, Landon carved up an old Rover 2000 on the inside lane, moved further across on to the hard shoulder and, applying the breaks spasmodically, left the motorway at a hundred, tyres screaming in protest. By the time he reached the first bend in the road the speedometer was reading fifty.

'Stop the goddamned car and let me out,' Ensley screamed.

'You just sit tight.'

Landon switched off all the lights as he drove round the curve, then went on for another fifty yards before pulling over on to the grass verge and shifting into neutral.

'I hope the police come looking for you and take away your goddamned driving licence for ever.'

'We were being followed — '

'Bullshit.' Ensley opened her handbag, took out a packet of Marlboro and managed to light a cigarette at the fourth attempt. 'I'll tell you this much, Mr Landon, you're not driving me to the airport tomorrow.'

It was the last thing Ensley said to him that night. Fifteen minutes later Landon pulled up outside Roseland Cottage.

6

Landon followed the Volvo all the way from Roseland Cottage in Bosham to Amberley Lodge outside Petersfield. Ensley Holsinger had been as good as her word: Heathrow might be off the agenda but she sure as hell hadn't allowed Landon to drive her to the Training School.

Landon supposed he should be grateful that it was Ashton who'd had to inform her that the SIS had cancelled her flight reservation for today. Ensley had given a fair impression of a volcano about to erupt, then Ashton had told her Amelia Cazelet's body had been recovered from the East River on Monday afternoon, and she had been too stunned to say anything. What followed had been the quietest late night dinner Landon had ever sat through, and it had been no surprise to find her equally subdued over breakfast that morning.

On arrival, the administrative officer had met them in the hall and conducted Ensley up to her room, the only one with a bathroom en suite, on the top floor overlooking the inner courtyard. The rooms on either side were unoccupied as yet. Come nightfall she would have company in the persons of two security guards, the younger of whom would be a woman not much older than herself. Landon had been given the room beyond the seismic pad under the carpet, which would alert him should Ensley attempt to sneak out during the hours of darkness.

Landon had needed barely five minutes to hang up his things; admittedly Ensley Holsinger had a lot more clothes than he did, but so far she had taken more than half an hour to unpack one bag. Landon was on the point of sending one of the security guards up to her room to see what Ensley was up to when she walked into the library, which had been set aside for them.

'Where is Mr Ashton?' she asked, addressing him for the first time since their altercation last night.

'He went into Hazelmere to catch a train to London.' Landon smiled. 'I'm afraid you're stuck with me.'

'So it would seem.'

She walked round the library, pausing every now and then to pluck a leather-bound volume from one of the shelves.

'If you're looking for a bestseller,' Landon said, 'you won't find one amongst them. They were a job lot purchased at an auction in order to furnish the library.'

'Pure window-dressing, huh?'

'You could say that.'

'Like the sign at the top of the drive, which indicates this place is the International Studies Centre?'

The sign, planted at knee height on the grass verge, displayed the initials I.S.C. in red against a green background. Nowhere did it spell out what the block capitals stood for. When Landon had attended the SIS Induction Course Amberley Lodge was supposed to house the Crown

Property Agency. Subsequently it had been metamorphosed into the Government Statistics Office, Central Region and had only become the International Studies Centre in September 1993, four years after Ross Frazer had been killed.

'What's your point?' Landon asked her quietly.

'I'm trying to establish what is for real. For instance, this business about Amelia Cazelet . . . '

'She's dead, Miss Holsinger, and consequently very little of what you told us about her stands up.'

'I'm sorry, I lied to you. Amelia gave me the script on the twenty-fourth of April, six weeks ago today.'

'And?'

'I was trying to make a name for myself with the agency.'

She had read the script several times over that first weekend and had then shown it to Evan, hoping he would share her enthusiasm. Instead, he'd called her into his office four days later and told her the script was total garbage, good only for the shredder.

'Alternatively I could send it back to Ross Frazer with a note informing him he had absolutely no talent and should give up the idea of becoming a writer.'

'But you didn't agree?'

'Damn right I didn't,' Ensley said forcefully. 'I thought Frazer told one hell of a good story. Tony Grimaldi might have been the villain of the piece in Frazer's book but as I see it, he was just the CIA agent in the field following orders. It was the executives of Aramco who were behind the trouble, first in Buraimi then in Muscat and Oman from 1957 to 1959. To be fair to the oil company, it was the Sultan himself who was responsible for the rebellion against his rule.'

By 1957 Sultan Said bin Taimur's government in Muscat had come to be regarded as the most reactionary in the whole world. Slavery was still common, and many medieval prohibitions were in force. All the inhabitants of the city had to be inside the walls at sunset when the gates were locked or remain outside until morning. There was no electricity and any citizen who had occasion to leave his house after dark had to carry an oil lamp or face arrest and incarceration. But it had been the Sultan's insistence that revenues from the oil exploration concessions be used exclusively on defence that had caused the insurrection in the interior.

'The insurrection was led by the Imam of Nizwa, Ghalib bin Ali,' Ensley continued. 'Because of the various treaties of friendship, commerce and navigation which you British had signed from the nineteenth century onwards, the Sultan felt entitled to call on the UK for military assistance. Do I have to spell it out for you?'

'Yes, you do. I want to know what was in that typescript which cost two people their lives.'

'Your Crown agents hired what they called contract officers from among the ex-servicemen they contacted. In my country we would call them mercenaries. Anyway, under their leadership the Sultan's armed forces reoccupied Nizwa, and Ghalib bin Ali sought foreign aid to establish a separate principality.'

Saudi Arabia had been happy to supply Ghalib bin Ali's followers with arms and ammunition, particularly anti-personnel and anti-tank mines. Their motive, according to Frazer, was not altruistic. What constituted the precise frontier between Oman and Saudi Arabia was in dispute and since British Petroleum was looking for oil near the border, the Saudi executives of Aramco obtained similar concessions from the rebels as the price of their support. Whatever the truth of the matter, the munitions supplied by the Saudi Arabian government had enabled the rebels to wage a successful guerrilla war from their mountain stronghold on the Jabal Akhdar.

'The rebels would come down from the mountain at night to mine the tracks around Nizwa and sometimes they would mortar the military base. The war gradually hotted up, RAF Shackletons bombed the hell out of the irrigation system on the high plateau and forced the dissidents to become cave dwellers. The Sultan's army expanded rapidly but the rank and file were reluctant to do any serious fighting.'

In response to yet another appeal for military assistance, NCOs from the Royal Marines and junior officers from infantry battalions, armour and artillery regiments were encouraged to volunteer for six months' active duty in Oman. There had been no shortage of applicants, and under their direction the Sultan's armed forces had developed a more aggressive spirit. But it hadn't all been one-sided. The rebels had enjoyed a considerable amount of success with their mining campaign, and a number of British service personnel had been seriously wounded. The rebels had also started to attack the British Petroleum exploration team.

'That was when Frazer was sent in. He was given the task of winning the hearts and minds of the people on the Jabal Akhdar.' Ensley shook her head in disbelief. 'As he said, it wasn't exactly an easy job after the RAF had dumped everything bar the kitchen sink on the local population.'

'And where was Grimaldi at the time?' Landon asked.

'He was running dates, rice and mines up the mountain from a base in the Saudi region of the Jabal Akhdar. Not every mine found a target; quite a few more were lifted intact. Frazer says the anti-personnel and anti-tank mines were American, left over from World War Two. He claims the Saudi army got them from us, and officials at the State Department were lying when they said it was impossible to discover where the ammunition had come from.' Ensley frowned. 'Something to do with numbers?'

'Lot and batch numbers,' Landon told her. 'They indicate where the mines were manufactured and which production run they were part of. If any mines in a batch are subsequently found to be faulty, Ordnance must be able to say which unit or units received them.'

'I guess that's why Frazer decided to teach the State Department a lesson,' Ensley said quietly.

Grimaldi was pretty much a creature of habit. Every other morning he left his base camp in the foothills of the Jabal Akhdar and drove to the Aramco exploration site to collect the mail, clean laundry and fresh vegetables for his small team. Under cover of darkness Frazer had crossed the frontier on foot and alone carrying four American M7 anti-tank mines in his Bergen rucksack. He had planted the mines at staggered intervals along the track habitually used by Grimaldi.

'The Jeep Grimaldi was travelling in was blown to pieces and he was killed instantly along with the Saudi driver.'

'What did we do about Frazer?' Landon asked.

'Nothing. He says he got a pat on the back.'

'I don't believe it.'

'Well, you would say that. In Frazer's shoes I think we would have done the same.' Ensley spread her lips in a thin smile. 'Look at the bright side, it might just be a novel after all.'

'The Buraimi incident, the riots in Bahrain and the business in the Oman — do they constitute the first fifteen chapters?'

'Yes.'

'How about the outline for the rest of the book? In what year does it finish?'

'December thirty-first 1996.'

'Then it can't have been written by Ross Frazer.'

'Oh, why not?'

'He was murdered in Paris on the twenty-second of August 1989. Rumour has it he was knocked down and killed by the CIA.'

'My God, first Frazer, then George Ventris and

Amelia Cazelet. The same sort of thing happened to all those people who witnessed the Kennedy assassination in Dallas. One by one they all died violently.'

'There is no similarity,' Landon said brusquely, 'and I'm not going to be sidetracked. Did Amelia tell you how the script came to be in her possession?'

'She said a friend whom she met every year at the literary festival at Edgartown gave it to her.'

'Where's Edgartown?'

'On Martha's Vineyard. I don't know whether this friend was a man or a woman. Amelia simply referred to him or her as J.S.'

'You're quite sure Amelia never put a name to this friend?'

'I can't recall her ever doing so.'

'OK. When is this literary festival held?'

'The first week in July.'

'And the first time you saw the script was six weeks ago,' Landon said, and deliberately raised his voice to convey astonishment. 'What was Amelia doing with it for nine months?'

'It was mailed to her just a few days before she gave it to me. She and J.S. talked about the book at the festival when it was a germ of an idea.'

'The script was delivered to you in a Jiffy bag. Right?'

'Yes.' Ensley frowned. 'Why do you ask?'

'Was there anything to show that it had come to Cazelet through the post? Had it been addressed to her?'

'I don't know . . . Wait a minute, there was no writing on the bag; it looked as if it had just been

89

purchased from an office supplier.'

'So you've only Amelia's word that the typescript reached her through the mail?'

'Yes, but why would she lie to me?'

'I'm damned if I know,' Landon said. 'How long have you two been friends?'

'Almost three years, in fact ever since I arrived in New York.'

'So tell me about her. How old was she? What was her marital status? How often did you two go out together? Details like that.'

Ensley told him Amelia would have been thirty-three in September. She had been roughly an inch taller than herself, had broad shoulders and large bones but had kept her weight down to a hundred and ten pounds through careful dieting. The fact that she had been a fitness fanatic had also helped. Amelia's parents had left Frederick, Maryland, where she had been born, and moved to New York when she was eight, settling in Queens. She had gone to NYU, married a fellow student and divorced him fourteen months later.

'She didn't like men,' Ensley said, and avoided his gaze.

'Yes?'

'OK, Amelia was gay.'

'Do I gather you didn't see quite so much of Amelia after you discovered her sexual predilections?'

'I couldn't really say.'

'Oh!'

'What do you mean, 'oh'?' Ensley asked, the colour rising in her cheeks. 'And why are you looking at me like that?'

'You think I'm censuring you in some way? Honest to God, I'm not interested in your private life.'

'It was my fault. I put out the wrong signals very early on in our friendship, and no one could have been more mortified when she discovered I wasn't inclined that way than Amelia. We continued to see each other because we both loved the theatre, the opera and going to concerts. OK?'

'You've been very helpful, Miss Holsinger, and I didn't mean to embarrass you.'

Landon meant every word but was still no nearer to identifying the author or discovering why 126 pages of A4 comprising the first fifteen chapters and an outline of the next twenty-one had led to the murder of two people. Considering what had happened at Buraimi, in Bahrain and the Oman, Frazer's security file had to be as thick as *Who's Who*. Yet the amount of information the DG had given Ashton was contained on a postcard. Landon needed to ring Peter and persuade him to do an Oliver Twist and ask for more. There was, however, one snag. The Training School was not provided with a Mozart secure-speech facility and the nearest one was in the Ashton household at Bosham. As soon as he had put Ensley Holsinger to work, he would call Harriet on his mobile and ask her when it might be convenient to use the secure-speech facility.

'You want to come with me, Miss Holsinger?' he asked.

'Where are we going?'

'To borrow a typewriter from the chief clerk. I'd like you to type out a résumé of the next twenty-one chapters.'

★ ★ ★

It was the first time since he had been promoted to Assistant Director that Ashton had missed morning prayers. In theory, nothing could have been simpler than to drive on to Hazelmere and catch a fast train into London. In practice he had missed one train by the skin of his teeth and there hadn't been a single parking space in the station yard. By the time Ashton had found somewhere to leave the Volvo where it wouldn't be clamped, he had missed another.

When eventually he walked into Vauxhall Cross the equivalent of a sighting report was flashed to Dilys Crowther by the ever-vigilant Enid Sly on the reception desk. Ashton's phone therefore started ringing before he could open the door to his office and it came as no surprise to learn that Hazelwood wanted to see him. As usual the extractor fan in the DG's office was working overtime to clear the cigar smoke eddying in a blue-grey haze below the ceiling.

'Tell me your diversion to Amberley Lodge was worthwhile,' he said as Ashton entered the room.

'If that's what you want to hear, Victor. The fact is there was no way Ensley Holsinger was going to get into a car with Will Landon behind the wheel. He frightened the life out of her last night taking evasive action to shake off the Seat Toledo.'

'Was it tailing him?'

'Nothing followed Will from the Dorchester to his flat in Stanhope Gardens but he's a pretty phlegmatic guy and has his imagination firmly under control. It's possible Miss Holsinger phoned somebody while he was collecting his car from the lockup in Gloucester Road and let slip they were going to Bosham.'

'Hardly likely, is it? I can't see Miss Holsinger deliberately putting herself in jeopardy.'

'Neither can I. Either Will was mistaken or it was some yob for whom an Aston Martin was like a red rag to a bull and was doing his best to harass him.' Ashton smiled. 'The man will never know how lucky he was not to catch up with Will.'

'So apart from antagonising the American girl and giving her heart failure what else did he achieve?'

'A synopsis of Anglo-American rivalry in the Persian Gulf during the fifties, but nothing anybody but a homicidal maniac would kill for. We've learned that Miss Holsinger is not entirely truthful about some things.'

'You mean we can't believe what she tells us?'

'Only in respect of when and how the typescript came into her possession. I told Will to question her about that.'

'Good,' Hazelwood said, and brushed the lapels of his jacket with his fingers to remove the ash he'd dropped on them. 'Anything else?'

'Only that whoever wrote the book has a

detailed knowledge of the Mid-East, which in a curious way brings me to Jill Sheridan. Harriet reckons she saw her on television last night in some travel programme. Apparently Jill was leaving Saks on Fifth Avenue.'

'I don't see the connection, Peter.'

'Well, if I had written a book which infringed the Official Secrets Act I wouldn't attempt to sell it in this country.'

'Are you inferring Jill Sheridan is the author?'

'I wouldn't dismiss the possibility out of hand. She was not a happy lady when she resigned from the Service.'

'Forget her.'

'I already have.'

'You're agreeing too readily: that's always a bad sign.' Hazelwood helped himself to another Burma cheroot and lit it most lovingly. 'What did you want to do about Jill Sheridan?'

'I'd like to make sure she is still domiciled in this country.'

'I suppose there's no harm in doing that provided you don't spend too much time on it.'

'Right.'

'Chris Neighbour stood in for you at the daily conference this morning.'

'I know. I rang him at home last night and told him he would have to.'

'It has been a troublesome twenty-four hours in Kosovo,' Hazelwood said pensively. 'The Serbs shelled a couple of Albanian villages a dozen miles from Pristina, the Kosovo capital; there are reports of four surface-to-surface missiles being launched at some unpronounce-able hamlet; and last but not least, armoured personnel carriers and tanks are said to be surrounding various enclaves. I think we are about to witness the sort of ethnic cleansing that went on in Bosnia.'

'Unless NATO does something about it,' Ashton said.

'Assuming we do intervene, how many Albanian speakers do we have, Peter?'

'One on the desk and a couple of translators who read the local papers but, of course, they are not security cleared.'

'What about the services?'

'I doubt if they have much call for them but I will check with Military Operations, Special Projects. We're better off for Serbo-Croat linguists.'

'We're going to need every interpreter we can lay our hands on, Peter.'

Ashton was already ahead of him. NATO was unlikely to commit ground troops in any numbers because there was nothing like the sight of body bags coming home to curb the enthusiasm of gung ho politicians. NATO's war would be waged by allied air power, the planes being guided on to pinpoint targets by deep-penetration patrols obtaining information from the local population. Hence the need for interpreters.

'I've got a list of former intelligence officers with the appropriate language qualifications whom I approached towards the back end of last year. Soon as we learn what the commitment is

I'll get in touch with them again and ascertain how many are still available.'

'You're learning fast,' Hazelwood said with a condescending smile.

'I should hope so,' Ashton told him. 'I've been in this game long enough to realise it pays to be one jump ahead of your superiors.'

The smile rapidly vanished and the atmosphere became somewhat chilly, with Hazelwood asking him to send in Dilys Crowther on his way out.

Back in his own office, Ashton looked up Jill Sheridan's ex-directory number in his Filofax and rang it on the BT line, only to get an unobtainable signal. Undeterred, he raised the operator, reported a fault on the line and was informed the number was no longer in service. There were two possible explanations. Jill had either moved house or had changed her phone number so that former colleagues who had known her ex-directory one would be unable to get in touch.

There was only one way to find out. Lifting the receiver again, he rang the Motor Transport Section, told the supervisor he had urgent business in Highgate and asked for a staff car to be ready at eleven forty-five. Five minutes before the departure time Will Landon called him on the Mozart secure-speech facility.

Before he even raised the subject Ashton knew he was going to ask for more information on Ross Frazer, which he wanted to have up his sleeve ready for Ensley Holsinger when she finished her résumé of the next twenty-one chapters. Much as Ashton regretted it, he had to inform Landon the DG would not release any additional information on the strength of what Ensley Holsinger had told him thus far. It might, however, be a different story once they learned what the rest of the book was about. The doubting tone in his voice when Landon said he understood, told Ashton he was disappointed in him and felt let down. Before he became head of a department Ashton wouldn't have hesitated to tackle Hazelwood head on, but times change and people with them and he was no exception. Leaving his office, Ashton walked down the corridor to the bank of lifts and took the first available car down to the Transport Section in the basement.

★ ★ ★

Considering Jill Sheridan had only been married to Henry Clayburn for eighteen months Ashton thought she had done pretty well for herself out of her ex. She had kept the four-bedroom house in Bisham Gardens, which overlooked Waterlow Park at the top of Highgate Hill, that had set her husband back all of four hundred thousand. But the bitterest blow must have been the loss of his pride and joy, the top-of-the-range Porsche 928 GTS. The car had depreciated in value since their divorce to the point where these days it was probably worth less than five grand. Nevertheless, Jill had still been driving around in it when he'd seen her last.

The house had obviously been repainted

sometime during the past year but outwardly little else had changed. The powerful security light just below the roofline was still in place, as was the Sentinel burglar alarm, but this was no longer connected to the police station in Archway Road. Terry Hicks from the Security Vetting and Technical Services Division had also removed the infrared intruder system the day after Jill's resignation had taken effect.

After telling the driver to wait for him, Ashton got out of the car, walked up the front path and rang the bell. The blonde woman who came to the door was in her early thirties and was, he judged, approximately six months pregnant. Reaching inside the breast pocket of his jacket, he produced the standard Ministry of Defence ID card with his head and shoulder passport-size photo in the top right-hand corner.

'My name is Richard Ash,' he said, holding the card far enough away from her to ensure she couldn't read what was on it. 'I'm an insurance investigator with Citibank International . . . '

'We don't want any insurance, thank you,' the woman said, and started to close the door in his face.

'Actually I was hoping to meet Mrs Henry Clayburn, who used to live here.'

'I've never heard of her.'

'She recently divorced her husband and may now be using her maiden name. Perhaps you knew her as Jill Sheridan? Anyway, this was her last known address and Citibank International agreed to let Mrs Clayburn have a bridging loan for a hundred thousand on call to make a down payment on a small hotel she wished to purchase in the Cotswolds. The bank was happy to do this because it was known this house was on the market for seven hundred and fifty thousand and was not subject to a mortgage.'

Recognition had already shown in her eyes; now the woman also looked wary as if she felt threatened. 'We paid a million two for this house,' she murmured.

'Oh, well, Mrs Clayburn asked for the bridging loan to be paid into her bank account four months ago and since then we've not heard from her. I don't suppose Mrs Clayburn gave you a forwarding address by any chance?'

'She did but we moved in last June and I'm afraid I threw it away roughly three months later.' The woman frowned. 'As I recall it was somewhere in Yorkshire. Harrogate comes to mind, or is it Knaresborough?'

'Thank you,' Ashton said. 'I'm sorry to have troubled you but you've been most helpful if that's any consolation.'

He turned about and walked back to the car. You could, he thought, go a long way with a million two in the bank, never mind the golden handshake Jill had received from the SIS.

7

Harrogate and Knaresborough? Neither seemed right for the Jill Sheridan Ashton knew. Anywhere north of Watford was alien territory to her and he couldn't see Jill choosing to settle in Yorkshire. There was a rudimentary way of partially substantiating his contention. Once back at Vauxhall Cross, Ashton went up to the reference library on the second floor and looked up the number of the phone book covering Harrogate and District. Of the Sheridans listed, there weren't all that many with the initial letter J. However, to be on the safe side he wrote down the phone number of every J. Clayburn in case Jill was using the surname of her former husband. He then spent the next twenty minutes working his way through the list, withholding each time the number of the BT phone in the library.

Hazelwood had been less than enthusiastic about ascertaining whether or not Jill Sheridan was still domiciled in the UK. Although Victor had seen no harm in doing that, he'd added a proviso that Ashton shouldn't spend too much time making enquiries. Never one to appreciate the value of negative information, he implied Ashton had been away from his desk far too long for such a meagre return.

'Contrary to standing orders, Jill sold up and moved house,' Ashton said forcefully. 'She also deliberately led the new occupants to believe she would be living in Yorkshire. Of course, Jill could have gone ex-directory again but I'm damned sure she hasn't bought a house in Harrogate or Knaresborough. Now we can either leave it like that or go a stage further. It's entirely up to you.'

'What in your terms would be the next stage?' Hazelwood asked.

'Jill receives a modified pension, which is paid into her bank account once a month. I would get Roy Kelso to phone Paymaster Limited at Crawley, West Sussex and ask for her new address. He can tell them Jill is no longer residing at the Highgate address and it's vital we get in touch with her. I'm sure Roy can invent a convincing reason.'

'No doubt he can but what if all Paymaster Limited will give him is the bank where her account is held?'

'We would have to get her new address out of the bank. That's something best left to MI5; they've got the necessary connections.'

'I don't want Five involved,' Hazelwood told him sharply. 'Same goes for Special Branch.'

'Then let's take one step at a time and see what we get from Crawley.'

'I'm happy with that, Peter. You can brief Roy Kelso accordingly.'

'And he will be rapping on your door five minutes later. Roy is by far and away the most senior assistant director we have. He's not going to take orders from me.'

Hazelwood sighed as if the whole weight of the world was on his shoulders. 'All right, I'll brief him,' he said wearily. 'Anything else?'

'Yes. Will called me just before I left for Highgate.'

'And?'

'Ms Holsinger admitted that the typescript had been in her possession for six weeks before it was stolen. She also said Ross Frazer had confessed to killing his American counterpart in the Oman. He blew Grimaldi up using an American M7 anti-tank mine. This was in 1958, and while it wouldn't have made him Top of the Pops with the CIA, I can't see them waiting thirty-one years to exact revenge.'

'Perhaps not. When can I expect to see a précis of the last twenty-one chapters of this saga?'

'Landon should have completed his part by the end of the day. I plan to stop off at Amberley Lodge to pick up the résumé and then phone you from home.'

'Make it before seven or after eleven thirty. Alice has organised one of her dinner parties.'

There was a noticeable sigh in Hazelwood's voice. It was common knowledge that on the day after the knighthood had appeared in the New Year Honours list of 1997, Alice had placed an order with their local printer for five hundred invitation cards beginning with the regal phrase 'Sir Victor and Lady Hazelwood'. Since that auspicious occasion, it seemed Alice was hellbent on using them up as soon as possible.

'The Home Office have been exerting pressure on me through the Cabinet Secretary while you've been gallivanting around,' Hazelwood continued morosely. 'DCI Ogden claims it is vital he reinterviews Ms Holsinger and I've been obliged to make her available tomorrow morning at nine.'

'Is Ogden coming down to Amberley Lodge?' Ashton asked.

'No, we have to deliver her safely to New Scotland Yard. I'm not expecting trouble but it doesn't pay to leave anything to chance. Who's the best driver for the job?'

'That's easy,' Ashton told him. 'You want Eric Daniels.'

Daniels had joined the SIS in 1979 after completing twelve years' service in the Royal Military Police. The army had taught him the skills of defensive driving and he was one of the very few people who'd had occasion to put theory into practice. In 1985, while serving with the British Embassy in Athens as a specialist driver, he had saved the then Head of Station from assassination when terrorists had tried to ambush the SIS man on the way to the international airport. The terrorists had opened fire much too soon and Daniels had been able to execute a hundred-and-eighty-degree turn at speed. He had then run down and killed the gunman the terrorists had put out as a backstop.

'Daniels it is then, Peter. Please speak to the transport supervisor and arrange it.'

Ashton had only one slight reservation. Daniels was now rising fifty and inevitably his reactions were bound to be a touch slower. But this could be compensated for.

'I'll accompany Ms Holsinger,' Ashton said.

'No, Will Landon can play nursemaid. If I

have to come through on the Mozart this weekend, I want to hear your voice on the line, not Harriet's. It could be you will have to mobilise your Albanian and Serbo-Croat linguists.'

'Do I understand the government is sending deep penetration patrols into Kosovo?'

'We'll know the answer to that sometime this evening after the House of Commons has adjourned for the weekend and the MPs are returning to their constituencies.' A broad smile appeared on Hazelwood's face. 'I've just realised this could play havoc with the dinner party. Alice isn't going to like that one bit.'

★ ★ ★

The big Four O, a benchmark in life long dreaded by Jill Sheridan, had come and gone a few weeks ago. The mirror told her she did not look her age and had worn better than a number of acquaintances who were in their mid-thirties. There were no marks under her eyes, no lines on the forehead or creasemarks around the neck. And there were other minor compensations: a bust that had not begun to sag, a flat stomach, hips that showed no sign of spreading and thighs anything but flabby. But nothing could assuage the bitterness she felt about the way her career had been terminated. From being the youngest assistant director in charge of the largest and most important department in the SIS she had become the first woman to hold down the appointment of Deputy Director General.

Everybody had thought she would succeed Victor when he retired on 30 June 1997, but they had reckoned without the all-male cabal who had given her no option but to resign.

If there was one man she really despised it was Ashton. He owed everything to her but he couldn't forget that, faced with a stark choice, she had put her career first and had broken off their engagement. Ashton had professed to be devastated but he had found consolation soon enough with that airhead Harriet Egan. And when the SIS had eased her out who was it who had volunteered to remind her of her obligation under the Official Secrets Act? Why Ashton, of course. He had never got over the fact that she had dumped him and he had waited nine years for a suitable opportunity to pay her back.

For the umpteenth time Jill told herself to blank Ashton out of her mind. It was good advice but difficult to put into practice at six forty in the morning, lying there wide awake in a hotel bedroom overlooking East Monroe Street on the fourth floor of the Palmer House Hotel. It was especially difficult when every two minutes you could hear a train on the el above Wabash Avenue one block east, and the man next to you in bed was snoring his head off. His name was Brad something or other. No matter, he had been a guest at the wedding she had gatecrashed at his instigation: She had returned to the Palmer House shortly after four o'clock yesterday afternoon to find the lobby crowded with people dressed for a funeral except they had all looked too young and happy to be mourners. Then one of the young unattached men had told her it was a wedding party and that wearing black was not so idiosyncratic as she might suppose. One thing had led to another and she had joined the legitimate wedding guests in one of the large reception rooms on the mezzanine floor, dancing to a six-piece jazz combo and drinking champagne until the witching hour of midnight, courtesy of the bride's parents.

Taking Brad up to her room had seemed the natural thing to do after he had been paying her compliments all evening in between boasting how good she would find him in bed. In the event his performance between the sheets had been less than satisfactory and, had she not been feeling quite so delicate, Jill would have kicked him out of bed.

A hand suddenly came to rest on her stomach and she instinctively turned over on to her left side to face the window. A little wriggle put her out of reach in the king-size bed. It was only then that Jill noticed the winking amber-coloured light on the telephone, which indicated somebody had left a message for her. Careful not to arouse the unsatisfactory lover, Jill reached out and lifted the receiver. The recorded voice of the operator informed her that Mr Alvin Dombas had tried to call her and would she please phone him a.s.a.p.

Jill slipped out of bed, collected her tote bag from the armchair where she had dumped it last night, then tiptoed into the dressing room and attempted to open the bathroom door quietly.

'Where are you going?' Brad asked sleepily.

'To the toilet.'

'Wh-a-a . . . ?'

'I want to use the can,' she snapped.

'OK. Just don't sit on it all night.'

'To hell with you.'

Entering the bathroom, Jill locked the door behind her, opened the tote bag and took out her mobile. A very tetchy Alvin Dombas answered almost immediately.

'Are you hellbent on committing suicide?' he demanded. 'I've been trying to reach you ever since six thirty yesterday evening.'

'Well, you've got me now so why don't you get on with it?'

'Your lesbian friend has been murdered.'

'Who?' Jill asked startled.

'Amelia Cazelet — how many lesbian friends have you got for chrissakes?'

'Just the one.' Jill tried to swallow but her mouth had suddenly gone bone dry. 'When did this happen?'

'Her body was pulled out of the East River on Monday afternoon. I didn't get to hear about it until late on Wednesday and then it was only by a fluke.'

It was a fluke because Amelia Cazelet had come to the notice of the FBI as a result of her fund-raising activities on behalf of Palestinian refugees living in Ramallah. Although not kept under surveillance round the clock, the Bureau nevertheless read her e-mail, had a phone-tap in place and checked on her movements to and from the bookstore on 7th Avenue, where she was the manager. Her absence from the bookstore on the Friday before her body had been recovered from the East River had been noted.

'Cazelet was also known to us,' Dombas continued. 'Naturally the Bureau was aware of this, that's why they notified the CIA.'

'And subsequently the notification passed across your desk?'

'Luckily for you, Jill.'

'What do you mean?'

'Cazelet had been tortured. Two of her fingernails had been ripped off. The men who drowned her wanted to know where to find you and she gave them the address of the place you are renting in Edgartown.'

'You're guessing,' Jill said in a hollow voice.

'I had the local police check out the clapboard house on Morse Street.'

Dombas paused briefly to clear his throat, then said, 'They told me it had been burgled. The room you use as a study-cum-workplace was the worst affected. The intruders had broken into your filing cabinet and been through all the papers. They also emptied all the desk drawers on to the floor. I hope they didn't find anything in your diary.'

'I may have made the odd note concerning travel arrangements.'

'Yeah?'

'Flight timings, possible hotels. I didn't mention Chicago.'

'Listen to me, Jill. The people who took out Cazelet aren't stupid. They can match the flight times and the hotels to a particular city.'

108

The implication sank in and she began to panic. How many hotels had she listed in addition to the Palmer House? The Drake, Ambassador West, Best Western Inn, The Fairmount, Chicago Hilton and Tower. Jesus Christ, they didn't have to match anything, she had given them the name of the city. Jill took a deep breath and exhaled slowly, only to find her pulse was still racing like a runaway train.

'I've got to get out of here,' she said wildly.

'You do that,' Dombas told her. 'Call me from San Francisco and I'll put you in touch with the local office.'

'Right.'

'Don't go direct, cover your tracks.'

'I was going to,' Jill said, but Dombas had already switched off his mobile.

There was no time to stand under a shower, Jill simply rinsed her face in cold water to freshen up and brushed her teeth. She dressed just as quickly, choosing low heels, beige-coloured slacks and a white cotton blouse, then packed her clothes and returned to the bedroom.

'About time.' Brad raised himself up on his elbows and stared at her, bleary-eyed. It slowly dawned on him that she was no longer wearing her satin nightshirt. 'Where the hell are you going?' he mumbled.

'Newark, New Jersey.'

'What for?'

'I have an appointment with the senior editor of *Who's Who in the Literary World*.' The excuse came tripping off her tongue. The hours she had passed in Edgartown's public library

109

creating a legend for herself had been time well spent. 'That was the message my agent left for me,' she added.

Jill checked the contents of the minibar, put down two brandies and a can of ginger ale on the chit, and then removed the key.

'You mean your pimp, don't you?'

Picking up the Hartmann business case, she shouldered her tote bag and walked towards the door. 'You know what your trouble is, Brad? You've got a pea-size brain and a dick to match,' Jill said, and left the room while the inadequate lover was still speechless.

It took less than five minutes to check out of the hotel; there was, however, the usual buildup of traffic on the John F. Kennedy Expressway to Chicago O'Hare, which put an extra quarter of an hour on what, with any luck, should have been a thirty-minute journey. At 10.57 hours Jill Sheridan departed on American Airlines Flight A2221 to Dallas Fort Worth, where it was scheduled to arrive at 13.16.

★   ★   ★

The outline of the last twenty-one chapters, which Ensley Holsinger had produced from memory, ran to eight pages of A4, double-spaced. Landon thought it was a somewhat meagre offering, considering the author had apparently hoped to secure a hefty advance before completing the book. The one really attention-grabbing section was the chapter devoted to the events that had occurred on

110

4 June 1968, during the California primary election when Robert Kennedy had been a contender for the Democratic presidential nomination. Frazer claimed to have been present in the kitchen of the Ambassador Hotel when Sirhan Bishara Sirhan, a Jordanian Arab, had shot Kennedy in the head.

The way Frazer had proposed to write the chapter, a reader could be forgiven for thinking the SIS man was behind the assassination and had provided the murder weapon. On the day of the primary, Frazer had kept Kennedy under observation as he rested at film director John Frankenheimer's Malibu home in case it became necessary to make alternative arrangements for the hit. Kennedy had been shot on the fourth and died on the sixth. If you could believe him, Frazer had got clean away during those forty-eight hours without arousing suspicion or drawing attention to himself. If you could believe Ensley's recollection of the original typescript, there was a clear inference that Frazer was far from being a rogue agent, though why Her Majesty's Government should want Kennedy dead had not been explained.

A lot would depend on how convincingly the chapter was written; if it read like a documentary the political fallout could be devastating. Landon could quite see that HMG would do everything in their power to stop publication but would they sanction murder? He liked to believe the idea would never have entered their minds.

'You've certainly got a memory for details,' Landon observed.

'Am I meant to take that as a compliment?' Ensley asked, her back still towards him as she gazed out of the window on the west side of the lodge.

'Yes, you are. I mean it would be easier to recall events if you'd actually lived through them but I doubt your parents had even met when the Saudis were ejected from Buraimi Oasis. And let's face it, I was only twelve months old when Robert Kennedy was assassinated.'

'What's your point, Mr Landon?'

'Have you thought about writing the book yourself?'

'What?'

'Well, you told me you had no idea who the author is or what the initials J.S. stand for. And now that Amelia Cazelet is dead you've lost the only means of contacting the author you had. Incidentally, I was surprised how calmly you took the news of her death.'

'Now I know you're being sarcastic,' Ensley said coolly.

'I tell you Amelia is dead and you say, 'Oh, I'm sorry I lied to you, she gave me the script six weeks ago today.' I'd call that pretty cool.'

'You forget Mr Ashton broke the news to me last night during that little inquisition in his study after dinner.'

'That's right, and you caught your breath. But you didn't look particularly shocked to me.'

'Amelia wasn't the most stable person in the world. She often suffered from fits of depression, especially when she had been rejected by another woman when she would

112

then talk about ending it all.'

'It wasn't suicide,' Landon said curtly. 'She was murdered. Her wrists and her ankles had been tied with baling wire. Or didn't you take that in?'

'Of course I did but I didn't come to the same conclusion as you.'

'NYPD is saying it was murder, not me.'

'OK, but I want a lot more proof before I share their opinion. It so happens that during one of her black moods Amelia told me how she would take her own life.'

The disclosure had occurred after Ensley had let it be known that she wasn't gay. Amelia appeared to have taken the gentle rebuff well and had persuaded Ensley to keep her company while she drowned her sorrows, as she had jokingly put it. Ensley had had a couple of drinks over her limit and had become mildly tipsy whereas Amelia Cazelet had really tied one on and had become maudlin drunk in the process.

'That was when she began to discuss the less stressful ways of taking her life. To OD with cocaine was out because she was too squeamish to stick a needle in a vein, and swallowing barbiturates wasn't the answer because she wasn't strong enough to lie there and wait for death to come to her. She would make a 911 call long before she became unconscious.'

'So what was her preferred solution?' Landon asked quietly.

'Drowning,' Ensley said in a matter of fact voice. 'Her idea was to jump off a bridge

113

somewhere, weighted down so that she couldn't change her mind and swim for the shore. The ballast would be attached to her ankles and naturally her hands would have to be tied to prevent her releasing the dead weight.'

'Did you believe her?'

'At first I thought Amelia was joking. I changed my mind later when I learned she was seeing a psychiatrist once a week. If Amelia had been less promiscuous and settled for one partner she wouldn't have had all those black moods every time she was rebuffed.'

Ensley fell silent for a few moments, then asked if Amelia's hands had been tied in front or behind her back. Her voice sounded remote, devoid of all expression. Her eyes could have told Landon a lot but she was still gazing out of the window, her back towards him. He sensed Ensley wanted to believe that her friend had committed suicide and that wouldn't have been possible if Amelia's hands had been secured behind her back.

'You know as well as I do that Mr Ashton didn't go into any details when he broke the news of her death last night.'

'I didn't take in everything he said. Do you mind if I smoke?' she asked. 'Or isn't it allowed?'

'Go ahead, I won't object. You'll find an ashtray on the mantelpiece.'

'Thanks.' Ensley turned away from the window, returned to the chair facing Landon where she had left her handbag and sat down. 'Out of curiosity, how long are you guys planning to keep me here?'

'Are you in a hurry to get back to New York?' Landon countered.

Ensley lit a cigarette. 'Let's say I won't be very popular with the agency if I'm still in this country on Tuesday morning,' she said, and slowly exhaled.

'It doesn't bother you that your life could be at risk?'

'I don't think I am at risk now.'

'Think again. Nicholson, Leach and people like them haven't gone away.'

'Why should they hang around? They've got what they were after.'

'Did you make a photocopy of the typescript during the six weeks it was in your possession?'

'No I did not.' Her eyes narrowed angrily. 'What are you inferring? That I was planning to set up a deal on my account without the agency knowing?'

Landon didn't know her well enough to make a judgement. Furthermore he wasn't interested in discovering what her motives might or might not have been.

'This man at Shubert who told you the book was a load of rubbish — '

'Evan,' Ensley said, interrupting him.

'Yeah, Evan. Would he have made a copy?'

'After telling me to return the book to the author, informing him he had no talent as a writer? We may not see eye to eye but Evan couldn't be that two-faced.'

'Listen to me,' Landon told her. 'I don't believe you are capable of doing anything underhand and Evan is probably as straight as a

115

die, but my opinion doesn't count. What counts is what the people who killed George Ventris and Amelia Cazelet believe.'

Landon had no need to dot every i and cross every t. The worried frown was a clear sign that he had got through to Ensley.

'So what are we going to do?' she asked in a husky voice.

'First thing you are going to do is put that cigarette out before it burns your fingers. Then it's back to the typewriter and a much fuller statement than you've given me so far.'

Landon wanted to know when was the last time Ensley had seen Amelia Cazelet. It was also essential to have a record of Ensley's exact movements on Monday, 1 June from the moment she had woken up to her time of departure from JFK that evening.

8

Miles Delacombe had been the SIS Head of Station, Washington, longer than any other previous encumbent. A small man, no taller than five feet seven and definitely overweight for his height, he had a smooth round face, the makings of a double chin, and a stomach that made him look four months pregnant. Delacombe had thin sandy hair and affected a trim military-style moustache, which he had started to cultivate when he had been a subaltern in the Royal Highland Fusiliers before being seconded to the Intelligence Corps. Gossip had it that the regiment had wasted no time unloading him on to 87 Field Security Section, Bielefeld, because he had little or no control over the Jocks in his platoon. Whatever the truth, the fact was Delacombe had proved himself to be a very able Intelligence Corps officer and had been taken on by the SIS on completion of his short service commission. He was forty-two years old and a leading light of the Caledonian Society in Washington.

The CIA thought highly of Delacombe, principally because he made no secret of his admiration of all things American and believed the US intelligence community should be kept fully informed whenever the Foreign and Commonwealth Office favoured a different approach to that advocated by the State

Department. This was especially true of the situation in the Middle East, where traditionally the FCO was inclined to support the Arabs and were noticeably cooler towards the Israelis. A great socialite, Delacombe frequently entertained the Director, the CIA's Executive Director, the Deputy Directors in charge of Operations, Intelligence, Administration, Science and Technology. He made a point of being especially close to officers like Alvin Dombas, who had overall responsibility for Humint requirements worldwide. In effect this meant he was responsible for evaluating the usefulness and financial worth of foreign agents recruited by CIA case officers on the ground. Foreign agents in place cost money, and Dombas was the man who controlled the purse strings. Needless to say the funds at his disposal dwarfed that of his British counterpart.

As Head of Station, Miles Delacombe saw it as his duty to maintain close contact with the Americans on the grounds that you could anticipate events if you learned where the CIA was spending money like there was no tomorrow. There was always an entry fee, which Delacombe sometimes paid by disclosing snippets of information that were meant for UK Eyes Only. He saw no harm in this because Dombas did the same as a come-on whenever he wanted to know what the British were up to. On such occasions the two men would meet on neutral ground. Otherwise Delacombe saw him when he paid a routine visit to the CIA complex at Langley, which he did once a month. He was therefore intrigued when Dombas made an appointment to see him in the British Embassy at four o'clock that Friday afternoon.

The American was some five inches taller than Delacombe and a great deal thinner. He weighed just over a hundred and forty pounds, and in Delacombe's eyes looked decidedly emaciated. He had a dry sense of humour, a quick nimble brain and there was enough of the actor in his makeup to be all things to all men.

'Jill Sheridan, Miles,' Dombas said tentatively after they had shaken hands. 'Are you aware that she has been living over here since May of last year?'

'No, I'm not aware. What is she doing?'

'Working for me and writing a book. She's pretty mad with you guys, reckons she had a raw deal.'

'She did,' Delacombe told him.

'You want to tell me why she felt compelled to resign?'

'You've obviously met her since she arrived in America.'

'Several times,' Dombas admitted cheerfully.

'So what did she have to say for herself, Alvin?'

'That she had made a minor error of judgement which would probably have resulted in a reprimand had Sir Victor Hazelwood not been the Director General. It was common knowledge that she would step into his shoes when he was obliged to retire at age sixty. For several personal reasons Hazelwood wanted to be extended in post a year at a time. This could

119

only happen if she was no longer in the running. But the man who really hounded her out of office was Jill's former lover, Peter Ashton. She claims he had never forgiven her for dumping him and had only been too happy to be Hazelwood's axeman.' Dombas smiled lopsidedly as if wryly amused. 'Any truth in that, Miles?' he asked.

'I have no difficulty in believing her account,' Delacombe told him.

'She was really good at her job then?'

'There was never a better assistant director in charge of the Mid-East Department.'

'Some people say she got there by fluttering her eyelashes.'

'Absolute nonsense. Jill had no need to flirt with anybody in order to get ahead. She was quite exceptional and had thoroughly deserved her promotion to Deputy Director General.' Delacombe paused. It was, he thought, about time Alvin explained his interest in Jill Sheridan. 'A few minutes ago you said she was working for you. How did that come about, Alvin?'

'Jill got in touch with Walter Maryck, our Station Chief in London.'

Walter Maryck had been in London almost as long as Delacombe had been Head of Station in Washington. A man to gladden the hearts of every tailor in Savile Row, Maryck did not care for loud checks or clothes that were supposed to make some kind of statement about the wearer. Instead he affected a style of dress much favoured by senior officers in the Brigade of Guards, which meant that, in addition to being

120

extremely well cut, his suits were of varying shades of grey. Delacombe had heard it said that he looked especially at home in green Wellingtons, corduroys, a waterproof jacket and a peaked cap when invited to join a shoot or attend a point-to-point. Walter's enemies within the CIA frequently accused him of being too pro-British, a charge so far removed from the truth as to be laughable. Maryck was a patriot through and through; he had enlisted in the army straight from college and had completed two tours of duty in Vietnam with the Green Berets, winning a Distinguished Service Cross and Silver Star in the process. Unfortunately the mud had stuck in the end and Maryck had been recalled to Washington in November 1997.

'She told Maryck she was off to America shortly and had certain Humint material she wished to share with us concerning Mid-East terrorist groups,' Dombas continued. 'We had never met, but she knew of me by reputation and Maryck put us in touch before she left for New York. I made Jill's acquaintance the morning after she arrived in New York at the offices of the Zenith Corporation on Battery Place, one of our front organisations in the States. We had a very interesting conversation about the kind of asylum seekers the UK is harbouring right now — radicals from Saudi Arabia who incite their fellow countrymen to murder the Royal Family from the safety of London; Kurds who are responsible for the bombing campaign in Turkey; Chechens with suitcases full of dollar bills who are trying to buy the latest weaponry.'

But it seemed not all the asylum seekers would be at risk should they return to their own countries. Among the refugees from Palestine, Iraq and Iran there were terrorist cells from Hezbollah, Islamic Jihad, Hamas and the Palestine Liberation Front whose objective was to wage war against the West from within.

'Ali Mohammed Khalef; there's a name for you to conjure with, Miles.'

'You've lost me,' Delacombe said, perplexed.

'He is one of your Iraqis who was granted political asylum because of his opposition to Saddam Hussein. Khalef is supposedly on Saddam's death list; however, Jill Sheridan claims he is a plant. For every newsletter he writes denouncing the Iraqi president, he produces a dozen soliciting funds allegedly to buy food and medicines for the marsh people in the South. The money is actually used to send young British Muslims to Libya for military training. Jill told me there is hard evidence on record to support this allegation but your Home Office refuses to deport him.'

'This is all very interesting, Alvin, but exactly what is it you want from me?'

'A while ago you said there had never been a better assistant director in charge of the Mid-East Department. How come? Did she bring some kind of special expertise to the job?'

As if quoting from her curriculum vitae Delacombe told the American that because Jill's father had been an executive vice president with the Qatar General Petroleum Company, she had spent much of her childhood and adolescence in

122

the Persian Gulf. Consequently Arabic had become her second tongue while Persian was an additional language qualification that she had obtained at the School of Oriental and African Studies when at university.

'It all sounds pretty academic, Miles. Does she have any practical experience in the field?'

Delacombe nodded. 'Jill ran the intelligence setup in the United Arab Emirates from Bahrain. But where she really shone was the way she ran her case officers and directed the Heads of Station throughout the Middle East. Nobody before or since has measured up to Jill.'

'That's quite a eulogy.'

Delacombe bridled, his lips compressed in a thin straight line, his small eyes narrowing. 'That was the last thing I intended,' he said coldly, then forced a smile on to his face, suddenly remembering that his self-appointed mission was the furtherance of the special relationship and snapping at Alvin was not the way to go about it. 'I wouldn't want you to think I am the president of the Jill Sheridan Fan Club.'

'Never entered my head, Miles.' Dombas reached inside his jacket and produced a slip of paper, then pushed it across the desk. 'What I would like you to do is run Ali Mohammed Khalef past your people in London and see what they come up with. I've listed his date and place of birth and other personal details on that piece of paper you're holding.'

'Why do I get the impression you are putting Jill Sheridan through some kind of test?'

'Because I am,' Dombas said, grinning. 'If she

passes we'll have a lot more to talk about.'

'What's all this about a book you said Jill was writing?'

'You might call it a one-sided view of power brokering, set in the Gulf sheikdoms during the mid- to late fifties where a nasty little war was going on with the Saudis, who were trying to lay claim to potential oil strikes in the disputed frontier zones.'

'Is it damaging?'

'To the SIS?' Dombas thought about it for a moment or so. 'Yeah, I reckon it is,' he said, and got to his feet. 'You want to escort me out of the secure area, Miles?'

Delacombe left his desk and walked the American to the steel gate that separated the chancery from the rest of the embassy. 'This book, Alvin,' he said while they were still out of earshot from the security officer manning the gate. 'How dangerous is it?'

'Dangerous enough to get a woman called Amelia Cazelet murdered. And dangerous enough for Jill Sheridan to go into hiding.' Dombas smiled. 'You guys aren't planning to put her in the ground, are you?'

'Wha-a-at?'

'Relax, Miles, it was just a joke.'

Delacombe thought it was a damned bad one and for a moment was tempted to say so. Returning to his office he drafted a long signal to London, setting out everything the CIA man had told him concerning Ali Mohammed Khalef and Jill Sheridan. Since the content of the transmission could seriously damage the nation if the

124

signal was intercepted he graded the text Secret. There was, he decided, nothing in the signal that demanded Action This Day by the recipient. Mindful too that in London it was now eight o'clock on Friday night, he unhesitatingly marked it Priority, which was just one precedence higher than Routine.

★　★　★

Landon watched the Volvo until it turned on to a road leading to Petersfield, then went back inside the lodge. Ashton had arrived in a tearing great hurry and had departed half an hour later just as quickly, taking with him a copy of the next twenty-one chapters of the Frazer saga in outline and Ensley Holsinger's account of her movements on Monday, 1 June. Apart from Frazer's claim that he had been involved in the assassination of Robert Kennedy, the only other story of note was a boast that under his patronage a substantial number of British Muslim volunteers had been and still were receiving military training in Iran, Iraq and Libya. The first such cadre had been due to pass out before the beginning of Ramadan in May 1996 and would be tasked to strike at American bases in Europe. In the absence of any kind of detail that could be checked against another source, the story had all the authenticity of the wildest rumour imaginable.

Ensley Holsinger was waiting for him in the anteroom and still nursing the gin and tonic he had ordered for her when the bar had opened at

125

six o'clock. She had her nose buried in the pages of the *Field*, which Landon suspected was entirely for his benefit and was intended to show she wasn't the least bit interested to learn what he and Ashton had been discussing when they had been alone together in the library.

'We're off to London early tomorrow morning,' Landon said abruptly. 'DCI Ogden wants to reinterview you.'

'And you're coming with me,' she said, turning a page.

'Yes. Mr Ashton has arranged for a chauffeur-driven car to pick us up.'

'That's a relief.'

'I thought you'd be pleased.'

'I'll be pleased when I can go home.'

'Unless the police object, there's no reason why you shouldn't take up that reservation you have for Monday with American Airlines.'

'You mean you guys are not going to stop me?' Ensley said in mock amazement.

'Well, let me tell you something about the way we classify informants. A source is graded from 'A' through to 'F'. At the top end of the scale, 'A' means the source is reliable while 'F' indicates the informant is too imaginative and should be treated with suspicion. The information provided by a source is rated on a scale of one to six. One means the report is probably true, six stands for uncorroborated and likely to be false. You are F6, Miss Holsinger.'

The explosive effect was immediate. Launching herself from the armchair, Ensley stalked across the room and tossed the copy of the *Field*

126

on to the round table, where it came to rest among the other periodicals. The gin and tonic that had been on the small side table by her armchair had been accidentally dislodged and was now on the floor, seeping into the Axminster carpet.

'At least you didn't throw it at me,' Landon observed mildly, then picked up the empty glass and set it down on the side table.

'Are you calling me a liar, Mr Landon?' she asked in an abrasive voice.

'That sign at the top of the drive — who told you the initials I.S.C. stand for International Study Centre?'

'What!'

'I asked you who told — '

'I heard what you said. I just don't understand how anybody with half a brain could ask such a damn fool question.'

'Humour me.'

'OK, if it means that much to you.' Her eyebrows met briefly in a frown. 'I guess I asked your Mr Ashton and he told me.'

'Wrong,' Landon said quietly. 'I put the same question to him a few minutes ago before he drove off and he said you weren't the least bit curious about the sign.'

'All right, I was mistaken but somebody must have told me what it meant.'

'I think it was on the list of questions you gave Amelia Cazelet,' he said, taking her completely aback.

The way Landon saw it, Ensley Holsinger had begun to suspect that the script she was reading was not a work of fiction. She had therefore made a note of the points that puzzled her and had passed them to Cazelet for clarification. The fact that she didn't once interrupt him persuaded Landon he was on the right lines.

'What you actually gave Amelia could be likened to the editorial notes an author might expect to receive from his publisher. There were minor points of detail to be answered such as, 'What does I.S.C. stand for?'. But the main queries were hidden in those parts of the script which you suggested would need to be fleshed out if the reader was to follow what was going on. And all those passages occurred in the outline of the last twenty-one chapters. Right?'

'Yes.'

'So let's hear it.'

'Well, you've heard my précis of the material which must have intrigued you, especially the section dealing with the recruitment and training of British Muslims. I wanted Frazer to say where these military camps were located and exactly what they were being trained to do.'

Ensley had also been puzzled by a reference to a counterfeit terrorist cell operating out of the Gaza Strip that had been betrayed by the Foreign and Commonwealth Office. Reading between the lines she had got the impression its secret mission had been to identify the cell leaders of Hezbollah, Hamas and Islamic Jihad, pinpointing the safe houses where they sheltered and passing the information to Shin Beth, the Israeli Security Service. In order to win the trust of the disparate Palestinian groups it had been

128

necessary for the counterfeit cell to bomb markets, restaurants, nightclubs and discos in the densely populated districts of Tel Aviv and Haifa. At some stage the FCO had evidently got wind of the operation and had ordered the Intelligence Service to disband the unit.

'This was all pure guesswork on my part,' Ensley told him. 'Frazer merely hinted at what had been going on and the outcome is very much a hunch. The only thing Frazer committed to paper was the bald statement that none of the British Muslims were ever heard of again. I assumed this meant they had been executed.'

'I don't remember seeing this in the précis you produced.'

'I'm not infallible, Mr Landon. I simply forgot Frazer's allusion to their subsequent execution. Anyway, the author didn't condescend to answer any of the questions I submitted to Amelia.'

'How long ago was that?'

'It must have been in late April. I'd had the script for roughly a week.'

'When you didn't get an answer did you ask Amelia what was happening?'

'Yeah, and she got pretty heated about it.' A smile appeared at the corners of Ensley's mouth. 'Matter of fact we almost broke up over it.'

'And you last saw her when?' Ashton asked.

'I've been thinking about that ever since I heard Amelia had been murdered. It must have been Thursday evening, May twenty-eighth. She was off on a long weekend to Martha's Vineyard the following day.'

Landon was prepared to bet a month's pay

that Amelia had not reached Martha's Vineyard. If he was right it meant she must have been lifted sometime on the Friday soon after leaving the bookstore. He wondered how long she had held out before telling the killers what they wanted to know.

Landon could understand why the killers hadn't got to Ensley on 1 June. She had taken her bag into the Julian H. Shubert Agency that day, had worked right through to six thirty, earning herself a few Brownie points in the process, and had then gone straight to JFK two hours before the departure of her American Airlines flight. But over the previous weekend was a different matter; according to the New York press Amelia Cazelet had been in the water two or three days when her body was recovered from the East River. It stood to reason the killers wouldn't have drowned her until she had answered their questions, which meant Ensley Holsinger had been at risk from Saturday at the latest.

'I don't mean to be intrusive,' Landon said, 'but could you tell me how you spent the weekend of the thirtieth, thirty-first of May? I wouldn't normally ask but it is important.'

'I stayed at The Inn on the Sound, Shoreham.'

'Where's that?'

'On Long Island.'

'Were you alone?'

Her eyes started glinting again. Ensley Holsinger was, he thought, easily the feistiest woman he had ever met or was likely to.

'I don't see what business it is of yours,

130

mister,' she snapped.

'I'm just trying to figure out why the killers didn't get to you twenty-four hours after they'd finished with Amelia.'

'I was with Evan. We left New York on Friday evening and drove straight to the office on Monday morning.' Ensley lowered her eyes and looked down at the carpet. 'Actually that isn't strictly true. Evan dropped me off outside the Main Street/Flushing subway station in Brooklyn and I finished the journey by train.'

'That was gallant of him,' Landon said drily.

Her head came up again, a defiant expression on her face. 'He's married, we're having an affair. OK?'

'Anybody at the agency know about it?'

'No. We've been very discreet.'

'What about Amelia, did you tell her?' Landon saw Ensley hesitate and supplied the answer himself. 'She knew,' he said tersely.

'She wouldn't have told anybody.'

'Don't you believe it. When those men went to work on her, as they surely did, she would have betrayed her own mother.'

Ensley put her hand to her mouth. 'Oh, my God,' she murmured, 'I told her Evan didn't like the script.'

'Why don't you put your mind at rest and phone the agency? It's still only eight minutes past two in New York. Ask for Evan; if he's not there find out when anybody saw him last.'

'What'll I say?'

'Use you imagination, you're in fiction.'

'I guess I can try.'

131

'Good. Use the phone in the commandant's office — he won't mind, he's gone home.' Landon got to his feet. 'Meantime I'm going to take a stroll round the grounds.'

It was one of those lovely evenings in early June when the sun was still well above the horizon and the shadows were only just beginning to creep across the lawn. Hands clasped loosely behind his back because he didn't know what else to do with them, Landon walked towards the indoor firing range, which was in the old stable block on the north side of the house. Nothing made sense. Neither George Ventris nor Amelia Cazelet had had anything to do with the events described by Ross Frazer, yet both had been brutally murdered simply because the typescript had passed through their hands. To Landon that suggested there must be something buried within the notes that could betray a major operation that was still in the planning stage. Of one thing he was certain: Hazelwood had withheld a good deal of information about Frazer that could prove useful. They had been given his date and place of birth, his military career, when he had joined the SIS and the date he had been murdered in Paris. What they didn't know was whether Frazer had ever been married, raised a family or had a list of character defects as long as your arm.

9

It was said of Eric Daniels that, like Big Ben in the clock tower opposite Parliament Square, you could set your watch by him. The transport supervisor had instructed him to report to Amberley Lodge at 07.00 hours and he arrived not a minute before or after the appointed hour but exactly on time. Punctuality wasn't the only thing he was noted for. The SIS car fleet had recently switched to Volvos; Daniels, however, was still driving around in a seven-year-old Ford Granada, which was not a little eccentric as some members of the Motor Transport Section thought. After conversion to unleaded, the 2.9 litre V6 fuel-injected engine had been souped up, giving it a top speed of 140 miles an hour and a zero-to-sixty m.p.h. in 8.9 seconds. There were other refinements, like a VHF transceiver, run-flat tyres, Chobham armour to protect the chassis, reinforced doors and toughened glass. Under the dashboard and to the right of the steering column a spring clip had been fitted to hold a Ruger .357 Speed Six revolver.

'Am I overdressed, Will?' Daniels asked after Landon had greeted him.

'I hope we both are,' Landon said, and patted the Speed Six nestling in the holster on his right hip. 'Ms Holsinger would have been seriously at risk had she remained in London but nobody has traced her to this place.'

'Cross fingers.'

'Amen to that, Eric.'

'So what's this American girl like?'

Landon glanced over his shoulder at the house but there was still no sign of Ensley. 'Well, obviously punctuality isn't one of her strong suits. That said, she's bright, very sure of herself and feisty with it.'

'You're slipping, Will. You forgot to mention Ms Holsinger is a real show stopper.'

Ensley would have been equally at home on the catwalk or at the Southampton Boat Show. She was wearing open-toed low-heeled sandals, white linen slacks and a long-sleeve sweat shirt that sported alternative blue and white hoops. Dark sunglasses masked her eyes.

In the time it took Landon to turn about, Daniels had got out of the Granada and moved round the front to open the rear door on the nearside.

'This is Eric,' Landon said.

'Hi, Eric.' Ensley gave him a dazzling smile. 'Why don't I sit up front with you?'

'It wouldn't be a good idea, miss.'

'Why's that?'

'Because you would be a distraction,' Landon told her. 'If there's trouble Eric can't afford to look out for you. That's my job.'

'I thought we had put that behind us yesterday evening. Nothing has happened to Evan. I recorded our conversation on the commandant's phone and played it back to you later. Remember?'

He certainly did, and the affectionate tone in

Ensley's voice had made him jealous, which was absurd considering they had been at loggerheads ever since they had met on Thursday evening. So what if she was a real show stopper, as Eric had observed, she was still too damned feisty for his liking.

'I don't believe in taking unnecessary chances,' Landon said.

'Don't I know it.' Ensley gave Daniels another of her dazzling smiles, told him he was a gentleman and settled herself in the back. 'I trust you are satisfied now, Mr Landon,' she said quietly when he got in beside her.

'Take it from me, you're a lot safer on the nearside next to the kerb.'

'Safer from what?'

'Two riders on a motorbike,' Landon said laconically.

In urban areas and wherever else there was heavy traffic on the road, the motorcycle duo was a tactical innovation currently in vogue with terrorists the world over. Also in vogue was the 9mm Micro-Uzi sub-machine-gun weighing just 2.36 kilograms when loaded with a 20-round box magazine. After drawing alongside the target vehicle, the motorcyclist would make a quick getaway, weaving in and out of the traffic as soon as his pillion rider had raked the car and passengers with one long burst of fire at close range from the sub-machine-gun. To get a clear shot at Ensley such a duo would have to draw level on the inside which was an impossibility provided Daniels hugged the kerb, or kept to the inside lane when on a motorway. The one

135

potential trouble spot today was the bottleneck in Hindhead where inevitably there were always long queues at the traffic lights controlling the intersection of the A287 with the A3 trunk route in the centre of town.

To take advantage of this bottleneck the killers would have to know Ensley would be travelling up to London on the A3 and, in addition, the estimated time of arrival of the car in Hindhead. Both pieces of information would be hard to come by. The fact that Leach and Nicholson had been able to pass themselves off as police officers suggested they might have had inside help. If that should be the case it was only prudent to assume the same source would have told them the date and time Ensley Holsinger was expected to meet DCI Ogden at New Scotland Yard.

'That's where we'll need to be on our toes,' Landon said, voicing his thoughts.

'Were you talking to me?' Ensley asked.

'No, just myself.'

'First sign of madness,' she said, and laughed.

And that was another thing he didn't like about Ensley: she was too damned cocksure and aggressive. Except towards that son of a bitch Evan; he could drop her off in the middle of Brooklyn in order to keep their affair a secret and it was evident she would come back to him for more of the same kind of treatment.

Landon told himself to forget about the American girl and concentrate on the job in hand. Although Daniels would have automatically carried out a radio check before leaving Vauxhall Cross, he told him to call up control again to make sure they were still within voice range of the radio room at New Scotland Yard.

'Give them our present location while you're at it,' he added.

Hindhead was approximately seventeen miles from Amberley Lodge and for once the tailback from the lights at the intersection was not excessive. Unlike the traffic heading south to the coast, they had a clear run through the bottleneck.

★   ★   ★

If it hadn't been for the situation in Kosovo the routine signal from Head of Station, Washington would have lain dormant until Monday morning. As a result of the decision to send deep-penetration patrols into the province, the chief archivist had come into the office that morning to deal with the additional cablegrams the operation was bound to generate. His first act on arrival was to read all the signals that had been received by the duty clerk during silent hours. His second act was to seek out Ashton, for whom Kosovo was very much part of his bailiwick.

'I thought you would want to see this,' he said, and handed the decoded text to Ashton.

The signal from Miles Delacombe was long enough to have compromised the cryptogram that had been in force until 00.01 hours Greenwich Meantime 06 June 98. With Fort Meade, home of the National Security Agency, the US equivalent of Government Communications Headquarters, practically on the embassy's

137

doorstep, it was odds on the Americans had captured and read the entire signal. However, no great harm would have been done because it appeared most of the information had been supplied by the CIA.

'Thank you, Donald, you did the right thing,' Ashton said, then told the chief archivist he would give the signal to the Director General as soon as he arrived.

Sooner or later the signal would find its way to the Mid-East Department but in the meantime it would do no harm to see what Delacombe had been offered. Seating himself in front of the computer, Ashton tapped in the entry code for MIDAS, the acronym for the Multi-Information Data Access System. He then looked to see if the SIS had a file on Ali Mohammed Khalef.

Delacombe had been informed by the source that Khalef had been born on 19 March 1953 at Mosul in northern Iraq, had allegedly been on Saddam Hussein's death list and had fled to the UK in 1982. MIDAS contained the same information but included a red star symbol, which indicated that certain material had been withheld to protect the source, even though the file itself was crypto-protected and could not be accessed by anybody outside Vauxhall Cross. To learn more about Ali Mohammed Khalef, Ashton would have to go cap in hand to the acting Head of the Mid-East Department, who would decide whether or not to grant him access.

'Bugger that,' Ashton said.

'Feeling out of sorts, are we?'

Ashton switched off the computer and stood up. For a large man Hazelwood was surprisingly light on his feet.

'You'll want to see this signal, Victor,' he said.

'Looks like an essay,' Hazelwood complained.

'Well, that's Miles for you; he's apt to be long-winded.'

'And he is sending us a letter in the diplomatic bag.'

'So I noticed.'

'Do we know the name of Delacombe's source in the CIA?'

'At a guess I would say it's Alvin Dombas. He runs the Humint Department and is said to have the ear of the Director.' Ashton frowned. 'All the same I wouldn't go a hundred per cent on everything he told Delacombe, especially where Jill Sheridan is concerned. For instance, I find it hard to believe she's been living in America since May last year. I visited her on polling day, Thursday, May the first, and there was no 'For Sale' sign outside her house.'

'What did Jill get for the property?'

'A million two, according to the new owner.'

'Well, there's your answer,' Hazelwood said triumphantly. 'Estate agents don't stick a notice outside a property where the asking price is in excess of a million. They advertise them in glossy magazines like *Harpers and Queen*, *Vogue*, the *Field* and *Country Life*.'

It didn't matter how the property was advertised. From personal experience Ashton knew you would be lucky to exchange contracts within a month of accepting an offer. Furthermore, as a born survivor who had come through other crises, it simply wouldn't have occurred to Jill to put the house up for sale while the necessity of her resignation was still in doubt.

'At least Roy Kelso won't have to bother Paymaster Limited now,' Hazelwood said.

'I hope he is already doing that, Victor. It would be useful to know where Jill's pension is going. It might give us an insight into her future plans.'

'Quite.'

'Frankly, I don't see her ever returning to this country. Dombas says Jill told him Ali Mohammed Khalef is a plant. Although we have him on file, MIDAS shows it's in the red star category, meaning people like me can't access the information without special permission. But that ruling didn't apply to Jill because she was the Deputy Director General, and prior to her promotion had been Head of the Mid-East Department. Whichever way you look at it, she committed a wilful breach of security and is liable to prosecution under the Official Secrets Act.'

'Let's continue this conversation in my office,' Hazelwood said tersely.

Ashton stacked the in, out and pending trays on top of one another, then placed them in the safe, closed the locking bar and spun the combination dial. With no Dilys Crowther on duty to act as a glorified major-domo, he entered the DG's office from the corridor.

'What's the situation regarding your Albanian

and Serbo-Croat interpreters?' Hazelwood asked, completely changing the subject of their conversation.

'I've got enough linguists to cover the eight patrols the SAS are sending in. Unfortunately there are only two Albanian speakers amongst them.'

'You should try to do better than that, Peter.'

'I can't provide what we don't have. There has not been much call for Albanian linguists, especially since we have been without consular representation since 1939.'

'Are you seriously telling me we've only got two Albanian interpreters?'

Hazelwood was obviously in a mood to be difficult. As patiently as he knew how Ashton told him that of course there were more than two interpreters. However, the veterans of World War Two who had been in the Special Operations Executive were now too old or too unfit to go into the field again. The Cold War generation was not so numerous and many of those who had been traced were either out of the country on business or had emigrated.

'So where are your interpreters now?' Hazelwood asked.

'Three have already reported to Headquarters, Special Forces at the Duke of York barracks, the other five are on their way there. Soon as I hear they've all arrived I'll go across and brief them.'

'Are you making full use of Max Brabazon?'

It was, Ashton thought, the sort of question usually put to a probationer fresh from the Induction Course at the Training School. As such it was a transparent attempt by Victor to keep him off the subject of Ali Mohammed Khalef. Max Brabazon was the retired commander, Royal Navy in charge of the SIS element in Military Operations, Special Projects. He had, in fact, worked his way through the list of interpreters that Ashton had produced, contacting them one by one to inform each man where and when he was required to report.

'Ali Mohammed Khalef,' Ashton said before Hazelwood could think of another distraction. 'Is he part of the Ross Frazer story?'

'No, Mohammed Khalef came on the scene long after Frazer had been murdered.'

'Can I see Khalef's file?'

'That would not be appropriate. Either Winston Reid or the Head of the Mid-East Department will reply to Delacombe's signal.'

Reid was a Foreign and Commonwealth man who had spent his entire diplomatic career in the Middle East. He had therefore been a natural to take over Jill Sheridan's old department when she had been promoted to Deputy Director General.

'What about the Ross Frazer file then?'

'Nice try, Peter,' Hazelwood said affably, 'but it's still off limits to you. Nothing Landon has learned from the American girl warrants opening the file for your perusal.'

'You're right, Ms Holsinger is economical when it comes to revealing the content of Frazer's memoirs. She doles it out a bit at a time and then only when she has to. Anyway, Will came to see me late last night with another morsel he'd prised out of her. This time it was a pseudo-terrorist gang belonging to Hezbollah. They were working hand in glove with Shin Beth, betraying the whereabouts of the Hezbollah leadership.' Ashton looked hard at Hazelwood, hoping to catch some kind of reaction but his old guide and mentor remained totally impassive. 'It's alleged the pseudo gang was eventually betrayed by the FCO. Any truth in that?'

'Only in so far as the Foreign Office withdrew their financial support. However, no official told Arafat where to find the group.'

'Maybe he simply passed the information on to Ali Mohammed Khalef?' Ashton suggested.

'You have a very vivid imagination,' Hazelwood told him dismissively.

Ashton recognised it for what it was, the kind of defensive riposte Victor resorted to instinctively when he was walking on glass.

'Is that a 'no', Victor?'

'What Ali Mohammed Khalef has or has not done is no business of yours.'

'All right, let's talk about Ross Frazer. Was he ever married? Did he have a family?'

'Listen to me, Peter. What Frazer did before he was killed in '89 doesn't provide a motive for the murder of George Ventris and Amelia Cazelet. Forget what may be in the book and look at the signal again. Dombas claims Jill Sheridan is working for him. The question we should be asking ourselves is, what has she stumbled upon?'

Ashton made no comment, even though, on

143

the strength of what Landon had told him about the book, he had previously informed Victor that in his opinion there was nothing in the memoirs anybody other than a homicidal maniac could kill for. The book was Jill's method of paying the SIS back for the way she had been treated by The Service. The people who were stalking Jill clearly believed that anybody who had a copy of the typescript knew how to get in touch with her.

'You've gone very silent, Peter.'

'I was just wondering whether Dombas will allow us to question Jill when they reel her in.'

'You can leave that to me,' Hazelwood said. 'I will spell it out to Delacombe when we reply to his signal.' Hazelwood opened the cigar box on his desk and took out a Burma cheroot. 'Anything else on your mind?'

'Only Ensley Holsinger. I think the FBI should take her into their Witness Protection programme. Her life is going to be at risk from the moment she steps off the plane at JFK. On no account should Miss Holsinger return to her apartment on East 71st Street.'

'All right, Peter, you've made your point. I'll see what can be done.'

There was an air of resignation about the undertaking as if Hazelwood half expected to be rebuffed.

★   ★   ★

If ever Daniels should want a licence to drive a Hackney carriage he would not have to go on 'The Knowledge', as it was colloquially known.

144

Like every taxi driver who had passed the test he knew the streets of central London as if they were simply an extension of his own neighbourhood south of the river. He stayed on the A3 as far as the New Kent Road where he turned left into St George's Road and thence across Westminster Bridge to Parliament Square. From there he cut through to Broadway, then went on down towards the junction with Victoria Street and stopped outside the entrance to New Scotland Yard just short of the revolving triangular sign.

Alighting from the Granada, Daniels walked round the front and opened the rear nearside door for Ensley. As she started to get out of the car, Landon drew the Ruger Speed Six from the hip holster and slipped the revolver underneath the driver's seat. There was no secure parking area in the vicinity and, in any case, with two loaded weapons on board the vehicle, Daniels would have to stay with the car. In the circumstance there was only one solution.

'You'd better wait for us at Vauxhall Cross, Eric,' Landon said. 'I'll ring the Transport Section when we're ready to leave and you can then pick us up.'

Like a sheepdog herding a stray back to the flock, Landon ushered Ensley into the building and steered her to reception.

'This is Miss Ensley Holsinger,' he told the civilian behind the counter. 'DCI Ogden is expecting her. I'm afraid we are a little early.'

'Only by an hour,' Ensley said, chipping in. 'My friend doesn't like to be late.'

145

The civilian receptionist rewarded her with a thin smile, lifted the transceiver on one of the internal phones and tapped out a three-digit number. After a brief monosyllabic conversation, the civilian informed them that DCI Ogden had not arrived yet but was on his way from the Holborn divisional station at Theobald's Road. Fifteen minutes later the investigating officer walked into the entrance hall, recognised Ensley immediately and came over to where she and Landon were sitting in the visitors' waiting area to greet her warmly. He was noticeably less enthusiastic when Landon introduced himself.

Nature had given Bernard Ogden a forehead like a wrinkled prune and light brown hair that resembled a field of stubble after the wheat had been harvested. A shade under six feet, he was the right weight for his height. His rank and lined face suggested to Landon that he was well into his forties; the flat stomach, however, belonged to a younger man.

There was no interview room as such but an office on the fourth floor had been set aside for Ogden's use. He did not want nor did he think it necessary for Landon to be present.

'I can understand your objection,' Landon told him politely, 'and in your position I wouldn't like it either. But the Leach, Nicholson case has security implications and it's possible certain questions may have to be ruled out.'

'I don't like having one hand tied behind my back,' Ogden said coldly.

'And I'm not about to do that. I'm the man who put you on to Lawrence and Jacklin at the

Dorchester. Remember?'

'And then whisked Miss Holsinger into hiding before we could reinterview her.' Ogden turned to Ensley and adopted a more conciliatory tone. 'I gather you saw the woman who called herself Nicholson? Is that correct, Miss Holsinger?'

'Yes.'

Landon blinked. He had said nothing about Ensley's brief encounter with Nicholson when he had made a 999 call from her hotel room. But he had told Ashton and had left it to him to pass the information on to the DG, who presumably had informed his political masters. He could understand now why Hazelwood had been pressured by the Home Office to produce the American girl.

'Could you describe her?' Ogden asked.

'Not in any detail. She just said good evening to me and walked on down the corridor.'

'Would you recognise Nicholson if you saw her again?'

'I think so.'

Ogden unzipped the thin black leather briefcase he had been carrying and took out a photofit, which he passed across the desk to Ensley. 'Would you say this is a good likeness?' he asked.

'That's the woman I saw. Her dark brown hair was drawn back in a ponytail, which made her face look really hard.'

'Have you seen this likeness anywhere else this morning?'

'No. I mean, how could I?'

'It appeared in every newspaper this morning,

147

broadsheet and tabloid.'

'The newspapers hadn't been delivered when we left,' Landon told him.

Ogden ignored him, dipped into his briefcase a second time and produced another photofit. 'This is Leach, he's also on the front pages. Did you notice him in the Dorchester at any time?'

'No.'

'OK. What I propose to do now, Miss Holsinger, is take a statement from you concerning your encounter with Nicholson.'

'That's fine by me. Does it matter that I wouldn't have known who she was if it hadn't been for Landon.'

'Hold it,' Landon said. 'You can't refer to me by name in your statement.'

'What?' Ensley's voice rose a full octave.

'The SIS are essentially a very modest bunch,' Ogden told her drily. 'They don't like to see their names in print.'

★ ★ ★

Despite the name, Seaside Terrace was not situated in what could be described as one of Brighton's desirable neighbourhoods. The transient residents included seasonal hotel workers earning less than the minimum wage, dropouts from the College of Technology, and people on social security benefits who had no intention of finding employment during the summer when lazing on the beach was infinitely preferable. The area also had more than its fair share of drug dealers, pimps and prostitutes, male and female.

The local shops consisted of a mini market, off-licence, Indian takeaway, tobacconist and newsagent, just round the corner from 8 Seaside Terrace, where Leach and Nicholson were staying in a bedsit on the second floor.

The tobacconist and newsagent was owned by the Khans, a Pakistani family comprising three generations, all of whom, from the grandfather to the youngest grandson aged twelve, worked in the shop. With people constantly moving into and out of the area, the Khans did not provide a delivery service, nor did they allow their customers to run up newspaper bills. Today was only the second time Leach had collected the morning papers from the newsagent. As on the previous occasion, he was not the only customer.

Leach took a copy of the *Telegraph* and *Daily Mail* from the display on the counter and paid the old man on the till. He was on his way out of the shop when he heard the younger of the two Khans say he was sure he had seen that woman somewhere before.

That woman — meaning what? A stranger whose face looked vaguely familiar? Somebody whose picture Khan had spotted this morning? But where? In the newspapers? Somehow Leach managed to hold out until he turned the corner into Seaside Terrace before he unfolded the *Daily Telegraph* and felt his bowels turn to water.

10

Mouth dry with apprehension, Leach pushed open the door of number 8 Seaside Terrace and went on up to their bedsit on the second floor. In his absence Nicholson had made up the sofa bed and, having stowed it away, was now relaxing in front of the portable TV with a cup of coffee. Telling her to start packing, Leach tossed the newspapers on to the sofa, then switched off the set. When he turned to face her again she had rearranged the papers and was staring at the photofits that had been placed side by side on the front pages of both the *Telegraph* and the *Daily Mail*. As she looked up at him with her lips parted, he knew exactly what was going through her mind.

'Save your breath,' Leach warned her. 'It is a good likeness of you. It was certainly good enough to remind one of the Khans of somebody he'd seen round these parts.'

'Those were his exact words?'

Leach hesitated. If you knew what was good for you, endeavouring to pull the wool over Borra Nicholson's eyes was not a good idea.

'Well, no. What Khan actually said was, 'I'm sure I have seen that woman somewhere before.' '

'Was Khan looking at the photofit when he said that?'

'I wouldn't know. I was on my way out of the shop.'

'So he wasn't necessarily referring to me?'

'The newspapers were on the counter right under his fucking nose,' Leach said furiously.

'Keep your voice down,' Nicholson told him. 'Do you want everybody in the house to hear you?'

'Oh, that's real good. We wouldn't be in this shitty mess if you hadn't been so stupid. Why the hell did you have to follow the Holsinger woman up to her room on the fourth floor? You'd already made sure Lawrence and Jacklin were unlikely to forget your face in a hurry with all that crap about Special Branch. Then for good measure you assure Jacklin that if we are ordered to detain Ms Holsinger, her arrest will not be effected inside the hotel. Next thing Lawrence sees is you following her into the lift. A few minutes later you reappear in the lobby and Lawrence is watching us like a hawk as I hurry after you. That's why your photofit is as good as a photograph.'

'Calm down.'

'Calm down,' Leach echoed shrilly. 'I'll calm down when I'm out of here.'

There were two backpacks on top of the hanging cupboard; standing on tiptoe, Leach lifted one of them down. 'Start packing if you're coming with me.'

'Where are you going?'

'Paris. There are people in the Algerian quarter who will shelter us.'

'As there are in Finsbury Park, but setting off

151

to either place is too dangerous at the moment.' Nicholson pointed to the photofits in the *Daily Mail*. 'The police will cover all the bus depots and mainline stations; Immigration at Heathrow, Gatwick, Stansted, Folkestone, Dover and every port of embarkation you can think of will have been warned to be on the lookout for us. This is day one and everybody will be alert; give it a week or so without any sightings and they won't be quite so sharp. Meantime, we stay put.'

Leach hated to admit it but she was right, the police and immigration service would be ultravigilant for a time. A week or so, according to Borra Nicholson, but that was just for his benefit. For week, read months. No way was he going to remain cooped up in a cesspit like 8 Seaside Terrace for that long, especially when Mr Nosy Khan and his brood were living just around the corner. Sooner or later that Asian business tycoon was going to remember where he had seen Nicholson before. They needed to be long gone before that happened but how were they going to break cover and get clean away?

It suddenly occurred to Leach that he knew of one man who could help them. 'Ali Mohammed Khalef,' he said, voicing his thoughts.

'What about him?' Nicholson demanded.

'He owes us. We're the people who recovered the script and mailed it to a poste restante in Paris.'

And on Borra's instructions he had killed Ventris and all because the literary agent had been too damned clever for his own good. He'd calculated the market value of the property

152

and maybe he'd also realised it wasn't a work of fiction. If Ventris had just accepted their story and had handed over the typescript he would still be alive today. But no, he'd had to play the hero and had paid the price.

'What are you suggesting?'

'Khalef has a van and he could pick us up. All we've got to do is make a phone call and tell him when and where we will be waiting.'

'If only it were that simple,' Nicholson said. 'The fact is we won't be able to raise him.'

'How do you know?'

Nicholson opened her handbag, took out a mobile and tossed it to Leach.

'You know his number — try it and see what you get.'

Leach did so and got absolutely nothing. 'It's not even ringing out,' he complained.

'That's because Ali Mohammed Khalef will have destroyed his mobile. Naturally he will have reported it stolen by some mugger who'd jumped him from behind. Khalef knows he is being watched by Special Branch, so he immediately put himself in quarantine. It's good security. What the police can't hear can't hurt us.'

'They don't need to overhear anything,' Leach said angrily. 'We're on the front page and there's an army of readers out there who are ready to pick up the phone.'

'Yeah, we had bad luck with the victim.'

'What?'

'He was too famous,' Nicholson said, and proceeded to enlighten him.

George Ventris was no minnow amongst the big fish in the publishing world. He had enjoyed a huge reputation with literary agents in London and New York and had represented a stable of bestselling international authors. He had also been on firstname terms with a number of former cabinet ministers on both sides of The House who had decided to write their memoirs and had heard there was no one better at extracting a six-figure advance from a cost-conscious publisher.

'They were talking about Ventris on Radio Four,' Nicholson continued. 'This was on Thursday morning, less than a day after he had been killed.'

Leach could understand why the two photofits had been released to the press the day after Jacklin and Lawrence had been interviewed. In life Ventris had not been without influential friends and they had obviously exerted pressure on New Scotland Yard to involve the public forthwith in the hunt for his killers. Had Ventris been the ordinary man in the street, the police would have waited until they had enough hard evidence that would stand up in court before they embarked on such a course of action.

'What did New York have to say about Ventris?' he asked.

'My information came from Ali Mohammed Khalef.'

'OK, Borra, so what did they tell him?'

'That Ventris was head of Warwick Thompson Associates, which handles clients of Julian H.

154

Shubert, who are looking for a British publisher. It followed that if anybody was going to sell the Ross Frazer book in London it would be him. They also told Khalef when the courier would be arriving in London.'

'But New York didn't name the courier?'

Nicholson shrugged her shoulders. 'Perhaps they didn't know who was going from the Shubert agency.'

'It stinks. When did Khalef tell you to retrieve the script from Ventris?'

'Two hours before I briefed you.'

Nicholson had arrived at his lodgings in West Ealing shortly after eight o'clock on Tuesday night to inform him what Khalef expected of them. It was their first operation together and they had less than twenty-four hours' notice.

'New York must have been sitting on the information.'

'They had planned to deal with the situation themselves but the opportunity never arose.'

'Now we're getting to it,' Leach said. 'We were required to kill Holsinger. Right?'

'The decision was left to me,' Nicholson told him. 'I came to the conclusion we were too exposed.'

In that instant Leach knew she had been ordered to silence Ventris; that it wouldn't have made the slightest difference if he had meekly handed over the typescript. What was it she had whispered to him out on the landing just as they were about to leave the literary agency? 'Ventris has seen through our charade and he can put us away for ten years minimum.' What really

155

sickened Leach was how easily she manipulated him.

'Pity you didn't think of that before you chatted up Lawrence and Jacklin,' he snapped.

'I gave Asir her room number, description and the date of her departure from the UK. The rest was up to him.'

Asir, meaning 'inaccessible' in Arabic, was the codename of their cell leader. Leach thought it was not wholly inappropriate. He had never met Asir or even spoken to him on the phone. For all he knew the man could be another Brit who'd converted to Islam and had then become a fundamentalist. It was the path he and Nicholson had taken, though unlike her, Leach was not yet ready for martyrdom. Maybe that was the reason why he was not trusted by Ali Mohammed Khalef while she was. Asir was another who obviously trusted her, and suddenly Leach thought he could see a way out.

'Will Asir have put himself in quarantine?' he asked casually.

'What's on your mind?'

'I think you should get in touch with Asir and make it clear that if he knows what is good for him he will get the two of us out of the country pretty damn quick.'

'If he knows what's good for him,' Nicholson repeated. 'I don't think he will like that.'

'Too bad. I've a hunch Asir won't respond unless he feels threatened.'

'You could be right.'

'So what are you going to do?'

'I'll phone Asir and tell him the score,'

Nicholson said in a voice that was somehow full of menace.

★ ★ ★

Richard Neagle had cut his teeth in the Irish Section of MI5, which he had joined in 1979 after spending four years in K1, popularly known within the Security Service as the Kremlin Watchers. From the Irish Section he had graduated to the wider field of Counter-Intelligence Ops with special responsibility for homing in on Mid-East terrorist groups suspected of using the UK as a secure base. He had taken over from Colin Wales as Head of the Anti-Terrorist Branch in November 1997, when the latter had been promoted to Deputy Director General of the service.

Neagle was forty-four but most people would never think it to look at him. Something in his genes had given him the round puckish face of a mischievous child, which time was unlikely to ravage. The same could not be said for his wispy fair hair, which he carefully brushed across the scalp to disguise the number of bald patches that were steadily increasing year on year.

For senior officers like Neagle the Security Service was not a nine-to-five, Monday-to-Friday job. Any terrorist incident and every incoming signal that had been given a precedence of Operation Immediate and above had to be dealt with personally by him a.s.a.p. Consequently there was hardly a Saturday when he wasn't to be found at his desk in Gower

Street. Today was no exception, but for once none of the usual reasons applied: his presence in Gower Street had been occasioned by a photofit in the *Independent*. He had never seen the man before but the woman had looked vaguely familiar, even though her name didn't ring a bell with him. If he was right her photograph would be in an envelope attached to the file of a suspected terrorist. Neagle was certain of one thing: the woman had no connection with the Provisional IRA, Continuity IRA, the Real IRA, the Irish National Liberation Army, the Ulster Freedom Fighters, the Red Hand of Ulster or any other terrorist group in Northern Ireland.

Concentrating on the Mid-East terrorist groups, Neagle pulled the files relating to suspected members of Hezbollah, Hamas, Islamic Jihad, Black September Second Generation and the Popular Front for the Liberation of Palestine who were resident in the UK. Three hours into what was beginning to seem a thankless task, he struck gold with Ali Mohammed Khalef, who was believed to be active in Islamic Jihad. Nicholson's photograph was among the twenty-eight in an envelope attached to the file.

The photographs were of six Caucasians whose only connection with one another was the fact they had been observed in the company of Mohammed Khalef on various occasions. Each photo had been colour-coded on the reverse to indicate how closely the subject might be associated with Islamic Jihad. Nicholson's colour code was off-white, which meant that, while there was no evidence to connect her with a terrorist movement, Special Branch and MI5 were not wholly convinced her relationship with Ali Mohammed Khalef was entirely innocent.

According to the card index maintained by the clerks, she was Gina Nichols, born Newcastle-under-Lyme 30 December 1963, current address 6 Denbigh Close, Denbigh Road, Ealing, National Insurance Number TX 177665B. She was a self-employed shorthand typist on the Brook Street Bureau and had worked as a temp for Shell, BT and various National Health trusts. She had also advertised for secretarial services in the *Author* and had done similar work for Ali Mohammed Khalef, editing and producing clean copies of his periodic diatribes against Saddam Hussein. Neagle believed these propaganda leaflets and letters to the press were simply a cover for his other activities; the question that had perplexed him up to now was whether Nichols or Nicholson had been aware of this.

That issue was no longer in doubt, though how the late George Ventris became part of the equation was beyond Neagle. There was, however, one way to find out. Lifting the receiver Neagle rang the commander (Operations) Special Branch and got the duty detective chief superintendent instead. Specifically he wanted to know who was in charge of the murder investigation, how it was progressing and what security implications, if any, were likely to arise. The chief super rang back fifteen minutes later on the secure-speech facility to inform him that

159

a Mr Will Landon of the SIS had insisted on being present when a key witness was being interviewed by Detective Chief Inspector Ogden.

Will Landon was the SIS member of CATO, the Combined Anti-Terrorist Organisation, which included representatives from Special Branch, MI5 and the Defence Intelligence Staff. They met once a week to exchange information on terrorist activities. Given his ingrained suspicion of 'The Friends', Neagle instinctively came to the conclusion that the SIS was intentionally withholding information. Ashton was Landon's superior officer and CATO was still part of his bailiwick, two very good reasons for calling him to account.

Neagle lifted the transceiver on the Mozart and tapped out the Vauxhall Cross number on the off chance that, even though it was Saturday, Ashton might have come into the office. If there was no reply he would ring him at home. The number rang out just twice before someone picked up the phone and rattled off the six-digit extension at machine-gun speed.

'Is that you, Peter?' Neagle asked.

'Yes, what can I do for you, Richard?'

'Perhaps you would care to tell me why Landon won't let Miss Ensley Holsinger out of his sight?'

'What are you offering me in exchange?'

'The woman who calls herself Nicholson is really Gina Nichols, a Muslim convert and fully paid-up member of Islamic Jihad.'

'Well, OK, Ms Holsinger is a literary agent and Will has written his memoirs.'

160

'That's not even remotely funny.'

'Take my advice,' Ashton said, pre-empting a slanging match, 'get your director to have a word with mine. It's the only way ahead.'

There was a loud clunk as Ashton put the phone down with unnecessary force as if to underline what he had just said. It took a little time for Neagle to decode the message but he finally got it and realised someone in the SIS had written a book people were prepared to kill for.

★   ★   ★

Ogden took close on two hours to interview Ensley Holsinger, which Landon thought had everything to do with the fact that she was a very attractive young woman and the DCI was definitely smitten with her. Since her recorded statement was subsequently transcribed, signed and witnessed inside twenty minutes this was, in Landon's opinion, proof of his contention. All things being equal they should have been on their way back to Amberley Lodge by eleven forty-five at the latest, and that was allowing Daniels more than enough time for the journey from Vauxhall Cross to New Scotland Yard. Landon, however, had reckoned without Special Branch.

The duty detective chief superintendent had intercepted him in the lobby demanding to know what the SIS was up to and just why the murder of a literary agent should concern them. When Landon had refused to answer his questions on

161

the grounds that he was not on the need-to-know list, the chief super had contacted the commander (Operations) at home and had asked him to come into the office. This hadn't gone down at all well and the situation had become even more heated after Landon had suggested they should talk to Ashton. Unfortunately Ashton had been away from his desk and the call had gone unanswered. By the time they did manage to run him to ground in Hazelwood's office, the Special Branch officers were threatening to charge Landon with obstructing the police in the investigation of a crime.

The issue had not been resolved there and then but it was as soon as Hazelwood came on the line. There was, of course, a further delay while they waited for Daniels to make his second trip from Vauxhall Cross to pick them up. At twenty-five past four they finally left New Scotland Yard and headed out of London on the A3.

'You know something,' Ensley said presently, 'the more I see of Chief Inspector Ogden the more I like him.'

'Yeah, I know, our police are wonderful.'

'I guess Special Branch must have given you a hard time.'

'Things got a little sticky for a while,' Landon said, and left it at that.

'The strong silent type,' Ensley observed.

'What about you? Do you intend to fly home on Monday?'

'You heard Inspector Ogden — he doesn't need me at any identity parade. The trial is a

162

different matter, but even if they pick up Leach and Nicholson tomorrow it would be a good ten months before I was required to give evidence in court.'

'We need more time,' Landon said.

'To do what?'

'To firm up the FBI. You need protecting.'

'You are trying to frighten me again, Mr Landon, but it won't work. Watch my lips — Monday, June eighth, American Airlines Flight 215; I'll be on that plane when it departs for New York at 14.05 hours.'

'There's no chance you will change your mind?'

'Absolutely none. But just to set your mind at rest, I won't go near my apartment on East 71st Street. Instead I'll stay with my mom in New Milton.'

It was the instant, off-the-top-of-her-head solution that made him doubt if she had any intention of basing herself in Connecticut.

'Forty-seven hours and thirteen minutes from now.' Landon sucked on his teeth. 'It's going to be very tight but maybe Ashton can do it.'

'Do what?'

'Go private and hire you a couple of watchdogs,' Landon told her.

★   ★   ★

As the passport control officer at the British Consulate in New York, Jack Boothroyd worked a five-and-a-half-day week, finishing on Saturday afternoon at twelve thirty. Allowing for the time zone difference Ashton calculated he had roughly twenty-four minutes in which to contact him before he called it a day and went home. Time wasn't the problem, security was, because there was no way he could tell Boothroyd in veiled speech what he wanted him to do. On the other hand he didn't know Boothroyd's plans for the weekend and he could draw a blank if he tried to ring him at home later in the day.

He didn't know what, if anything, Hazelwood had arranged with the FBI or even if he'd been in touch with Director Louis Freeh before he was called away. After committing eight SAS patrols to operate in Kosovo, the Cabinet Office briefing room had been activated so that the government could have second thoughts. Leastways that was how Hazelwood had acidly put it on learning he was expected to attend. Victor wouldn't approve of what he was about to do but, what the hell, it wasn't in his nature to sit tight and hope for the best. Hesitating no longer he rang Boothroyd in New York.

'I've got a job for you,' Ashton told him. 'There's a VIP arriving JFK this coming Monday on American Airlines Flight 215. I want you to hire a reception committee from a reputable firm. Like the Burns Agency, for instance.'

'I hear they don't come cheap,' Boothroyd said.

Ashton knew that. He had hired the agency once before to run an ex-pat to ground and had been impressed by their discretion and efficiency.

'Don't worry about it, Jack. You tell me what

164

it'll cost and I'll wire you the money afterwards.'

'How many crowd controllers do you have in mind?'

'Three should do it. We shall also need accommodation out of town but within commutable distance. Hopefully Burns can provide this?'

'I don't think that will be a problem.'

'There are a lot of points we need to discuss.'

'I imagine there are,' Boothroyd said drily. 'Shall I call you back after I've spoken to the agency?'

'You do that.'

'Right. I believe I have your home number.'

'I've certainly got yours,' Ashton said, and put the phone down, confident that Boothroyd had read the veiled message correctly and would return the call from his home in Queens.

11

The Training School at Amberley Lodge was sponsored by 17 Maritime Regiment Royal Logistics Corps based at Gosport. The sponsor unit was responsible for routine administration support, ranging from replacement of domestic electrical appliances to the provision of a special dispatch service on demand. The demand that Sunday afternoon had been initiated by Ashton, and the driver of the SDS Land Rover had driven from Gosport to Bosham to pick up the communication and had then delivered it to Landon at Amberley Lodge.

Graded Secret, the envelope contained a copy of the head-and-shoulders photograph of Jack Boothroyd that appeared in his security file. The copy had been stapled to a description of Boothroyd's physical characteristics written in longhand by Ashton. He had also included a note detailing the arrangements for Ensley Holsinger's protection that would be in place when she arrived at JFK International Airport. All Landon had to do was brief Ms Holsinger and persuade her to comply with the measures taken for her safety.

It was, Landon thought, a pretty tall order. She had spent practically the whole of the last three days in his company and it was pretty obvious she couldn't wait to see the back of him. They were, in fact, incompatible. Whatever he asked Ensley to do she invariably did the opposite. This afternoon was no exception. To avoid making herself a target for a sniper, Landon had asked her to stay indoors unless she was accompanied by two prowler guards. When he eventually found Ensley she was stretched out on a sun lounger facing the old stable block on the north side of the house where she was in full view of anybody on the high ground six hundred yards away. There was, of course, not a watchdog in sight.

'There's nothing like living dangerously,' he said, and pointed to the wooded slope. 'You're a gift to any sniper out there.'

'Here we go again,' she said wearily. 'First you do a hundred miles an hour to get away from some car you think is following us but isn't. Then we have to watch out for a couple of killers on a motorbike who don't appear, now it's a sniper prowling the woods. What will you think of next?'

Landon ignored the jibe. Crouching beside Ensley, he produced the head-and-shoulders copy and handed it to her. 'This is Jack Boothroyd. He will be waiting for you in the baggage claim area at JFK. Look for him at the carousel serving American Airlines Flight 215.'

'Aged thirty-nine, five feet seven, and one hundred and forty-two pounds.' Ensley intoned, then looked at Landon with contrived astonishment. 'And this is the man who is going to protect me? What is he, a karate king?'

'He has won medals at clay-pigeon shooting,' Landon told her, straight-faced.

167

'So has my mother and she's drunk half the time.'

'Well, Jack will be sober when he hands you over to the men from the Burns Agency. They will take you to a safe house within commuting distance of New York.'

'Lucky me. What time do we leave tomorrow?'

'Ten a.m. Eric Daniels will drive you to the airport and you'll have one of the security guards for company.'

'What about you?'

'I'll be following in the Aston Martin. OK?'

'One question. What if Mr Boothroyd isn't there to meet me?'

'He will be.'

'You're avoiding the issue, Mr Landon,' she said, smiling.

'Well, all right, if he's not there you don't go looking for the Agency men. Go stay with your mother in New Milton or with someone you can trust implicitly if she isn't at home. Phone me the moment you take refuge.'

Landon retrieved the combined photo and physical description of Boothroyd, then wrote down the international code for dialling the UK, area code and subscriber's number on the back. 'That's my home number,' he said. 'If I don't pick up the phone, leave a message on the answer machine and I'll get back to you.'

'And do what?'

'Raise all kinds of hell on both sides of the pond.'

Ensley gazed at him thoughtfully. 'Yeah, I do believe you would do just that,' she said quietly.

★ ★ ★

Jill Sheridan followed the signs to the baggage claim area, located the carousel dealing with American Airlines Flight 1659 from Dallas Fort Worth and waited patiently for her dark brown Hartmann business case to arrive. Ten minutes later she joined the queue at the cab rank outside San Francisco International Airport. She had arrived in Dallas with nowhere to stay and it was only by a stroke of good fortune that she had managed to take advantage of a last-minute cancellation at the Hyatt Regency. The thought of arriving in San Francisco on a Sunday afternoon and being faced with the same sort of situation had persuaded her to take a chance and use the services of the concierge to book her into the Hyatt on Union Square. The risk that the people who had murdered Amelia Cazelet might trace her to the hotel in San Francisco seemed minimal. As of that morning she had had no reason to fear they had traced her movements since checking out of the Palmer House in Chicago.

The cab driver who picked her up when she reached the head of the queue was a Hispanic with a poor command of English. It was either that or else he couldn't understand her accent. She was still trying to explain she wanted the Hyatt on Union Square, Stockton at Sutton long after he had joined the Bayshore Freeway, which she discovered also happened to be the US Highway 101. A little later the freeway was signed for Oakland and she endeavoured to make him understand that she didn't want to go there.

'You change your mind, no want hotel now?' he asked.

'Just take me to the Hyatt on Union Square,' Jill said, emphasising every word in a loud voice.

The cab driver took the right hand off the wheel and slapped his forehead. 'OK, OK,' he sighed.

They left the freeway at the 4th Street exit, headed northeast on Bryant, then made a left into 3rd.

'Market Street,' the cab driver informed her. 'Soon be there.'

He turned left on to a street the name of which she didn't catch, crossed Stockton and made a right up Powell, passing a cable car on the way. After that Jill lost her bearings and was both somewhat surprised and relieved when the cab driver stopped outside the hotel. It was normal to give a fifteen per cent tip; because he merely opened the trunk from inside the cab and left it to the doorman to collect her case and tote bag she reduced the gratuity to twelve and a half.

Jill checked in at the desk, had an impression taken of her credit card and, accompanied by a bellhop, went up to her room on the seventh floor. Once the bellhop had left after the usual welcome to the Hyatt and have a nice day speech, she unpacked, plugged her mobile into a power point to recharge the battery and then stripped off. Donning a shower cap to protect her hair, Jill adjusted the mixer until the temperature of the water suited her, then

170

freshened up under the shower. Wearing only a towelling bath robe, she returned to her bedroom, disconnected the mobile and called Alvin Dombas.

'It's me,' Jill said when he answered the phone. 'I'm here.'

'Where are you?'

'San Francisco.'

'I already guessed that. Where are you staying?'

'First things first, Alvin. You said you would put me in touch with your local office.'

'It's like that, is it?'

'You told me to cover my tracks,' Jill reminded him.

'Smart girl. The guy you want works from home. Name's Spencer, 162 Bay View, Sausalito. He can be reached on 547-4000. OK?'

Jill added the phone number to the address she had scribbled on the memo pad supplied by the hotel, then asked him how to get to Sausalito.

'Take a Red and White ferry from Fisherman's Wharf on Pier forty-three and a half or go by road over the Golden Gate Bridge.'

'Thanks.'

'You're welcome. Now tell me what you made of Abbas Sayed Alijani?'

The Abbas Sayed Alijani Jill Sheridan knew of was an Iranian diplomat who had walked into the British Embassy in Bonn fourteen years ago and asked for political asylum. He had been debriefed over a period of twenty-one months by the SIS and put to work as a linguist, which

171

meant he read and translated every newspaper and magazine published in Iran. Although the SIS was his paymaster he had not required even minimal security clearance. There had been no prospect of a career in the SIS for the Iranian and after a while the appointment had ceased to give him any kind of job satisfaction. In October 1989 an opening had been found for him in the World Service of the BBC. Four years later he had disappeared, leaving no trace. When the police searched his flat in St John's Wood some eight weeks after he had vanished they had found a pocket notebook listing the names and addresses of Iranian dissidents who had sought refuge in the West.

'I'm still waiting for an answer,' Dombas said, yapping like a small aggressive dog.

'Well, OK, the Iranian I saw in Chicago is not Abbas Sayed Alijani.'

'Are you absolutely sure?'

'Of course I am; the Mid-East was my fiefdom. Furthermore I am fluent in Farsi and was a member of the team which debriefed Alijani. I actually submitted a minority report on him because I believed he was an agent of Ayatollah Khomeini.'

'That was a long time ago, Jill, and maybe the Iranian has changed out of all recognition — '

'Now you listen to me, Alvin. There's nothing wrong with my memory, as even my worst enemies would tell you.'

It was not an idle boast. Jill had a photographic memory; she had only to read a document once for the salient points to be filed away in her mind.

'Do me a favour, Jill. Forget I said that.'

'OK, you're forgiven. Now do me a favour.'

'Name it.'

'I'm travelling on my passport and using my credit cards. I need a completely new identity because right now I'm too easy to trace.'

'I need you out there, Jill, as large as life.'

'What does that mean?'

'It means we'll cover you,' Dombas said, and broke the connection.

'We'll cover you': Jill didn't like the sound of that. It was too damned ambiguous.

★ ★ ★

The house in Seaside Terrace where Leach and Nicholson were staying was subdivided into six self-contained bedsits. The two on the top floor were currently occupied by an unknown number of asylum seekers from Bosnia, Albania and Macedonia, some of whom had escaped from the detention centre outside Ashford in Kent where they were being held while their applications were processed by the Home Office. The remaining bedsits were, in Nicholson's opinion, rented by college dropouts and the homeless on social security benefits.

For the first time Nicholson was conscious of just what a noisy place the house was — raised voices from the floor above, a music centre going full blast in the bedsit across the landing, doors banging, people coming and going. Normally her own portable TV contributed to the noise level

173

but tonight she was too keyed up to watch anything on the small screen. Early yesterday afternoon she had contacted Asir and had told him what Leach had implied he would do if steps weren't taken to get them out of the country pretty damn quick. Contrary to what she thought would happen Asir had reacted calmly to the possibility that Leach would betray them. Twenty-four hours later Asir had returned her call to explain how he would collect them separately using two vehicles this Sunday evening after dark.

Leach had already left the house and by now would be waiting on the seafront opposite the Palace Pier. He had packed his clothes and left them behind with her because there was nothing more suspicious in this town than a man standing around with a backpack on his shoulders. They would meet just once more when they rendezvoused in Ashdown Forest, and Leach collected his backpack. After that they would go their separate ways, which was fine by her. Leach couldn't be relied upon. He had nerves of steel when it came to killing a helpless man in cold blood but when his own life was in danger she had learned he wouldn't hesitate to betray his comrades.

Nicholson glanced at her wristwatch: six minutes to ten, not much longer now. She had heard the sound of footsteps on the landing, then loud voices in a foreign tongue and knew it was some of the asylum seekers from the top floor on their way out of the house. There was another false alarm a couple of minutes later

174

when some drunk tried to call on the neighbours across the landing and got very abusive when he was turned away. Suddenly in need of a cigarette to help her relax, Nicholson opened her handbag and took out a packet of Silk Cut. However, before she could light one, someone tapped out the letter 'V' in morse, the recognition signal Asir had told her to listen for. The cigarette still between her lips she went to the door and let him into her bedsit.

Asir was about five feet eight and slim. He had straight black hair parted on the left side, brown eyes and by any standard was very good-looking, especially when he smiled. He was dressed in black from head to toe with a thin poloneck sweatshirt, close-fitting Italian slacks and soft leather slip-on shoes.

'Are you OK, Gina?' Asir asked, as he removed the cigarette from her lips and crushed it in the saucer she had been using for an ashtray.

'I'm all the better for seeing you,' she said, and closed the door behind him.

'Did you think I wouldn't come?'

'Of course not. I meant how good it was to see you again. I like being with you, surely you know that?'

'And I you,' Asir assured her. 'You will be glad to leave this house, I think?'

'Well, it's not a particularly nice place but it was the best Mohammed Khalef could do for us at short notice.'

'I'm sure it was; it will, however, be necessary to stay here a little longer.'

'A little longer?' Nicholson echoed.

175

'Until things quieten down. There are too many people coming and going.' He smiled and hugged her close. 'We have time for a cup of coffee, I think.'

'I've no milk.'

'That's OK, I like it black,' Asir said, and released her.

Nicholson had felt the hardness of him against her and wished he hadn't let her go quite so quickly. They had made love twice fifteen weeks ago when she had gone to Paris to give him maps of the Birmingham Conference Centre and the surrounding area. Asir had made her do things no other man would have dared to dream about and she had revelled in it.

The tiny kitchenette measured approximately seventy-two square feet and was concealed from the living room by a floral patterned curtain suspended from a wire. Nicholson filled the electric kettle, plugged it into a power point and switched it on, then looked out a jar of instant coffee and two chipped enamel mugs.

'When are we going to have a decent summer?' Asir called from the other side of the curtain.

'These last few days haven't been too bad.'

'That's the trouble with you English, you are too easily pleased.'

'That shows you don't really know us. The weather is our number-one topic of conversation.'

'And what is number two, Gina?'

Nicholson turned about, and there was Asir, stark naked and sporting a rampant erection.

176

'Sex, I guess,' she said in a husky voice.

'It is better to have sex than talk about it, is it not?'

'Definitely.'

Asir turned Nicholson about to face the sink again and made her bend forward at the waist, then unzipped and pulled her jeans down around her ankles.

'Let's go into the other room,' Nicholson murmured, 'it'll be more comfy on the sofa bed.'

'But not so exciting.'

Asir slipped his left arm around her waist and began to caress her thighs while simultaneously reaching out with his free hand to open the kitchen drawer under the draining board as stealthily as he could, then groped for a sharp knife. The cutlery had been thrust into the drawer anyhow and he had to rely on a sense of touch to find a kitchen knife with a blade long enough for the job. Unfortunately the blade was entangled with an egg whisk and there was no way he could separate the two implements without making a noise.

The clatter alarmed Nicholson and, straightening up, she broke free and spun round to face him. Her eyes fastened on the carving knife in his right hand and she instinctively threw up her left arm to ward off the serrated blade. In that same instant a high-pitched scream erupted from her mouth.

Asir stabbed her just below the breast, the blade penetrating two to three inches before it snapped in two. The left arm that had been

177

guarding her chest dropped and she automatically placed the hand over the wound as if hoping to stem the flow of blood seeping through the T-shirt. Grabbing a fistful of her dark brown hair with his free hand, Asir turned her until once more she was in front of him. He rammed a knee into the small of Nicholson's back and retaining a grip on her hair, bent her like a drawn bow. She screamed again, then clutched her neck in an effort to protect the jugular.

'Gina, Gina,' Asir said as if reasoning with a fractious child, 'you are only making things more difficult for yourself.'

He used what was left of the carving knife like a saw, hacking through the fingers of the right hand until she involuntarily let go of her throat. He had planned to slit her throat with one surgical incision before she knew what was happening to her. Unfortunately the surprise element had been lost. He slashed through the jugular, almost decapitating her in the process. The blood pulsated from the severed artery in a fine spray like a garden hose. Asir let go of her and stepped aside as she fell backwards on to the floor. He did not move fast enough or far enough and flecks of blood splattered him from navel to ankles. That did not greatly worry him since he had stripped naked in anticipation of such an accident.

As soon as the fountain effect had ceased, Asir dragged the body clear of the pool of blood on the floor and adjusted the clothing, zipping up the jeans once he had got them to hip level

178

again. The murderous attack had to look as if it had started in the living room; leaving the kitchenette he opened both backpacks and tipped the contents out on the sofa bed. He took a pair of cotton slacks and a sweatshirt belonging to Leach, returned to the kitchenette and dipped both items into the pool of blood. He then daubed the carpet and armchair in the living room and cleaned himself on the cotton slacks before dumping them with the sweatshirt in the bin liner that served as a laundry basket.

After killing her Leach would have changed and fled the house; opening the bottom drawer of the tallboy, he stuffed the rest of the clothing inside to give the impression of a man in a blind panic. Nicholson's underwear, spare bra and T-shirts he neatly folded and put away in the top drawer. Finally Asir placed both backpacks on top of the hanging cupboard, something he only managed to do by standing on tiptoe.

He dressed unhurriedly, glanced one more time round the room, then, satisfied he hadn't overlooked anything, he went out on to the landing. No one saw him leave the house nor did he pass anybody until he turned the corner into Trafalgar Street. The car was where he had left it in Terminus Road right by the station.

★ ★ ★

Four minutes past ten: the day trippers from London and the Home Counties south of the Thames had gone home but the sea front was still pretty lively. Leach counted three beach

179

parties huddled round driftwood fires, the nearest no more than twenty yards away to his left. Come morning the beach above the high-water mark would resemble a municipal rubbish dump with the usual litter of discarded beer cans, empty cigarette packets and polystyrene beakers and food cartons, some containing leftovers from Indian and Chinese takeaways. Scavengers combing the foreshore in search of coins, cigarette lighters and anything else absent-minded owners might have left behind would probably find the odd syringe and used condoms under the pier itself.

Although it was too late to do anything about it Leach nevertheless checked the inside of his bomber jacket to make sure he had his mobile on him, then turned his back on the revellers and walked off towards the derelict West Pier. He had been told to wait ten minutes in the area of the Sea Life Centre before moving on to the final rendezvous, and the fact that he had shaved the time practically in half didn't bother him one bit. If they were any good at their job Asir's people would know within minutes whether or not he was being shadowed by the police. Besides, to have stayed any longer would have sent the wrong signal to the gay who had been sizing him up ever since he'd arrived in the area and that could have led to a very awkward incident.

Harry's was just up the road from the amusement arcade in Middle Street. It was the kind of bar that appealed to single men under forty whose idea of a good night out involved lap dancing, serious drinking and gambling machines. Nobody was yet paralytic when Leach arrived, and neither of the two bouncers had been called on to do anything remotely energetic. A redhead in a strapless black dress and three-inch-high heels was gyrating on a small stage, pressing herself against a vertical steel pole and acting as if she were about to have an orgasm. Finding a niche for himself at the bar, Leach ordered a Bacardi and Coke.

The man who had followed Leach to Harry's called himself Abu Nidal in honour of the Palestinian terrorist whom he regarded as a freedom fighter. His brother-in-arms, Ahmed Zia, was standing by the Ford Escort in the car park on West Street, ready to move off at a moment's notice. Since it was evident the Englishman was not being followed, Abu Nidal decided there was no point delaying matters unnecessarily; taking out his mobile phone he bleeped the ten-digit number he had committed to memory and got an immediate answer.

'Mr Leach?'

'Yes, who is this?'

'Asir sent me to collect you,' Abu Nidal told him. 'Leave now.'

'But I've just ordered a drink and it's going to look funny if I don't touch it.'

'Make some excuse and finish it quickly.'

'OK. How will I recognise you?' Leach asked in a low voice.

'Turn left outside the bar, go into West Street and make your way to the car park. I will call out to you when it is safe to do so.'

Abu Nidal terminated the call, drifted into the

amusement arcade, and fed a pound coin into the first available fruit machine near the entrance. He did not have to feed the machine a second time; the symbols were still revolving when Leach walked past the amusement arcade and turned the corner into West Street. After allowing the Englishman a head start Abu Nidal left the amusement arcade to follow him.

Leach had almost reached the car park before he became aware that somebody was following him. Fearing the worst, he clenched his hands, ready to lash out if some mugger tried to jump him. Then the man he'd spoken to only a few moments ago said, 'Wait for me Sabri al-Banna,' and he immediately slowed down.

Sabri al-Banna was the real name of the freedom fighter Abu Nidal. It was also the name given to Leach when he had become a Muslim.

'Who are you?' Leach asked when the stranger caught up with him. 'I mean, what is your name?'

'It is better you don't know.'

'For reasons of security. Right?'

'Did you learn nothing at the Oruzgan Training Camp?'

A red Ford Escort nosed its way out of the car park, made a left and drew up alongside them. Leach got into the back and, on the stranger's instructions, moved across to sit behind the driver.

'Where are we off to?' he asked as the driver pulled away from the kerb.

'To meet Asir,' the stranger said.

They headed out of Brighton on the road to Lewes where the driver left the A27 trunk road and picked up a minor road. Between Lewes and the junction with the A22 south-east of Uckfield they encountered just three vehicles. Roughly twenty minutes later the driver turned off the main road to follow a track that led deep into Ashdown Forest where Asir was waiting for them in a clearing.

Asir watched Leach get out of the Escort and went forward to meet him. This was the point where every move was fraught with risk. If the Englishman sensed danger and ran off into the forest, finding him again might be impossible on such a dark night as this.

'Greetings, Sabri al-Banna,' he said, addressing Leach by his Arab name. 'I have your clothes in my car.'

'Good. Where are we going?'

'To a safe house not far from here.' Asir smiled. 'By this time tomorrow you will be in France.'

Abu Nidal came up behind Leach silent as a big cat stalking its prey until he stepped on a twig and snapped it, but by then it was too late for Leach to do anything. While Ahmed Zia held the Englishman, Abu Nidal clapped a sanitary towel soaked with chloroform over his nose and mouth. Thereafter it was simple enough to pick up Leach, carry him over to the Ford Escort and position his body behind the wheel. Asir donned a pair of surgical gloves, fetched a .357 Colt revolver from his car and, forcing the unconscious Leach to open his mouth, rammed the barrel inside. He then squeezed the trigger and blew away the back of his skull.

183

12

The Ford Escort had been left in a clearing
north of the Ridge Road in Ashdown Forest
roughly four hundred yards beyond one of the
visitor car parks. The vehicle could not be seen
from Ridge Road and, but for a retired Post
Office engineer out walking his Labrador, several
days might have passed before it was discovered.
In fact it was the dog who actually found the car
and refused to come to heel when the owner
whistled for him. The reason for his disobedience
became clear when the engineer reached the
Ford and looked inside.

The dead man would have toppled right over
to his left had the seat belt not been fastened
across his chest to hold him more or less in place
behind the steering wheel. The interior was
literally swarming with flies eagerly dipping their
probosces into the congealed blood and brain
matter on the upholstery. Others were exploring
the matted hair on the back of the skull where a
sizeable piece of bone was missing. How the flies
had got inside the Escort was no big mystery;
they had entered through the elongated hole in
the roof midway between the rear window and
the courtesy light. No one had to tell the retired
Post Office engineer what had made the gash.
He had done twelve years in the Royal Signals
and recognised a bullet hole when he saw one.
He pressed the left side of his face against the

front off-side window and could just see a revolver on the floor between the brake pedal and the accelerator.

The engineer prided himself on having a strong stomach. While a soldier he had done four years of duty in Northern Ireland in the early seventies when the bombing campaign waged by the Provisional IRA had been at its height. He had seen the blood-spattered interior of a Saracen armoured personnel carrier that had been blown up in South Armagh by a five-hundred-pound bomb placed under a culvert. He had been serving in Belfast when thirteen bombs had been simultaneously detonated in different areas of the city and had just passed the bus depot in a Land Rover when the first one had exploded. He had stopped and tried to give first aid to a young woman whose arm had been blown off at the shoulder but it had proved impossible to stop the arterial bleeding with a tourniquet and he had nursed her in his arms, giving what comfort he could until she died. Nothing, however, had prepared him for the loud and sudden eruption of gas from the corpse and the frantic activity it provoked amongst the swarm of flies. The bile rose in his throat and, backing away from the Ford Escort, he folded at the waist and threw up. It was some minutes before he was sufficiently composed to phone the police on his mobile.

★ ★ ★

Ensley Holsinger was a taboo subject. Her name had never been mentioned at morning prayers and, so far as Ashton knew, none of the other department heads had ever heard of her. He thought it possible that even Winston Reid, the Deputy DG, was unaware of her existence. Certainly the former Foreign Office man had never been present when he and Victor Hazelwood had discussed what the SIS should do about her. Morning prayers had finished at three minutes past nine and it was now twenty to eleven. Landon had left Amberley Lodge at ten o'clock sharp and would shortly arrive at Heathrow and still there was no word from Hazelwood, even though Victor had been told by his PA that he wanted to see him. Ashton decided he would give it another five minutes before he walked in on the DG, regardless of whether or not anyone happened to be with him. In the event Dilys Crowther rang to inform him that Sir Victor was now free before his self-imposed time limit expired.

The moment Ashton walked into his office it was evident that the subject of Ensley Holsinger was not uppermost in Hazelwood's mind. In one fluid movement Victor waved him to a chair with the slip of paper he was holding in his right hand.

'Here's the answer to your query,' he said, and pushed the memo at him.

The note was from Roy Kelso, handwritten in his familiar backward-sloping style and was headed 'Jill Sheridan — banking arrangements modified pension'.

186

'Bit of a shaker, isn't it?' Hazelwood observed. 'Must bring back old memories for you.'

Ashton nodded. 'Ones I would prefer to forget.'

The year's tax-free salary Jill had received on leaving the SIS had been paid into her current account with the Highgate branch of Lloyd's Bank PLC on 2 May 1997, the day after she had resigned from the service. Her modified pension was credited to her account on the first of the month commencing 1 June. Before this, however, Jill had closed the Highgate account and transferred everything to Surbiton where she had banked when she and Ashton had been engaged and living together in a flat on Victoria Road.

'Why do you suppose she did that, Peter?'

'I haven't the faintest idea. I moved out of the flat when Jill returned from Bahrain with Henry Clayburn in tow. Maybe when they moved to Highgate she kept the account in Surbiton open.'

'For what purpose?'

'I don't know — perhaps because she married Clayburn with divorce in mind. When we sold the flat, she may have banked her share in Surbiton against that rainy day.' Ashton placed the memo on the desk within Hazelwood's reach. 'Be interesting to know what she has done about her pension. Is it piling up in Surbiton or has she arranged for it to be transferred each month to a bank in the States?'

'I don't think we need to waste any further time on Jill,' Hazelwood said crisply. 'Same

187

applies to Ensley Holsinger now that she is on her way home.'

'I assume the FBI will be looking out for her?'

'What have you been up to, Peter?'

It was the exact expression young mothers used to their offspring when the latter were looking too angelic for words. Hazelwood was not in a benevolent mood and Ashton knew he would have to do some fancy footwork.

'I got Jack Boothroyd to hire three men from the Burns Agency. I figured that with all those meetings you had to attend concerning our operations in Kosovo you wouldn't have time to set things in motion with the FBI.'

'That was thoughtful of you,' Hazelwood said acidly. 'Who's paying for this?'

'Jack Boothroyd, initially. I said I would reimburse him from my contingency fund.'

'I see. And how much is the Burns Agency charging for their services?'

'Twenty-five hundred dollars a day, say one thousand six hundred and fifty pounds. I hired them for a maximum of four days.'

'In the hope that the Bureau will have taken Ms Holsinger under their wing by then?'

'I think I may have been overgenerous in allowing four days,' Ashton said. 'The FBI shouldn't need more than forty-eight hours' notice.'

'And what if the Bureau doesn't come through?'

'Is there a chance they won't?'

Hazelwood snorted, 'Of course there is.'

When talking to Director Freeh he intended to

stick to the known facts and leave it to the American to draw his own conclusions. There would be no allusion to a possible terrorist involvement when Hazelwood related the conversation between Nicholson and the desk clerk at the Dorchester. And nothing would be said about the Ross Frazer file.

'Because it is politically damaging,' Ashton said flatly.

'That's one reason,' Hazelwood agreed, 'but it's not the principal one. The Ross Frazer story is a distraction. There is nothing in it that is worth killing for. You said so yourself.'

'I also said Will Landon was convinced Ms Holsinger was being pretty economical with the information she disclosed to him. He had to wrest it out of her a bit at a time.'

'And the same applies to the résumé she produced covering the last twenty-one chapters?'

'Yes. There are another seven chapters after the one dealing with the assassination of Robert Kennedy in '68. There has to be at least one other startling revelation after that.'

'But neither you nor Will Landon felt sufficiently confident to recommend delaying Holsinger's departure beyond today.' Hazelwood wagged an admonishing finger at him. 'Don't bother to deny it,' he added.

Ashton wasn't about to, even though the accusation was unjust. No way would Hazelwood have supported him had he recommended detaining Ensley Holsinger for further questioning. After taking a second statement from her the police had raised no objection to her returning home. This meant the SIS would have to brief the Foreign and Commonwealth Office, which in turn would have to make a case with the American Ambassador. There would be no suppressing the Ross Frazer file then and that was something Victor and the Permanent Under-Secretary would never contemplate.

'I presume the Burns Agency is providing a safe house for Ms Holsinger?'

'Yes. New Haven, Connecticut, 196 Orange Street.'

'I will, of course, let you know what Director Freeh has to say.' Hazelwood made a note of the address on his memo pad, then looked up. 'Whatever his decision you are not to renew contact with the Burns Agency. We are not in the business of providing bodyguards for American citizens. Clear?'

'Perfectly,' Ashton said, masking his anger.

'As far as your department is concerned, Kosovo is now the number-one priority. Leave Nicholson and Leach to the police and MI5. Ralph Meacher will handle any further queries raised by Alvin Dombas and will decide what is of interest to members of the CATO committee.'

Ralph Meacher was the acting Head of the Mid-East Department and was rumoured to be keeping the seat warm for some Foreign Office mandarin. He was certainly keeping it warm for somebody; more than twelve months had passed since Winston Reid had moved up to Deputy DG following Jill Sheridan's resignation. Meacher was not without ambition and still entertained the hope of being confirmed in the appointment, and that made it easy for Victor and his deputy to manipulate him. Meacher would no more decide what was of interest to CATO than fly to the moon.

'Something on your mind, Peter?' Hazelwood asked.

'I was just wondering if Colin Wales knows of Jill's literary pretensions.'

'Why should he be interested?'

'Because everything started with her and that damned book. Now do I gag Will Landon in case Neagle raises the matter at the next CATO meeting or what?'

'You worry too much,' Hazelwood told him.

It was not the guidance Ashton had sought.

⋆　⋆　⋆

At the height of the Cold War the Grade I intelligence officer in charge of the Russian Desk was regarded by his peer group as a man who was definitely going places. That had certainly applied to Hazelwood, but thereafter perestroika and glasnost had reduced the kudos attached to the appointment. Perestroika had also led to the downsizing of the post from a Grade I appointment to a Grade II at the insistence of the Treasury, eager to impose the so-called peace dividend on every government ministry except theirs.

It was true Ashton had made it to assistant director but he had advanced sideways via the Combined Anti-Terrorist Organisation, which had earned him his initial promotion. Chris

Neighbour, the latest incumbent of the Russian Desk, doubted if he could ever emulate Ashton. For one thing, Will Landon had been a member of the CATO committee from its inception and was now the SIS representative; for another, the appointment had become a Grade II post since Ashton had held it.

Despite his limited career prospects, Neighbour was a long way from being disgruntled. He enjoyed what he was doing, liked working for Ashton, and knew he was good at his job, thanks to his practical experience. In 1994 he had been posted to the British Embassy in Moscow where he had made a name for himself. Two years later he had been deported after spiriting an A. P. correspondent out of the capital, whose life was in danger from both the Mafiozniki and officers belonging to the Criminal Investigation Division of the Moscow Police Force.

Many of the names that appeared from time to time on communications from George Elphinstone, Head of Station, Moscow, were familiar to Neighbour. That afternoon one name in particular made him sit up and take notice. After reading the intelligence report a second time, he left his office, locked the door behind him and walked the report up to Ashton on the top floor.

'I think this intelligence report will be of particular interest to you, Peter,' he said, and placed the flimsy on the desk and pointed to the subject heading.

'Vassily Semyonovich Malinovsky, brother of the late Katya Malinovskaya,' Ashton intoned,

192

and looked up frowning. 'I didn't know she had a brother in the diplomatic.'

'Neither did I.'

Eight years ago Katya Malinovskaya would not have looked out of place on the front cover of any of Moscow's fashion magazines, which had burgeoned with the coming of perestroika. On the changed circumstances of the former Soviet Union she had been chosen to represent the more acceptable face of the KGB's Second Chief Directorate. Back in those days Katya had been more than an attractive-looking young woman; in fact, until a nearly fatal knife wound in the back had put paid to her career, she had been one of the rising stars in the Criminal Investigation Division, which had grown out of the former Twelfth Department.

Ashton had become acquainted with her when she had been one of the police officers protecting Elena Andrianova, a member of the locally employed support staff at the British Embassy whose life was at risk from hard-line members of the KGB. The threat had been real enough. Katya Malinovskaya had, in fact, been knifed in the back by one of her colleagues while on duty. Invalided out of the police force she had used the skills acquired in the service to set up her own security agency, specialising in protecting valuables, property and people. Ashton had employed her in '93 to provide electronic and physical protection for the Moscow-based representative of Stilson Manufacturing, a front company operated by the SIS. He had employed Katya again two years later, this time to find a

193

barman at the Golden Nugget who might or might not have overhead a conversation between a Russian informer and his case officer from the British Embassy.

Neighbour knew of her reputation before she had phoned him at the embassy when on the run from the Mafiozniki in '96. She had had information for sale and the price had been relocation in England, provision of a fully furnished house of her choosing and enough start-up capital to launch a new business. Head of Station hadn't bought it and Katya had sought refuge in the apartment rented by Walter Iremonger of Associated Press. Moments after her arrival she had been shot dead by a sniper from an apartment across the street. As a direct result of his involvement with both parties, Neighbour had been served with an expulsion order.

'Head of Station seems to be very impressed with Malinovsky's curriculum vitae,' Neighbour observed.

'Yes, that is unusual. George Elphinstone isn't exactly noted for his enthusiasm. Have you run Malinovsky through MIDAS to see if he's genuine?'

Neighbour shook his head. 'I'm afraid it didn't occur to me. I mean, George Elphinstone was Head of Station, Cairo at the time when Malinovsky was serving in the Russian Embassy. I assumed he would have picked up on that if the information was false.'

'Read the CV again Chris. This guy has served in Baghdad, Beirut, Cairo and New York with the United Nations Delegation. That should tell you something.'

'It does.'

Neighbour mentally kicked himself for not seeing the implication until Ashton drew his attention to it. Rarely did a Russian diplomat do so many tours abroad unless he or she was an officer in the Foreign Intelligence Service.

'Malinovsky's language qualifications are out of this world — Arabic, Farsi, English, French, German.' Ashton paused then said, 'Katya would be thirty-three going on thirty-four had she still been alive; whatever else he might be, Vassily Semyonovich can't be her younger brother. Look at the time he must have spent acquiring those language qualifications, never mind the number of foreign postings. He's got to be at least fifty. Could be he is not even related to her. After all, Malinovsky is a pretty common name.'

'He made a big thing about your relationship with Katya,' Neighbour said quietly. 'Says she told him you could be trusted implicitly.'

'That doesn't make Katya his sister. You can bet the Russian Security Service has a file an inch thick on the two of us. They could have given Malinovsky all the information he needed to hoodwink George Elphinstone.'

Malinovsky had approached the Head of Chancery during a reception held at the German Embassy hosted by the newly appointed ambassador. The Russian, who was reputed to be a senior political adviser in the Ministry of Foreign Affairs, had spoken of the concern shared by their two countries with regard to

195

Muslim extremists and had suggested an exchange of information would be of mutual benefit. Malinovsky had made only one stipulation: Ashton was the sole person he was prepared to deal with.

'And another thing,' Ashton continued, 'the way Vassily Semyonovich tells it, Katya and I got on like a house on fire but it wasn't like that at all. She had a vocabulary of epithets that would have made a whore blush and all of them applied to me at one time or another.'

'What exactly does that prove?' Neighbour asked.

'Nothing. Use my terminal, tap in Vassily Semyonovich Malinovsky and let's see what MIDAS has on him.'

The answer was not a lot. His date and place of birth were not known, and if he had served in Baghdad and Beirut, nobody in the diplomatic had noticed him. There were no photographs of Malinovsky on record but it was possible the FBI or the CIA had taken his picture when he had been serving with the Russian delegation to the United Nations from 1978 to 1981. The only description had been provided by George Elphinstone, who had met him in Cairo. Malinovsky was said to be approximately six feet tall, between one sixty and one seventy-five pounds in weight, had blond hair and the bluest eyes Elphinstone had ever seen. In '92 he had been married to Lydia Petrukova.

'Take a printout and attach it to the intelligence report,' Ashton said, peering over Neighbour's shoulder.

'Right.'

'And what would you recommend in my shoes, Chris?'

'I think we need to know a hell of a lot more about Vassily Semyonovich before having anything to do with him. We should ask Head of Chancery for an up-to-date description. After all, he was face to face with him at the German Embassy do.'

'Then write me a memo to that effect and I'll waltz it into the DG,' Ashton told him.

★ ★ ★

Jill had been warned that San Francisco could often be cold and damp even in summer, but not today. Today there was no sea mist rolling in to obscure the Golden Gate Bridge, today the sky was aquamarine blue and the temperature was in the mid-seventies. Sausalito was a twenty-minute boat ride from Pier 43½, and if she hadn't been on edge, the ferry trip across the bay would have been enjoyable. Other than the fact that Spencer worked from home at 162 Bay View, Jill knew next to nothing about the man she was going to meet. A voice on the telephone could sometimes provide a clue to the caller's age and possible disposition but any mental image formed as a result was wide of the mark nine times out of ten.

The guidebook described Sausalito as a quaint yet sophisticated village, which looked like a transplant from the French Riviera. That certainly applied to Spencer's house on the waterfront, with its spectacular view of Alcatraz Island and the former legendary federal prison.

The man who opened the door to Jill when she pressed the bell button was distinctly unimpressive. Thin as a rake, with birdlike features, he was barely five feet eight inches tall. Half a dozen strands of fair hair were trained across the crown of his head in an effort to disguise the fact that he was rapidly going bald. Jill thought he was in his early fifties and suffered with very poor eyesight if the thickness of the lenses in his spectacles was any guide.

'Mr Spencer?' Jill asked tentatively.

'Yes indeed. Won't you please come in, Miss Sheridan.' Spencer opened the door wider and stepped aside to give her more room. 'If you'd like to lead the way, it's the second door on your left.'

The room was at the back of the house and looked as if it was rarely lived in. It was austerely furnished with a couple of armchairs, a steel desk and swivel chair that had obviously been purchased from an office supplier, and three rugs arranged in haphazard fashion on the parquet floor. There were no pictures on the walls and the fitted bookcase behind the desk was three-parts empty. Although the Venetian blind was lowered, individual slats had been opened just wide enough to allow shafts of sunlight into the room and reveal the dust moats drifting in the air. The temperature was subarctic.

'I think I'd better turn the air conditioning down, don't you?'

Jill flinched. She had not heard Spencer enter

198

the room and, without knowing why, believed he had deliberately set out to frighten her.

'Yes, it is a little cold in here,' she said in a small voice, and sat down in the nearest armchair without waiting to be invited.

'That's right, make yourself at home, Miss Sheridan.'

She didn't know whether or not she was imagining it but his tone of voice sounded a touch sarcastic. Like a rabbit transfixed by the headlights of an oncoming vehicle, Jill watched Spencer use the wall-mounted control panel to adjust the air-conditioning unit before seating himself at the desk.

'Let's talk about Walter Maryck,' he said brusquely.

'Maryck?' she echoed.

'Yeah, good old pro-Brit Walter, who'd swallowed more horseshit from you guys than the previous five station chiefs put together.'

'That's ridiculous. You obviously don't know Walter — '

'I know this much: you contacted Maryck the day you resigned from the SIS and persuaded him it was in our interest to make you feel at home in the States. So you end up with a long-stay visa and work permit but what did we get in return . . . ?'

'A lot of good information,' Jill snapped.

'Yeah, all of it ancient history. Interesting, I admit, but none of it worth the asking price.'

'I don't know what it is you want from me.'

'The truth, lady, the goddamned fucking truth.'

The violence of Spencer's language shocked her. You didn't expect that kind of thing from a fifty-something puny man who looked as if he wouldn't harm a fly. The diatribe continued relentlessly; when it came to the present day she was accused of feeding the CIA a load of crap about how Ali Mohammed Khalef, the Iraqi cleric and member of Islamic Jihad, was allowed to operate from a safe haven in the UK.

'And then there is Abbas Sayed Alijani, the one guy we can trace. And what happens when you go to Chicago to identify him? You tell Alvin Dombas that he is not the man you debriefed.'

'Because he wasn't,' Jill said angrily.

'Next thing I know you will be telling me you had no idea Amelia Cazelet was an active supporter of the Popular Front for the Liberation of Palestine.'

'I'm not going to listen to any more of this nonsense.'

'What were you getting from Amelia, apart from sex? More material for that book we know you are writing? Whatever it was, did you deliberately set out to compromise Cazelet and get her killed?'

'That's it, I'm leaving.'

'The hell you are.'

'Try and stop me,' Jill snarled and stood up.

'There are two FBI agents in the next room, Miss Sheridan, and they're just aching to take you into custody.'

'I'd like to see them try.'

'Stay where you are.'

As she turned away and moved towards the

door, Spencer reached under the desk and pressed a buzzer. Up to a point what happened then was all very civilised. The FBI agents were in their mid- to late thirties, and were very polite, the taller of the two men addressing her as 'mam' when he informed her why she was being arrested. Things became less friendly after that as they manacled her wrists in front, linking them with a heavy chain to the leg irons that shackled her ankles. The length of her stride was reduced to a few inches and she had to gather in the slack on the linking chain for fear of tripping over it. Feeling totally humiliated, Jill shuffled out of the room, across the hall, and through the kitchen into the integral garage. Unable to raise her legs, Jill had to be lifted into the closed van. Neither man would say where they were taking her.

13

The room was a concrete box some twelve feet long by nine feet wide. Lacking any windows, light was provided by a powerful halogen lamp in the ceiling, which, although out of reach, was protected by a metal grille. There were just two items of furniture: a chemical toilet, and an iron bedstead, the legs of which had been anchored to the floor. Jill Sheridan had no idea how long she had been incarcerated in the box because on arrival at this hellhole they had taken her wristwatch and other personal belongings away. If that wasn't enough, Jill hadn't the faintest notion of her present whereabouts. The journey from Spencer's house to the detention centre had taken thirty-five minutes, but she had been unable to see a damned thing from inside the van. And on arrival, she had been blindfolded before they took her out of the vehicle.

Jill Sheridan had attended the SIS Induction Course in 1981, a year before Ashton had gone to Amberley Lodge. Resistance to Interrogation had been part of the curriculum, the cardinal lesson being that before a prisoner could resist effectively it was vital to know what to expect from the interrogation. She had learned about disorientation and sensory deprivation, about psychological and physical intimidation but it had been entirely theoretical. The instructors hadn't put a bucket over her head and hammered it with truncheons until her ears seemed to pick up the sound of Bow Bells. Her only experience with physical intimidation had involved embracing the wall. This was a subtle form of torture whereby the victim had to stand with legs wide apart some four feet away from the wall and lean forward to within touching distance when they then had to support their weight on fingertips. Jill had been allowed to quit whenever it got too much for her but out of pride had managed to hold the position for just under four minutes.

There had been no easy opt-out clause from the two goons who had brought her to this garbage dump. She had been forced to embrace the wall until both arms from the fingertips to shoulder blades ached intolerably and she begged them for permission to stand upright again. So far they hadn't resorted to head banging but she was learning what disorientation, sensory deprivation and psychological intimidation really meant. When the halogen lamp was switched off, the cell was pitch-black and it was literally impossible for her to see a hand in front of her face. Without a watch it was also impossible to keep track of time; it was night when the lamp was off, daytime when it was on. She was fed at irregular intervals and deprived of sleep, woken at all hours to answer the same damn questions over and over again. And more often than not they roused her when her pattern of sleep was at its deepest.

However, when the light came on this time she was already half awake. A key rattled in the lock, the bolts top and bottom were withdrawn and the steel door swung open. Familiar with the drill by now, Jill stood up, held out both arms and waited patiently for her wrists to be manacled while the second man shackled the leg irons about her ankles. It was all part of the intimidation process like the orange coveralls and slippers they made her wear. As was her usual practice, Jill gathered up the slack in the wrist-to-ankle chain and shuffled into the interrogation room next door.

Instead of the iron bedstead to sit on there was a wooden ladderback chair. There was also a window but it was strictly one way and the light was still artificial, but it was less glaring than the one in her cell and therefore easier on the eyes. The interrogator was a disembodied voice; the man running this session had a Texan drawl.

'We'll talk about Amelia Cazelet,' he informed her.

'Just for a change,' Jill said, imitating his accent.

'Starting with how and when you met her, Miss Sheridan.'

'That's easy. I walked into the bookstore on 7th Avenue where she worked in early June last year. I was browsing through the reference section and had picked up a copy of *The Authors' Year Book 1997*. I must have had my nose buried between the covers for about ten minutes when she approached me.'

'Was this before or after you had started to write your hard-luck story?'

'I'll ignore that,' Jill said, tight-lipped with anger.

Hard-luck story? After the disgraceful way she had been treated by the SIS? Her temper had started to boil over the day the Permanent Under-Secretary at the Foreign and Commonwealth Office had called for her resignation and it hadn't diminished one iota since then.

'You were residing in New York City at the time?'

Jill nodded to the window. 'The Shakespeare in downtown Manhattan. It was very convenient for the Zenith Corporation, your front organisation in New York, as I'm sure you are aware.'

The decision to get even with her former colleagues had, in part, to do with the offhand treatment she had received from the CIA. Maryck had led her to believe she would be welcomed with open arms by 'The Company', and certainly Alvin Dombas had been quick to debrief her. Not at Langley, Virginia, but in New York at the offices of the dummy corporation that made it that much easier for the CIA to dump her if they had a mind to. And for a while it had looked as if they intended to do so.

'What exactly did Cazelet offer to do for you?'

'Amelia volunteered to put me in touch with a literary agent who was a friend of hers and lived in the same apartment house.'

'Right off the bat?'

'No, of course it didn't happen quite like that,' Jill said wearily. 'How many more times do I have to tell you that we met for a drink after the bookstore closed that evening? Amelia was good company, I liked her and we saw each other roughly twice a week. It was towards the end of June when she offered to put me in touch with Ensley Holsinger of the Julian H. Shubert Agency.'

'Was this before or after she had invited you to spend some time at her love nest in Edgartown?'

'You guys must be pretty dim but I'll say it one more time. I never met Ensley Holsinger and she never knew who she was dealing with. I used Amelia Cazelet as a go-between. And for the record, I didn't have a lesbian affair with her.'

'Did I say you did, Miss Sheridan?'

'It sounded like it to me.'

'You're too sensitive. All the same you want to be careful what you say to people. For example, take the conversation you had with this man last Friday.'

A moment later she heard Dombas say that her lesbian friend had been murdered and her own startled reaction to the news had provoked him to ask how many lesbian friends she had. 'Just the one,' she had told him.

'OK, it sounds bad,' Jill admitted. 'And yes, I knew Amelia was gay but I'm not. We slept in separate bedrooms when I stayed with her at the cottage she'd rented in Edgartown for her summer vacation.'

'You returned to New York two days ahead of Cazelet. Why was that?'

'You already know the reason. I'd left my mobile number with the people at Zenith and after weeks of silence, Alvin sent word he wanted to see me a.s.a.p.'

'Because some of the information you had given him about Islamic fundamentalists had checked out?'

'Yes. He also wanted to know what I made of Amelia Cazelet. I told him of her concern for the plight of the Palestinians living in Ramallah. I also said I believed Amelia was anti-Semitic. Truth was she didn't have a good word to say for the Israelis. What I passed on was really tittle-tattle but Alvin was very keen for me to cultivate Amelia. So after I had acquired a place in Edgartown I used to invite her to spend a weekend up there roughly once a month. And of course I also saw Amelia whenever Alvin summoned me to attend a briefing session in New York.'

'What did you talk about during those friendly get-togethers?'

'Books, movies, Amelia's fund-raising activities and her helpers whose names I passed on to Alvin, our families, holidays abroad, my early life in the Persian Gulf, politics, in fact everything under the sun.'

'Are you sure you gave Mr Dombas all the names of her helpers?'

They were, Jill thought, getting to the crunch point now. Sooner or later every interrogator who had questioned her wanted to know how much of the stuff from Amelia had gone into the book she was writing.

'I held nothing back from Alvin,' Jill informed the faceless Texan. 'And before you ask, not one of Amelia's fund-raisers had come to the FBI's notice, or so Mr Dombas informed me. That includes Talal Asir.'

'Who's he?'

'A Saudi businessman, lives in Paris but is a frequent visitor to America.'

'Did you put him in your book?'

'No.'

'Then you'd better figure out what was in your script that got Amelia Cazelet killed. And while you are racking your brains just remember we can hold you indefinitely. Nobody will miss you. We've packed your things and checked you out of the Hyatt on Union Square.'

The Texan was right. She had cut herself off from her family, friends and former colleagues. Nobody was going to look for her. The realisation that she was alone made her blood run cold.

★   ★   ★

The CATO committee routinely met once a week at the Gower Street headquarters of MI5 on a Tuesday morning at ten a.m., a time chosen for the convenience of the representative from Government Communications Headquarters who had the furthest to come but still had to catch the 06.53 hours train from Cheltenham Spa to Paddington. Emergency sessions were called whenever there was an occurrence that MI5 considered should be discussed forthwith. Richard Neagle, in his capacity as chairman, had called one for midday that Thursday, 11 June

1998. Half the familiar faces were missing for one reason or another and Landon found himself sitting between a lieutenant commander, Royal Navy, from Defence Intelligence at the MoD, and a detective superintendent from Special Branch, neither of whom he'd met before. Neagle simply introduced them as Kenneth and Mal respectively. Landon assumed their surnames would appear in the minutes of the meeting, but it wasn't something he could get worked up about.

For the benefit of the naval commander from Defence Intelligence, who hadn't attended the meeting on Tuesday, Neagle told him why the Security Service believed the murder of a literary agent in Red Lion Square had been the work of Islamic fundamentalists.

'The killers were identified as Gina Nichols, also known as Borra Nicholson, and Leach, first name unknown,' Neagle continued. 'Leach was found in Ashdown Forest seated behind the wheel of a red Ford Escort, which incidentally had been stolen from a parking lot in Brighton. He had apparently committed suicide with a .357 Colt revolver that had slipped from his grasp after it was discharged in his mouth. Prints of his middle and fourth finger as well as his thumb were found on the pistol grip.'

'I would have said that was fairly conclusive evidence of suicide,' the naval commander observed with a faintly condescending smile.

'Until last night I would have agreed with you, Kenneth.' Neagle glanced at the detective superintendent. 'Perhaps you would bring us up to date, Mal?'

'OK. The body of Gina Nichols, a.k.a. Borra Nicholson, was found at 8 Seaside Terrace, Brighton, last night at approximately 21.30 hours. One of the Bosnian asylum seekers from the floor above broke into her bedsit to steal the money in the gas and electric meters. He, of course, tells a different story, claims there was a sickly smell coming from the bedsit and he had broken in, thinking there was a gas leak. Nicholson was lying on the floor in the kitchenette, her throat cut from ear to ear with a carving knife. The murderer had wanted the local police to believe that he had attacked Nicholson in the living room and finished her off in the kitchenette. A blood-stained pair of cotton slacks and a sweatshirt belonging to a man were found in the bin liner.

'Both items had been dipped in a pool of blood and then used to smear the furniture and floor in the living room. Proof of this contention was provided by the fibres found on the slacks and sweatshirt that had come from the carpet. The detective was sure DNA tests would prove that both items had been worn by Leach.

'The killer or killers wanted us to believe that he had murdered Nicholson and then committed suicide. The idea might have had some merit but the execution was poor.' Mal paused, looked pointedly at Landon, then said, 'Two questions interest us — what did the killer hope to gain, and what was their motive?'

'Any thoughts, Will?' Neagle asked casually.

There was nothing spontaneous about the invitation. The way Landon saw it, both men were convinced the SIS knew a great deal more than the high-priced help were prepared to admit. The detective superintendent from Special Branch had undoubtedly arrived at Gower Street well before the meeting was scheduled and he and Neagle had discussed ways and means of applying pressure on him.

'I'd only be guessing,' Landon told them dismissively.

'Don't tell me the four days you spent questioning Ensley Holsinger was a complete waste of time, Will?'

'Spending four days in the company of an attractive young woman is never a waste of time,' Landon said, and drew a ripple of laughter.

'This is no joking matter.'

Neagle was right. Unfortunately he had a knack for rubbing Landon up the wrong way. The truth was he should have ignored the jibe and if they were going to move forward the time had come to take a deep breath and offer some kind of olive branch.

'OK, Richard, you'll hear no more jokes from me — just guesswork.'

'Well, I really started it, so let's try again?'

'Why not? It seems to me that there has to be some major terrorist incident in the offing. I can't even begin to guess what it will be or where it will take place, but if you were to ask me when it will happen, I'd have to say pretty damn soon.'

'Pretty damn soon,' Neagle mused. 'That's

quite explicit considering you're only guessing.'

'Four people have been killed in a little over a week,' Landon said, and ticked them off one by one on his fingers. 'Amelia Cazelet in New York, George Ventris in London, Borra Nicholson in Brighton and plain Mr Leach in Ashdown Forest. All of them had one thing in common — access to part of a book supposedly written by a dead man. Leach and Nicholson were engaged in a clean-up operation in the sense that they were tasked to retrieve the typescript, which they did. I'm willing to bet a month's pay that one of them panicked when their photofits appeared in the national press. It happened to be an extremely accurate likeness in both cases, thanks to Messrs Jacklin and Lawrence of the Dorchester, and there was a good chance one or both of them would be recognised.'

Landon believed they had got in touch with their cell leader and delivered what had mounted to an ultimatum. Either they were smuggled out of the country or they would cut the best deal they could for themselves, should they be arrested.

'In effect they signed their own death warrants.'

'Where does that leave Ms Holsinger?' Neagle asked. 'Is she still at risk? Yes or no?'

Landon shrugged. 'I can't say. The FBI doesn't appear to think she is.'

Ensley Holsinger had left a message on his answer machine late on Tuesday morning when she knew he wouldn't be at home. She had wanted him to know she had arrived safely and

212

would have phoned yesterday had she not been quite so tired. This morning Ashton had told him the security guards from the Burns Agency had been withdrawn and would not be replaced by the FBI.

'But what do you think, Will?'

'Well, if Special Branch hasn't recovered the typescript we have to assume Leach and Nicholson sent it on to their people. In which case the terrorists will know their forthcoming operation has not been compromised so far because everything in the Ross Frazer book is ancient history.'

'So who is responsible for this bloodbath if it isn't anything to do with Frazer?' Neagle said, and looked around the table.

Landon presumed it was a purely rhetorical question that Neagle would answer but not a bit of it. A polite 'whenever you're ready, Will' told him different.

'It has to be Amelia Cazelet,' he said. 'She was the channel of communication between Ensley Holsinger and the real author. The lady was involved with the Popular Front for the Liberation of Palestine, and may have unwittingly disclosed some vital piece of information to the author that set the whole train of events in motion.'

The naval commander had been wearing a puzzled frown from the moment Neagle had called the meeting to order. It was therefore almost inevitable that he should ask if the identity of the author was known.

'Only by the initials J.S.,' Landon said

213

smoothly, effectively killing any speculation before it arose.

The CIA had got their hooks into Jill Sheridan and if she was giving them anything of value, Dombas was keeping it within the Agency. CATO couldn't afford to wait for what scraps of information Dombas might eventually throw their way. They had to start digging for it themselves, which meant that any minute now Neagle would go round the table apportioning tasks. With this in mind Landon assessed what the other intelligence services might tackle and then tried to fill in the gaps.

The only potential source this side of the Atlantic was Ali Mohammed Khalef, whom Special Branch had lost track of. Finding him again would be the number-one priority for MI5 and their foot soldiers. Defence Intelligence would alert all navy, army and air force attachés to be on the lookout for terrorists whose details and photographs appeared on the Most Wanted list. Eavesdropping on those Mid-East states with an ambivalent attitude towards acts of terrorism was down to GCHQ. Just how valuable their intelligence-gathering would prove was problematical. As a general rule terrorist groups kept their radio traffic to an absolute minimum, the same applied to mobile phone calls. The odds against GCHQ intercepting anything of significance were therefore pretty high.

'So would you like to lead off, Will?' Neagle asked blandly.

Landon had expected him to start with

Defence Intelligence followed by GCHQ before calling on the SIS. The batting order was, however, irrelevant so far as he was concerned.

'I'm sure we will buy what we can where we can. Heads of Stations throughout the Mid-East and North Africa will be encouraged to go down into the souk and listen to the bazaar gossip. We shall also be asking the Board of Trade to pay particular attention to certain rogue countries in Africa, the Middle, Near and Far East. We want to know if any of these rogue states are purchasing materials which could be used to further their chemical, nuclear and biological weapons programmes. The Saddam Hussein regime already has the capability of producing most weapons of mass destruction and they wouldn't hesitate to supply a terrorist organisation with them if they could get away with it.'

Neagle thanked him for his contribution and turned to Defence Intelligence. Nothing that was said thereafter was new to Landon except for the chairman's closing remarks.

'Remember this, the enemy is already among us,' Neagle said, and repeated it just in case somebody round the table might have missed the point.

Landon thought the observation would give the race relations industry a bad case of collective heartburn if that particular homily should appear in the press.

* * *

215

Some people never fade away. One such person was Vassily Semyonovich Malinovsky, alleged brother of the late Katya Malinovskaya. Three days ago Malinovsky had got word to Head of Station, Moscow and suggested that an exchange of information on Muslim extremists would be of mutual benefit. He had made one stipulation: he would deal with Ashton and no one else. However, the Russian had not said where or when they should meet, though George Elphinstone, Head of Station, had taken it for granted that it would be in Moscow on the grounds that Malinovsky was a big wheel in the Ministry of Foreign Affairs and could not leave town. Ashton had made it equally clear to Hazelwood that no way would he be persuaded to set foot in Moscow again and that it was Geneva or nothing. And there the matter had rested until two minutes ago when Dilys Crowther had rung him to ask if he would kindly meet Sir Victor in the conference room.

The housekeeping element of the Property Service Agency had decreed that the Director General of the SIS should have two leather armchairs for visiting dignitaries. Common sense therefore told Ashton that more than three would be attending the meeting. That Winston Reid should be present was no surprise. A former member of the Diplomatic before transferring to the SIS, he had been the foremost expert on the Middle East political scene in the Foreign and Commonwealth Office. The one person Ashton hadn't expected to see was Robin Urquhart, the senior of four

216

deputy under-secretaries at the FCO.

'I believe you two know one another,' Hazelwood said by way of introduction.

'Only by reputation,' Urquhart said with a tight smile.

'Likewise,' Ashton agreed.

Urquhart was one of those hugely intelligent men who had come down from Cambridge with a Double First in Modern Languages and an uncanny talent for falling in love with the wrong woman. His first wife, Rosalind, had walked out on him after sixteen years of marriage to live with a junior but well-heeled partner in the biggest firm of commercial lawyers in the city. The relationship had foundered when she had been paralysed from the waist down following an accident while riding to hounds with the Withersfield Hunt in November 1989. Urquhart had taken Rosalind back, purchased a four-bedroom house in the better part of Islington, which he then had specially adapted for a wheelchair, and had hired a live-in nurse and a resident cook-housekeeper to take care of her every need. And all Rosalind had done in return was to remind him, especially when they had company, that it was largely her money that had paid for the structural alterations. His colleagues had been unable to understand why Urquhart put up with such a spiteful woman and it had been no surprise to them when he had taken up with Jill Sheridan.

It was Urquhart who had saved Jill's career after she had requested to be relieved of her post in Bahrain. As a woman she had been treated as a second-class citizen in the Arab world and had found it almost impossible to be an effective Head of Intelligence in the Persian Gulf. Urquhart had blamed the then Director General for selecting Jill to fill such a difficult appointment and had done everything in his power to ensure she was not penalised. Her eventual promotion to Assistant Director in charge of the Mid-East Department owed a lot to Urquhart's influence behind the scenes. They had become lovers shortly thereafter but from the very beginning it had been apparent to neutral observers that Jill was emotionally detached and was simply using him to further her career. After years of misery Urquhart had finally divorced his wife to leave him free to marry Jill Sheridan. Unfortunately she had had other ideas and had taken herself off to America a year ago, severing all contact with Urquhart.

'Malinovsky has agreed to meet you in Geneva,' Hazelwood announced abruptly. 'You have Robin to thank for that.'

'I'm indebted,' Ashton said drily. 'When does Katya's brother suggest we meet?'

'Tomorrow, Friday, June the twelfth at eleven a.m.,' Urquhart informed him.

'Will he be on his own?'

'No one else will be present . . . '

'That means Vassily Semyonovich will have a minder watching his back.'

'I think we have to trust Malinovsky.'

'Are you coming with me, Mr Urquhart?'

'No.'

'Well, let's have less of the royal 'we' then. And

218

for the record, I don't take anything or anyone on trust. The meeting will take place on Monday, eleven thirty a.m. at the Au Bec Fin. I'll send Will Landon over to Geneva first thing tomorrow and he can do a little plane spotting.'

'Plane spotting?' Urquhart echoed.

'I assume Vassily Semyonovich will be travelling on Aeroflot.'

'Oh!'

'I think you are coming on a bit strong,' Reid said. 'What if Malinovsky won't accept your conditions?'

'We grin and bear it. But I don't believe Vassily Semyonovich will object. After all, he's the one who suggested a tête-à-tête.'

Reid pursed his lips, then hinted that perhaps Ashton was being a little simplistic.

'You could be right,' Ashton told him, 'but to my simple way of thinking the Russians want something from us. They never give anything away for nothing. The question is, how much are we prepared to pay?'

'I think I can safely say that he would be ready to promote another financial aid package with our European partners.' Urquhart smiled. 'Naturally the extent of the package will depend on the value of their information.'

'Money may not have been part of their calculations,' Ashton said.

'In my experience the Russians are always after money.'

'Malinovsky said he had information on Muslim extremists we should know about. Moscow is having a lot of trouble with their own

219

brand of Islamic terrorists especially down in Chechnya. It could be some of their most wanted terrorists are here in London.'

Hazelwood didn't say anything; neither did Reid. Both men evidently thought this was one for the FCO, though Victor had been giving a pretty fair impression of a Trappist monk for the past fifteen minutes. Urquhart cleared his throat several times before he responded.

'All Moscow has to do is to produce the necessary evidence and apply for extradition.'

'That will take for ever,' Ashton said, 'and we can't afford to wait. If extradition is granted the judgement will be referred to the Appeal Court, the House of Lords and the European Court for Human Rights before the lawyers are through.'

'We shall do our best to speed things up,' Urquhart assured him.

'The Russians may give us something to whet the appetite but they won't deliver the rest until we pay up.'

'What exactly are you suggesting?' Urquhart enquired coldly

'We lift the wanted men and hand them over to the Russians at some out-of-the-way airfield in this country.'

It was, Ashton knew, the kind of proposition calculated to give Urquhart a blue fit. However, nobody asked him to commit the FCO to anything, and he ceased to raise objections after Hazelwood agreed there would be no record of the meeting on file.

14

Landon returned from the CATO meeting in Gower Street shortly after one fifteen. Before he had time to open the combination safe, Ashton rang to ask if he could spare him a few minutes. When he had been in charge of the South American Desk the kind of summons he had been used to receiving from Roger Benton, Head of the Pacific Basin and Rest of the World Department, had been very different. More often than not it had been a case of 'my office now', which in practice meant Landon had taken his time about getting there. With Ashton he responded like a 100-metre sprint champion determined to leave his fellow competitors standing.

Landon figured Peter wanted to learn what had come out of the CATO meeting. To be told he was going to Geneva was the last thing he had expected to hear.

'Roy Kelso has booked you on the first British Airways flight out of Heathrow tomorrow,' Ashton told him. 'I'll be joining you the following day.'

'Do I take it Vassily Malinovsky has agreed to meet you there?' Landon asked.

'You do.'

Earlier in the week Ashton had told him all about Vassily Semyonovich, the alleged brother of Katya Malinovskaya. Actually he had talked

221

more about the sister than the brother and how her death had led to Chris Neighbour being declared *persona non grata* by Moscow.

'And what am I required to do?'

'Your job, Will, is to watch my back when I meet Malinovsky at the Au Bec Fin on Monday. Chris Neighbour can't do it because his face is too well known to Russian Intelligence.' Ashton opened the centre drawer, took out a photocopy of a head-and-shoulders snapshot and passed it across the desk to Landon. 'This is Malinovsky. It's the best Head of Station, Moscow, could come up with at short notice. The picture only arrived this morning in the diplomatic bag. A Queen's messenger is taking other photocopies to our house martins in Berne.'

House martins was jargon for the SIS station in a quiet, non-active country. During World War Two, Switzerland, like Portugal, had been a hotbed of espionage. However, nothing too exciting had happened in the land of the cuckoo clock since 1945, which meant Head of Station, Berne wasn't a particularly taxing appointment.

'One of the house martins will be waiting for you at Geneva airport,' Ashton continued. 'Head of Station, Berne had been told to hire a maximum of six inquiry agents from amongst the local talent. It will be their job to find out where Malinovsky is staying and then follow him wherever he goes until told otherwise. As far as they are concerned, the Russian has been divorced by his English wife who was granted custody of their only child. The husband, however, did have visitation rights and he has taken advantage of this to abduct his three-year-old son. None of the hired help will know who they are really working for.'

Their instructions would come from a bogus firm of solicitors in London with an impressive letterhead showing an accommodation address, all courtesy of the Technical Services Division. Their fees would be settled by the same bogus firm with cheques drawn on a secret bank account. If anyone decided to ring the phone number on the letterhead they would come straight through to Roy Kelso.

'You, Will, are an articled clerk at Jerome, Hayes, Baldock and Peterson, and the senior partner has sent you over to keep an eye on things. The inquiry agents will report to you daily, and in theory you will keep the firm informed and take your instructions from them. In reality you will be working for me.'

'How do we communicate?' Landon asked.

'You draw a Haydn from Tech Services.'

A Haydn was a miniature battery-operated radio that resembled a mobile phone but was slightly smaller in size. It had a transmitting range in excess of five miles, had eleven pre-set frequencies and was crypto-protected for up to seven days, the cipher being changed once every twenty-four hours. There was a pager button to warn the recipients to switch on, and thereafter the radio was used as if it were a telephone. The beauty of Haydn was that it was totally secure in every respect.

'Do you have any questions, Will?'

'Yeah, where am I staying in Geneva?'

'Roy Kelso will tell you when he issues you the flight tickets.'

'Fine.'

'OK. Now tell me what happened at the CATO meeting?'

There wasn't much Ashton didn't already know. Before leaving for Gower Street Landon had told him that the body of the woman who had called herself Detective Sergeant Nicholson had been found in a rooming house on Seaside Terrace in Brighton with her throat slashed from ear to ear.

'I'm afraid I more or less guaranteed that Heads of Stations throughout the Mid-East would be getting a lot more dosh to buy information where and whenever they can,' Landon confessed.

'No harm in that,' Ashton told him. 'Of course it will probably give the financial branch a bad case of gastroenteritis.'

'MI5 kept hinting that we were holding data back which could shed light on what is going on. Specifically, Neagle would like to know what's in the Ross Frazer file.'

'So would I,' Ashton told him. 'But all we'll get out of it will be a load of dirty laundry. Nothing between those file covers is going to tell us what is about to go down. OK, so a number of people have been killed because they have read a script supposedly written by Frazer and therefore what's in his file must be relevant. However, the fact is we tend to think the opposition is so much cleverer than us but they are just as likely to go down a blind alley. The rule in this game is to keep an open mind and refrain from bending the facts to fit with a preconceived theory.' Ashton smiled. 'End of lesson,' he added.

'Thanks for the tip.'

Landon excused himself, went down to Technical Services and signed for a Haydn, then took the first available lift up to the fourth floor. He had just opened the combination safe and was about to remove the filing trays when Nancy Wilkins arrived bearing a grubby-looking folder.

'What have you got there?' he asked.

'Frazer's Record of Service before he went to Sandhurst. I got it from the Historical Records Office in Hayes. It's a remarkable establishment. They can even produce the nominal rolls of the regiments which fought in the American War of Independence.'

'Are you sure you've got the right Frazer? It's my understanding that the MoD gave us his Record of Service when he joined the SIS. The papers included the six months he had spent in the ranks from June to December '46 before going to Sandhurst.'

'He had prior service in the ranks before 1946,' Nancy informed him calmly. 'He enlisted in July 1943 aged fifteen.'

Landon frowned. 'Well, I suppose he could have signed on as a boy soldier having been accepted for training as a military bandsman, but it seems unlikely.'

'Frazer enlisted under the name of Simmonds. He told the recruiting sergeant he was eighteen.'

'And the sergeant believed him?'

'Yes. Apparently Frazer was tall for his age and well built.'

'Even so, Nancy, somebody must have turned a blind eye.'

'Frazer was clever enough to hoodwink the military authorities for twenty months. Read the report from his company commander in the 9th Royal Fusiliers.'

'Oh, I will.' Landon tapped the folder she had placed on his desk. 'You're not going to get into trouble over this, are you, Nancy? I mean, Frazer's security file is a red-hot number. Except for the DG and his deputy, nobody is allowed to see it. This folder would be under lock and key if Sir Victor were aware of its existence.'

'But he isn't,' Nancy said. 'You and I are the only people who are.'

'So how did you get on to it?' Landon asked.

'I was talking to Bob Marlow, my contact in the army's Directorate of Security, a few days ago and during the course of our conversation Bob told me he was destroying a lot of files relating to people aged sixty-six or over. He said it was easy to get sidetracked because sometimes the content was enthralling.'

Marlow had quoted a case of fraudulent enlistment, which had set her thinking, and she had rung the Historical Records Office to see what, if anything, they had on fraudulent enlistments by underage males.

'I said we were endeavouring to trace an arms broker called Ross also known as Frazer spelt with an S or a Z whose father was thought to have served briefly in the army during the

1940s.' Nancy smiled. 'The rest was pure luck.'

'Luck or not, how would I manage without you, Nancy?'

'I'll remind you of that when I want to leave the Armed Forces Desk,' she said lightly, and left him to it.

Enlisting in the army at fifteen had been made slightly easier for Ross Frazer in that his parents had been divorced early in 1942 on the grounds that Evelyn Frazer had committed adultery with an RAF flight lieutenant. The divorce had been acrimonious and his parents had ceased to communicate even through their respective solicitors, once the decree absolute had been granted. In July 1942 Keith Frazer had been posted to the 51st Highland Division in Egypt, which meant one parent had been effectively removed from the scene.

A year later Ross Frazer had forged a letter from his mother to the headmaster of Taunton School, informing him that her son would not be returning after the summer holiday. Frazer had packed his school trunk, taken it down to the station and sent it down to left luggage at Euston. He had then gone to London the day school started back, had altered the personal details of his civilian identity card and presented himself to the recruiting centre in Acton where he had enlisted on a regular engagement, signing up for seven years with the colours and five on the reserve.

The report submitted by Frazer's company commander in Italy did not say how he had deceived his parents for so long but his

227

fraudulent enlistment had only come to light because he had volunteered the information to Major Rousell, the officer commanding A Company, 9th Royal Fusiliers. Frazer had joined the battalion in November 1944 when the Allied front had settled down for the winter on a line north of Viareggio in the west, across the Apennines to the Senio River behind Ravenna on the Adriatic. It had been an incredibly hard and miserable winter of sleet, snow and rain. The battalion had sent reconnaissance and fighting patrols across the river, gradually establishing a presence on the shore of Lake Comacchio. In return they had been shelled and mortared and sniped at. At stand to one morning, a Private Costello, who had shared the same slit trench as Frazer, had been shot in the throat and killed instantly.

In Rousell's opinion the incident had unnerved Frazer and, guessing the fighting was bound to intensify with the coming of spring, he had attempted to get out of it by claiming he had enlisted underage. Nevertheless, Rousell had recorded everything Frazer told him and had sent a written report to battalion headquarters. The report had gone all the way up the chain of command to Eighth Army, where it had rested while details of Frazer's story were checked out in the UK. The answer was received on 3 April 1945, two days after the 9th Royal Fusiliers and the rest of the 56th (London) Infantry Division attacked across Lake Comacchio in Fantail tracked amphibians. A week later Frazer was on his way home on board a navy supply ship.

Landon thought Bob Marlow was right: old files could be distracting and there was nothing in this one that was relevant today. It was only as he tucked Rousell's report back inside the folder that he noticed the handwritten memo from the commanding officer Fields Records, British Forces Italy. Dated 8 September 1945 and addressed to Headquarters 56th Infantry Division with a copy to 9th Royal Fusiliers, the writer wanted to know what action the battalion proposed to take with regard to the paternity suit filed by Clara Sophia Roffi. Below the signature block, in her unmistakable hand, Jill Sheridan had written, 'What happened to mother and child?'

★ ★ ★

The incandescent light from the halogen lamp in the ceiling roused Jill Sheridan immediately, even though she was bone tired. Like a robot she rolled off the bed and straightened up, hands outstretched ready to be manacled even as the door swung open and the two guards entered her cell. Neither man spoke to her as they shackled her ankles and wrists before leading her into the interrogation room next door. Instead of the Texan there was a new inquisitor behind the one-way window. The synthesised electronic voice was such an obvious disguise that Jill automatically assumed she was pitted against Spencer.

'We will talk about Ensley Holsinger,' the relief interrogator told her.

229

'That makes a change.'

'Did you ever meet her?'

'No, I've already told you, Amelia Cazelet was our go-between.'

'Ever talk to her on the phone?'

'No.'

'But you knew which literary agency she worked for?'

'Of course I did. Amelia told me why she thought the Julian H. Shubert Agency would be the most receptive. She also gave me the number of Ensley Holsinger's extension but I saw no point in using it until a publisher expressed an interest in the book.'

'Incomplete as it was?'

'I'm told it's not unknown for a publisher to pay a substantial non-returnable advance before the script is delivered.'

'Especially if the author already has a name the public will immediately recognise?'

Jill wondered just where this line of questioning was going. 'I suppose so,' she said listlessly.

'But you don't have a name outside the intelligence community. Right?'

'It depends what you mean by a name. I was rubbished by the press when a senior member of the FCO divorced his paraplegic wife to marry me. The reporters changed their opinion when they learned what a bitch she was but the damage had been done.'

'We all know about Robin Urquhart and his wife, Rosalind.'

'Then why ask?'

'Because we are curious to know why you

chose to write under the name of Ross Frazer.'

'A scandal is never dead,' Jill told him. 'Should the book be published under my own name the press would resurrect the whole sorry business.'

'It would have done your sales no harm and made you a rich woman into the bargain,' the inquisitor said, not unreasonably.

'I can do without that kind of publicity.'

'Why choose Ross Frazer as a pseudonym?'

Jill sensed a trap but couldn't see a way to avoid it. Woken at all hours of the day and night, she doubted if they had allowed her to sleep more than a couple hours at a time. Consequently she was too exhausted to think straight.

'Frazer existed, didn't he?'

'You know he did. You people murdered him in Paris on Tuesday, the twenty-second of August 1989.'

'So, using his name was an act of revenge, was it?'

'Yes.'

'Against whom — not us, surely? Judging by what you told Mr Dombas your disclosures would have been a major embarrassment for the SIS, never mind the British government. Seems to me you wanted to damage your former colleagues.'

He was right but Jill wasn't about to admit it. On the basis that attack was the best means of defence she told the metallic voice she wasn't going to answer another question until she received better treatment.

'I'm in a mess, I smell, I'm unwashed, my hair must look like a ravaged bird's nest and these

231

orange coveralls I'm wearing need to be changed. I want to stand under a hot shower and shampoo my hair. I want — '

'A little co-operation wouldn't come amiss. Help us and we'll help you.'

'Go to hell.'

'Maybe you'd better go back to your little room and think about that.'

She wanted to lash out, to kick and scream but it would get her nowhere because they had the whip hand. Tears of anger and frustration welled in her eyes.

'What is it you want from me?' she asked in a voice strained with emotion.

'Was Frazer married at any time?'

Jill sensed the interrogator already knew the answer, though how he could defied explanation. Only a minute ago he had told her a little co-operation wouldn't come amiss and if she really wanted to stand under a hot shower, now was the time to show it. Compared with what the CIA already knew about Frazer, disclosing what he had been up to in Italy during the war would hardly bring down the government.

'Frazer wasn't married but fathered a child in September 1945.'

'This was in his security file?'

'There was an oblique reference to it.'

The procedures to determine whether an individual should have constant access to Top Secret material had been examined in 1960 by the Radcliffe Committee. One of their recommendations had been the introduction of a subject interview by an experienced interrogator before Positive Vetting clearance was given. The recommendation had been accepted by the government of the day, which had meant that catch-up interviews had had to be arranged for several hundred intelligence officers who already had constant access. Ross Frazer was one such individual.

'Frazer's subject interview was a farce,' Jill continued. 'It was more like a cosy chat between friends than a probing assessment. In writing his report the interviewer gave the impression that he admired Frazer and thought there couldn't be much wrong with a chap who'd enlisted under age to fight for his country. Since there had been no reference to his wartime service in the papers the Ministry of Defence had sent to the SIS, I sought advice from the Historical Records Office at Hayes. A very helpful senior executive officer suggested Frazer had probably enlisted under another name but if I could give him Frazer's real date and place of birth he would see what he could do. The SEO was brilliant. A fortnight later the documents relating to a Private Simmonds, otherwise known as Ross Frazer, pitched up on my desk.'

'Why the interest in the man?'

'The file on Ross Frazer is one of seven the SIS has retained in perpetuity because of their sensitivity. These files can only be accessed by the Director General and his deputy. I read all of them the day I took over from my predecessor.' Jill smiled lopsidedly at the one-way window. 'You can't be responsible for the safe custody of those particular files without knowing why they

233

are held in perpetuity.'

'It doesn't explain why Amelia Cazelet was murdered, does it?'

'No. I'm beginning to think Talal Asir is responsible for her death.'

'The Saudi businessman you said was one of the fundraisers for the Palestinians in Ramallah?' There was a loud rasping noise that sounded like a file grating on metal. What followed suggested it was more of a derisive snort. 'The FBI have never heard of him.'

'So in your book the Bureau is the fount of all knowledge, is it?' Jill snapped. 'Well, for the record we've long suspected Talal Asir is one of the paymasters funding Islamic Jihad. For all her faults I liked Amelia and I warned her not to get involved with Talal Asir.' Jill paused, then said, 'I told Amelia a whole chapter would be devoted to him later in the book and consequently she could find herself in serious trouble with the FBI. It's possible she may have done something stupid and confided in Asir.'

'In other words, you could have been responsible for her murder.'

'I suppose so,' Jill agreed reluctantly.

'You know something, Ms Sheridan? I think you have earned yourself a hot shower and a change of clothing.'

*　　*　　*

Landon checked the clothes he had laid on the bed to make sure he had three of everything, shirts, socks, underpants plus a pair of pyjamas,

234

then packed the items into the carry-on bag. The alarm clock on the bedside locker was showing thirteen minutes past eight; he had already eaten, there was nothing on TV he wanted to see and the rest of the night stretched before him. Late that afternoon he had instructed Nancy Wilkins to phone Bob Marlow at the army's Directorate of Security and ask for the phone number of the Julian H. Shubert Agency. If questioned why the SIS wanted it he had ordered her to tell Marlow gently but firmly that he ought to know better than to ask. He had also left Nancy in no doubt that the same stricture applied to her.

It was not something he was proud of when he recalled how she had gone out of her way to help him over Frazer's wartime service. What made him feel even more guilty was the knowledge that he simply wanted to get in touch with Ensley Holsinger for entirely personal reasons. The slip of paper on which Nancy had written the phone number of the agency was tucked under the phone on the small table that served as a desk. Ever since he had returned to the flat, Landon had resisted the temptation to call the agency. His resistance had taken the form of busying himself with household chores and thus postpone the need to come to a decision. Now that he had run out of things to do, he could no longer avoid the issue. Contemptuous of himself for being so wet, he crossed the room, lifted the transceiver and tapped out the international code for the USA, followed by the area, zone and subscriber's number.

When the switchboard operator at Julian H. Shubert answered, he said, 'Hi, my name's Landon. I'd like to talk to Ensley Holsinger, please.'

'I'm afraid Ms Holsinger is no longer with the agency.'

The news didn't greatly surprise him. In taking the script to George Ventris, Ensley had tried to put one over on the agency and had been found out, probably by lover boy.

'OK. In that case put me through to Evan.'

'What did you say your name is, sir?'

'Landon, Mike Landon.'

'And you represent?'

'Warwick Thompson Associates in London.'

'I don't think we have your name on our list — '

'I've just been taken on,' Landon said, hustling her.

'Well, I guess it's no big secret. Mr Vance is in hospital. He was mugged on his way home last night.'

'My God, how is he?'

'Mr Vance is in a coma,' the operator informed him, and hung up.

Mr Vance: Ensley Holsinger had allowed him to believe Evan was the surname of her boss. It was yet one more example of how Ensley never disclosed more than she absolutely had to. Landon picked up the receiver again and rang Ashton at home to give him the latest news on Ms Holsinger before he left for Geneva in the morning.

15

Will Landon arrived in Geneva on British Airways flight BA2736 at 10.45 hours local time, five minutes ahead of schedule. With only a carry-on bag to worry about, he avoided the customary delay in the baggage claim area so that after passing through Immigration and Customs, he made straight for the exit. The house martin from Berne who was waiting for him, was Mr Average, medium height, medium build, no distinguishing marks. If the definition of a successful spy was somebody who would pass unnoticed by the waiters in an otherwise empty restaurant, then he was the prime example of the species. Landon only noticed him because he was holding a placard across his chest which read 'Mr Clerk', and in brackets underneath, 'Jerome, Hayes, Baldock and Peterson'.

'I'm Will,' Landon said, walking up to him, 'Will Landon. And you are?'

'Bill Browne with an e.'

Landon supposed he might have known the invisible spy would have a surname like Smith, Jones or even Brown with an e.

'Shall we go?' Browne suggested. 'My car is right outside, parked in a fifteen-minutes waiting area and time is running on.'

'I take your point,' Landon told him.

In keeping with its owner the car was

inconspicuous, a six-year-old Citroën AX hatch-back with no CD plates. Aiming the remote control at the vehicle, Browne tripped the central locking, opened the offside front door and tossed the placard he had been carrying on to the back seat before getting into the Citroën. Landon joined him, drew the seat belt across his chest and slipped it into the housing.

'Where are you staying, Will?' Browne asked as he cranked the engine into life.

'The Pension Albert.'

'Where's that?'

'Hang on a minute.' Landon reached inside the breast pocket of his jacket and produced the slip of paper Kelso had given him. On it, apart from the address, the ever-cost-conscious Admin King had written, 'A small, modest but comfy hotel suitable for a legal clerk.' 'It's on the Rue Verdeine de la Tour Maitresse in the old part of the city.'

'I think I can find the street.' Browne smiled apologetically. 'I'm not in Geneva all that often.'

'No matter, you'll probably know the city like the back of your hand before this coming weekend is over.'

'Are we expecting trouble?'

'We'll be doing everything we can to avoid it, that's why your Head of Station was told to hire up to six freelance inquiry agents.'

'And he gave the job to me,' Browne told him.

Everything had had to be done in a hurry and whether Landon liked it or not, private inquiry agents were not exactly thick on the ground in Geneva. Consequently Browne had been forced to go to Suter Sécurité National, the biggest security company in Switzerland with branches in Basle, Berne, Lausanne and Zurich.

'I don't know whether the people I dealt with believed my story concerning the marital affairs of Vassily Semyonovich Malinovsky.'

'You didn't mention him by name, did you?' Landon asked casually.

'No, I simply referred to him as the Russian. Anyway, the company was able to provide six operatives at short notice and I got them together for a briefing this morning at eight o'clock. Each man has one of the photocopies of Malinovsky's head and shoulders the Queen's messenger delivered yesterday afternoon.'

Browne had divided the men into two watches to cover the international airport, the Gare de Cornavin, in case Malinovsky flew into Zurich and completed the rest of the journey by train, and the offices of the Russian Consulate General on the Boulevard Helvetique. Their only means of communicating with Browne and one another was by mobile telephone.

'It's not a great plan,' Browne continued. 'As surveillance operations go, this one has every chance of being a real bummer. A whale could slip through the net I've cast.'

'You're being too hard on yourself,' Landon told him. 'Look at it another way; if Malinovsky's desire for a meeting is genuine he won't attempt to slip through the net and arrive in Geneva unnoticed. Should he do so, we'll assume he's up to no good and take appropriate measures.'

'Appropriate measures,' Browne murmured

239

thoughtfully. 'And what do we mean by that?'

'It's up to my boss, Peter Ashton. My advice to him would be either to turn round and go straight back to London or call for backup from the heavy mob.'

'You mean the SAS?'

'Who else?'

'I thought you said you would be doing everything you can to avoid trouble?'

'We shall be,' Landon said unperturbed. 'The backup won't be armed. Incidentally, how much further is it to the Pension Albert now?'

'Not much, say ten, maybe fifteen minutes, depending on the traffic.'

They had left the airport on the Avenue Louis Casai, which had then become the Route de Meyrin before changing yet again to the Rue de la Servelte. Browne turned right then left, passed under the railway and made yet another left to head up towards the Central station.

'I lost my way there for a moment,' Browne murmured, embarrassed.

'It happens to all of us,' Landon assured him, and lapsed into silence.

They turned into the Rue du Mont-Blanc and went on down the street past the Bristol-Minerva and Alba Hotels. It was, as Landon recalled, the second time he had been to Geneva, the first being when he and three fellow students from Nottingham University had gone skiing in Chamonix-Mont Blanc. They had flown into the city by Dan Air, commonly referred to as the Dan Dare Airline, and had completed the rest of the journey by coach. Back in '87 Geneva had struck him as a wholly antiseptic place, worthy but dull. Maybe his negative reaction had been due to the fact that it had been the first week in January on a particularly grey afternoon but even now on this bright sunny morning, he saw no reason to change his opinion. The most remarkable thing about Geneva was the water jet fountaining out of the lake off the Jetée des Eaux-Vives, but once you had seen one water spout you had seen them all.

'I don't think your room at the hotel will be ready for occupation before three p.m.,' Browne said presently.

'No problem, I'll leave my bag with the concierge while we take a look at the Au Bec Fin.'

'Where's that?'

'In the Rue de Berne. Ring any bells with you?'

'Can't say it does.' Browne paused, then brightened visibly. 'But I've got a street map,' he added.

Browne was wrong about checking into the Pension Albert. This establishment was three-parts empty and the desk clerk had no problem about providing Landon with accommodation there and then. Small, modest, comfy were the adjectives Kelso had used to describe the hotel; he had omitted the major attraction for him — the fact that the room rate was dirt cheap for Switzerland.

★　★　★

The postman had been very early that morning and the newspapers wrapped up in brown paper had been delivered to the house before Ashton left for the office. The parcel had remained unopened throughout morning prayers and had subsequently lain dormant in the pending tray while he dealt with a whole raft of signals received during silent hours that carried a precedence of Op Immediate and above. The most time-consuming one concerned the replacement of an Albanian interpreter attached to one of the SAS deep-penetration patrols operating in Kosovo. Five days after arriving in the country the man had fallen into a slit trench and broken his left leg.

Ashton had contacted Max Brabazon, the retired commander RN in Military Operations (Special Projects) and told him to dig out the list of Albanian interpreters and start ringing them. Brabazon had been through the list once before when they were putting the teams together a week ago and only two Albanian speakers had been available. There was, however, a chance that one or two of the possibles who had been holidaying abroad or out of the country on business might have returned in the meantime.

At the height of the Cold War the SIS had maintained a list of sales executives who frequently went behind the Iron Curtain on business, spoke the appropriate language and were prepared to do their bit out of patriotism or for a small financial consideration. In those days the SIS had been spoiled for choice, with a small army of businessmen doing the rounds in Russia, Czechoslovakia, Poland, Hungary, Romania and Bulgaria. But they never had any takers for Albania.

Neagle at MI5 had been unable to help when Ashton had approached him. 'Of course there were Albanians among the thousands of refugees screened by the Security Service and Special Branch, but I assure you, Peter, none would measure up to your requirements. Why don't you try the World Service of the BBC?'

Ashton had already thought of that. Even supposing the BBC would release one of their newsreaders to go foot-slogging around Kosovo, he wanted somebody who would be politically neutral, a quality he was unlikely to find in an Albanian national.

Just for a change the Mozart rang again and he knew it was Max Brabazon even before he answered the phone; knew too that the retired commander RN was unlikely to be the bearer of good news.

'I'm afraid there's no change, Peter,' he said when Ashton came on the line. 'The situation is the same as it was a week ago. Well, to be precise one of the wandering sheep has returned but he's not interested in going to Kosovo.'

'I don't blame him.'

'He told me he had too many business commitments. Personally I don't believe him.'

'It doesn't matter what we believe, Max. We can't order him into Kosovo.'

'I've had the brigadier, Special Forces, on the phone all morning wanting to know what we are

243

doing about the shortfall,' Brabazon said gloomily.

'Snap. He's rung me several times. I told him soon as I had a body for him he would be the first to know.' Ashton smiled to himself. 'I think he got the message.'

'So what happens now?'

'There is one resource we haven't tapped yet but what we do about it is up to Hazelwood.' Ashton paused. 'I'll call you when he has made a decision,' he added, then hung up.

Ashton walked into the PA's office, checked that the red light wasn't showing above the communicating door and asked Dilys Crowther to announce him. 'Sir Victor', she informed him, was on line two and couldn't be disturbed. Then a light started winking on the cradle of her telephone, a sign that Hazelwood had finished his conversation. However, as Dilys cleared line two the red light above the door suddenly lit up.

'I don't believe it,' Ashton told her. 'How did anybody get past you?'

Dilys Crowther muttered something about dictation and grabbed her notebook and Biro, but he beat her to the communicating door.

Hazelwood was standing at the window gazing out across the river, both hands stuffed deep into his trouser pockets when Ashton entered the adjoining office.

'Found your Albanian speaker yet?' he asked, his back still turned.

'There is none to be had.'

'Nonsense. What about those linguists in Defence Intelligence who spend their entire time reading every technical and scientific journal they can lay their hands on? Has Brabazon tried them?'

'There is only one Albanian and she's in her fifties. Anyway, we don't want an Albanian national.'

'Who said so?'

'You did,' Ashton told him.

It was all part of the window-dressing. Albanian and Serbian nationals could not be members of the deep-penetration patrols because the local population would never believe they were unbiased. This edict had been issued by the FCO on tablets of stone.

'As I see it, we are left with three options. Assuming GCHQ has no objection we could raid the RAF Squadron in 9 Signal Regiment based on Cyprus — '

'You can rule that out,' Hazelwood snapped. 'It would create an imbalance of seven Serb to one Albanian speaker, which would be politically unacceptable.'

'OK, persuade the politicians to reduce the number of patrols to seven and thereby cut the odds to six to one.'

Hazelwood turned about to face him. 'Are you trying to be funny?' he growled.

'No, I'm being deadly serious. Are you interested in hearing the third option?'

'It had better be good.'

'Why not go to the FCO? They have three Albanian linguists, the youngest of whom is twenty-six and is in the Territorial Army.'

'What's his name?'

245

'It's a her,' Ashton said, and watched the eager expression on Hazelwood's face rapidly fade away.

'Don't be ridiculous, Peter.'

'This girl is a very unusual career diplomat. She is the assistant adjutant of a reserve artillery regiment, is single, unattached and lists mountaineering as one of her pastimes. She is, I'm told, as tough as old boots and can certainly hold her own with any SAS trooper. Come Monday, October the fifth, Valerie Cogland will be joining the embassy in Belgrade. OK, so we'd only have her for three months but surely that's better than nothing?'

'Would she volunteer for the job?'

'I think she would jump at it,' Ashton said.

'What is her name again?'

'Valerie Cogland.'

'All right, leave it with me, I'll have a word with Robin Urquhart.' Hazelwood returned to his desk and sat down. 'Have you heard from Will Landon?'

It was the opportunity Ashton had been waiting for. 'As a matter of fact he rang me yesterday evening,' he said, deliberately misinterpreting Hazelwood's question. 'Will tried to contact Miss Holsinger earlier that evening and rang Evan Vance, her boss at the Julian H. Shubert Agency. From their switchboard operator he learned that Vance had been mugged on his way home on Wednesday evening — '

'You're being disingenuous,' Hazelwood snapped, interrupting him. 'You're answering a question I didn't ask and you know it.'

246

'Vance was knocked unconscious and taken into hospital,' Ashton continued remorselessly. 'He's still in a coma.'

'And you believe the attack on Vance is somehow connected with the murders of Ventris and Cazelet?'

'Yes. The connection is Ensley Holsinger. She told Cazelet that her boss had read the Ross Frazer book and rejected it.' Ashton raised a hand like a police officer on point duty. 'I know what you are going to say, Victor. We all agree that there is nothing in the script worth killing for and I can't explain why anyone should have waited a whole week before striking at Evan Vance. It's likely he was simply the victim of a particularly vicious street crime. Nevertheless, I recommend we make a few discreet enquiries to find out what Vance was doing between the third and tenth of June.'

'As long as you don't make a meal of it,' Hazelwood told him.

'Right.'

'Now please answer my original question.'

'I haven't heard from Will Landon and I didn't expect to. Will drew a Haydn from Technical Services, which had a transmitting range in excess of five miles. If he had failed to make contact with the house martin at Geneva airport, Head of Station, Berne would have signalled me before now.'

'So you're happy with the way things are going?'

'Yes.'

'Thank you, Peter, that's all I wanted to know.'

Ashton returned to his office, opened the roll of newspapers Boothroyd had sent him and spread them out on the desk. The passport control officer had made the task of reading them easier for him by highlighting points of detail. Amelia Cazelet was last seen on Friday, 29 May at approximately four thirty-five p.m. The last person to talk to her had been the assistant manager of the 7th Avenue bookstore. Amelia Cazelet had asked her deputy to cover for her while she returned to her apartment on East 71st Street, which apparently had been broken into. The neighbour who had reported the incident to her was Miss Ensley Holsinger who, according to Amelia Cazelet, was working at home that day.

But Ms Holsinger had not been working at home that Friday. She had spent the weekend with Evan Vance at The Inn on the Sound, Shoreham, and had gone straight there from the office. She had also given Will to understand that Amelia Cazelet, whom she had last seen on the Thursday evening, was spending a few days on Martha's Vineyard starting that Friday the twenty-ninth. Ashton decided it was important to establish which of the two women had been telling the truth and there was only one person who could do that for him. He glanced at his wristwatch, subtracted five hours and reckoned he might just catch Jack Boothroyd before he left his house in Queens and walked to the subway station.

★　★　★

For the first time since she had been incarcerated in the detention centre Jill Sheridan had not felt exhausted when she was woken by the halogen lamp in the ceiling. She had asked for clean coveralls and a hot shower; they had respected her wishes and a lot more. She had been allowed to wallow in a hot bath and had then been transferred to a much larger cell. Although it too lacked a window, tucked away in an alcove there was a shower, a flush toilet and a vanitory unit with a mirror fixed to the wall above it. The room was also better furnished, with a comfortable divan bed, a hanging cupboard and a chest of drawers. As a final touch they had collected her clothes from wherever it was they had stored her travelling bag and had unpacked them. When the warders, as she mentally called them, came to collect her it was evident there was a limit to the softer approach. As on every other occasion, her wrists and ankles were shackled before she was taken into the interrogation room. Jill recognised the treatment for what it was, a psychological reminder that unless she behaved herself and co-operated, the old regime would be reinstated.

This time the hidden interrogator was not the Texan or the synthesised electronic voice but a woman who sounded breathless as if she suffered with asthma. Almost inevitably she wanted to talk about Talal Asir.

'You've told us that British Intelligence has long suspected he was one of the paymasters funding Islamic Jihad. My question is how long is long, Ms Sheridan? And when exactly did the

SIS open a file on him?'

'The last part of the question is easy. The file was opened on Monday, August the sixth 1990. I actually met Talal Asir in November 1989 shortly after I was posted to Bahrain. I automatically carded him because he was distantly related to the Saudi ruling family. In those days he was the vice president in charge of overseas investments at the National Bank of Saudi Arabia in Riyadh.'

Throughout 1989 and the first six months of 1990 Talal Asir had travelled extensively in the Middle East and Europe investing heavily in telecommunications and information technology. He was known to have acquired property in Switzerland and the south of France on behalf of his relatives. It was also beyond doubt that if it hadn't been for the subsidies he had channelled to Yasser Arafat, the Palestine Liberation Organisation would have collapsed.

'It's presumed he did this with the approval of the ruling family,' Jill continued.

'How could you possibly know this, Ms Sheridan? You were responsible for intelligence-gathering in Kuwait, Muscat and Oman and the United Arab Emirates.'

'I had a very good source, an entrepreneur who made it his business — '

'You are referring to Henry Clayburn, the pimp you later married, aren't you, missy?'

Jill felt the colour suffusing in her cheeks and looked down at her lap, reluctant to show her face to the hidden interrogator concealed behind the one-way window. 'We all make mistakes,' she muttered, 'and, as you well know, I divorced

Henry within eighteen months. Anyway, it doesn't alter the fact that his information was A1, the best you could have. Furthermore the only reason why the Head of the Mid-East Department opened a file on Talal Asir was because I had pressed him to do so.'

'It had nothing to do with the fact that Iraq had invaded Kuwait only a matter of three weeks prior to that?'

'That may be your opinion,' Jill said heatedly, 'but it isn't mine and I doubt many of my former colleagues would agree with you.'

There were, she thought, always exceptions, like the unspeakable Ashton and Will Landon, his pet Rottweiler. And, of course, Sir Victor Hazelwood, the biggest misogynist of them all. He had orchestrated the demand for her resignation for personal gain.

'When did Talal Asir arrive in London?'

Jill looked up startled. 'I'm sorry, what did you say?'

'I want to know when Talal Asir arrived in London.'

'Early in May 1993. I can't remember the exact date. He had lost his job with the National Bank of Saudi Arabia. Some said it was because he had been embezzling the bank by inflating the cost of properties he had bought, others maintained the family had grown tired of his sexual antics with foreign women.'

In London Asir had become a currency speculator buying Deutschmarks and Swiss francs to force up their value, then playing it safe by selling them just before they peaked and

251

started to fall back. He had come to the notice of MI5 because he was regularly transferring large sums of money to offshore banking accounts and was a frequent visitor to the Lebanon, the West Bank, Syria and Iraq. In March '96 he had moved to Paris.

'The activities of the Security Service was making life difficult for him. Both MI5 and ourselves alerted the French authorities and asked them to keep us informed of his movements, but their attitude had been one of *laissez-faire*. Consequently we have had no feedback from the French and Head of Station, Paris has had to do the best he could with his own resources.'

'Do you have Asir's address in Paris?'

Jill nodded to the window. 'Yes, it's Rue de Ponthieu in the eighth *arrondissement*.'

'You people don't get along with the French too well.'

'We have our differences,' Jill said.

'Well, maybe they will do things for us they would never do for you Brits.'

'You've got to be joking. They hate you even more than they do us.'

16

June was supposed to be the month for really good weather. It used to be said that if you wanted to get away to the seaside and be sure of acquiring a suntan the Wimbledon fortnight was the best time to take a holiday. The Lawn Tennis Championship was still ten days off, which Ashton thought was just as well because it was blowing a gale outside and there had been no need to set the alarm when the rain was lashing so noisily against the window. He had slept restlessly — left side, right side and on his back, the bedclothes winding around his body as if he were mummified. At least twice during the night Harriet had asked him what the hell he was playing at as she fought to retain her share of the bedclothes.

He reached out with his left hand and turned the clock on the bedside table towards him so that he could see the face. Ten after seven, another twenty minutes before the alarm started ringing. In truth he didn't need to get up at seven thirty. His British Airways flight to Geneva departed at 12.50 hours and he could easily make Heathrow in an hour forty, especially since this was a Saturday and the traffic heading into London would be that much lighter.

'What time is it?' Harriet asked drowsily.

'Eleven minutes past seven.'

'You don't want to go to Geneva.'

253

In the absence of any kind of inflection of her voice Ashton wasn't sure whether it was a question, an assertion or a statement of fact. 'I'm not expecting trouble, if that is what is on your mind,' he said.

'Trouble has a way of sneaking up on you, Peter.'

'Not this time. Malinovsky wants to trade information; the days when the KGB and subsequently the Russian Foreign Intelligence Service wanted my head on a platter are over. Besides, what have I got to worry about when Landon is watching my back?'

'Not a lot, provided he keeps his mind on the job a hundred per cent of the time.'

'What are you implying?'

'Will is enamoured of Ensley Holsinger.'

'That, my love, is absolute rubbish,' Ashton said quietly. 'They fight like cat and dog. Anyway, you must have noticed she didn't say a word to Will all through dinner the night they stayed under our roof?'

'I didn't say she was smitten with Will, but I noticed the way he kept stealing glances at her.'

'The first time Will met Ensley Holsinger he had a funny feeling she was a bit of a liar. Those were his words, more or less, and that impression was subsequently reinforced. And, by the way, I didn't see him giving her the eye.'

'That's because you are not very good at people watching,' Harriet countered.

'Well, OK, if he did keep gazing at Ms Holsinger he must have been wondering how much of her life story, which she was relating to

254

you, bore any resemblance to the truth. Anyone who allowed himself to be taken in by her is asking for — '

Harriet leaned over Ashton and planted a kiss on his lips, silencing him before he could finish what he was saying. 'You just take care,' she murmured. 'Absolutely no heroics.' Her left hand fingered the hollow in the left shoulder immediately below the collarbone. 'I don't want you coming home with a piece of you still in Geneva.'

Four years ago up at Lake Arrowhead, California, a man called Gillespie had put a bullet in his shoulder with a 6.35 Walther PPK semi-automatic.

'You hear me?' Harriet whispered.

'I hear you.'

'Good, because I don't fancy being a single mother of three.'

'What!'

'I'm pregnant, and the answer to your next question is the second week in December.'

They hadn't discussed the possibility of having a third child and she had taken the decision unilaterally. Maybe it was an accident? After all, Harriet hadn't sounded exactly overjoyed. Ashton frowned — what did it matter how she had conceived? She was the most exciting woman he had ever met and he considered himself lucky to have her. As if it was only yesterday he could remember the day Harriet had walked into his office, this tall, dark-haired girl on an exchange posting from MI5, which she hadn't wanted. He remembered too how he had nearly lost her five years ago in Berlin when her skull had been fractured by a Turkish *Gastarbeiter* during a race riot in the Kreuzberg District. She had been rushed to St Thomas's Hospital in Mittenhofstrasse and had been on the operating table for over three hours. Harriet had looked awful, her face had been the colour of marble and had resembled a skull, the skin stretched tight as a drum, the cheeks sunken. The woman he loved had been just a mess of tubes, drips and wires, her hair, or what was left of it, concealed under a white turban. This was not the time to suggest she might have consulted him first before increasing the family. Life had been tough on Harriet. Her mother had committed suicide after learning she had terminal cancer, and barely two years ago, her father had succumbed to Alzheimer's. It was also a fact that Carolyn really was their third child after Harriet had miscarried their second when she was four months pregnant.

'Well, say something,' Harriet urged, a note of desperation in her voice.

'It's a heck of a surprise,' Ashton told her, 'but a damned nice one.'

'Do you really mean that?'

'You know I do. Three are better than two.'

Her feeling of relief was almost physical and he knew he had found the right words even before she kissed him again with lips slightly apart, her tongue seeking out his. Occasionally, and without any forewarning, Harriet would take the lead in bed. She did so now, first straddling and then mounting him. In their frenzy neither

256

of them realised they were no longer alone until a small voice asked Harriet if she was playing horsey. Harriet froze at the sight of four-year-old Edward standing by the bed gazing at her in wonderment with eyes as big as saucers. There was a brief pause and then Harriet said, 'Yes, darling, I suppose I am,' before collapsing on to Ashton's chest, shaking with suppressed laughter.

Edward contemplated his mother for all of ten seconds and in the next moment announced he was hungry.

'Well, I tell you what,' Ashton said, 'why don't you go downstairs, put the TV on and lay the kitchen table while Mummy and I get dressed?'

Children's programmes on BBC1 and ITV started at 6.00 a.m. on a Saturday morning and no one in the house knew this better than Edward. He turned away from them, left the bedroom and ran downstairs. A few minutes later the peace and quiet was shattered by a Disney cartoon on full blast. The noise woke eighteen-months-old Carolyn, who added to the din.

Asking Edward to lay the breakfast table was not the greatest idea Ashton had had. In the process of getting some milk from the fridge for their Coco-Pops, Edward had dropped the bottle on to the floor and never had a pint spread so far and so wide. Ashton fetched a dustpan and brush from the broom cupboard and swept up the shards of glass. He was standing there, mop in hand, contemplating the mess and wondering where to begin when Harriet seized it from him and did the job in half the time he would have taken. Normal service was resumed shortly after Harriet had put the mop and bucket away in the broom cupboard.

As was usual on Saturdays and Sundays Ashton sat at the table with the children, Carolyn in a high chair, Edward with a couple of cushions on his seat to raise him up. As was usual seven days a week Harriet ate a bowl of cornflakes standing up at the sink. She was wearing a cotton housecoat, which she had left unbuttoned to reveal a dark blue, ankle-length satin nightdress that hugged her figure. Ashton couldn't take his eyes off her.

'It will be at least another month before anything shows,' Harriet said, as if reading his thoughts.

'And you will look marvellous.'

'Flatterer.'

'Admirer is a more appropriate word,' Ashton said.

'Save the compliments for when you come back from Geneva in one piece,' Harriet told him.

'Right.'

'Now go upstairs and get changed.'

When Ashton left the cottage an hour later, it was no longer raining, the Force 8 gale had abated, the sun was shining and the sky was mostly blue. Although not superstitious by nature, he hoped it was a portent of his meeting with Vassily Semyonovich Malinovsky.

★　★　★

The diplomatic staff at the British Embassy on Massachusetts Avenue were always formally attired in dark, tailor-made two-piece suits, conservative shirts that looked as if this was the first time of wearing, discreet ties and black lace-up shoes. The dress code at the British Consulate at 845 Third Avenue, New York, was much more relaxed, a style epitomised by Jack Boothroyd, whose wardrobe consisted almost entirely of sport jackets, slacks, checked shirts, knitted ties and a range of loafers. That hot Saturday morning he was wearing off-white cotton slacks, a plain dark blue T-shirt and moccasins, a get-up that would not have looked out of place on Coney Island.

The private investigator from the Burns Agency, who was waiting for Boothroyd in the Irish pub on Lexington Avenue, answered to the name of Jordan. He was a big man, six feet three, two hundred and twenty-odd pounds, large feet, large hands. Flecks of grey in his short black hair and a thickening waistline suggested he had left forty behind some four to five years ago. Jordan was therefore at least four years older than himself. Against that, he was taller by eight inches and was some eighty pounds heavier. His mere presence was physically intimidating and Boothroyd reckoned nobody in their right mind would want to make an enemy of him. The American was perched on a bar stool in the one area of the pub where smoking was allowed. His whole attention appeared to be concentrated on the 27-inch TV screen, high up on the back wall behind the bar, which was tuned to a sports channel. Boothroyd knew different when Jordan turned about and tipped him a salute before he reached the bar.

'What'll you have, Mr B?'

It was Jordan's annoying habit that he always addressed Boothroyd as Mr B. He had been one of the three PIs from the Burns Agency who had met Ensley Holsinger off American Airlines flight 215 when it had arrived at JFK on Monday, 8 June, and the habit had started there and then.

'A bottle of Miller Lite,' Boothroyd said, and perched himself on a bar stool the American had been keeping for him.

The beer arrived ice cold with dewdrops trickling down the outside of the bottle. Boothroyd picked up the Miller Lite and drank half of it in one go. He would, of course, pay for it later. In spite of all the years he had spent in New York he still hadn't got acclimatised to being hot and clammy one minute, then feeling chilly the next after walking into an air-conditioned building. There wasn't a summer went by that he didn't end up with at least two streaming head colds.

'So what have you got for me?' he asked Jordan.

Jordan produced a slip of paper from his shirt pocket and passed it to Boothroyd. 'A list of expenses. You don't get anything for nothing in this world and I had to grease a couple of palms.'

'One hundred and seventy-five dollars?' Boothroyd's voice rose a full octave in disbelief. 'That's kind of steep, isn't it?'

'We're talking homicide. You think the

260

detective squad at the nineteenth precinct was going to let me see what they had on Amelia Cazelet for free?'

'No, I guess they wouldn't.'

'Damn right,' Jordan said emphatically.

'And what did you learn?'

'There is nothing to indicate Amelia Cazelet planned to spend the weekend of twenty-ninth, thirty-first of May on Martha's Vineyard. She had said nothing about going away to the assistant manager of the bookstore, which was her usual practice. And that message Cazelet was supposed to have received? Nobody broke into her apartment. And Ensley Holsinger wasn't working at home that Friday, she was in the office from nine thirty to six.'

'Do you know where Ms Holsinger is now?' Boothroyd asked.

'I know where she isn't, Mr B. She never returned to her apartment on East 71st Street when she left the safe house the agency had provided in New Haven.' Jordan lit a cigarette, drew the smoke down into his lungs and slowly exhaled. 'I'll tell you another thing, she hasn't been near her mother's place in New Milton either.'

'In other words she's gone missing?'

'That's about the size of it,' Jordan agreed.

'Is there anyone else she might have sought out? I understand her father is a hot-shot lawyer in Chicago.'

'I don't recall you mentioning her father when you briefed me yesterday, Mr B.'

'No, you're right. I didn't think it would be

261

necessary to involve him.'

'But it is now?'

'Yes.'

'It's going to cost you.'

Boothroyd was sure it would and was the reason why he didn't pick up the tab when Jordan ordered two more beers.

'Did you hear what I said, Mr B?'

'Yes. I want you to run down her father and see if he knows where she has got to. If he hasn't the faintest idea, find out the names and addresses of any other relatives Ms Holsinger might have looked up.'

'I can't do that over the phone. Is it OK if I fly into Chicago?'

'I guess so.'

Boothroyd could hear the till ringing up every time Jordan opened his mouth. He didn't know how Ashton was going to cover it but that would be his problem.

'I might have to stay over, Mr B.'

'For how long?'

'No more than a day or two.'

'Fine. Try not to stay at the Drake.'

'What's the matter with it?'

'Nothing, it's a great hotel. Princess Di stayed there when she visited Chicago and I haven't got a bottomless purse.'

'Point taken.'

'Good. Ensley is on friendly terms with Evan Vance at the Shubert Agency. He might know her present whereabouts or at least point you in the right direction.'

Boothroyd reached for his beer and took a

long pull from the bottle. He'd hoped Jordan would volunteer the information he was after but the PI had ignored the hint. Finally Boothroyd was forced to ask Jordan if he had discovered which hospital Vance had been taken to after being mugged.

'The Roosevelt on 10th Avenue and he's no longer in a coma.'

'That's good news.'

'Savour it because it's all the news you'll get from me where Vance is concerned.' Jordan placed a hand on Boothroyd's leg close to the kneecap and crushed the tendon in a grip of steel. 'Don't even think about asking me to go back to the cops and milk them for more information.'

'The thought never entered my mind.'

'Keep it that way.'

'Can I have my leg back now?'

Jordan removed his hand. 'Those guys gave me a real hard time,' he said reflectively. 'They hadn't linked Cazelet with Vance and couldn't see why I should think there was a connection. Same precinct, two different crimes; Cazelet was murdered, Vance was mugged. We had a simple and believable story until you had to drag Vance into it.'

The cover story, like all good legends, had been partially based on truth. An American couple living in London who were friends of Ensley Holsinger had expected to see her before she flew back to New York. They had known she would be seeing George Ventris, head of Warwick Thompson Associates and when they learned he

263

had been murdered they were naturally alarmed, especially when there was no word from Ensley. They had rung her apartment in New York, her home in New Milton and, aware of her friendship with Amelia Cazelet, they had called the bookshop on 7th Avenue. Following their conversation with the assistant manager, they'd had good cause to be thoroughly alarmed. They had therefore gone to the London office of the Burns Agency and sought advice. Hence Jordan had been hired to ascertain Ensley Holsinger's present whereabouts.

'The one thing that puzzled the cops about this story, Mr B, was why her mother didn't call the police.'

'And how did you explain that?'

'You told me she was a lush and I passed it on, said the mother was more interested in the bottle than her daughter and they hadn't spoken in six months.'

'And they believed you?'

'Sure they did. The cops are used to dealing with dysfunctional families. It was when I started to question them about Evan Vance that they got suspicious.' Jordan shook his head. 'Big mistake,' he muttered.

Boothroyd thought he was right and the way he saw it, he was the one who was to blame for the mistake. What was it Ashton had said when they spoke yesterday morning? 'It's almost certain the attack on Vance was not premeditated. I mean, why wait nine days from the first to the tenth before dealing with him? It doesn't make sense unless he was out of town for the whole of that period.' He had assumed Ashton wanted to know if this had been the case whereas what he had actually said had been more in the nature of a soliloquy than a request for information. He should have known that if Ashton had wanted him to go down that road he would have come straight out and said so.

'The cops wanted to know who I was working for,' Jordan said quietly. 'Of course I didn't tell them but I can see a time coming when I might have to.'

'Do you want to call it a day?' Boothroyd asked.

'Hell, no. I'll find Mr Holsinger, his ex-wife and Ensley for you, Mr B, but not Vance. OK?'

'Yes.'

'But if the Feebies come knocking — '

'Feebies?'

'FBI, the Bureau. Once they question me your anonymity goes. Understood?'

'Yes.'

'Good. Now pay me my expenses to date and I'm out of here.'

'I've only a hundred and twenty on me.'

'That will do for the time being,' Jordan told him.

★ ★ ★

Occasionally, when somebody told you there was nothing to report, the information could be significant. In a battlefield context it meant the enemy was inactive. However, Landon knew full well that in his case 'nothing to report' had no

265

significance whatever. As he waited for Ashton to appear in the Arrivals hall at Geneva airport, Landon wished he had something positive to impart. For once in his life he wouldn't have minded if the plane was late but, of course, British Airways flight 728 had to be bang on time and Ashton was the first to clear Immigration and Customs. There was no need for Landon to hold a placard in front of his chest; Ashton spotted him immediately and homed in.

'Hello, Will,' he said cheerfully. 'How's it going? Is Malinovsky here yet?'

This was Ashton for you, Landon thought. No beating about the bush, direct and to the point.

'If he is, we failed to spot him. He wasn't on the Aeroflot plane which arrived yesterday and there isn't another until Monday.' Landon walked Ashton towards the exit. 'I rented a car from Hertz,' he continued. 'I thought you might need one.'

'I expect I will.'

'Roy Kelso forgot to tell me where you would be staying.'

'The Angleterre in the Quai du Mont-Blanc.' Ashton smiled. 'Not wholly inappropriate,' he added.

In more ways than one, Landon thought. The Angleterre was a four-star hotel, the Pension Albert wasn't even classified. Roy Kelso might not like Ashton but he was an assistant director and the Admin King believed in maintaining the pecking order.

'About Malinovsky,' Ashton continued as they

266

drove away from the airport, 'have you checked to see if he is in town?'

'I rang all the hotels in Geneva this morning. If Vassily Semyonovich is with us he's registered under a different name.'

'What else have you done, Will?'

'I've stepped up the watch on the airport in case he flies in today, tomorrow or even first thing on Monday. Anyway, we're covering every inbound flight. Malinovsky may leave Moscow by Aeroflot but that doesn't necessarily mean he will use the same carrier to get here. He could break his journey in Berlin or Paris and switch to Lufthansa or Air France.'

'What's wrong with going via Italy?'

'Nothing. Paris and Berlin were just two examples.'

'What time does the Aeroflot plane arrive on Monday?'

'Too late for your meeting.'

'That's disturbing,' Ashton scowled. 'In a way I hope Malinovsky has already slipped through the net and is staying with the Russian Consul. Switching airlines and all that stuff could mean he is concerned for his own safety.'

'What are we talking about? The Russian Foreign Intelligence Service?'

'Possibly, but I fancy the Chechens. According to Head of Chancery, Moscow, Vassily Semyonovich shares our concern regarding Muslim extremists.' Ashton shrugged. 'I'd say the Chechens were in that category. Incidentally, have you had a look at the Au Bec Fin?'

The question almost threw Landon and for

several moments, he couldn't see the connection. He had assumed Ashton's reason for choosing the place was based on prior knowledge. Then it dawned on him that Ashton wasn't interested in the cuisine, he wanted to know if the restaurant could be a deathtrap in the event of a terrorist attack.

'The Rue du Berne is hardly a quiet backwater but the Au Bec Fin gives the impression that it is at odds with the other buildings in the immediate neighbourhood. It has a Dickensian look about it — mullioned windows, narrow entrance, a signboard hanging from a wall-mounted bracket, candles on the tables — that sort of thing. I'm not sure it would be the place I'd choose as a rendezvous if I were in Malinovsky's shoes.'

'He'll have sent his security people on ahead,' Ashton said thoughtfully. 'In fact they may have already given the r.v. a thumbs down. If that should be the case, they will probably spring an alternative venue on us late on Monday morning.'

'Assuming they know where to find you.'

'They will,' Ashton said. 'Chris Neighbour will have sent Head of Station, Moscow a signal informing him I would be staying at the Angleterre. George Elphinstone has been asked to pass this on to the interested party.'

'Whose bright idea was that?'

'Mine.'

He had his reasons, though after listening to them Landon thought he was mistaken. Since Malinovsky had agreed they should meet in

Geneva instead of Moscow, Ashton was willing to agree to a last-minute change of venue. There was, Ashton claimed, method in his madness. He was prepared to go out on a limb once but not twice. The meeting therefore either took place on Monday, 15 June or not at all.

'The risk is negligible, Will. What have I got to worry about? You'll be watching my back with that fella from the embassy.

'Browne, Bill Browne.'

'Yeah. Where is he now?'

'In the British Airways office at the airport, running the hired help from Suter Sécurité National.'

As they were covering every inbound flight, Landon had assigned all six operatives to Geneva airport, rotating them at ninety-minute intervals to minimise the risk of attracting the attention of the police officers on duty. Keeping Browne out of sight would have been impossible if BA hadn't allowed him to squat in the supervisor's office.

'You can pay the hired help off after the last inbound flight tomorrow, Will.'

'I'd already planned to do that,' Landon told him. 'I also intend to spell Browne tomorrow.'

'Right.'

'I understand Head of Station, Berne has a couple of .38 revolvers in his office safe — '

'And that's where they are going to stay,' Ashton said, cutting him short. 'We're not going to start a war in neutral Switzerland.'

So much for the SAS. There would be no sending for the heavy mob even if it began to look as if there could be trouble with a capital T.

'First stop is the Angleterre, Will, then you can take me to the Russian Consul.'

'What?'

'A belt and braces job,' Ashton said coolly. 'I want to make sure my message is received by Malinovsky.'

17

Jill Sheridan's rehabilitation began when she was led out of her cell without her wrists and ankles being shackled. She had no idea of the time, day or date. Despite the more liberal regime, her wristwatch had not been returned with her other possessions and she had not been allowed to see a newspaper. Furthermore, Jill had no idea whether her removal from the detention centre was being conducted during the hours of daylight or under cover of darkness. Before leading her out of the cell the shorter of the two warders blindfolded her with a cloth.

'Sorry about this,' he said, 'but you won't be wearing it for long.'

Whenever she had been taken into the interrogation room they had always turned left on leaving the cell; this time they walked her in the opposite direction, then stopped after ten paces. Jill heard them open a door and felt warm air on her face as she turned to her left. Two paces and she was outside the building, six more and she was halted a second time.

'There's a step right in front of you,' the smaller man told her. 'Feel for it with your foot and step up.'

Jill did so and felt herself swaying and was told to raise her other foot and plant it higher. A hand grabbed her left arm above the elbow and hauled her into the vehicle. A man whose voice she didn't recognise said to trust him while he steered her backwards on to a bench seat.

'And don't remove the blindfold until you are told to,' he added.

Jill mentally counted off the seconds, one thousand, two thousand, three thousand, four thousand, five thousand, six thousand, and calculated three minutes had passed when somebody tossed her bag into the back and slammed the doors shut one at a time. A starter motor whirred briefly and the engine caught, then a panel at the rear of the cab was slid open and somebody up front told Jill she could now remove the blindfold.

The hand that had pulled Jill into the van belonged to the breathless interrogator who sounded as if she suffered with asthma. Seeing her in the flesh for the first time, Jill reckoned the woman was in her middle to late forties. She was a blonde, no more than five six but heavy with it, broad shoulders, thick waist, with the arms and thighs of a wrestler.

'Nice to meet you at last,' Jill said tartly. 'What do I call you?'

'You don't need to know my name.'

'I see, it's like that, is it? You mind telling me what time it is?'

'My wristwatch has stopped,' the interrogator told her.

'OK. Here's an easier question. Where are we going?'

'You'll know soon enough, Miss Sheridan.'

'I can tell we are going to have a scintillating conversation.'

'I prefer to keep myself to myself. I suggest you do the same.'

'If that's what you want.'

Jill turned her attention to the Hartmann business case on the floor and wondered what had happened to her handbag.

'What have you done with the rest of my things? she demanded loudly.

'What things?'

'My Gucci handbag, is it in the suitcase?'

'How would I know? I didn't pack it.'

'What have you done with my Omega wristwatch? I bet you've stolen it.'

The asthmatic interrogator started wheezing. 'If I knew where it was, I'd smash the damned thing to pieces,' she gasped, a paroxysm of coughing punctuating her every word.

The panel at the rear of the cab slid back again and a loud voice with a Texan accent said, 'Are you OK, Carol?'

'Carol's all right,' Jill yelled back, 'but she could do with a drink of water.'

'No water. 7 Up OK?'

'Yes.'

Carol: learning her first name represented a victory in Jill's eyes. It had been a slip of the tongue on the Texan's part but she had little difficulty in persuading herself she had deliberately engineered the disclosure. Jill did not consider what use could be made of the information; she had got her own back on these people and that was enough for the time being.

The regular drumbeat of the tyres on concrete suggested they were on a freeway and, based on

273

this assumption, she figured they were travelling at fifty-five to sixty miles an hour. Jill began counting the seconds again, starting from scratch every three minutes, hoping in this way to gauge the passage of time mentally. Approximately twelve minutes into the count, the driver eased his foot on the pedal and their speed fell back to something in the region of thirty miles an hour. Until then the noise level had indicated that traffic on the road was moderately light, but now it was evident they were in a built-up area. The assumption was confirmed for Jill by the number of times they came to a halt for a few brief moments. A Mensa-level IQ was not required to deduce the driver had caught a red light on each occasion.

Presently their speed fell even further away, dropping, Jill estimated, to below twenty. As the vehicle slowed to a walking pace, the driver put the wheel over to the right, then stopped and, shifting into reverse, backed the vehicle into what she thought had to be a driveway. The engine died, two doors up front opened and closed, then somebody walked round to the back of the van and hammered on the panelling.

Carol said, 'All right, lady, on your feet. Turn about and keep perfectly still.'

'Surely to God you're not going to blindfold me again?'

'You bet I am.'

'This is ridiculous.'

'You give me any trouble and I will have you wearing handcuffs and leg irons again.'

'And get a kick out of doing it,' Jill said

caustically before meekly surrendering.

The scarf was tied unnecessarily tight over her eyes and, just in case Jill thought it was unintentional, Carol made sure she knew it was deliberate. Pushed unceremoniously towards the double doors, she feared she was going to be shoved out of the vehicle. Two pairs of hands reached up, took hold of both arms and helped her down.

'We walk straight forward now,' the Texan said, still holding on to her right arm. 'You are approaching two concrete steps. Mind you don't stub your toes.'

One step, two steps. Jill felt the Texan reach past her and open a door to enable her to cross the threshold and enter the house.

A woman with a kindly voice said, 'Please put that suitcase down and close the door behind you.'

'Where am I?' Jill asked, and was told she was in safe hands, then in the next breath she was politely asked not to remove the blindfold just yet.

'It's supposed to be a surprise; your friends were very insistent about that.'

'What's your name?' Jill snapped.

'Damaris Theophilus. My great-grandparents come from Piraeus.'

'Well, Damaris Theophilus, you should know the people who brought me to this place are no friends of mine. You should also know it doesn't matter whether I can see or not; this is Spencer's place, isn't it?'

'Spencer? I don't think I know a Mr Spencer.'

'He owns this house.'

'Really?'

'Please don't play games with me, Damaris. This is 162 Bay View, Sausalito?'

'Yes, it is, honey, but I own the property and my agent hasn't rented it out to anybody called Spencer.'

'I'm sorry, I don't believe you.'

'Well, I'm equally sorry because there is no way I can prove it to your satisfaction. Incidentally, you can remove that blindfold now.'

'I thought I heard them drive away.' Jill reached behind her and tried to undo the scarf, breaking a nail in the process. 'I can't loosen the damned knot,' she said.

'Here, let me try.' Damaris Theophilus came to her assistance and picked at the knot with her fingers, talking all the time about the stupid tricks some people play on their friends. A week at the house with all expenses paid was to have been a surprise present for Jill but had it been necessary to blindfold her? Damaris Theophilus didn't think so, especially as the knot wouldn't budge.

'I'm afraid I'll have to cut it off,' Damaris said apologetically. 'It's going to ruin the scarf.'

'I don't care,' Jill told her. 'It doesn't belong to me.'

She heard Theophilus open the drawer, moments later the American woman returned and cut the scarf in two with a pair of scissors. The sudden influx of light dazzled Jill and for a while she could hardly see anything, such was the haze that had been induced by the scarf.

Then gradually her eyes began to focus properly and she could make out the Hartmann business case on the kitchen floor by the back door.

'Are you OK, honey?'

'Yes, I'm fine.'

Damaris Theophilus was the mirror image of how Jill had pictured her. She had short, curly black hair liberally streaked with grey crowning a kindly-looking face. She was approximately five feet six in high heels and was roughly ten pounds heavier than she should have been for her height. Jill thought Damaris was in her early fifties.

'I'm fine,' Jill repeated, and looked up at the fluorescent tube in the ceiling. 'Why is the light on?'

'It's dark outside.'

'Dark?'

'It's five after ten at night,' Damaris said, and pointed to the kitchen clock. 'Now let me show you to your room,' she added, and picked up the Hartmann business case.

'What's today?'

'Are you sure you're OK, honey?'

'Just answer the question,' Jill said wearily.

'It's Sunday — Sunday, June fourteenth. Where have you been?'

'I wish I knew.'

'You ought to go to bed, you look all in.'

Damaris led her into a bedroom that would have compared favourably with anything the Hyatt on Union Square had to offer. Jill opened her suitcase, found it contained the tote bag and the Gucci handbag. The Omega wristwatch had been wrapped in tissue paper and placed on top of her clothes. After unwrapping the tissue she saw it was recording seven minutes past ten. Still in doubt she switched on the TV, found CNN news and learned it was indeed Sunday, 14 June. She had been detained for six days. It felt more like six weeks.

★ ★ ★

The meeting had been set for 11.30 a.m. Monday; 15 June at the Au Bec Fin. It was now five minutes to eleven and there had been no word from Vassily Malinovsky. There were several explanations for his tardiness, the most comforting being that he was quite happy with the chosen rendezvous, which Ashton did not believe. The second and most alarming possibility was that, for some reason he had had second thoughts and had turned back. There was some justification for thinking this might be the case. When the hired help from Suter Sécurité National had been stood down late on Sunday night there had still been no sign of the Russian. It was also conceivable that Malinovsky didn't know how to get in touch with Ashton because the Russian Consul had deliberately failed to inform him he was staying at the Angleterre.

Ashton had had breakfast in his room and had then hung a 'Do No Disturb' sign on the door to ensure a chambermaid didn't enter at precisely the wrong moment. At 08.00 hours he had established contact with Landon on the crypto-protected Haydn short-range transmitter. They had carried out a radio check every hour on the

278

hour and had reported loud and clear each time. That their communications were good was no more than Ashton had expected. With Landon and Browne only a mile and a half away in the car park between the Quai Général-Guisan and the Rue du Rhône they were well inside the maximum operating range of the Haydn.

Eleven o'clock came and went. Then just as Ashton decided he should set off for the Au Bec Fin, the telephone rang. When he answered it the caller spoke to him in Russian. He had no idea whether the caller was Malinovsky himself or one of his bodyguards; their conversation was however, brief and largely one-sided. Malinovsky didn't like the look of the Au Bec Fin and proposed instead they should meet at the Simplon Café in the Botanical Gardens. The time remained unchanged: Ashton was to be there at eleven thirty.

'How will I recognise you?' Ashton asked.

'I'm sure you have many photographs of me,' Malinovsky said, and chuckled. 'But no matter, I know you very well, Peter James.'

Ashton frowned. Some people had been doing their homework. James was his second Christian name and he had dropped it a lifetime ago after his mother had married a second time and he had acquired a singularly unpleasant stepfather with the same Christian name.

'So how many security men are looking after you, Vassily Semyonovich? And please don't tell me you will be alone because I won't believe you.'

'Two,' Malinovsky said after hesitating

momentarily. 'And you?'

'I also have two men, both of whom are unarmed. Make sure your people leave their weapons behind.'

'You have twenty-three minutes, Peter James,' Malinovsky said, and hung up.

Ashton replaced the phone, called up Landon on the Haydn, gave him the new r.v. and confirmed the eleven thirty deadline. There was no need to urge Landon to get a move on. Leaving his bedroom on the fourth floor, Ashton reversed the hanging sign on the door, and, rather than wait for a lift, ran down the staircase. He cut through the lobby, sidestepping and weaving past the other hotel guests. Out on the street he flagged down a passing cab.

★　★　★

Landon passed the Haydn to Browne, started the Audi and, shifting into gear, drove out of the car park with no regard at all for the ten-kilometre-an-hour speed limit.

'The Botanical Gardens,' he shouted to Browne. 'Give me directions.'

'You're the wrong side of the Rhône.'

'For Christ sake, I don't want to know where I am now, tell me how to get there.'

'Take the Pont du Mont-Blanc, then turn right and stick close to the lake.'

Although it wasn't nose to tail there was a lot of traffic on the road, and playing nip and tuck with an automatic drive wasn't easy. Landon reckoned that with a manual gearbox he could have changed up and down faster and would therefore have been able to move into a lot more gaps. Ashton had anticipated that Malinovsky would want to change the r.v., but in waiting until the last minute before informing him of the new one, the Russian had deliberately set out to put them on the back foot. At least he had in Landon's opinion. The hotel where Ashton was staying was nearer the Botanical Gardens than where they had been lying up, and he would reach the r.v. long before they did. That wasn't the way it was supposed to be. He and Browne should have got there first and looked the place over. As it was, Ashton would be going in blind. Turning right at the Quai du Mont-Blanc after crossing the bridge, Landon put his foot down and kept an eye out for the police in the rear-view mirror. The last thing he needed was to be pulled over for speeding.

★   ★   ★

From the Angleterre the taxi driver headed straight up the Quai du Mont-Blanc into the Quai Wilson, which in turn became the Avenue de France as the road skirted the lakeside park. At the junction with the Rue de Lausanne the taxi driver turned right for the International Labour Office facing Albert Thomas Square and the Botanical Gardens.

Alighting from the Peugeot, Ashton paid the cab off and took stock. In trainers, cotton slacks and dark blue sweatshirt, he blended in with most tourists. An observant bystander might

281

notice that he didn't have a camera, an experienced bodyguard would focus on his legs, knowing that an ankle holster was the only means of concealing a firearm on his person. A knife was a different matter; it could be taped to the inside of either thigh but getting at it in a hurry wouldn't be easy.

There was no sign of Landon and Browne yet, which didn't surprise him. Time, however, was running on and, with only eight minutes to go before the deadline, he couldn't afford to wait much longer. He couldn't spot the security men he assumed were protecting Malinovsky but they had undoubtedly picked him out and would have had a good look at him. He broke the radio silence to call up Landon, got Browne instead and asked him for their location.

'We're approaching the lakeside park and should be with you in five.'

It was, Browne added, their intention to park the Audi in the lane between the Botanical Gardens and the grounds of the UNO building.

To wait for them was, in Ashton's opinion, out of the question. The longer he dallied outside the Simplon Café, the more suspicious Malinovsky's security men would become.

'I'm off to meet our friends,' Ashton said. 'You and Will should enter the Simplon Café separately.'

'And then what?'

'You play it off the cuff.'

Ashton slipped the small transceiver into a trouser pocket, entered the grounds of the Botanical Gardens and walked down the narrow path leading to the café.

The Simplon was self-service, not unlike McDonald's in that respect, except it specialised in pastries and was far less crowded. Ashton ordered a large coffee from one of the girls behind the counter, paid for it at the till, then glanced round the café as if looking for a vacant table. The man who tipped a brief salute to him was wearing a loose-fitting jacket over a pale green shirt and dark grey slacks. When Ashton nodded back, the man sitting next to him got up and left the table.

'You are Vassily Semyonovich?' Ashton enquired in Russian.

'I am indeed, Peter James, and we will converse in English.'

'I don't see any family resemblance between you and your late sister, Katya.'

'That's because she was my father's bastard. She became part of the family and adopted our name after my mother died. Katya was then sixteen years old.'

'Neat,' Ashton told him. 'Very neat, just like the legends the old KGB used to produce.'

'Meaning?'

'Meaning I don't believe you but I will listen to what you have to say.'

'You will not regret it. We are in possession of information which leads us to believe Islamic Jihad is planning a major terrorist operation directed at the UK.'

'Can you be more specific like where, when, and what we can expect?'

'I can't tell you where but it will be soon and it

will be spectacular.'

'You're wasting my time,' Ashton told him bluntly and started to get up.

'Wait, I will give you a name.'

'I'm listening.'

'Ali Mohammed Khalef. I understand he is known to your Security Service?'

'Yeah. What do you want in exchange?'

'These two men,' Malinovsky said, and passed a slip of paper across the table.

The names didn't mean anything to Ashton but he had anticipated the Russian might well look for a quid pro quo for their co-operation. 'Khalef is not enough,' he said. 'Give me another name.'

★   ★   ★

Landon sent Bill Browne ahead, then locked the Audi and, mindful of the instructions Ashton had given them, sauntered back to the entrance to the Botanical Gardens. By the time he passed through the gate the house martin from Berne was no longer in sight.

Landon knew that among his own several character defects was an eye for a pretty girl and the one sitting on the park bench reminded him of Ensley Holsinger. Same dark brown glossy hair, same styling. Maybe her face wasn't quite so arresting, and it was difficult to gauge her height when she was sitting down but he would be surprised if she was shorter than the American girl. She was obviously heavier because, despite the thigh-length smock, there was no disguising the fact that she was carrying a child. Drawing near, Landon noticed how pale she looked.

'Are you OK?' he asked. The girl looked up at him, her eyes blank. 'Can I get you something to drink? A glass of water perhaps?'

There was no verbal response but she appeared to nod her head, which Landon took for a 'yes'.

'Don't go away,' Landon told her. 'I'll be right back.'

He went into the café, joined the short queue at the counter and asked one of the girls for a glass of iced water. When he went back outside there was no sign of the pregnant woman.

★   ★   ★

Malinovsky was a firm believer in the hard sell. For close on ten minutes he lectured Ashton nonstop on the threat posed by Islamic Jihad and similar terrorist organisations, which he believed should be described as movements since their adherents were not confined to a particular ethnic group. That was why Chechen rebels like Maskhadov and Zakayev were England's enemy just as much as they were Russia's. That was why they should be returned to Moscow to answer for the outrages they had committed.

'And you can have them,' Ashton told him. 'Produce the evidence and apply for extradition.'

'That will take months, perhaps years. Your lawyers are so clever.'

'You would like us to cut through the red tape,

285

pick up Maskhadov and Zakayev and put them on a RAF plane?'

'You would have our eternal gratitude,' Malinovsky assured him.

'I had the same conversation with my Director General and a deputy under-secretary at the Foreign and Commonwealth Office and they nearly had a fit. However, I believe I can turn them around. But, as I've already said, you've got to give me something more than Ali Mohammed Khalef to swing it.'

'All right, I give you one more name.'

'Make it two.'

Malinovsky laughed derisively, then just sat there at the table staring into space. It was, Ashton realised, a contest of wills to see who would be the first to give way. Out of the corner of his eye he saw Landon enter the café again, still clutching the polystyrene beaker he had taken outside a couple of minutes ago. Browne with an e was seated at a table on the far side of the room, seemingly in earnest conversation with two youngish backpackers.

'Abbas Sayed Alijani,' Malinovsky said, breaking the silence, 'and Asir.'

'Asir, just plain Asir?'

'I will tell you the rest when you deliver Maskhadov and Zakayev to a deserted but still serviceable airfield in the north-east of England. You will also supply the aircraft.'

'And when is this supposed to happen?'

'You have seven whole days.'

'Don't hold your breath,' Ashton told him. 'Nobody in Whitehall moves that fast.'

'We shall see, Peter James.' Malinovsky pushed his chair back and stood up. 'Meantime, you and I will leave this café together. It is for our mutual protection.'

'Who are you worried about? Us or the Chechens?'

'Compared with the SIS the Chechens are boy scouts.'

'A slight exaggeration, I think,' Ashton said, and followed Malinovsky towards the exit.

★　★　★

Landon watched the two men make their way towards the exit and waited for some kind of signal from Ashton that would tell him what to do. Ashton's right arm was hanging loosely by his side and although he continued to look straight ahead, he flipped his hand in a backward motion, then curled his fingers into the palm and pointed the thumb in the direction of the swing doors.

In that same instant four men seated in different areas of the café simultaneously rose to their feet and walked briskly to the exit. The effect was farcical, like something out of an old Benny Hill routine. The babble of conversation ceased abruptly; two of the Russians managed to get ahead of Malinovsky and there was a mix-up in the entrance and exit as they pulled the swing doors back instead of pushing them forward.

Landon tagged on to the end of the party of six, hoping that Browne would use his common sense and hang back until he was outside the café before attempting to join him.

When Landon emerged into the open air, two of the bodyguards were in front of Malinovsky while the other two were close behind him. Ashton was walking on the grass to the left of the tightly knit group of Russians and coming up the path was the pregnant young woman. Suddenly the significance of what was happening hit him like a thunderbolt.

'Peter,' Landon roared, 'break left and run.'

There was not even a momentary hesitation from Ashton; he had told Landon to watch his back, and unless you were a complete idiot, you assumed Will knew what he was doing and followed his instructions to the letter. The bodyguards surrounding Malinovsky reacted in the worst possible way, those behind him turned about and went for their firearms, those in front froze after drifting slightly apart. The woman came on unimpeded and was almost within touching distance of Malinovsky when she detonated the bomb under the hip-length smock and blew herself to pieces.

18

Landon's father had been a butcher with a couple of shops in Norwich. In the hope that his only son would one day take over the business, he had taught him a thing or two about the buying and selling of meat from the abattoir through the cold store to the display in the shop front window. But nothing Landon had seen during his many visits to the local slaughterhouse had prepared him for the bird's-eye view of the carnage outside the Simplon Café. There were bits of unrecognisable tissue, fragments of bone, brain matter, complete body parts and a lot of blood everywhere. He wondered why the mayhem was at eye level until it dawned on him that he was lying flat on the ground, the left side of his face pressed into the grass. He couldn't understand why all he could hear was a constant high-pitch humming noise like a swarm of bees on the move. Then, as he started to get up, his ears popped and there were people screaming behind him, the injured and the terrified.

The whole of his shirtfront was soaked in blood and at first Landon feared he had been seriously injured. His chest felt as if it had been used as a punchbag but to his relief there was no sign of an entry wound. He did not have to look very far to find the object that had punched him in the chest: lying on the grass near his feet was an arm that had been severed above the elbow. The security team assigned to protect Malinovsky had been decimated. Of the four men only one was still alive and he was in a bad way after losing a leg at thigh level. When Landon had last seen him Ashton had been to the left of the Russian party roughly in line with the suicide bomber. Now there was no sign of him.

'Peter.' Landon raised his voice even higher. 'Peter, where the fuck are you?'

'I'm over here,' Ashton shouted, and emerged from some pampas grass, his face and hands lacerated by the razor-sharp leaves. 'Are the emergency services on the way?'

'I don't know,' Landon confessed, shame-faced.

'Have you got a mobile?'

'No, but Browne has one.'

'Good. Ask him to call them, Will.'

But the house martin from Berne was in no fit state to call anybody. He was sitting on the path just outside the café holding a head between his hands as though it was a football.

'Say hello to Mr Malinovsky,' he said, and giggled inanely.

'Put it down,' Landon told him quietly, 'and give me your mobile.'

'Why?'

'Because we need to alert the emergency services. There are people here in urgent need of medical attention.'

'Yes, of course, I should have thought of that.'

Browne tossed the head over his left shoulder with the result that the grisly object hit a middle-aged woman who was nervously trying to pick her way through the shards of glass littering the path and the grass verge on either side. The woman shrieked in horror, then pitched forward in a dead faint and would have hit the ground face down had Landon not caught her in time. Browne was still sitting cross-legged on the path, his hands twitching spasmodically like a victim of Parkinson's disease. For the moment he was physically incapable of producing his mobile phone. As it happened, Landon no longer needed it; away in the distance but getting closer every minute, he could hear the 'blee ba' of a police siren and the more musical warble of an ambulance. Where there was one vehicle, others were bound to follow.

By now the middle-aged woman was the centre of attention for a crowd of onlookers and a man who knew something about first aid and was very voluble with it. Although French was not Landon's strong suit, he understood enough to realise the man was accusing him of being responsible for the incident. Landon figured it was not a good time to advertise the fact that he was English and told the inquisitor in fluent Spanish that he didn't understand what was being said. Turning his back on the Good Samaritan he walked down the path to join Ashton, who had removed the belt around his waist and was using it as a tourniquet on the left thigh of the surviving Russian.

'You should get out of here before the police arrive, Peter,' Landon said, and hunkered down beside him. 'There is nothing you can do for the Russian and there will be one hell of a political

291

stink if you are arrested and the authorities discover they have netted a big fish.'

'And what happens to you won't cause a ruckus?'

'I'm only a minnow,' Landon told him. 'Besides, I have to stay with Browne; he's in shock.' Landon dipped into a trouser pocket and produced an ignition key and remote control for the central locking. 'Here, take them, Peter. The Audi is parked in the lane between this place and the grounds of the UNO building. Do you remember the registration number?'

'More or less.' Ashton frowned. 'It's 6833 something . . . '

'The something is 4954. Now go while you've still got a chance. I'll look after your wounded Russian.'

Ashton didn't argue with him but it was already too late. The first police car had arrived outside the entrance to the Botanical Gardens before Ashton set off down the path, and the two officers had seen him crouching beside the Russian. Linking outstretched arms the two police officers advanced up the path towards the Simplon Café, sweeping all before them. Ashton was the first to be intercepted but some people from the café managed to slip past them on either flank. However, they didn't get very far; before they reached the gate, reinforcements arrived on the scene and they were rounded up like strays and driven back to join the herd.

'I should have made you go ahead,' Ashton said on rejoining Landon. 'I was a bit too conspicuous.'

It wasn't just the lacerations on Ashton's face that had attracted the unwelcome attention of the police. While rendering first aid to the surviving member of Malinovsky's bodyguard his cotton slacks had been soaked in blood from knee to ankle.

'The police are certain to question us,' Ashton continued. 'Eight men leaving the café together won't have gone unnoticed.'

'So what story do we give the police?'

'We stick to the truth; it's the only way to protect ourselves.'

Landon blinked. 'Are you inferring London might dump us?' he asked softly.

'Not exactly. I just don't want to give them an excuse to wash their hands of us. So, no story about an undercover op against an international drugs cartel.'

'Good, I'm all for plain talk.' Landon turned about and walked towards the Simplon Café.

'Where are you off to?' Ashton asked.

'I'm going to put the wind up Head Office,' Landon told him. 'Browne's the only one of us who's got a mobile.'

★   ★   ★

Rowan Garfield was the Assistant Director in charge of the European Department, a fiefdom that in the course of six years had expanded out of all proportion, only to contract to its original boundaries. At the height of the Cold War the department had been quite manageable, consisting as it had of the NATO countries plus the

293

fringe neutrals of Sweden, Switzerland and Spain. Following the demise of the Warsaw Pact the East European Bloc had been merged with Garfield's empire at the behest of the Treasury. In their determination to implement the so-called peace dividend, they had pared the number of desk officers to the bone. As a result Garfield had found himself in charge of intelligence-gathering from Lisbon in the west to Vladivostock in the east, from Hammerfest in the far north to Sicily in the south with a significantly reduced budget and a wholly inadequate number of intelligence officers. The situation had been finally remedied two years ago with the virtual resurrection of the old East European Bloc, except 'Bloc' was dropped in favour of 'Department'. To justify the about-face, Jill Sheridan had tagged on the SIS element of the MoD's Military Operations (Special Projects) with the added commitment of providing the SIS representative on the Combined Anti Terrorist Organisation.

That a stingy Treasury had refused to provide Ashton with any additional resources to run his establishment was a matter of quiet satisfaction for Garfield. He had done rather nicely out of the reorganisation, thank you. Very few of his desk officers had gone across to the new establishment and the name of his department had not been changed to reflect the reduced area of operations. Consequently his estimates for the financial year 1998/1999 had not been cut to any great extent by the Treasury Committee when reviewing the SIS budget requirements for the year. Best of all, in Garfield's opinion, was the fact that in the last two years nothing untoward had occurred in his fiefdom. At least it hadn't until 14.31 hours that afternoon, when a Top Secret signals with an Emergency precedence was received from Head of Station, Berne. Garfield read it twice, then having committed the details to memory he walked the signal along the corridor to Hazelwood.

'You'll want to see this, Victor,' he said after Dilys Crowther had announced him on the office intercom.

He was impatient to see what Hazelwood's reaction would be when he got to the paragraph concerning the murder of Vassily Semyonovich Malinovsky and his four bodyguards by a suicide bomber. The explosion should have occurred when Victor learned that Ashton, Browne and Landon had been detained by the police for questioning but his face gave nothing away.

'I'm not surprised the Swiss are already making a fuss,' Garfield observed. 'I mean, Peter is not the luckiest of men, is he?'

Hazelwood placed the flimsy to one side and looked up. 'Why don't you say what you mean, Rowan? You think he is a loose cannon, don't you?'

'Well, I'm sorry but wherever Ashton goes there's always blood on the carpet.'

It was also a fact that Ashton was not exactly top of the pops in America. In his capacity as Head of Station, Washington, Miles Delacombe had complained time and again that Ashton had damaged the special relationship he had

295

cultivated with the CIA, the State Department and the FBI. In Garfield's opinion, Delacombe had every right to be angry. Lake Arrowhead, St Louis, Richmond, New York, Denver, Chesapeake Bay: the list of flashpoints where there had been bloodshed was formidable by any yardstick but he knew better than to make this point to Hazelwood.

'I'd better prepare a brief for the Foreign and Commonwealth,' Garfield said presently.

'That won't be necessary, Rowan. The op was approved by the FCO.'

'So there's nothing you require of me?'

'You can open a branch memoranda and take a photocopy of this signal when I've finished with it.'

A branch memoranda or BM was simply an enclosure attached to whatever file was deemed appropriate. If the Simplon incident generated a spate of signals the BM would become a separate file in its own right and would acquire a registration number. If that should happen, Garfield was determined the file should be unloaded on to Ashton's department. The day would come when Hazelwood was forced to retire and he didn't want the new DG to get the impression that he had been responsible for the foul-up in Geneva.

'You look preoccupied, Rowan,' Hazelwood said abruptly, which had the effect of putting him on the back foot. 'What's the problem?'

'The signal.'

'I haven't finished with it yet.'

'Yes, of course . . . '

'However, if you are in that much of a hurry to open a BM see Mrs Crowther on your way out.' Hazelwood passed the signal across the desk. 'Ask her nicely and she will run one off on her photocopier.'

'Thank you.'

Garfield snatched the flimsy and stalked out of the office. There were not enough four-letter words in the English language to express his fury. Switzerland was in his fiefdom, for Christ's sake, but Hazelwood hadn't seen fit to brief him about the Malinovsky business until it was actually underway.

★　★　★

The month of June was living up to its historic reputation that Monday afternoon. In the early hours of Saturday the heavy rain driven by a howling gale had lashed the windows. As of now the sun was shining, there wasn't a cloud in the sky and the barometer in the hall was showing 76 degrees Fahrenheit. Harriet was dressed for the beach in a sleeveless cotton top, pale blue shorts, white ankle socks and a pair of trainers. After strapping Carolyn into the pushchair, Harriet called out to Edward and told him to come and join his sister. The only response was a short burst on BBC Radio 2 followed by Classic FM, a commercial station and then back to Radio 2 again as her four-year-old son played about with the Samsung in the kitchen. The sound of his mother's footsteps in the hall prompted Edward to switch off the radio at the beginning of the news headlines. Before the newsreader was silenced Harriet caught the phrase 'terrorist outrage in Geneva', and froze, rooted to the spot, a sinking feeling in the pit of her stomach.

Geneva: what sort of terrorist outrage? A car bomb or sustained bursts of fire from one or more Kalashnikov AK47 assault rifles? The momentary paralysis disappeared and she went into the kitchen, switched on the radio and found herself listening to Steve Wright in the Afternoon. At two o'clock you only got the headlines, and you had to wait till the early evening for the full news bulletin, and right now she couldn't remember what time of the day that was. She could see Peter half in, half out of the car, his legs two bloody stumps where his kneecaps had been or lying fatally wounded in a gutter somewhere with gunshot wounds in the stomach, chest and head. Then suddenly Harriet was aware of Edward tugging at her shorts and asking if she was cross with him.

'Of course Mummy isn't cross with you, darling,' she said and crouched down to give him a great big hug.

The telephone in the study rang while she was still hugging Edward. It was not the rapid burr burr she associated with British Telecom but the long-drawn-out single tone ring of the Mozart secure-speech facility that immediately filled her with dread.

Entering the study, she lifted the receiver to establish contact and was greeted with an

298

oscillating whistle. The crypto setting was good for seven days and was changed every Sunday by Peter at midnight. The Mozart had been charged with eight key variables on the seventeenth of May of which five had been used. To bring the sixth into play all Harriet had to do was open the trapdoor in the base of the instrument and move the selector wheel one click in a clockwise direction. It was something she could have done in a matter of seconds with her eyes blindfolded but not that afternoon. Nervous tension had got to her and she was all fingers and thumbs. The sudden intrusion of the BT phone didn't help and although Harriet tried to ignore the ringing tone its strident summons made her even more flummoxed. On the edge of losing her temper, she snatched at the receiver and greeted the caller with a sharp 'Yes?'

'Mrs Ashton?'

'Yes. Who are you?'

'My name is Jessica,' Dilys Crowther told her. 'I wonder if you have considered the advantages of our Call Minder service?'

Harriet recognised the voice and knew that in veiled speech she was being invited to change the crypto on the Mozart. 'Never mind the sales talk,' she said crisply. 'One of your engineers is here trying to service my phone. And we'd both get along much better if you would just let him do his job.'

Harriet put the phone down, changed the crypto setting and closed the trapdoor in the base. A few moments later the Mozart rang.

Bad news was usually conveyed by Roy Kelso; on this occasion, however, Hazelwood had taken it upon himself to call her.

'It's Victor,' he said. 'Have you been watching television by any chance, Harriet?'

'No. I heard the news on the radio but not in any detail.'

'Well, I want you to know Peter is all right. He hasn't been injured.'

'That's a relief. Was he deliberately targeted?'

'No. By rights I shouldn't tell you this but the bomber was definitely after Vassily Malinovsky.'

'Is Peter on the way home?'

'Not yet.' Hazelwood cleared his throat. 'I'm afraid the Swiss authorities have detained him for questioning. They're unhappy because they weren't consulted about the proposed meeting between your husband and the Russians — '

'And whose fault was that?' Harriet demanded, interrupting him.

'Well, it has to be said Peter was the one who insisted the meeting had to take place in Geneva or not at all.'

'I don't believe I'm hearing this, Victor.'

'I'm sorry but it happens to be true.'

'Oh, so Peter is at fault because he refused to go to Moscow as Robin Urquhart wanted.'

'Somebody has been talking out of turn,' Hazelwood growled.

'Just give me a straight answer to a straight question. When can I expect to see my husband again? Tomorrow? Next week?'

'I wouldn't like to guess but, rest assured, the

300

FCO is working quietly behind the scene.'

'That isn't good enough. I want Peter home by Wednesday at the latest and I expect Robin Urquhart to kick up a fuss.'

'Now you're being unreasonable.'

'If the Swiss are still holding Peter forty-eight hours from now, you'll discover just how unreasonable I can be,' Harriet said, and slammed the phone down.

★   ★   ★

In theory Jill Sheridan could have walked out of 162 Bay View any time she had felt like it. There were no guards to detain her and Damaris Theophilus had departed shortly after breakfast. If she had put it to the test Jill knew she wouldn't have got very far. Although there was twenty-three dollars in her purse, her passport, credit cards, international driving licence, bank card and cheque book had not been returned with her other possessions. There was also the note from Alvin Dombas, which Damaris Theophilus had passed to her before leaving the house. It had left Jill Sheridan in no doubt that Dombas expected to find her there when he arrived at three o'clock in the afternoon. For him to say how grateful he was that she had agreed to his request was to Jill sheer, breathtaking hypocrisy.

'An apology would be more appropriate,' Jill said icily.

'An apology?'

'For what you put me through at that hellhole

of an interrogation centre. I was rigorously questioned at all hours, deprived of sleep, made to live in squalor and humiliated at every opportunity.'

'I make no apologies for the way you were treated,' Dombas said, talking her down. 'Any one who is suspected of being a double agent is always subjected to a hostile interrogation.'

'Me, a double agent?' Jill said incredulously.

'We had reason to question your integrity. You claimed you were compelled to submit your resignation for a minor error of judgement which merited no more than a reprimand, but you didn't say what that mistake entailed, and if the FBI knew, they surely didn't bother to tell us. What intelligence you initially gave us was ancient history that would have damaged Anglo-American relations sixty-odd years ago had we known about the incidents at the time.' Dombas smiled lopsidedly. 'I guess my disappointment must have registered with you because you then gave us a couple of names.'

'Ali Mohammed Khalef, the Iraqi cleric allegedly opposed to Saddam Hussein,' Jill said listlessly.

'And let's not forget the Iranian dissident Abbas Sayed Alijani,' Dombas reminded her. 'Trouble is, your former colleagues at Vauxhall Cross maintain they don't have enough on Khalef to deport him. And as for Sayed Alijani, you swore the guy we had traced to Chicago was not the right man. I had you down as a grey person, someone who was neither one thing nor the other.'

'And now I'm black?'

Dombas shook his head. 'No, I'd say you were semiwhite.'

'What made the difference, Alvin?'

'Talal Asir. His address in Paris checked out, which was a plus point in your favour. There were others: you linked Amelia Cazelet to Asir and supplied the motive for her murder.'

'Some commendation,' Jill said bitterly.

'Don't feel badly about Cazelet. She was a waste of space. Isn't that how you Brits describe somebody who is useless?'

'I didn't mean to but I set her up.'

'And now I'm giving you the chance to do the same to Asir.'

'You are joking?'

'I was never more serious,' Dombas said.

'I'm forty years old; I'd like to see at least fifty.'

'You won't be out there on your own.'

'No? Who will be looking after me? Please tell me it won't be Carol the asthmatic, or the anaemic Spencer.'

'You've got the wrong idea, Jill, I'm not going to use you as a moving target. There is another way of getting to Asir.'

The other way was to freeze and then empty whatever numbered accounts Asir was using to bankroll Islamic Jihad. Amelia Cazelet had been one of his fund-raisers; it would be Jill's task to contact her friends and express an eagerness to make a substantial donation to improve the lot of the Ramallah Palestinians. The CIA would provide her with the necessary financial

303

resources, including a bogus contract with a major New York publisher that would hold up under investigation.

'We'll start with Ensley Holsinger,' Dombas continued. 'If anybody's in a position to name the friends of Amelia Cazelet, she is. Ms Holsinger was close to Amelia and lived in the same apartment block.'

'Getting the information you want might be difficult.' Jill shook her head. 'I don't know a damned thing about Ms Holsinger.'

'You'll know all about Ensley by the time you meet her. I'll get Miles Delacombe to ask your former colleagues in London what they make of Holsinger, especially the guy who interrogated her.'

'You make it sound so easy, Alvin.'

'The operation is not without risk, Jill.'

She didn't need Dombas to tell her that. Sooner rather than later, word of her generosity would get back to Asir and her survival would be entirely dependent on the quality of the cover story provided by the CIA.

'Do I have a choice?' Jill asked. 'Can I say no?'

'Sure you can. I don't believe in coercion.'

'And what would happen if I did?'

'Well, there we'd have a problem. See Miles Delacombe has told us that you're not too popular in London. In fact, your former colleagues would like to put you away for a very long time. But they are reluctant to apply for extradition, and we've dug our heels in on legal grounds because you're a valuable asset. Of

304

course all that could change any day and the Justice Department might well put you on a plane to London without going through the usual formalities of extradition.'

19

Will Landon had been released on Wednesday 17 June in time to catch the last British Airways flight out of Geneva departing at 19.05 hours. As if to make a point, the Swiss authorities had detained Ashton at the last minute for a further twenty-four hours. This unexpected development had required the prompt intervention of Robin Urquhart to placate Harriet and persuade her that Peter would be home a lot sooner if she left everything to the FCO as opposed to the press. When it came to eating humble pie, no one was better at it than Urquhart. He had gone straight to the Swiss Embassy at 16/18 Montagu Place and, in briefing His Excellency the Ambassador, had been far more open and candid than Hazelwood had bargained for. The fact was, Urquhart's diplomatic approach had paid off. After a flurry of cables between London and Berne, Ashton had been allowed to leave the country.

In order to shield him from the media Head of Station, Berne had issued Ashton with a new passport in the name of Peter James. On the assumption that Reuters, A.P., and local stringers would be looking for Ashton at Geneva International, he had booked him on Swissair flight SR808 departing from Zurich at 19.55 hours. His colleague at Vauxhall Cross had been equally cautious in that nobody from The Firm had been there to meet him in the Arrivals Hall of Terminal 3. That chore had been left to the senior duty officer, who had gone straight to the long-stay car park where Ashton had left the Volvo.

It was customary for an officer in Ashton's position to be debriefed immediately, no matter what time of the day or night it might be. Nothing, however, was written in tablets of stone and from the senior duty officer he'd learned that contrary to the usual practice the debriefing would be held after morning prayers on Friday.

When he walked into Vauxhall Cross the following morning, Will Landon, and Chris Neighbour, the Grade II intelligence officer in charge of the Russian Desk, were waiting for him in the lobby.

'So who's going to be first?' Ashton enquired as he continued walking towards the bank of lifts.

'I think it had better be me,' Landon said, and followed him into a vacant car with Neighbour in tow.

'Well, OK, Will, I'm listening.'

'Richard Neagle called a special meeting of the CATO committee yesterday afternoon. Apparently MI5 persuaded their French equivalent, the *Direction de la surveillance du territoire*, to enter Talal Asir's apartment on the Rue de Ponthielu in his absence. In turning the place over they found a small combination safe behind a painting of the Place de la Concorde by an unknown artist.'

The safe had contained statements from the

Hispaniola Bank, Port au Prince, Haiti, First National Trust and Investment, Grand Bahama, the Consolidated Bank, Bridgetown, Barbados, and two numbered accounts with the Grande Banque Estavayer-le-Lac. Without exceptions the accounts were extremely active and the transactions involved large sums of money. The statements had been mailed to various post office box numbers in France, Germany and Italy.

'None of the statements was addressed to Talal Asir,' Landon continued. 'The fact that they were in his possession suggests he was using more than one alias.'

'So we have a copy of these documents, Will?'

'MI5 has; the French photocopied them before their locksmith put the combination safe back in working order.'

Landon fell silent as their lift bumped to a stop at the top floor. He did not resume until they had reached Ashton's office situated on the west side of the building in a room that had once been occupied by the code breakers.

'Neagle is pretty excited. By the time the financial wizards at the Treasury have done their stuff, he believes the Security Service will be able to deny Islamic Jihad the financial support it has been receiving up till now.'

'Let's hope he's right.'

'There's more,' Landon said. 'Asir has a large old-fashioned writing desk in his apartment. When the French checked it out they found a secret compartment in the left-hand pillar on the inside.'

Hidden within had been a four-page leaflet about the National Conference Centre, Birmingham. It included a photograph of the centre plus a diagram showing the layout, together with a small-scale map of the surrounding area.

'The French sent MI5 photographs of the fingerprints they had lifted from both the leaflet and the map.' Landon smiled. 'And guess what, Nicholson's thumbprint was on the front cover of the leaflet and she had left enough of her index and first finger on the back page for Special Branch to clinch the identification.'

'And what conclusion did Richard Neagle draw from that?'

'He reckons Islamic Jihad were contemplating a major attack on the centre. This would have occurred during the G8 summit from the fifteenth to seventeenth of May. The operation didn't go ahead because of the security measures taken by the host nation.'

'There's nothing like giving yourself a pat on the back,' Ashton said drily. 'For the record I don't subscribe to that view.'

'I don't blame you. It's too damned complacent.'

'And another thing,' Landon continued, 'I'm absolutely sure the Ross Frazer memoirs had nothing to do with the decision to back off. The G8 summit had come and gone before that erupted on the scene. I think the decision was taken by someone with political savvy.'

Ashton had no quarrel with that suggestion. To take out the political leaders of the world's eight strongest economies might have been a major coup but the backlash against Islamic fundamentalists would have done irreparable damage to their cause. To Islamic Jihad, America was Satan while the UK was the devil's disciple. Attack these two countries and words of condemnation was the worst you had to fear from the rest of the world.

'Is there anything else I should know, Will?'

Landon hesitated then glanced sideways at Chris Neighbour as if looking for his support.

'Well, out with it,' Ashton said.

'You've received a lot of coverage in the press and on television . . . '

'So Harriet told me.'

'There was one very arresting photograph,' Landon continued doggedly. 'You were crouching beside one of the bodyguards, trying to keep him alive. Some amateur took a picture of you and caught the right side of your face in profile. It was a pretty fuzzy image but the photograph made the front page of the *Neue Berner Zeitung* as well as most of the local dailies in Geneva.'

Ashton could understand why the picture had been snapped up. By the time reporters, press photographers and a camera crew from the local TV station had arrived on the scene the police had cordoned off the immediate area and they'd had to content themselves with long-range shots. The media had had better luck later in the day when Ashton and the other witnesses to the incident had been released from the clinic where they had been taken for a check-up prior to being interviewed by the police. Even so, he had remained anonymous for over forty-eight hours before his identity had been discovered by a reporter working for the Associated Press.

'Some people are asking why you travelled to Geneva under your own name.'

'I can imagine.'

For 'some people' read 'one person in particular'. There was, Ashton thought, no prizes for guessing who that might be. He and Rowan Garfield had scarcely been the best of friends since 1993 when the Head of the European Department had been responsible for much of the former Soviet Union. Garfield had never run an operation in a high-risk area before, and Ashton had had the misfortune to be the man on the ground in Moscow when he'd cut his teeth. To kick-start the operation Garfield had sent their Russian contact a cable that had led the hardliners in the Russian Intelligence Service straight to him. Garfield had incurred Hazelwood's wrath for that and his career had suffered as a result, for which setback he continued to blame Ashton.

'I don't like snitching on people,' Landon said, colouring, 'but I thought you should know what's being said behind your back.'

'Thank you for that, Will. Forewarned is forearmed. The same applies to Islamic Jihad.'

'You've lost me.'

'We should look for another event similar to the G8 summit,' Ashton told him, 'one that only involves America and this country. Check with MI5, the Home Office and the FCO to see what they've got on their books on the next six to eight weeks. Any questions?'

311

'You don't believe Joe Public could be the target? I'm thinking of Centre Court during Wimbledon fortnight. Plenty of VIPs there on finals day.'

'What's wrong with the World Cup, or have you got something against football?'

'No, but it's being held in France and we've agreed they aren't a target nation.'

'I must be getting old.' Ashton glanced at his wristwatch, then turned to Neighbour. 'I'm pushed for time, Chris. Morning prayers is only five minutes away.'

'I only need a couple of minutes,' Neighbour told him. 'The Russians are pretty upset about their man. They are saying their Malinovsky would still be alive today if the meeting had taken place in Moscow as they'd wanted.'

'I can see this is going to be a fun morning,' Ashton observed wryly.

★   ★   ★

Nobody had asked Nancy Wilkins to find out what had happened to the child Ross Frazer had fathered as a result of his liaison with Clara Sophia Roffi. She had taken it upon herself to do so partly out of curiosity but also because the task represented a challenge that Jill Sheridan had avoided. There was one other attraction. Tracing the descendant of the seventeen-year-old Italian girl and the sixteen-year-old British soldier was a lot more interesting than the day-to-day routine on the Armed Forces Desk.

The only lead Nancy had to go on was the

memo from the commanding officer Field Records, British Forces, Italy addressed to 56th Infantry Division with a copy to the 9th Royal Fusiliers. As an executive officer on the Armed Forces Desk she dealt only with the individual security files relating to officers and senior NCOs. She therefore knew next to nothing about the organisation of the army. However, Nancy did have one source of information in the person of Bob Marlow, the desk officer at the army's Directorate of Security. From him she had learned that the 56th Infantry Division had been disbanded, as had the 9th Royal Fusiliers. On his advice she had gone to the Imperial War Museum during her lunch hour to seek assistance from the staff.

One of the curators had taken a shine to her and had been extremely helpful. The 9th Battalion of the Royal Fusiliers had been raised in January 1941 and had simply disappeared from the Order of Battle nine months after the war in Europe had ended. Unlike the regular and Territorial Army battalions, the 9th had no previous history and was unlikely to be reconstituted. All the museum had was a copy of the battalion's war diary, which the curator told her she was welcome to read. However, as he had already assured Nancy, the diary contained no reference to Private Ross Frazer alias Robert Simmonds and Signorina Clara Roffi. It did, though, record that Major Kenneth Rousell OC A Company had been killed in action on 10 April 1945. Since it appeared the lady had filed a paternity suit, the curator was of the opinion that the document would have ended up in the hands of the Army Legal Service long before Field Records, British Forces, Italy had been stood down.

The following morning Nancy had phoned Bob Marlow again, this time to enquire how she could obtain the papers relating to the paternity suit. She did not explain why the SIS was interested in the love life of a young British soldier that had happened fifty-four years ago and Marlow knew better than to ask. He had come back to her with the not unexpected information that the relevant papers were no longer held by the Army Legal Service. That they had been transferred to the Public Records Office in 1949 was something Nancy hadn't dared to hope for. To be told the documents were filed alphabetically in year order had been an added bonus.

The day before yesterday Nancy had telephoned the officer in charge at the Chancery Lane office, told him exactly what she wished to see and had arranged for a reader's ticket to be available at the desk on her arrival on Thursday, 18 June at one p.m. when the Record Office opened its doors to the public. She had told her supervisor that she had a dental appointment that afternoon and would take a half-day from her annual entitlement.

Nancy had gone to Chancery Lane with no great expectation. The Army Legal Service had a file on Frazer, all right, but after reading the first few pages it seemed to her that where Clara Roffi was concerned the military authorities had not been prepared to lift a finger to help her. In fact, there were grounds for thinking the army had gone out of its way to shield Frazer. He had enlisted under the name of Simmonds and even though he had disclosed his true identity to Rousell the Legal Service still referred to him as Simmonds, the name Clara Roffi had known him by. The papers included a certified-true copy of a birth certificate, and Nancy noted the Italian girl had given birth to a son whom she had named Anthony William Simmonds. The date and place of birth was 26 September 1945 at Ravenna, the nearest town of any consequence to Marco Comacchia, the village where she had been born and brought up.

There was one very interesting enclosure. Inside the back cover of the file, in a sworn affadavit to the British Consul General, Bologna, Clara had stated that she had met Simmonds in December 1944 when the 9th Royal Fusiliers had been resting out of the line in her village. She had further stated that she and Simmonds had been married by the village priest on Tuesday, 6 February 1945, when his battalion had been resting out of the line again shortly before the British offensive had opened at the beginning of April. In her affidavit Clara had admitted to being pregnant at the time, which had prompted the military authorities to wonder just whose child she had been carrying. They had been even more sceptical when she had accounted for her failure to produce a marriage certificate to the fact that it had been lost during a heavy raid on the village. No amount of scepticism could demolish her story. The Luftwaffe had indeed bombed Marco Comacchia on day two of the British offensive, destroying the church and the mayor's office as well as much of the village. Civilian casualties had been heavy and both the mayor and the priest had been among the dead. Clara had survived because she had been staying with her cousin in Ravenna at the time.

There had been one other indisputable piece of evidence that had tended to support her story. Two days after the war in Italy had ended a Warrant Officer Balcombe from the 9th Royal Fusiliers had returned to Marco Comacchia to see his Italian girlfriend and, in the presence of witnesses, had told Clara that Simmonds had been killed in action. Having read the file, Nancy believed this was yet another example of the army shielding its own. However, the Consul General, Bologna hadn't had the same amount of information at his fingertips and he had confirmed that Clara's son, Anthony William Simmonds, enjoyed dual nationality.

In Nancy's opinion Thursday afternoon had been extremely worthwhile. This morning she had to decide whether or not to continue with her self-appointed task. The question was academic, the investigative bug had got to her and the sheer pleasure of unravelling a mystery was all the justification she needed.

Every government department and agency had its own security officers. A list showing their names and telephone numbers had been compiled and issued to appropriate users by

MI5. Digging out the copy that had been received by the Armed Forces Desk, Nancy looked up the name and telephone number of the security officer at the Passport Office, Clive House, Petty France. Although Patrick Chambers was senior to her by at least three grades she didn't hesitate to phone him. When Chambers answered, she identified herself and, observing basic security procedures, drew his attention to the list and invited him to return her call. Two minutes later her extension trilled.

'So what can I do for you, Miss Wilkins?' Chambers asked after she had given her number.

'We're looking at a dual nationality who may or may not have applied for a British passport while living in Italy.'

Chambers sighed. 'I assume this is important?'

'It is,' Nancy told him coolly.

'Can I have his or her particulars?'

'His name is Anthony William Simmonds, he was born on the twenty-sixth of September 1945 at Ravenna. Dual Nationality was recognised on the fifth of May 1948 via the Consul General, Bologna. I assume his first passport would have been issued by the British Embassy?'

'You're right, unless, of course, his mother brought him to this country on her passport and was permitted to stay by the Home Secretary.'

'That possibility had occurred to me,' Nancy admitted. 'However, that's immaterial. Assuming Simmonds does have a passport, there are three things we would like to know. Is it current, when was it issued and where was he living then?'

317

'And I suppose you would like this information a.s.a.p?' Chambers said wearily.

'You've taken the words right out of my mouth,' Nancy told him cheerfully.

★ ★ ★

Contrary to what Ashton had anticipated, there had been no fireworks at morning prayers. Hazelwood had welcomed him back to the fold much as if he had just returned from one of the 'City Mini Breaks' on offer at Thomas Cook and other travel agents. All that had been required of him was a brief account of the suicide bombing outside the Simplon Café, at the end of which Garfield had been moved to congratulate Ashton on his lucky escape. So had Roger Benton who, in a roundabout way, had also implied that things could have been very different if he hadn't agreed to transfer Will Landon from his Rest of the World Department. Before anybody could ask what he had learned from Malinovsky, Hazelwood had turned the spotlight on the acting Head of the Mid-East Department.

His subsequent contribution could be encapsulated in a couple of sentences. Despite the injection of additional funds that had led to increased activity in the souks and coffee houses, Heads of Stations in Libya, Syria, Egypt, Jordan, the Lebanon, Saudi Arabia and the Gulf sheikdoms had virtually nothing to show for the money they had spent. 'It was early days yet,' the acting Department Head had claimed, and in one sense Ashton reckoned he was right. A lot of time and effort was required to find, recruit, cultivate and evaluate a source. Throwing money about haphazardly only bought you a load of rumours. On the other hand, time was probably the one thing they didn't have. As though conscious of this, Hazelwood had brought morning prayers to a close earlier than usual.

Ashton sensed that some of the people sitting round the table thought he had been let off the hook considering the political fallout that had been occasioned by the Simplon incident. But they were wrong. Before the day was over Hazelwood would summon him to attend a Board of Inquiry. When that happened it would be helpful to know how the Russians had reacted after they learned Malinovsky was dead. Returning to his office, Ashton rang Chris Neighbour and told him to bring every signal he had received from Head of Station, Moscow from 15 June onwards.

Before becoming Head of Station, Moscow, George Elphinstone had been doing exactly the same job in Cairo. While he had enjoyed his time in Egypt, Elphinstone was less than enthusiastic about serving in Russia, possibly because his command of the language was limited whereas he had been fluent in Arabic. The number of cables dispatched between the fifteenth and eighteenth was a reflection on his diligence. That they contained nothing that hadn't already appeared in the Moscow press or had been aired on TV newscasts was an indication of his limitations as a Head of Station in Russia. For Ashton's benefit Chris Neighbour had drawn up

319

a comparative table showing Elphinstone's input measured against that of the translators on the ground floor, whose tasks were to monitor TV newscasts and read every newspaper and magazine coming out of Russia. Had anyone from the Treasury seen the paper, they could have made a good case for downgrading Elphinstone's appointment.

The long-expected summons finally came shortly after three o'clock with a phone call from Dilys Crowther, who politely asked Ashton if he would join the DG in the conference room. Hazelwood was not alone, Winston Reid was seated on his right at the top of the table with Robin Urquhart next to him on his other side. When Dilys Crowther entered the room with notebook in hand and sat down at the small table in the far corner, Ashton knew there was nothing informal about this meeting.

'This is question-and-answer session, Peter.' Hazelwood smiled. 'Will Landon had told us what happened outside the Simplon Café. We want to know what passed between you and Malinovsky before he was assassinated. OK?'

'I'm happy with that. I assume Will told you Malinovsky changed the r.v. at the last minute?'

'He did. Were you surprised that our Russian friend objected to the Au Bec Fin?'

'No, with his background I expected him to do so.'

'What do you mean, 'with his background'?' Urquhart asked sharply.

'He's an ex-KGB man and inherently suspicious.'

320

'Did he tell you that?'

'Malinovsky didn't have to. You only had to look at his CV to know he wasn't a diplomat.'

'What exactly did he tell you when you were head to head?'

Ashton turned to face Hazelwood. 'Nothing we didn't already know. He gave me three names — Ali Mohammed Khalef, Abbas Sayed Alijani and Asir, all of whom are hardly strangers to us and MI5. Malinovsky claimed to be in possession of information which led his people to believe Islamic Jihad is planning a major terrorist operation directed at the UK. He couldn't say where it would be or when.'

'And for that morsel we end up with egg on our faces and a first-class row with the Swiss,' Urquhart snorted derisively. 'Hardly worth the journey, was it?'

'It wasn't my idea to meet Malinovsky,' Ashton told him.

'But going to Geneva was,' Urquhart insisted.

'What did Malinovsky expect to get for his information?' Reid asked quietly.

'Two Chechens — Maskhadov and Zakayev. He said they were England's enemy just as much as Russia's. Malinovsky inferred they were some-how involved in the Islamic Jihad operation.'

'Do we have them carded?' Hazelwood enquired.

'No.'

'What about MI5?'

'I haven't run their names past them yet. I thought you should be the first to know about the Chechens.'

'If I may go back to the beginning, Peter,' Reid said apologetically, 'I'd like to know by what means you advised Landon of the new r.v.'

'We were both equipped with a crypto-protected Haydn.'

'So how did the Chechen girl get to hear about it?'

'Malinovsky had four bodyguards. I think money changed hands and one of them kept her fully informed. I don't believe for a moment that he knew he was in danger of losing his life.'

'She could have struck before you arrived at the r.v.' Reid murmured.

'Maybe.'

'But she chose not to. What does that tell you?'

'She was hoping to get two for the price of one,' Ashton said jokingly.

'Yes, I believe you were also meant to die,' Reid said in a deadly calm voice that sent a shiver down Ashton's spine.

★   ★   ★

Six days had passed since Jack Boothroyd had met Jordan at the Irish pub on Lexington Avenue. This time around it was a working day and he was more formally attired in dark grey slacks, collar and tie and a lightweight sports jacket. It was also hotter than on the previous occasion, and he was sweating profusely when he came in off the street to find Jordan sitting up at the bar drinking an ice-cold beer.

'I'll have the same,' Boothroyd told the bartender, and perched himself on the adjoining stool next to the powerfully built American. 'So how are you doing?' he asked.

'I'm feeling good, Mr B,' Jordan told him, then reached inside his jacket and produced an envelope. 'My bill,' he said in a low voice.

The envelope wasn't sealed and Boothroyd sneaked a look at the itemised statement. 'Two thousand, eight hundred and seventy-five dollars!' he exclaimed. 'How the hell did you run up a bill like that?'

'I had to fly to Chicago, remember?'

'Yeah and I told you not to stay at the Drake Hotel.'

'I didn't. I chose the Palmer House on East Monroe.' A large meaty hand came to rest on Bothroyd's leg and crushed the tendon behind the left kneecap. 'That OK with you, Mr B?'

'You know it is,' Boothroyd said, and gritted his teeth. No way was he going to argue with a man who was eight inches taller and some eighty pounds heavier than he was.

'Good. You ever been to Chicago, Mr B?'

'Just the once. My wife and I spent five days there on vacation.'

'What's the ritziest part of town?'

'The Gold Coast?'

'You bet and that's where Zachery Holsinger lives in a fine apartment overlooking Lake Shore Drive. Guess where Ms Holsinger went after she ceased to be our responsibility?'

'Chicago?'

'Yep. I don't think Zachery was overjoyed to see her. His new wife is only two or three years older than Ensley. My guess is they went around

323

hissing at one another like a couple of cats. Maybe that was why he turned her in.'

'What?'

'The FBI came looking for Ensley. They took her into protective custody three days ago. I've a pretty good idea where she is being held.'

'And whereabouts is that?'

'It's in my report, which you will have after two thousand, eight hundred and seventy-five dollars is paid into my bank account.'

20

The house in Annapolis was on Maryland Avenue between Prince George and King George Streets and less than a block from the United States Naval Academy. Completed in 1779, it was the same age as the State Capitol, the oldest house in continuous legislative use in the United States. In the two hundred and nineteen years since then the property had changed hands sixteen times and was currently owned by the Van Murens, a middle-aged couple with numerous friends and a large extended family.

Hendrik Van Muren had been born in Michigan of Dutch parentage and had met his wife, Paula, when he'd moved to California. His circle of friends and neighbours in Annapolis understood he had been a successful insurance broker who had also played the stock market successfully enough for him to take early retirement. Not too much was known about Paula Van Muren, even though she had been living in Annapolis with her husband since 1989 and was active in the community. She was thought to have graduated from UCLA majoring in English Literature and had been awarded her Masters by the equally prestigious Berkeley. Thereafter Paula had taught for a year before marrying Hendrik when she had then happily settled down to being a housewife.

The facts were very different. Hendrik Van Muren had been neither an insurance broker nor had he ever played the stock market to any degree. Before moving to Annapolis he had been a teacher at a public school in St Louis, as had Paula. Contrary to the impression they had given, the Van Murens did not own the house on Maryland Avenue. Instead a peppercorn rent was deducted from their joint salary by Alvin Dombas in his capacity as Deputy Director, Humint. The extended family were the CIA operatives who were in residence whenever the Van Murens were required to play host and hostess to a VIP guest of the Intelligence Agency. Currently there were two VIP guests staying at the house. First and foremost was Ensley Holsinger, who had arrived on Thursday afternoon from Chicago where she had been detained by the FBI for just over forty-eight hours. The other was Jill Sheridan, who had flown in from San Francisco via Boston and Martha's Vineyard. They met for the first time shortly before dinner on Friday evening when Jill walked into the drawing room, a period piece with well-made but fake Hepplewhite and Sheraton furniture that was good enough to deceive anybody other than an expert. As she entered the room, Paula Van Muren stood up, welcomed Jill with a hesitant smile and announced that she ought to see how dinner was coming along, then left.

'Hi, I'm Jill Sheridan,' she said, introducing herself now that they were alone, 'and you must be Ensley Holsinger. I feel I already know you very well.'

'Have we met?'

Cool, arrogant, spoiled little rich girl; that was Ms Holsinger, Jill thought, taking an instant dislike to her. 'We had a mutual friend in Amelia Cazelet.'

The condescending smile that had been present on Ensley's lips rapidly disappeared and gave rise to a blank expression until eventually she made the connection.

'That's right,' Jill told her, 'I'm the J.S. who wrote the Ross Frazer memoirs and you're the overly ambitious literary agent who tried to put one over on the Julian H. Shubert Agency and got herself fired in the process. Still, that's the least of your problems.'

'I don't have to listen to this,' Ensley said, and started to get up.

Jill ignored her, went over to the drinks trolley that looked totally out of place in the room, and fixed herself a brandy and ginger with a slice of lemon.

'What'll you have to drink, Ensley?' she asked, her back still turned on the younger woman.

'I don't touch alcohol,' Ensley said contemptuously.

'Because your mother is an alcoholic? That never bothered you before, according to Amelia. She told me you were quite partial to a gin and tonic.'

'I don't want to drink with you.'

'Oh, so I'm some kind of leper, am I? Well, that's rich considering you've been playing footsy with a bunch of terrorists who have killed Amelia Cazelet and George Ventris and tried to do the same for your lover boy, Evan Vance.'

It was a blatant lie. Islamic Jihad had not attacked Evan Vance, he had simply been the victim of a mugging. And the Puerto Rican who had put him in hospital was now in jail awaiting trial because the cretin had continued his shopping spree with Vance's American Express card after it had been cancelled. Ensley Holsinger didn't know that and Jill wasn't about to enlighten her just yet. Fear could loosen the most recalcitrant of tongues and she had a vested interest in making Ensley sing like a bird, as officers in Special Branch were so fond of putting it.

'I don't believe you,' Ensley said in a low voice. 'I spoke — '

'Why don't you sit down?' Jill said interrupting her. 'You look ridiculous standing there.'

'I spoke to the girl on the switchboard,' Ensley told her and sat down involuntarily. 'And the secretary I shared with Evan. They both told me that he had been attacked and robbed on his way home after working late at the office. He was never attacked by a member of Islamic Jihad or any other damned terrorist group.'

'And you are thinking that's why the FBI didn't take you into protective custody when the British Secret Intelligence stopped paying the Burns Agency to do it.'

'Is there any other way of looking at it?' Ensley demanded.

'Well, yes, there is. You have to ask yourself

why the FBI traced you to Chicago and took you into custody a week after the Burns Agency had walked off the job. There are only two possible explanations for that; either the Bureau was guilty of an error of judgement the first time around or else additional evidence came to light that caused them to change their minds.'

'You're with British Intelligence, aren't you?'

'I used to be,' Jill said.

'Do you know a Will Landon?'

'Yes, he's one of the Rottweilers.'

'Well, you're just like him. He tried to put the fear of God in me.'

'You remind me of Amelia Cazelet, Ensley. I warned her about Talal Asir but she wouldn't listen to me.'

'Who's Talal Asir?' Ensley asked in a tone that suggested she was genuinely puzzled.

'A Saudi businessman who was supposedly one of her fund-raisers for the Palestinians in Ramallah. In reality he is one of the paymasters behind Islamic Jihad. Amelia read something into the Ross Frazer memoirs that wasn't there and suddenly she began to ask him too many questions and he either murdered her himself or he had someone else do it. Of course this was after Amelia had been kidnapped and tortured. Two of her fingernails had been ripped off but I guess you've already heard about that from Will Landon.'

'Not in such graphic detail,' Ensley murmured, and swallowed.

'The pity of it is, we believe there was nothing she could tell them. What passed between Amelia and the people who were torturing her is a matter of conjecture but it's likely she gave them your name in sheer desperation.'

Jill smiled at the younger woman with all the warmth of an Arctic winter. 'Cheer up, you're not alone. She gave them my name as well, plus the address of my place on Martha's Vineyard. They went through the clapboard house on Morse Street in Edgartown like a hurricane, stole the fair copy of the first fifteen chapters and removed the disk so that I would have to start from the beginning again.'

What the intruders had been looking for was the chapter she had told Amelia was devoted entirely to Talal Asir. It hadn't existed then, it didn't exist now. The chapter was merely an idea she had plucked out of the air in an attempt to whet the appetite of any would-be publisher.

The fact that Islamic Jihad had assumed the chapter contained details of an impending operation did not surprise Jill. Such false assumptions based on misleading information were not unknown in the intelligence world. She recalled a lecture given by a senior analyst, Special Intelligence during her induction course, who had illustrated this point by recounting the saga of dichlorodiphenyltrichloroethane, more commonly known as DDT. Towards the end of World War Two the Germans had added tabun to their armoury, an invisible, odourless nerve agent which, absorbed through the skin in liquid form or inhaled, caused death within a minute. There were, the lecturer had said, two reasons why the agent had never been used. Firstly, the

British government had made it clear through neutral countries that should poison gas be used against the civilian population, they would not hesitate to retaliate. And secondly, German scientists were convinced the British had already produced nerve agents on a massive scale. However, although the British had conducted research on the same lines they had come up with DDT, an insecticide that attacked the nervous system.

'We think there is a good chance Amelia expressed her doubts about Talal Asir to a third party before she tackled him.'

'A third party?' Ensley repeated in disbelief. 'Are you inferring she confided in me?'

'You both lived in the same apartment house on East 71st and you continued to see Amelia after it became evident she was gay because you both loved the theatre, the opera and going to concerts.' Jill paused, and then said, 'Sound familiar to you? It should, it's the explanation you gave Will Landon.'

'How do you know?'

'The SIS Head of Station in Washington makes it his business to keep the CIA fully informed and in this instance my former colleagues in London have been very co-operative.'

Holsinger was rattled; she was bright enough to realise how her conversation with Landon could be twisted to imply she had been particularly close to Amelia Cazelet. Savouring every moment Jill reminded her just how economical she had been when describing her relationship with the murdered woman and of the many lies she had told concerning the Frazer memoirs.

'What is it you want from me, Miss Sheridan?' she asked faintly at the first opportunity to do so.

'That's easy. We'd like the names of those people who helped to raise money for the population of Ramallah. You want to know why? Because one of them might have warned our Saudi businessman that Amelia was thinking of reporting him to the FBI.'

'I'm not sure I can — '

'Listen to me,' Jill said, interrupting her. 'There are indications that Talal Asir has been engaged in planning a major terrorist attack that could happen any day now. I wouldn't be in your position if subsequently it could be shown the attack would have failed if you had been a little more co-operative. Somehow I don't think you would last a year in a federal prison.'

'My father — '

'Forget him,' Jill said contemptuously. 'This will be the first time in your life when he will be powerless to help you.'

★   ★   ★

The note from the chief archivist that awaited Nancy Wilkins on Monday morning was addressed to the Supervisor, Armed Forces Desk. It referred to 10299037 Private Simmonds R. and stated that the Historical Records Office, Hayes, wanted to know what had happened to their file on the above named soldier. Below the chief archivist's signature, Rona, the supervisor of the Armed Forces Desk had written 'Any ideas, Elizabeth? Nancy?' Against her name, Elizabeth, the deputy head, had written 'Sorry, can't help you.' Nancy had given the file to Will Landon a week ago last Thursday and, having read the document quickly, he had transferred it to his out tray to await collection. Had she not told Landon's clerical assistant to return the file to her when she had finished with it, the document would have been returned to Hayes the following day. Jill Sheridan had been the last person to see the file before she had requested it and that had been over a year ago. She remembered what Landon had said when she had presented him with the file. It boiled down to the fact that he hoped she wouldn't get into trouble with the high-priced help because if the DG had known of the document's existence he would have had it under lock and key.

There was, she decided, only one way to find out who was after the file; lifting the receiver on the BT phone she obtained an outside line and rang the senior executive officer at the Historical Records Office, Hayes with whom she had previously dealt. When he answered she identified herself and told him she had a problem concerning 10299037 Private Simmonds R.

'How can I help you, Nancy?' he asked.

'Well, I understand you want us to return the file?'

'And would you like to know who has called for it?'

Nancy caught her breath. If the friendly officer

at Hayes could read her motives like a book she was really in trouble. 'Actually, that does puzzle me,' she admitted reluctantly.

'I'm not surprised. The request came from a Mrs Dilys Crowther on behalf of your Director General. She submitted it in writing.'

'Oh!'

'I don't want to know what is going on. However, the file is obviously regarded as extremely sensitive because it is to be taken permanently out of circulation. My enquiry was intended to give you advanced warning.'

'Thank you.'

'Look, if you can send the file back to me without going through your post room, I'll turn it around and explain the document was put in the wrong filing cabinet after it was returned the last time.'

'Why would you do this for me?' Nancy asked. 'We've never met.'

'Let's say I like the sound of your voice.'

'That's a cockeyed reason for doing something that could harm your career.'

'You let me worry about my career. The question is, are you going to take me up on the offer?'

'I'm tempted but it would mean deceiving people I like and admire, and that's something I can't do.'

'At least think about it. OK?'

'OK.' Nancy paused then said, 'Thank you is so inadequate but I do thank you.'

'Yeah. I can stall Mrs Crowther for a couple more days but if I haven't heard from you by

Wednesday afternoon, that will be it.'

'I understand,' Nancy told him, and put the phone down.

There was nothing to think about. She had obtained the file on her own initiative and then retained the document without authority. Will Landon hadn't considered the file important enough to hang on to but, of course, what did he know! The trouble she was in was of her own making and she had to face the consequences. On the memo slip from the chief archivist Nancy wrote, 'I have the file' against her name and signed it. That was the easiest part. Handing the slip to Rona was more daunting. An incoming call came to her rescue and postponed that inevitable moment. Lifting the receiver she gave the number of her extension.

'Nancy Wilkins?' a vaguely familiar voice asked.

'That's me.'

'I'm Patrick Chambers, Passport Office, Petty France, remember?'

'Yes, of course. Forgive me, I'm not really with it this morning.'

'I know the feeling. However, this is your lucky day. Anthony William Simmonds born Ravenna, Italy on the twenty-sixth of September 1945 has held a British passport continuously since 1964. He renewed it yet again seven years ago when he was then living in the Greater London area. Is this of any help to you?'

'Indeed it is,' Nancy told him, 'and thank you very much for all your help.'

It was decision time again, the second in

almost as many minutes. The issue was clear enough. Whatever she did Nancy knew that she would be dismissed. On the principle you might as well be hung for a sheep as a lamb, she took out the MI5 list of security officers in government departments. The man she wanted looked after the Department of Health and Social Security in Newcastle upon Tyne. Through him she could obtain Simmonds' National Insurance number and perhaps his home address.

With his National Insurance number she could phone the appropriate tax office, speak to the civil servant in charge and convince him the SIS needed to know everything the Inland Revenue had on Anthony Simmonds — his marital status, home address and what he did for a living. But before calling the Inland Revenue she would see Will Landon and confess her sins.

★   ★   ★

If material possessions were a yardstick, then Anthony William Simmonds was a highly successful businessman. His mother had brought him to England on her passport shortly after his fourth birthday and had been lucky enough to find lodgings in Hounslow at a time when there was a chronic shortage of housing. A bright boy, he had won a scholarship to Merchant Taylors'. By that time his mother had married a childless widower and the family had moved to Wembley. Leaving school at sixteen he had been articled to a firm of chartered accountants, a profession

336

with which he had gradually become less and less enthralled.

Two events had rescued Simmonds from what would have been a life of unremitting boredom. In 1996 his elderly step-father, who had been a buyer for British Silks, had suffered a fatal heart attack, leaving his widow a large semi-detached house and nearly four thousand on deposit in the local branch of the Midland Bank plus eight hundred pounds in Premium Bonds. Eleven months later his mother, Clara, had died of cervical cancer and the whole estate had passed to Simmonds.

If his time as an articled clerk had taught him one thing it was that money begat money. Throughout the sixties there had been a boom in housing and Simmonds had gone into the property market at the right time. He had had the vision to see that working class areas such as Islington, where the local population was moving out of London to places like Milton Keynes, could become the desirable neighbourhoods of tomorrow. He had bought up terraced houses as they became available and had them renovated by self-employed artisans, which had saved him from paying the employer's share of National Insurance contributions. As soon as work had been completed on a property it was put on the market and sold for a minimum profit of a hundred and fifty per cent. The fact that Simmonds never overreached himself was the secret of his success.

Simmonds was also adept at anticipating trends and had branched out into package

337

holidays as more and more Britons took their vacations abroad. Trading under the name Go Easy Go Getaway he had, by the early eighties, established a chain of shops across North London with branches in Acton, Brent, Finsbury Park, Hammersmith, Harringay and Southall.

The semi-detached house in Wembley had been sold long ago. These days he had a seven-bedroom waterfront house outside Goring-on-Thames in the so-called stockbroker belt. There was a Ferrari 550M and a top-of-the-range BMW in the double garage, a wife, and two children in their mid-teens and a luxury flat in the Barbican where he spent Monday to Friday every week in order to keep on top of his business. Some wags, who nevertheless knew Simmonds better than most, claimed the flat enabled him to stay on top of his mistress. Currently he was worth twenty-one million on paper.

Simmonds attributed his success in the travel business to his staffing policy of horses for courses. In practice this meant the branch manager reflected the ethnic majority of the population in that particular area. As a result there were Hindus, Muslims and West Indians working for him. He also believed in descending on a branch without warning to see for himself how the staff handled their clients. That morning it was the turn of the Finsbury Park branch managed by Ahmed Zia. Unbeknown to Simmonds, the manager was a soldier of Islamic Jihad and had participated in the execution of Leach, also know as Sabri al-Banna.

338

Ashton put the phone down, reached for his millboard and crossed off 'Albanian Interpreters' from the list of queries he had compiled. He had intended to phone Military Operations (Special Projects) but as it happened Max Brabazon had called him first with the news that the FCO had agreed reluctantly to release Valerie Cogland until Sunday, 27 of September. Everybody was happy: the brigadier, Special Forces, who could now field eight deep-penetration patrols in Kosovo, and Max Brabazon, who no longer had to put up with the brigadier bellyaching in his ear every day. According to Max, Valerie Cogland, the mountaineering assistant adjutant of a Territorial Army artillery regiment and career diplomat, was absolutely delighted. Ashton assumed the FCO wasn't too down-hearted because Ms Cogland would be returning to the fold eight days before she was due to join the embassy in Belgrade.

The next item on the list was to check whether Jack Boothroyd had been reimbursed yet for the expenditure he had incurred in looking after Ensley Holsinger. Ashton was on the point of ringing Roy Kelso to find out what had happened when Landon rapped on the door of his office and asked if he could spare him a few minutes.

'Of course I can,' Ashton told him. 'What's on your mind, Will?'

'Nancy Wilkins.'

Ashton raised a quizzical eyebrow. 'A very

attractive young woman.'

'Who happens to be in big trouble,' Landon said.

'So tell me about it, Will.'

In a few concise sentences Landon told him exactly what Nancy had done, how she had involved the Historical Records Office, Hayes, the Passport Office, Petty France and the Department of Social Security, Newcastle upon Tyne in an endeavour to find the son Ross Frazer had sired.

'Who else knows about this?' Ashton asked when Landon paused.

'The DG has asked for the record of service relating to Private Simmonds.'

'Shit.'

'Nancy is resigned to the fact that she will be dismissed.'

'I'm afraid that's inevitable, Will. In going to the Passport Office and the DHSS office at Newcastle upon Tyne she has infringed the Data Protection Act. You and I might get away with that but not an executive officer.'

'She obtained the information for me.'

'Are you saying you asked her to break the law, Will?'

'Not in so many words.' Landon slowly exhaled. 'Look, in this instance Nancy went a step too far.'

'Just a step?'

'Well, OK, several yards but the fact is Nancy is a bright young woman and I would hate to see her kicked out of the service. She's learned her lesson and if she is given another chance, I

340

guarantee she will never make the same mistake again.'

'She can't stay on the Armed Forces Desk, and the DG will bump her down a grade to clerical officer.' Ashton pursed his lips. 'I could find a niche for her in this department,' he added thoughtfully.

'You won't regret it, Peter.'

'Don't get too excited. I've got to persuade Victor Hazelwood to see it our way and that isn't going to be easy.'

'I know.'

'Did you say Nancy obtained Simmonds' National Insurance number from Newcastle?'

'Yes.'

'Good. Write it down on a slip of paper,' Ashton told him. 'Then I'll see what the Inland Revenue can tell us about Simmonds.'

21

As was always the case with Richard Neagle in the chair, the CATO meeting held routinely every Tuesday morning at the Gower Street address of MI5 started on the dot of 10 a.m. The fact that Neagle asked the rep from Government Communications Headquarters to lead off suggested to Landon that he had something to impart that would have had a much greater impact if it was held over until the other intelligence agencies had had their moment of fame.

The eavesdroppers of Cheltenham had been monitoring radio transmissions from the Ministry of Defence in Belgrade to Serbian police units and irregular forces operating in Kosovo. Although each transmission had been encrypted the cipher was pretty basic and the code breakers at Cheltenham had experienced little difficulty in reading everything that came out of Belgrade and vice versa. The messages from the Ministry of Defence promised that all police and military units on the ground would shortly be reinforced by volunteers from the Yugoslav National Army. They had also been promised heavy mortars and an indeterminate number of the 76mm mountain gun often known as the Tito gun.

Then Defence Intelligence got into the act. Specifically the army wanted to know when and in what order the Serbian police and irregular units might expect to receive the promised reinforcements and equipment. If it were possible for the eavesdroppers to provide this information, the SAS deep-penetration patrols would be more effective. By effective, Defence Intelligence meant that if a patrol was in the right place at the right time, the commander would be able to call in an air strike. The man from the eavesdroppers reckoned there was a fifty-fifty chance the promised reinforcements and equipment had been broadcast either for propaganda purposes or as part of some deception plan, a suggestion that immediately spawned a debate between the two intelligence agencies.

Landon had nothing to contribute and listened to the exchange with half an ear, his thoughts touching on another matter. Sometimes things could happen with breathtaking speed at Vauxhall Cross. While he and Ashton had been discussing how to retain Nancy Wilkins, Rona had returned the memo slip to the chief archivist. At the same time Roy Kelso had received a telephone call from an indignant deputy chief executive at the Department of Health and Social Security, Newcastle upon Tyne, who'd wanted to know why a junior officer had seen fit to breach the Data Protection Act.

The Admin King had moved swiftly. He had summoned Nancy to his cubbyhole of an office on the top floor and demanded an explanation. After learning she had also involved the Passport Office, Kelso had marched straight down the corridor and into Hazelwood's office. Within the next twenty minutes Nancy's Positive Vetting clearance had been cancelled, her ID card had been withdrawn and after signing the Official Secrets Act again, a mandatory requirement on leaving the service, she had been escorted off the premises. And neither Landon nor Ashton had been able to do a damned thing about it.

The truth was he'd had an opportunity to put a stop to the whole sorry business when Nancy had produced the file she had obtained from the Historical Records Office. What was it he had said to her after she had assured him no one else knew the document existed? 'How would I manage without you, Nancy?' With the benefit of hindsight Landon could see now that his chance remark had been all the encouragement she had needed.

'Are you with us, Will?' Neagle asked.

'No, I'm afraid not,' Landon told him. 'What were you saying?'

'I was talking about Maskhadov and Zakayev, the two Chechens whom, according to you, Malinovsky was eager to get his hands on. The fact is they haven't come to our notice and Immigration has no record of them entering the country. Do you have their full names and where they came from?'

'I'm sorry I can't help you there,' Landon told him. 'They haven't come to our notice either. Naturally, we've asked Head of Station, Moscow to find out all he can but the Russian Intelligence Service is being very coy at the moment. We've also approached the Russian Ambassador through diplomatic channels but he claims he is unable to help us.'

'So where does that leave us?'

Although Landon wasn't sure whether or not the question was addressed to him, he answered it nevertheless. 'Looking for two illegals, which won't be easy,' he suggested.

Provided Maskhadov and Zakayev didn't seek regular employment, kept themselves to themselves, didn't fall ill, were circumspect where they worshipped and didn't claim benefit, they could remain lost indefinitely.

'Anything else to report, Will?'

Landon nodded, then told Neagle that the money the SIS had been spreading around might have borne fruit. During silent hours last night the duty watch-keeper from the Mid-East Department had received a signal from Head of Station, Beirut to the effect that Mubarak Al-Massad had flown Middle East Airlines from Kuwait to Athens via Beirut.

'Mubarak Al-Massad is number one on the Israel hit list,' Landon continued. 'According to Shin Beth, when it comes to making a blockbuster, he's the best man the Palestinians have.'

'How good is this information?'

'The source is graded B3 by Head of Station.'

'Meaning the source has a better-than-average track record and the story might possibly be true,' Neagle mused, then said, 'Why Athens?'

'Your guess is as good as mine, Richard.'

'Do we have a photograph of this man?'

'We do. It was taken in the departure lounge at Beirut by the source. The subject was among a crowd photographed in the airport café. Although he was seated at a table with three other people, the source is adamant they weren't acquainted. It's not a good picture of Mubarak Al-Massad — you can only see the left side of his face and that's not well defined either. Furthermore, the photograph bears little resemblance to the artist's impression we received from the Israelis in 1996. Consequently we have sent both images so that you can run off however many copies are needed for Immigration, Customs and Special Branch.'

'Do we get a physical description of him?'

'Yes, one is included with the images. As descriptions go this one is not particularly helpful.' Landon smiled dismissively. 'Mubarak is said to be aged twenty-eight to thirty-one, medium height, medium build, brown eyes, dark hair, no visible blemishes, could pass for a Caucasian.'

'In other words he doesn't look like an Arab,' Neagle said. Among his peers he was known as a man who had no time for euphemisms and took great delight in calling a spade a shovel at every opportunity. 'Anything else, Will, before we move on?'

'Athens has been instructed to track Mubarak and report his movements. What we want from Head of Station, Kuwait is confirmation that he was on a Middle East Airlines flight to Beirut. The trouble is the source waited six days before passing the information on to his case officer.'

'Six days!' Neagle shook his head in disgust. 'A month's salary says Mubarak is no longer in

Greece, never mind Athens.'

Neagle wanted them all to know that with Ali Mohammed Khalef it was an entirely different story. The imam from Finsbury Park had been spotted in Bahrain and reported to the MI5 security officer at the British Embassy in Manama. What he was doing on the island was not yet clear but he was staying quite openly at the Tyhos Hotel and had been seen coffee housing in the local souk. It was believed Khalef had arrived in Bahrain on Sunday, 21 June. Where he had been and what he had been doing during the nineteen days between Monday, 1 June, when he had disappeared from Finsbury Park, and the twenty-first was a complete mystery. Neagle was, however, absolutely confident there was no way he could slip out of Bahrain without being noticed. Landon wasn't inclined to bet on it. MI5 had lost Khalef once, they could lose him again.

★   ★   ★

If you were to persuade Hazelwood to reverse a decision he'd made after hearing all the facts it was vital to catch him at the right moment. Before or immediately after morning prayers was not the right time. Before the meeting with heads of departments he was too busy reading the incoming signals received by the watchkeepers during silent hours to listen to any argument. After morning prayers his mood was frequently uncertain, especially if there had been an inter-departmental dispute or in his opinion the

347

meeting had gone on for far too long.

That morning had been a case in point, thanks to Roy Kelso, who had objected to the transfer of the equivalent of eight thousand pounds in US dollars from the monies allocated to the East European Department to the passport control officer, British Consulate, New York. Kelso maintained that Ashton had no right to do this, especially as Boothroyd was financed by Head of Station, Washington, under a different vote. In a matter of a few minutes Hazelwood was at loggerheads with the Admin King.

A department head, he thundered, didn't have to seek Kelso's permission before he authorised payment from his contingency fund, especially when the sum involved was a miserable eight thousand pounds.

It was a little more than that, as Ashton had learned on Monday night when Boothroyd had phoned him at home. Much to Boothroyd's embarrassment he had just received an additional invoice from the Burns Agency. This was in respect of rental charges for the safe house on Orange Street, New Haven, which had apparently not been included in the original quote.

Morning prayers had continued until four minutes to ten and there had been the mother and father of an inter-departmental dispute, two reasons why Ashton had waited until gone eleven before he delivered his bombshell. Even so, Hazelwood sounded less than overjoyed when Dilys Crowther announced over the office intercom that Mr Ashton would like to see him.

'Nothing contentious, I hope,' he said as

348

Ashton entered the room.

'I hope so too,' Ashton told him, and placed a memo slip on his desk the right way up, then sat down in one of the leather armchairs the Property Service Agency had provided for visitors.

'What's this, Peter?'

'Information provided by the Inland Revenue concerning Anthony William Simmonds, the illegitimate son of Ross Frazer. It's all there: home address, business address, tax liability on his salary as managing director and principal shareholder of Go Easy Go Getaway.'

'Are you out of your mind?' Hazelwood spluttered. 'I assume you have heard of the Data Protection Act?'

'Many times. The Inspector of Taxes, District 6 spent a good ten minutes lecturing me about it before I managed to persuade him this was a matter of national security and it was his duty to disclose the information we needed.'

'Nancy Wilkins — ' Hazelwood began.

'You should have talked to me before you sacked her.'

'You told her to ring Newcastle upon Tyne?' Hazelwood's voice was sharply registering incredulity and mounting anger.

'No, I'm afraid Nancy went a step too far by involving the Department of Health and Social Security. I had a hunch Ross Frazer had seen action before he went to Sandhurst. There were a number of incidents in the first fifteen chapters of his alleged memoirs to suggest he had, and I asked Nancy to look into that possibility. She was clever enough to discover he had enlisted under an assumed name at the age of fifteen. That was thanks to the Records Office at Hayes. She also had a lot of help and advice from the Imperial War Museum and the Public Records Office. There is no rule to prevent her consulting either of those establishments.'

'When did you call the Inland Revenue, Peter? Was it before or after Miss Wilkins was dismissed? And think carefully before you answer.'

'I don't need to. I wasn't aware that we had dispensed with her services until after I had made the call.'

'I won't ask the obvious question,' Hazelwood growled, 'because I already know why you went to the Inland Revenue. You did it to put yourself in the line of fire. You can dismiss an executive officer for ignoring the strictures of the Data Protection Act any day of the week but getting rid of an assistant director is a lot more difficult. I can't fire Miss Wilkins and keep you. That's what you're banking on, isn't it?'

'Nancy is the best entrant we've had for the last three years. She stands head and shoulders above the others. By all means bust her down to clerical officer and give the girl an official warning in writing but don't let her go.'

'You're asking me to take her back,' Hazelwood said bleakly.

'Yes I am.'

'I don't know.' Hazelwood opened the ornate cigar box on his desk, took out a Burma cheroot and lit it. 'Who the hell would trust her not to do

350

something equally stupid a second time?'

'I would,' Ashton told him promptly. 'My department is understaffed.'

'I don't know, Peter . . . '

Two years ago Hazelwood wouldn't have hesitated to reinstate Nancy Wilkins but then, two years ago he wouldn't have fired her in the first place.

Hazelwood had been extended in post for twelve months beyond the retirement age of sixty because his successor had been a Foreign Office man who had only recently joined the SIS. In exactly three days' time Victor would know whether or not he had been lucky enough to be given a further extension of twelve months. To blot his copybook at this juncture was the last thing he wanted. Thinking about it, Ashton came to the conclusion this was the principal reason why Hazelwood had refused to let him see the Ross Frazer file.

'All right, Peter, you can have her.' Hazelwood sighed. 'I know I'm going to regret this.'

'And I guarantee you won't.' Ashton got to his feet and moved towards the communicating door, then looked back. 'Just for the record, Victor, I didn't go to the Inland Revenue to put you on the spot. It's simply that I don't like leaving a job half completed.'

'Neither do I. My question is, was it worth completing?'

'It's too early to tell but we could be on to something. Simmonds is in the travel business, and is pretty successful, given that he has branches all over North London. One of them is

351

located in Finsbury Park. It would be interesting to know if Ali Mohammed Khalef has ever availed himself of their services.'

★ ★ ★

Jill Sheridan left the house on Michigan Avenue and headed in the direction of State Circle before turning left into Prince George Street. From there it was a mere two hundred yards to Annapolis Harbour, crossing East Street, Randal and passing Sands House on the way. Carol, the short, heavily built blonde interrogator from the detention centre, was waiting for her, seated at a table on the decking outside the Bay View Café, her back to the sea. A waitress appeared at the table the moment Jill sat down.

'What'll you have to drink?' Carol asked, in a voice that no longer wheezed as if she suffered from asthma.

'Coffee,' Jill told the waitress. 'With cream, medium-size cup,' she added before the girl could recite the usual rigmarole.

'We're not very happy with you, lady,' Carol said when they were alone. 'You haven't got a single name from Ms Holsinger we weren't already familiar with.'

'You think I'm not aware of that? I'm the one who gave Alvin Dombas the list of fund-raisers who were among Amelia's circle of friends and acquaintances.'

'And they were all whiter than white when we checked them out. We couldn't find anything to link a single one of them with your Saudi

352

businessman.' Carol glanced sideways to her right and suddenly changed the subject, making small talk about the annual boat show when the harbour would be crowded with yachts and dinghies. She continued in the same vein until the waitress walked away after serving Jill. Only then did she revert to the subject of Talal Asir. 'Matter of fact we don't believe he exists.'

'Yes, I know the FBI has never heard of him. But as I've said to you people before, that law enforcement agency is not the fount of all knowledge.'

'We have to rely on the FBI. Counter-intelligence operations in continental America is strictly off limits to the CIA.'

'So you would have the public believe,' Jill said curtly. 'That's why Spencer pretended the two men who lifted me from the house in Sausalito were FBI agents. You, Spencer, the Texan and the guards at the detention centre — all of you are CIA. It was a charade to protect Alvin Dombas in case the British government learned what was going on and took exception to the way a UK citizen was being treated.'

'OK, if it pleases you, lady, Talal Asir exists. Try his name on Ms Holsinger and let's see how she reacts.'

'She may never have heard of him.'

'Fine. Then she will be in good company, along with all the fund-raisers you name who, of course, have never heard of the Saudi either. There was an equally negative reaction when we showed these people an artist's impression of the Saudi businessman based on your description.

At the end of the day we have only your word that Amelia Cazelet knew him.'

Jill made no comment, gazed instead at the small craft becalmed in Chesapeake Bay on this hot, airless morning. 'Maybe we can go down another track,' she said when finally Carol paused to draw breath.

'You know what I admire about you, lady?' Carol said, resuming the onslaught. 'Whenever you are backed in a corner, you find a way to wriggle out of it. Now try worming your way out of this one. Remember Abbas Sayed Alijani, the Iranian you went to see in Chicago? He's disappeared, leaving no trace.'

'So what? The man I saw in Chicago was not, repeat, not Abbas Sayed Alijani. Have you got that?'

'Oh yeah, and Alvin Dombas believed your assertion. He took the surveillance team off Abbas on Monday, June eighth and the Iranian waited three whole days before he took off. Pretty cool, huh?'

'How do you know all this if you haven't been keeping him under observation?'

'We checked his place on West Hollander Street from time to time.'

Number 4131 West Hollander. Jill could see the terraced house now, similar to a brownstone in New York, steps up to the front door, basement and two floors above, a long, narrow back yard with a double garage at the bottom that opened into a parallel lane.

'Abbas Sayed Alijani lived alone,' Carol went on, 'worked for a firm of accountants in the

354

Evanstone District and owned a ten-year-old Mercury Lynx that stayed in the garage most of the time because he bussed to his workplace. The car was there when agents from the Chicago office visited the house on Thursday, June eleventh, when they called again five days later, the Mercury Lynx had gone. None of the neighbours recalled seeing him after Friday, June twelfth.' Carol leaned forward over the table, her eyes narrowing. 'Now where do you suppose he has gone?'

'I don't know and I don't care,' Jill told her. 'Talking about Alijani is a waste of breath. We should concentrate on Ensley Holsinger because she is definitely holding something back. I mean, Spencer and the Texan have been listening to our every word and they must have noticed the distinct pause which followed every time she was asked a difficult question about her time in London. Ensley told me she had never been in London before.'

'Is this leading anywhere?' Carol demanded impatiently.

'Yes, I think she may have a close friend living in the UK whom she wants to protect.'

'Yeah? You mind telling me how we persuade Ms Holsinger to talk about this friend?'

'We have to confront her with something.' Jill frowned, then snapped her fingers. 'Why don't you phone the Julian H. Shubert Agency and ask them when they expected her to return from London?'

★ ★ ★

Until the beginning of April, Nancy Wilkins had shared a four-bedroom, two-bathroom furnished flat in Ilchester Place with three other girls. Her share of the rent had been three fifty pounds a month, which even with the Inner London Weighting Allowance still made a big dent in her salary. She had moved out and returned to her parents' house for two reasons. In March '98 her father had suffered a heart attack and had needed a bypass operation. The other cause was the fact that the real leaseholder had broken the covenant he'd signed by subletting the flat to four tenants whose combined rent exceeded the amount charged by the company that owned the apartment house. The property company had cancelled the existing lease and given the four girls three months' notice to quit with effect from the thirty-first of March.

The Wilkinses lived in Burnt Oak, one of the outer suburbs in North London. That evening was the first time Landon had occasion to visit their house in Market Lane. He had, however, looked up the directions in the *A to Z* street finder. Exiting from the Northern Line station, he walked up Watling Avenue and turned left into Market Lane, which looped round to rejoin the thoroughfare just short of the crossroads at the top of the hill.

The only thing that distinguished the semi-detached owned by the Wilkinses from the other houses was a small ornamental pond with a solar-powered fountain in the front garden. Nancy was twenty-six; the woman who opened the door to Landon when he rang looked to be in her sixties.

'Mrs Wilkins?' he asked smiling, and got an answering nod. 'I'm Will Landon, one of Nancy's colleagues. Could I please see her if she is in?'

'I doubt she will want to see you, Mr Landon.'

'Could you tell her I'm here? You never know she might agree to see me.'

'All right, wait here,' Mrs Wilkins told him and then closed the door in his face.

He wasn't kept waiting. A few moments later a wan-looking Nancy appeared and invited him into the house. 'You'll find the sitting room is the second on your right,' she said and stepped aside to allow him to pass down the hall while she closed the front door.

The sitting room was roughly sixteen by eleven feet and looked a mite crowded with a three-piece suite arranged in front of a gas fire with a twenty-one-inch TV on one side of the chimney breast and a music centre on the other. French windows opened on to a well-kept lawn, free of clover, daisies and other weeds. The flowerbeds were laid out with military precision, dwarf dahlias and geraniums in the front, hybrid roses in the centre and in the rear rank, a mass of sweet peas trained against a chicken-wire fence. Each row was dressed off by the right like so many guardsmen on parade. Cupressus planted close together formed a tall hedge enclosing the garden on all three sides.

'Who's the keen gardener?' Landon asked as Nancy entered the room.

'My father. Unfortunately he can't do as much nowadays as he would like and we'll have to get somebody in to top the cupressus before the neighbours start complaining. But you didn't come here this evening to talk about gardening.'

'No, I'm here to tell you the DG has changed his mind,' Landon said, and watched her eyes grow wider.

'Would you mind repeating that, Will?'

Landon did so and told her of the negative aspects as well, the downgrading to clerical officer, the severe reprimand and the official warning in writing concerning her future conduct.

'You will be working for me again and I wouldn't blame you if you told me what to do with the job.'

'Why did the DG change his mind?'

'Ashton had a word with him. He did what you were thinking of doing and talked to the Inland Revenue about Simmonds. I don't think Ashton had much use for the information they gave him and I don't know what he said to the DG. But I can make a pretty shrewd guess.'

'Which is?'

'That he more or less invited Sir Victor to sack him for ignoring the Data Protection Act or reinstate you.'

'He did that for me?'

'Or something like it.'

'My God, I love that man.'

'Better not tell Harriet that,' Landon said jokingly.

22

Mubarak Al-Massad said goodbye to the Dutch driver who had transported him from Calais to the Toddington Service Area approximately sixty miles north of London on the M1 motorway. He then climbed down from the Volvo rig and, braving the heavy shower of rain, ran across the parking lot to the Little Chef restaurant. There was a bank of pay phones in the entrance hall; opting for the nearest one that was available, he lifted the receiver, fed the meter with a fifty-pence coin and tapped out the number he had committed to memory. Although he had never met the man who answered, they shared a commitment to Islam, nursed a lasting hatred for all non-believers, and had a sufficient command of the English language to be able to communicate to one another.

'Guess who this is?' Mubarak said.

'Saladin?'

'You're right, Michael.'

The brief exchange was a simple recognition code based on two passwords. Saladin represented the challenge, 'Michael' the correct response. Had Michael failed to give the correct challenge, Mubarak would have put the phone down and walked away.

'Where are you calling from?' Michael asked.

'The place where we arranged to meet. It's not like you to be late.'

'But you are early. Still, no matter, stay where you are and I will meet you in one hour from now.'

'Good. Look for me in the restaurant,' Mubarak said, and put the phone down.

It had taken him eight days to get this far and for the first time since leaving Kuwait, Mubarak felt threatened. He had spent four days in Athens where sympathisers had provided him with a new identity and a Lebanese passport. During the stopover he had also acquired a lightweight two-piece suit and other items of clothing a civil servant might take with him while away on business. Security at Hellenikon Airport had always been lax, and the girl on the check-in desk had paid scant attention to the head and shoulders photograph in his passport. The same lack of curiosity had been shown by Immigration Control and the security officer when he had gone through the departure lounge. As befitted his assumed status he had flown business class to Rome.

Security had been tighter at the Leonardo da Vinci airport and as a Lebanese citizen Mubarak had had to fill in a landing form. The Immigration officer had compared him with the likeness in the passport, then asked where he had studied civil engineering, a question that hadn't perturbed him in the least since he had a degree from Cairo University. Customs had searched his suitcase and carry-on bag but that was standard procedure for everybody hailing from the Middle East and North Africa.

From Rome, Mubarak had caught a train to

Livorno where he had spent a night before going on to Genoa. Continuing by rail he had made his way to Calais via Avignon, Lyon and Paris, which had involved a further stop over in the Algerian quarter of the city. While there Mubarak had got rid of everything that had marked him as a successful civil engineer to become an asylum seeker in a faded pair of jeans, red and white check shirt and leather jacket. He had also destroyed the Lebanese passport.

Calais was the place where he had begun to feel exposed. Up until then he had been passed from one active member of the Islamic Jihad network to another. The Dutch truck driver who was to take him across the Channel was not a member of the network and therefore could not be trusted implicitly. He was a professional smuggler and a very discreet one. Although as a regular user of the cross-Channel Ferry Service his face was, of course, known to British Customs and Excise, he had never been caught. Unlike some drivers he did not transport upwards of forty asylum seekers at a time, attempt to bring in heroin with a street value in excess of five million or convey enough small arms on a single trip to set up in business as an arms dealer. It was the Dutchman who decided what would be transported and when, not the customer.

The Volvo rig was fitted with a combined chest of drawers and bunk bed across the width of the cab. Between the mattress and chest of drawers there was a false compartment that was just large enough to accommodate a man of average height and build lying flat on his back. Mubarak had spent ten claustrophobic hours in the coffin and hadn't been released until the Dutchman had pulled into a layby ostensibly to check his tyre pressures before joining the motorway. Thereafter he had sat up front, acting the part of a co-driver all the way to the Toddington Service Area via the M20, Orbital and M1 motorways.

Mubarak finished the chicken salad he had taken from self-service and attacked the slice of chocolate cake, his nose still buried in the *Sun* newspaper, a prop to safeguard his privacy. It was his first time in England and he didn't like it. The longest day had passed but there was no sign of summer. All it had done since he arrived at Dover was rain on and off.

He finished the chocolate cake and put the plate aside. He wondered how long he could spend over a cup of coffee without it becoming obvious that he was killing time while he waited for somebody. What had happened to Michael? An hour, he'd said, and that had come and gone a good twenty minutes ago. He raised his eyes from the newspaper again and glanced in the direction of the entrance and suddenly there was Michael. Slim, face like a fox, thick black moustache just like the photograph Ali Mohammed Khalef had given him in Bahrain before he flew on to Kuwait. In that same instant Michael recognised him and waved a hand discreetly.

Mubarak left the table and headed towards the exit. As he drew near Michael, he signalled him to follow on, then dumped the newspaper in the litter bin in the entrance hall. Neither man said a word until they were outside.

'You were beginning to worry me,' Mubarak told him. 'What delayed you?'

'The traffic, it was heavier than I had expected,' Michael said, and led Mubarak to a four-year-old Ford Fiesta that had seen better days.

'I will be quicker going back,' he added.

'Be careful. We do not want to find ourselves in trouble with the police.'

'You worry too much, my friend,' Michael said dismissively.

'I don't want us to be caught speeding.' Mubarak opened the nearside door and got into the car. 'You hear me?'

'I am not deaf.'

'Good. Where are you taking me?'

'To a nice place in Hackney.'

'So what is your real name, Michael?'

'Lev Maskhadov,' the Chechen told him.

★ ★ ★

It was the end of the road for him. Hazelwood knew that even before he opened the plain blue envelope marked 'Personal for Sir Victor Hazelwood' and extracted the unctuous letter from the Cabinet Secretary. The Secretary of State, Foreign and Commonwealth Office had been more than a little tardy in informing him that his services would no longer be required after Friday, 26 June. Out of common courtesy they should have given him a month's notice instead of a mere three days, which was inexcusable. After May had passed without any word as to his future, Hazelwood had begun to think a further extension of twelve months in post was virtually in the bag. In less optimistic moments he knew it to be wishful thinking.

Hazelwood read the letter a second time, then buzzed Winston Reid on the intercom and asked him to drop by when he had a few minutes to spare because there were things they needed to discuss.

With nothing to do but to wait for a subordinate who was either snowed under with work or was demonstrating a new-found independence, Hazelwood swivelled his chair round to face the window and gazed at the river. It was a truly miserable day in more ways than one. It was the sort of chilly, overcast day with frequent showers that made you wonder if summer would ever come.

'Admiring the view, Victor?'

'No, just gathering my thoughts.' Hazelwood swung the chair round to face his deputy, who was already comfortably seated in one of the leather armchairs.

'First things first. Heartiest congratulations, Winston. With you in charge I'm sure The Firm is in good hands.'

'Thank you.'

'Well, as you must know, this coming Friday is my last day in — '

'Actually I was going to ask if you would consider staying on until the following Friday?'

'The third of July?'

'Yes. Is that a problem, Victor? I mean, do say if it will interfere with your plans because I can take over here and now.'

Reid simply wanted an opportunity to pick his brains and the finance people at the FCO had raised no objection to the proposal. Naturally Reid did not expect him to be there all the time and there was really no point coming into Vauxhall Cross before morning prayers had been concluded.

'I assume you will want to use this office, Winston?'

'Well, I will be the Director General.' Reid smiled. 'I thought you could use my old office.'

Hazelwood caught him eyeing the paintings he'd always had in his office dating from the time when he had been appointed to head the Eastern Bloc Department. The signed print of Terrence Cuneo's *The Bridge of Arnhem*, the battered-looking corvette on a storm-tossed Atlantic entitled *Convoy Escort* and *Enemy Coast Ahead*, which depicted a vic of three Wellington bombers on a moonlit night approaching a smudge of land on the horizon reflected his admiration of the armed forces. While the paintings appealed to him, he recognised that they were not to everyone's taste.

'I imagine you will want to change the pictures?'

'That's all in hand, Victor. I saw the man from the Property Service Agency last week. If it's all right with you, I have arranged to have them changed this coming Friday afternoon.'

'Ready for the big day?'

'Something like that.'

Hazelwood had thought he knew his deputy rather well. Now Reid was showing him there was a side to his character he hadn't seen before and it definitely wasn't attractive.

'You look very pensive, Victor.'

'I was thinking about your deputy and wondering who it might be.' Although no such thought had occurred to him, his answer was seized upon by Reid.

'I'd welcome your advice about that, Victor,' he said eagerly.

'You mean your replacement is to be found within The Firm?'

'Yes. I want to know who you think would be the best man for the job?'

'That's easy. You need look no further than Peter Ashton.'

'I don't think so, Victor. The FCO would never wear it. Off the record, I've been instructed to rein him in.'

'Good luck. You're going to need it.'

'You're wrong. Luck doesn't enter into it. Ashton will be sacked if he fails to curb his cavalier attitude.' Sensing that Hazelwood was about to defend his former protégé, Reid hastily changed tack. 'I want someone who is experienced, is steady under pressure and has an eye for detail like Roy Kelso.'

'You would be mad to choose Roy,' Hazelwood told him bluntly. 'He would have everybody up in arms before you could blink an eye.'

'I've no intention of choosing him. Roger

Benton is steady enough but the Pacific Basin and Rest of the World Department is hardly a testing appointment. That leaves us with Rowan Garfield.' Reid pursed his lips. 'How do you rate him, Victor?'

'He's been around a long time.'

'And is set in his ways?' Reid suggested.

'Rowan is never going to set the world on fire but he's competent. I found him to be a bit of a moaner at times.'

'This would be when he had far and away the largest department?'

'Yes, he had a lot on his plate.'

'A testing appointment then.' Reid slapped both knees simultaneously and stood up. 'Thank you, Victor, you've been most helpful.'

'I have?'

'Oh yes, your endorsement of Rowan Garfield has convinced me he is the right man for the job.'

Hazelwood knew he hadn't tipped the scales in Rowan's favour. Reid had already made up his mind who he wanted. Winston needed him to stay on until 3 July so that if there should be any dissension about the appointment among the other department heads, he would claim to have had his predecessor's approval.

★ ★ ★

Ever since Winston Reid had been elevated to Deputy Director General a year ago, Ralph Meacher had been the acting Head of the Mid-East department. A Grade I Intelligence

367

Officer, Meacher was reconciled to the fact that he would never be promoted to Assistant Director. Although he was in receipt of extra responsibility pay, his job was simply to keep the chair warm for Winston Reid's designated successor, who happened to be another Foreign Office man. It was common knowledge that the Foreign and Commonwealth Office was determined to exercise control over the SIS; filling the key appointments as they became vacant with one of their own was the obvious way to do it. Had everything gone according to plan the new man should have taken over from Meacher on 31 January. However, filling a vacancy always involved moving several people into different slots and somewhere down the line there had been a hiccup.

Those who worked for Meacher thought he had every reason to feel cheated. Maybe he wasn't so authoritative as Winston Reid had been but for sheer competence there wasn't much to choose between him and Jill Sheridan when she had been in charge of the Mid-East Department. No matter how much he resented being sidelined Meacher never took it out on the more junior officers. However, Landon had noticed a certain coolness between him and Ashton; Meacher was the elder of the two by three years and he had never rocked the boat like the younger man had, yet he was the one who had been unjustly penalised while the other had been given a lift up the ladder.

In his capacity as the SIS rep on the Combined Anti-Terrorist Organisation Landon had always found him easy to get on with. Today, however, was the first time he had had to go back to Meacher and question the information he had been given, and he wondered how the acting Head of the Mid-East Department would react. It began amicably enough when he rang to ask when it might be convenient to see him and was cheerfully told to come on up to the top floor. It looked set to continue in the same vein when he walked into Meacher's office.

'What can I do for you, Will?' Meacher asked, and waved him to a chair.

'I'm not sure you are going to like this,' Landon told him, 'but here goes. The fact is, I have been asked to find out why the source in Beirut waited six days before informing his case officer he had seen Mubarak Al-Massad at the airport.'

The welcoming smile rapidly faded. 'Who wants to know?' Meacher demanded.

'MI5. Well, to be more accurate, Richard Neagle. He would also be grateful for anything else you could tell him about Mubarak. What he is like — that sort of thing.'

'The source was protecting himself. He plays for both sides.'

'To what extent?'

'He has killed the odd Israeli, which gives him a certain amount of street cred with Hamas. With Shin Beth on his tail, things got too hot for him in Haifa and he fled to Beirut.'

After lying low for several months the source had taken up arms again, this time in southern Lebanon. In his very first engagement with an

Israeli patrol, he had been winged in the shoulder and had taken a second bullet in the left thigh. He had been rushed to a makeshift hospital on the outskirts of Beirut that was run by the Green Crescent.

'One of the volunteer doctors from France managed to save his leg.' Meacher smiled. 'Didn't save him from our Head of Station, though,' he added.

'Are you saying our man recruited him while he was lying in hospital?'

'He most certainly did, Will. Just how he achieved this is no concern of yours or Richard Neagle. OK?'

'Sure.'

Landon wasn't interested in the tactical coercion of the source. Once the SIS had got their hooks into him he had become a puppet on a string. It would have been made clear to him Shin Beth would know where to find him, so too would his fellow freedom fighters in Hamas, Hezbollah, Islamic Jihad or whatever terrorist group it was he had belonged to.

'You look thoughtful, Will,' Meacher told him.

'I was wondering how the source happened to know Mubarak Al-Massad.'

'They were at the same training camp in Pakistan. Anything else you want to know?'

'Yes, a whole lot more about Mubarak. What drives him?'

'Hatred, Will, pure hatred. Seems he witnessed a particularly brutal murder. Of course, this is according to the source who claims he had heard it from his own lips when they had been learning

370

how to blow people up.'

The incident that had been a catalyst for Mubarak had happened near Ramallah in the West Bank administered by Israel, roughly twelve kilometres north of Jerusalem. The population of Israel had increased dramatically with the influx of immigrants from eastern Europe, all of whom had needed somewhere to live. Land that was not being worked was seized and colonised by Israeli settlers. One such incursion had been an olive grove that appeared to have been abandoned.

'It was one land grab too many for the Palestinian population,' Meacher continued. 'Stoning the Israeli settlers and construction workers became such a daily occurrence that units of the Israeli army were sent in to sort things out. Inevitably there were fatalities among the rioters. Then somebody had the bright idea of getting the children out on to the streets. The ten- to fifteen-year-olds threw the rocks, Palestinian snipers used them as cover to engage the Israeli troops. You can't shoot children without attracting universal condemnation so the Israelis tried to use CS gas to disperse them. It wasn't entirely successful. The agent rapidly dispersed into the air, the kids took to wearing goggles and masking the nose and mouth. The army countered this by using armoured personnel carriers to break up the mob.'

The rioters had simply melted into the narrow sidestreets and alleyways where the APCs were physically unable to follow them. They had then reformed to ambush the infantrymen as they

371

dismounted from their vehicles.

'The incident Mubarak witnessed occurred on the fringe of the Israeli settlements. For once the soldiers managed to catch one of the youngsters. Two of them gave the boy one hell of a beating, after which they tied his hands behind his back and forced him to lie down in the footings that had been dug for a house. One of the infantrymen had fetched a couple of shovels from their armoured personnel carrier and thereafter they proceeded to bury the boy alive.'

'Jesus,' Landon breathed, 'how could they live with themselves after doing a thing like that?'

'We've only Mubarak's word for what happened Will, and that was through a third party.'

'Let's hope Mubarak embellished the story for propaganda purpose. Any guess where he is now?'

'On the way here,' Meacher said tersely. 'You want to know why?'

'I think I already know,' Landon said. 'Mubarak had no quarrel with Italy, Germany or France, but the way he probably sees it, without American support Israel would cease to exist. We are America's closest ally and most certainly the easier target to hit. It's called guilty by association.'

'Full marks,' Meacher told him laconically. 'Go to the top of the class.'

★ ★ ★

It was evident to Jill Sheridan that even if they lived in each other's pockets for a whole year she and Carol would never get along. Her attitude grated on Jill like squeaky chalk on a blackboard. Carol blamed her for every little setback as though she had allied herself with Ensley Holsinger and was determined to sabotage the interrogation. If she had entertained any doubt about that supposition, the way the American woman greeted her when she walked into Starbucks on Market Square only confirmed her impression.

'What kept you?' Carol demanded in a low but angry voice. 'Been cooking up another story with Ms Holsinger?'

'Something tells me the people at Julian H. Shubert Agency were not very helpful.'

'I spoke to Evan Vance and he told me Ensley Holsinger was going to fly back to New York on Friday, June fifth. However, she did ask him if it would be OK to stay on in London over the weekend. Vance said he had no objection provided she was back in the office bright and early on the Tuesday morning. He was under the impression she wanted to do some sightseeing. Nothing was said about staying with friends, as you would have us believe.'

'What about her friends at the agency?' Jill asked. 'Did you speak to them?'

'According to Mr Vance Ms Holsinger has no friends at the Julian H. Shubert Agency. Matter of fact she is regarded as pushy, overly ambitious and self-centred.'

'Will Landon was the SIS officer who

interrogated her,' Jill said thoughtfully.

'So what?'

'So it would be advantageous to know what Ensley Holsinger said to him about her plans for the weekend. If Alvin Dombas approached Miles Delacombe he would get the information out of London. You can depend on it.'

'I think this is another of your diversions.'

'You know what, Carol? You think too much and do too little.' Jill finished her cup of coffee and stood up. 'Go see Alvin Dombas and do us both a favour.'

23

The nice place in Hackney was a run-down housing estate on the fringe of London Fields. The flats were purpose built in blocks four storeys high and there was nothing to distinguish one mean street from the next, other than the name. The shopping precinct in the centre of the estate had in the past consisted of a greengrocer's, minimarket, a bakery, butcher's, laundrette, newsagent, barber's shop, ladies' hair dressing salon, betting shop, off-licence and a discount store selling electrical goods. Now only the newsagent, laundrette, minimarket and heavily fortified off-licence remained. The rest were boarded up and covered in graffiti like so many of the empty flats in Elm Tree Road where Mubarak Al-Massad was staying.

The ethnic mix in Hackney embraced the Caribbean, Asia, North Africa, Middle East and Eastern Europe. The real Londoners, as a significant number liked to call themselves, accounted for a shade under fifty per cent of the borough's total population. On the housing estate itself the Caribbean was not represented, neither was North Africa and the Middle East. The Asian element, which accounted for over fifty-one per cent of the residents, originated from Pakistan while the Caucasian minority included Bulgarians, Latvians, Ukrainians and a handful of Chechens. In an area of high unemployment the indigenous population was responsible for over eighty per cent of the street crime. The police were hardly ever seen on the estate during daylight hours; at night they were totally invisible. The neighbourhood was, in fact, a law unto itself, which was the major attraction for Lev Maskhadov and Boris Zakayev, who had been assimilated into the community.

'But my face is not going to fit,' Mubarak told them. 'I will stand out like a sore thumb in this neighbourhood.'

'I don't see why,' Zakayev said, his eyes still glued to the black-and-white portable television set perched on an upturned milk crate.

'You don't? Just how many Arabs are living in Elm Tree Road?'

'You worry too much. With your dark looks you could pass for one of us or a Bulgarian.'

The two Chechens worried Mubarak. They were far too casual and so far they had shown scant regard for security. The registration number on the Ford Fiesta was another case in point. He couldn't shake off the feeling it didn't belong to that particular car. He had come to London to build a bomb, not to idle away the time cooped up in a flat.

'How much longer are we going to sit around here?' Mubarak demanded impatiently.

'We go soon,' Maskhadov informed him.

'Why not now?'

'Because the man cannot meet us before noon.'

'The man?'

'We are not allowed to know his name.'

376

It was the first reassuring thing the Chechen had told him since they'd met at the service station yesterday morning. 'And where do we say hello to this Mr No Name?' he asked.

'At Finsbury Park. The journey will take half an hour.'

Mubarak grunted. Thirty minutes and his wristwatch was showing nine after eleven. The next twenty-one minutes was going to seem like eternity. The flat was more squalid than the refugee camps he had seen in Jordan and the Lebanon. All the Chechens had were a few sticks of furniture: camp beds in the bedrooms and nowhere to hang their clothes except from the curtain rails, and in the living room, a card table and three upright wooden chairs that were moved into the kitchen at meal times. Linoleum covered the floorboards and there were a couple of rugs that were also mobile.

Mubarak made himself a hand-rolled cigarette from the packets lying on the card table and lit it. He rarely smoked and only did so now to pass the time. Unfortunately it did not work for him, cannabis never had, and he crushed the joint in the saucer his hosts used for an ashtray. What was showing on TV didn't interest him, and the temptation to keep looking at his wristwatch proved impossible to resist. He began to think eleven thirty would never come, then when he least expected it, Maskhadov switched off the set and announced it was time to go.

The Ford Fiesta was garaged in a lockup at the top of the street. The first thing Mubarak noticed about the car was the new registration number.

'Zakayev changed it last night,' Maskhadov told him before he could ask.

'What have you done with the old one?'

'I dumped it,' Zakayev said.

Maskhadov circled the estate, passing two abandoned cars that had been vandalised, before he picked up the main road leading to Canonbury. At the junction with Highbury Grove he turned right into the A1201 trunk route and stayed on it as far as the Seven Sisters Road. Glancing over his left shoulder Mubarak caught a glimpse of Finsbury Park station as Maskhadov turned off the main road to follow a potholed lane that ran parallel with the railway. Their final destination was a long concrete shed with a corrugated iron roof. A weathered-looking signboard indicated the property was currently in use by Kamal Allam, Printing and Stationery. Waiting to greet them was a youngish, dark-haired man with a pockmarked face.

'That is your Mr No Name,' Maskhadov informed him. 'You will be staying with him now.'

'And where are you going?'

'Into hiding until we strike.'

Mubarak got out of the car, slammed the door behind him and went forward to meet the man with the pockmarked face. As he did so, Maskhadov shifted into gear, let the clutch out and executed a U-turn at speed, the rear wheels of the Ford churning up the cinder track.

'Do you have a name?' Mubarak asked him

378

when they were alone.

'I'm Ahmed Zia.'

'And I am Mubarak Al-Massad. Ali Mohammed Khalef sends you greetings.'

'I'm honoured.'

Zia opened the door to the shed, invited Mubarak to lead the way, then followed him inside. The shed, which Zia said was forty feet long, was divided into two by a floor-to-roof steel partition. The front half was obviously where Kamal Allam conducted his printing and stationery business. There was, of course, no Kamal Allam but the boxes of A4 paper neatly arranged on the racking, and the printer, suggested otherwise.

A narrow well-camouflaged steel door set in the partition afforded access to the other half of the shed where a blue Ford Transit was garaged. On the driver's side of the vehicle, a workbench was positioned against the wall. On it was a vice, a hacksaw capable of cutting metal and a wide range of box, double-ended and ring spanners, adjustable monkey wrench, as well as screwdrivers of varying sizes.

'The materials you need are hidden beneath the floor,' Zia told him.

'What's down there?'

'Move the workbench away from the wall and you'll see.'

'Give me a hand then.'

Zia shook his head. 'This is something you will have to do on your own because I shan't be here.'

Mubarak tried dragging the workbench and

379

rapidly discovered it was a lot easier to move if he picked up one end at a time and moved it crabwise. It took him a lot longer to find the trapdoor, which had been painted to match the concrete floor complete with oil stains and grease. Slipping a finger into the counter-sunk D ring, he raised the board and laid it to one side. The cache was lined with bricks and was some nine feet long by three wide and six deep.

Zia said, 'You will find the pit containing an oxyacetylene torch, a cylinder of oxygen and acetylene, a number of tubular steel pipes and two hundred pounds of Semtex.'

'How did you acquire the explosive?' Mubarak asked.

'We purchased it from the Real IRA. The same applies to the electric detonators. A fishing boat brought it from Dundalk and transferred the cargo in the North Channel to a trawler out of Ayr. We collected the stuff from there in a van and brought it to London. This was four months ago.' Zia smiled. 'Is there anything else you want to know?'

Mubarak shook his head. 'I'd like to begin work on the bomb, if that is OK with you?'

'Of course it is. I will collect you at six.' Zia moved towards the steel door in the partition. 'One last thing,' he added. 'You will be staying with me from now on. I have a flat above a travel agency.'

Mubarak waited until Zia had left before he opened the rear doors of the Ford Transit. He would cut the tubular steel pipes into two-inch lengths, then split each ring down the middle prior to giving each metal piece a serrated edge. These metal barbs would be embedded in the Semtex bricks nearest the side walls of the van. The charge would be shaped in such a way that the blast travelled horizontally, with devastating effect on a dense crowd.

Mubarak reckoned it would take him eight days to build the bomb.

★ ★ ★

Landon could not recall a previous occasion when the Deputy Director General had sent for him. People who were next to God like Winston Reid were briefed by the appropriate assistant director, not by some lowly Grade II Intelligence Officer. There was, however, a first time for everything, as Dilys Crowther had pointed out when she had rung his extension and told him to come on up.

Among lesser mortals the top floor was jocularly known as the eyrie. Of the incumbents, only Roy Kelso could be accurately described as a bird of prey. As with any eyrie, the view was impressive from those offices that overlooked the river.

'This exchange of signals with Miles Delacombe,' Reid said, looking up from the flimsies he had been reading as Landon entered the room. 'Why would the CIA be interested to know what Miss Ensley Holsinger had planned to do over the weekend of the sixth and seventh of June?'

'I don't know, sir.'

'Well, I see you answered the question, Will.'

'Actually, I'm not sure Miss Holsinger has any close friends living in this country. The fact is, according to Ensley she was supposed to be dining with family friends the night before she was due to fly back to New York on Friday, June the fifth. DCI Ogden proposed to assign a couple of watchdogs to look after Ensley, which didn't suit her at all. She brokered a deal with Ogden; in return for cancelling the dinner date and a firm promise not to leave the hotel that night, he would withdraw his people when she returned to the Dorchester. Roy Kelso obtained a copy of her hotel bill and it shows she didn't make any calls from her room that night.'

'Did she have a mobile phone with her?'

'No.'

'Did Miss Holsinger mention the names of these friends at any time?'

'No.' Landon paused, then said, 'But that doesn't mean to say she invented them to get the police off her back. If Ensley does know an American couple living in London, they are possibly acquaintances of Amelia Cazelet.'

'That's a pretty wild assumption, Will. Would you care to substantiate it?'

Landon was reluctant to do so because in order to understand what made Ensley tick you had to spend some time in her company. To say she was a spoiled little rich girl was an over-simplification. Ensley was only too aware of the label and it did nothing for her self-esteem every time she had to go cap in hand to her father for something.

382

'She is hugely ambitious,' Landon said, 'and is quite ruthless in her determination to make a name for herself. Right from the moment Amelia Cazelet gave her the first fifteen chapters of the Ross Frazer memoirs, Ensley was convinced she was on to a winner. When Evan Vance hadn't agreed with her estimation of the script's potential, she had felt free to go it alone.'

Landon was convinced that every lie, every evasion, every economical version of the truth had been motivated by her resolve to safeguard the material in her possession.

'For all her statements to the contrary, I'm convinced that somewhere she has another copy of the typescript — '

'You've lost me, Will,' Reid said, interrupting him. 'How does anything you have just told me justify your assertion that Miss Holsinger's alleged friends are in fact acquaintances of Amelia Cazelet?'

'Before she left New York Ensley booked herself on to American Airlines Flight 215 departing Heathrow on Friday, June the fifth, and also on the same flight departing Monday the eighth. On her arrival in London, Ensley had three days in which to establish contact with the friends of Amelia Cazelet. If she had failed to do so by Thursday afternoon she would have departed on the Friday. Had she succeeded, Ensley would have stayed over the weekend. Our intervention screwed things up for her and from then on she was engaged in damage limitation. That's why Ensley never mentioned the people she was hoping to see. In a very real sense she was protecting them.'

'Protecting them,' Reid said with heavy irony.

'Yes. I'm betting Ensley Holsinger regards them as a valuable source of information.'

'Really.'

The way Reid shook his head suggested to Landon that the Deputy DC thought he was being ridiculous. The gesture provoked him into developing his hypothesis a stage further than he had intended.

'I'll go further,' Landon said rashly. 'I believe Ensley suspects these people are active supporters of Islamic Jihad.'

'Well, no one could accuse you of lacking imagination, Will.' Reid looked at the signal that had been sent to Head of Station, Washington. 'All the same I'm glad you didn't broadcast your view to Miles Delacombe. We don't want the CIA to get the impression we're certifiable.'

★ ★ ★

A number of disturbances had occurred on the estate where the Chechens lived during the night of 24 and 25 of June. A gang of youths had participated in stock-car racing in the vicinity of the shopping precinct between 10 p.m. and midnight. Sometime after midnight a car had been driven on to the waste ground between the housing estate and London Fields, where it had been set on fire. Persons unknown in search of free alcohol and cigarettes had attempted to break into the heavily fortified off-licence and had subsequently vented their frustration by

384

trying to set the shop on fire. When this too had failed, they had wrecked the last serviceable telephone kiosk on the estate. None of these incidents had been reported to the police until after the eight-to-four shift had come on duty.

Eight uniformed police officers under a sergeant had descended on the estate to conduct door-to-door enquiries while the Community Liaison Officer set up a meeting with the leaders of the various ethnic groups. It was an exercise the police and community leaders had conducted many times before with few long-term results. Almost without exception the mayhem on the estate was committed by ten- to eighteen-year-olds who virtually controlled the streets and so terrorised the residents that no one was prepared to identify the troublemakers for fear of retribution.

As was always the case, the door-to-door enquiries proved negative. Those interviewed fell into two categories: the ones who had neither seen nor heard anything, and the reluctant witnesses who were unable to recognise any of the perpetrators.

Both cars used for stock racing had been stolen. A brand new Audi A6 had been lifted in the more upmarket area of South Hackney, whereas the basic Fiat Cinquecento had been removed from Dutton Street in nearby Bethnal Green. The Fiat Cinquecento had ended up partially submerged in the algae-covered lake in Victoria Park while the Audi was now a burned-out wreck on the waste ground. The only thing that hadn't been destroyed in the fire was a number plate that originally belonged to a Volvo 244, more recently attached to a Ford Fiesta. It had clearly been tossed in the car after the fire had burned itself out.

★　★　★

For more than a week now Ashton had suspected that Victor Hazelwood had not been granted a further extension of twelve months. Nevertheless, it was still a shock to hear him say that tomorrow would be his final day in the office.

'Of course I'll be around on and off next week helping Winston to settle in.'

'Who turned your application down? The Cabinet Secretary or the Permanent Under-Secretary of State at the Foreign and Commonwealth Office?'

'It doesn't matter.'

'Well, whoever it was has made a big, big mistake.'

'It's nice of you to say so, Peter, but my time has come and gone. Anyway, if anyone has made a big mistake, it's me.'

'How's that?'

'The next Deputy DG is to be found within The Firm. I recommended you for the appointment but I'm afraid you didn't get it.'

'It's OK,' Ashton told him. 'You paid me a terrific compliment by putting my name forward but the mandarins made the right decision. I'm not cut out for the job.'

'That's a matter of opinion. The fact is, I

handled it badly. To me you were such an obvious choice, I did not begin to give my assessment of the other assistant directors until after Reid had turned you down. I should have done it the other way round. My recommendation would have had a much greater impact if your name had been the last one out of the hat. As it is, I have to tell you Rowan Garfield will be the next Deputy DG.'

'Rowan will do a good job.'

It was an automatic response but still genuine for all that. Rowan was steady, reliable and conscientious. At one point he had been in charge of the largest department and the world hadn't blown up as a result of his stewardship. On the other hand, he was a prickly character who was quick to take offence. Relations had been a little strained between them ever since Ashton had spent seventy-eight days in solitary confinement at Moscow's Lefortovo prison in 1993 because Rowan had tried to kick-start an operation that wasn't moving quickly enough for his liking. With the passage of years he could look back at the episode with wry humour but Rowan had never ceased to feel guilty and was forever on his guard. Life, Ashton thought, was likely to be a lot more difficult after Victor had gone.

'I'm going to miss you,' he said, voicing his thoughts.

'You'll be all right, Peter.'

'Of course I will. Monday morning should start with a bang when Roy Kelso learns that I have sent Jack Boothroyd another certified

387

cheque for the sterling equivalent of two thousand eight hundred and seventy-five US dollars plus bank charges.'

'I hope what you got in return was worth it,' Hazelwood observed mildly.

'I think so. The FBI detained Ensley Holsinger in Chicago and then turned her over to the CIA three days later. Right now she is an unwilling house guest in Annapolis with Jill Sheridan for company.'

'How good is your information?'

'Grade A1!' Ashton said. 'Jordan from the Burns Agency traced Ms Holsinger to Annapolis, the rest we got from Alvin Dombas, who was a little too frank with Miles Delacombe.'

'Do you still want somebody to take a crack at Jill now that he has reeled her in.'

Ashton shook his head. 'Things have changed. I'm more interested in Ms Holsinger these days. I've been talking to Alvin this morning. Hopefully he will let Ensley out of the cage. Then things might begin to happen.

★   ★   ★

The signal from London Communications Centre was addressed to Head of Station, Washington. The originator's reference was CATO/BM25/3/WL, a combination of letters and figures that told Jill Sheridan the name of the author at Vauxhall Cross and a lot more besides. Classified Secret, it had been accorded an Emergency precedence, one down from Flash, which was reserved for impending major crises with worldwide implications. Headed 'Security Risk — Miss Ensley Holsinger — American National', it referred to an earlier communication from Miles Delacombe. The text read:

First. Subject was placed under police protection early on Thursday 4 June when it became evident that her life was in danger following the murder of George Ventris. This did not meet with subject's approval who informed the officer in charge of the investigation she was dining with family friends that evening and asked if her escort could be withdrawn. A compromise was reached: subject agreed to cancel dinner date and spend night in hotel, in return escort was withdrawn. Second. Situation deteriorated later that same day and subject was taken to a safe house where she remained until departing from UK on Monday 8 June. At no time did subject call the family friends to cancel alleged dinner date, nor did she mention them by name. Third. Because of connection with Amelia Cazelet, consider subject to be a security risk.

The date/time group of the signal was 24June17.45Zulu. British Summer Time was an hour ahead of Greenwich Mean Time. Allowing for the time zone difference it was evident to Jill that Will Landon must have acted on Delacombe's request for information minutes after the signal had been decoded by the cipher experts at Vauxhall Cross. The SIS cell at the British Embassy hadn't been slow off the mark either; Delacombe would have received the signal from London shortly before 14.00 hours local time yesterday and within forty-five minutes had had it photocopied and delivered it to Alvin Dombas.

Thereafter things had moved at a more leisurely pace. Dombas had written guidelines for the way the next session with Ensley Holsinger was to be conducted. Then earlier this morning he had talked to Ashton over the crypto-protected satellite link and she had to suffer another briefing session, this time in the parking lot by the Arundel Center. It was a hot sticky day and walking back to the house on Maryland Avenue had left Jill in no mood to take any lip from the spoiled little rich bitch.

She found Ensley Holsinger in the small back yard relaxing on a sunlounger and dressed in trainers, white ankle socks, matching shorts that were almost indecent and a light blue top. Black polaroids concealed her eyes.

'Take those sunglasses off,' Jill snapped.

'Why should I?'

'Because there is a document you need to read.'

'The sun will be in my eyes.'

'Then come inside the goddamned house.'

'Someone's been poking a stick in your eye.'

It was Holsinger's innate air of superiority rather than what she had said that got to Jill and made her seethe with anger. They had disliked each other on sight but in her own mind Jill knew she had done her best to be civil towards the much younger woman. Holsinger had never missed an opportunity to score off her.

'If you know what is good for you, miss,' Jill grated, 'you'll get your arse off that sunlounger and follow me into the drawing room.'

The implied threat worked but only after Ensley had kept her waiting a good two minutes.

'OK, I'm here now,' Ensley said. 'What is it you want from me?'

'I want you to read this,' Jill said, and thrust the signal from the London Communications Centre at her.

Cool to the point of being insolent, Ensley glanced at the signal, then sat down in an armchair and crossed one leg over the other.

'Well?' Jill demanded after a longish silence from the younger woman.

'I don't have any friends living in London. How many times do I have to tell you?'

'So why did you lie to the police?'

'Haven't you ever told a white lie to get out of something you didn't want to do? Look, this was my first trip to London and I wanted to see something of the night life. Where would the fun have been with two great hairy police officers in tow?'

'Let me explain the significance of that reference at the top of the signal. CATO stands for Combined Anti-Terroist Organisation. BM two five means Branch Memorandum; two five, your own personal file; oblique stroke three indicates there are just three enclosures on the file at present and the initials WL is, of course, Will Landon.'

'Well, gee whizz, if you believe what Will Landon tells you, you will believe anything.'

'Let me spell it out for you, miss,' Jill said icily. 'The British have you down as a suspected terrorist. The CIA knows this, so does the FBI. From now on you will be followed everywhere, your mail will be intercepted, your phone tapped, and your apartment bugged wherever that might be. You won't be able to travel abroad because the State Department will withdraw your passport, but, hey, what does that matter? Ninety per cent of Americans don't have a passport and never want to spend a vacation overseas — '

Jill broke off. It suddenly occurred to her that the Abbas Sayad Alijani she had seen in Chicago could have been a plant, that the former Iranian diplomat was dead and an impostor had taken his place. What was so impossible about that? All the impostor needed was Abbas Sayed Alijani's social security number in order to get started.

'Mr and Mrs Carl Gartenfeld,' Ensley said quietly.

'What?'

'Mr and Mrs Gartenfeld. They are really Amelia Cazelet's friends but I was going to dine with them.'

'Where do they live?' Jill asked.

'I don't know, all I have is their phone number. I called them from Transworld when I visited the publisher on the Wednesday afternoon that George Ventris was murdered. I spoke to their manservant, and he told me they were vacationing on the Continent.'

Jill snapped her fingers. 'Forget the explanations,' she said, 'Just give me their telephone number.'

24

The signal from Head of Station, Washington, was classified Confidential and had been given a routine precedence that practically guaranteed it would only be dealt with marginally quicker than one that had been marked 'Deferred'. The signal was pinned to the front cover of BM25 and delivered to Landon by Nancy Wilkins when he arrived in the office on Friday morning. Headed 'Security Risk — Miss Ensley Holsinger — American National', it referred to CATO/BM25/3/WL dated 24 June. The text read:

First. Subject named a Mr and Mrs Carl Gartenfeld as friends of late Amelia Cazelet. Claims not to know their address but states their phone number is 0947 0193. Second. Gartenfelds said to be currently on holiday somewhere in Europe. Subject stated this info came from the Gartenfelds' manservant when she rang the house. Third. Description of couple to follow later by fax.

The comparatively low security classification and routine precedence suggested Delacombe had been out of the office when the information had been received and the matter had been dealt with by a junior officer who was not aware of its significance.

'I thought you might want the address,' Nancy

394

said, and placed a slip of paper on his desk, 'so I had a word with British Telecom. I hope that's OK?' she added in a subdued voice.

Nancy was obviously suffering from lack of confidence, which was hardly surprising. Demotion and an official warning in writing about your future conduct wasn't likely to do much for her self-esteem.

'It's more than OK, Nancy,' Landon told her. 'Don't ever be afraid to use your initiative. But if you're ever in doubt, come and see me first.'

Landon picked up the slip of paper and noted Gartenfeld's address was Montpelier House, Arthur Road, Wimbledon.

'The house number is not shown in the telephone directory,' Nancy told him, 'but wherever Montpelier is, it can't be far from the All England Lawn Tennis Club. Anyway, I've photocopied page one hundred and seven of the London Street Atlas, which covers the immediate area. You'll find it under the signal from Washington.'

'Thank you,' he said, feeling a complete fool for having just told her not to be afraid of using her initiative.

'I don't know if you are planning to go by car but parking is likely to be very difficult.'

'Are you a Wimbledon buff?' he asked.

'I follow it on the TV,' Nancy said on her way out of the office.

Wimbledon: the first week of the rain-affected lawn tennis championships was drawing to a close. A week ago he had discussed with Ashton the possibility that Joe Public might be the target

395

of a major terrorist attack and had suggested Finals Day would be a good time to strike. Now they had an address roughly half a mile from the club for two of Amelia Cazelet's friends. The connection at present was too thin to pass on to Richard Neagle. At his instigation MI5 was already keeping an eye on the Finsbury Park branch of the Go Easy Go Getaway travel agency. He had also alerted the Security Service to the possibility that Mubarak Al-Massad was heading for the UK. There was a limit to the number of surveillance operations Special Branch, the foot soldiers for MI5, could undertake simultaneously. In any event security was always tight throughout the Wimbledon fortnight because of the number of Royals and VIPs who attended the championships.

On reflection, Landon decided it would be prudent to have a look at Montpelier House before taking it any further. That, however, would have to wait until Ashton returned from morning prayers and he'd had a chance to brief him.

★   ★   ★

Dilys Crowther had lost count of the number of times she had attended morning prayers in the fifteen years since she had been selected to be personal assistant to the Directors General. But allowing for weekends and the thirty working days' holiday a year, which she rarely took in full, Dilys calculated she must have recorded and distributed at least three thousand five hundred separate minutes of meetings. None was sadder than the one she was attending this morning. Of all the Directors General she had served, Victor Hazelwood was her favourite, irascible though he was at times. This was his last official day in the office and she was going to miss him. Whether she could stomach Winston Reid as her boss was a moot point. Had anyone asked Dilys a week ago what she thought of him, quiet, dignified, thoughtful and brilliant were just a few of the adjectives that would have sprung to mind. Right now she didn't care for Reid at all. Power could change a man's character overnight and for the first time she saw him as someone who would always put himself first. And as for Rowan Garfield becoming the Deputy DG, words simply failed her. If Garfield was the best they could do, then the SIS was in big trouble. What really irked her was the fact that these people sitting round the table in the conference room were not prepared to give Sir Victor the send-off he deserved. Ashton was the exception. He had stumped up fifty pounds in cash and told her it was towards smoked salmon and champagne and to let him know if, with all the other donations, there still wasn't enough to put on a decent party. Everybody else had taken their lead from Winston Reid, who had wanted to know what precedent there was for holding a farewell drinks party for the out-going DG. Had they given one for Sir Stuart Dunglass, Victor's predecessor? And the short answer was, no they hadn't. But Dunglass was a different case altogether. He had been in and out of hospital for chemotherapy, leaving Victor to keep the chair warm for him until one day it had become apparent that he was never going to return. By then Sir Stuart Dunglass had been at death's door and a farewell party was no longer appropriate.

Dilys could not recall now what they had done about Malcolm Kirkbride when he had handed over the reins to Stuart. The answer was probably nothing, because he had been the man who had banned departments from celebrating Christmas with an office party, an edict that still persisted to this day.

A question addressed to her brought Dilys back to earth with a bump. Her jaw dropped as she looked at the others round the table, hoping one of these would give her a clue.

'It's all right, Winston,' Ashton said coolly. 'I saw Mrs Crowther before the meeting began and said I would write a memo detailing the action taken by MI5 and ourselves to freeze Talal Asir's accounts. I refer, of course, to the Hispaniola Bank, First National Trust and Investment, the Consolidated Bank and the two numbered accounts with the Grande Banque Estavayer-le-Lac.'

As of that moment Dilys Crowther joined the ranks of those SIS personnel who unhesitatingly would go the extra mile for Ashton without waiting to be asked.

* * *

Morning prayers rarely lasted more than three-quarters of an hour. That morning proved

398

to be the exception because Winston Reid had decided to interview the assistant directors and had started with Ashton. Landon had no idea what had passed between the two men but Ashton was looking pretty grim when he finally got to see him a few minutes after ten.

'Have you tried the Wimbledon phone number?' Ashton asked after glancing at the signal.

'No I didn't think that would be wise. Ensley is known to the Gartenfelds and their man-servant might not have suspected anything was wrong when she phoned the house. With me it could be very different.'

'Do you believe Ms Holsinger's story in this instance, Will?'

'I'm inclined to give her the benefit of the doubt,' Landon said cautiously.

'OK. Check the place out. If you think it looks promising, alert MI5.'

Landon said he would do that. Returning to his office, he cleared the desk and locked the filing trays away in the security cabinet. On the way out of the building he dropped by central registry and told Nancy Wilkins what to do should the physical descriptions of the Garten-felds arrive while he was out of the office. It took him only a few minutes to walk from Vauxhall Cross to the main line station; waiting for a stopping train to Guildford ate up a lot more time.

The rush hour was normally over by 9 a.m. but this was Wimbledon fortnight and the six-car unit was pretty crowded even though it was a weekday. Looking round the car he had boarded Landon was prepared to bet that for the most part anyone under retirement age was an overseas visitor.

The train went through Queenstown Road, Battersea, then stopped at Clapham Junction, Earlsfield and finally Wimbledon. Alighting from the car, Ashton went up the staircase leading to the concourse above and then made his way back down again on to the District Line platform. The street map Nancy had photo-copied showed that Arthur Road was directly opposite the Underground station at Wimbledon Park, one stop up the line. With the rush hour over, District Line trains were running at eight-minute intervals. It seemed more likely twenty minutes to Landon before the doors closed and the train pulled out of the station.

Arthur Road started on the flat at the Underground station and rose steadily up hill to the All England Lawn Tennis Club. As Landon discovered for himself, the higher up the hill you went the more solid and prosperous the houses looked. Montpelier was a large brick building, mock-Georgian style. Situated at a bend in the road, it was a good deal more isolated than many of the other properties in the immediate vicinity. It was partially screened from the road by a tall wooden fence and hidden from the adjacent property further up the hill by a row of trees higher than the roof line. There was a considerable gap between the entrance to the school, which separated Montpelier from the nearest house lower down the hill. The drive

400

fronting the house joined Arthur Road at a very acute angle of no more than thirty degrees. Driving in was not a problem, getting out on to the main road certainly was when you couldn't see what was coming down the hill. To overcome this difficulty a mirror had been placed at the end of the drive, which enabled one to see back up the hill.

Landon went on up the road, feeling slightly conspicuous because he was the only man wearing a suit amongst the crowd walking to the All England Lawn Tennis Club. At the top of the hill he took out his mobile and called Nancy Wilkins.

'Hi,' he said, 'it's me. Any sign of that fax yet?'

'Yes, it arrived shortly after you departed.'

'Good. Please fax a copy to Richard, then phone to say I will be with him shortly after one o'clock to explain what it's all about. OK?'

'Yes, no problem.'

'One more thing. If Neagle isn't available, call me at this number.'

Landon collapsed the aerial and slipped the mobile into his jacket pocket.

During the run-up to an operation it was essential for a terrorist cell to keep a low profile and in that respect, Landon thought Montpelier House had a lot to offer.

★ ★ ★

Abu Nidal moved away from the window where he had been keeping watch on Arthur Road ever since Ali Jaffar had left the house. A deeply

401

religious man, he unfolded his prayer mat and positioned it in the direction of Mecca, then went down on his knees and bowed his head until it was touching the floor. Ten minutes later he rose to his feet and resumed his watch on the road from behind the net curtain.

The number of spectators making their way up the hill to watch the lawn tennis championships had increased significantly. All of them, men women and children alike, were casually dressed in complete contrast to the man in the two-piece suit he had seen an hour ago. Although the man had strolled past the house looking neither to his left or right, his very presence on the street had made Nidal uneasy. Had he reappeared some time later heading back down the hill on the opposite side of the road, Abu Nidal would have known for sure that he was looking for Montpelier House. Even so, the feeling persisted that the very tall stranger had come to Arthur Road for a definite purpose unconnected with the Wimbledon fortnight, as the English called it.

It was ridiculous. How could any of the neighbours know that Abu Nidal was sheltering in the house? For that matter, why would they ever have heard of him? He hadn't once set foot outside the house since he had arrived in the middle of the night eighteen days ago after taking part in the execution of Leach, who had disgraced his chosen name of Sabri al-Banna. No one knew where he was except Ali Jaffar. He could have betrayed him — God knows, he had had many opportunities to do so. Beginning on

Monday afternoon Jaffar had made his way to the lawn tennis club, joined the queue waiting to be admitted and had then spent hours prowling the grounds, ostensibly watching the matches on the outer courts. His task was to ascertain by observation the best place and time of day to launch the attack when they could be sure of inflicting the maximum of fatal casualties. To achieve this aim it was essential to watch the security guards covertly and discover their routine day by day, hour by hour. Ali Jaffar had been doing just that for the past five days. Plenty of time then for him to befriend one of the security guards and suggest it might be an idea to have a close look at Montpelier House.

Abu Nidal told himself to stop it. There would be no betrayal by Ali Jaffar. They were both soldiers of Islam and one week from today they would strike their enemies such a blow that, Allah be praised, their names would ring round the Muslim world and inspire other young men to emulate them.

★ ★ ★

Five minutes into the briefing Landon could tell Neagle wasn't in a receptive mood. There was an air of resignation about him like a man who had endured one sales talk too many on the benefits of double glazing and knew how much money it would save him in X years time, should he live that long.

'Am I boring you?' Landon asked in the face of total indifference.

403

'Not in the least. You tell a good story, Will.' Neagle raised a hand to fend off the inevitable protest. 'I'm sorry, I put that badly. I didn't mean to imply you had allowed yourself to be carried away by a few scraps of information from the CIA. But what have you really got? A house that offers a great deal of privacy — '

'That happens to be half a mile from the All England Lawn Tennis Club,' Landon said, interrupting him.

'Quite so. You also have an allegation by Ms Ensley Holsinger that the Gartenfelds were friends of the late Amelia Cazelet. As you yourself said not so very long ago, Ms Ensley Holsinger can be pretty economical with the truth. Gifted with a vivid imagination too. I mean, don't you think it odd that she didn't give the Gartenfelds' address while she was at it?'

'No, I don't. I bet if I leafed through your Filofax it would be the same as mine: lots of names and phone numbers, precious few addresses.'

Neagle plucked the head-and-shoulders print-outs from the pending tray and pushed them across the desk at Landon. 'You won't have seen these,' he said. 'Your clerical officer faxed them to me while you were out of the office. They are said to be the Gartenfelds.'

Carl Gartenfeld had been blessed with the most anonymous face Landon had ever seen. As described by Ensley Holsinger there was nothing remarkable about the set of his eyes, the shape of his eyebrows, ears, nose and mouth. There were no scars, no worry lines, no pockmarks. He had dark brown hair parted on the left side, grey-blue eyes and was approximately five feet ten and weighed between one sixty to one eighty pounds, which was a pretty generous bracket. His wife had received a more flattering appraisal from Ensley. The photofit showed a woman with prominent cheekbones, a patrician nose and small, perfectly shaped ears. Her dark brown curly hair had been cut short and back-combed. She was five feet four, weighed a hundred and five pounds and had an olive-skinned complexion.

'Mrs Gartenfeld obviously made an impression,' Neagle said acidly. 'Notice how precise she is about Mrs Gartenfeld's vital statistics? Doesn't show anything like the same interest in husband Carl.'

'You've got it wrong,' Landon told him. 'There is no lesbian relationship. Ensley made up both descriptions. The FBI had arrested her and now she was being interrogated by the CIA, and she knew they wouldn't be satisfied with just a name and a telephone number.'

'Well, I'm sorry, Will, I'm not doing anything about Montpelier House until you bring me something more definite. I don't have the resources to fritter away.' Neagle dipped into his pending tray again and produced two more facsimiles for Landon's inspection, which he had received that morning. 'Lev Maskhadov and Boris Zakayev,' he intoned. 'You people are deluging me with names.'

George Elphinstone, Head of Station, had

405

done his stuff. Following Malinovsky's assassination, the Russian Intelligence Service and Ministry of External Affairs had broken off all contact and appeared to hold the SIS responsible for his death. George had clearly mended a few fences and the Russians had coughed up photographs of the two Chechens together with bibliographical data.

'As you will see from the notes, the photos were taken six years ago and they've probably shaved off their beards by now. The Russians tell us they are in London, planning some terrorist outrage and would we please arrest them in order that they may apply for extradition and hang them up by their thumbs.' Neagle snorted. 'London, how precise can you get?'

'So what are you going to do about the Chechens?' Landon asked.

'I'll give the facsimiles to Special Branch and suggest they run off sufficient copies for distribution to every police district in the Metropolitan area. But do us a favour, Will, don't send us any more suspects unless you come up with something we can really get our teeth into. Islamic fundamentalists are not the only show in town. The peace settlement in Northern Ireland hasn't been accepted by the Irish National Liberation Army. The Real IRA and Continuity IRA, never mind the Red Hand, the Ulster Volunteer Force and sundry other protestant paramilitaries — '

'I'm sorry we are such a nuisance,' Landon said in a voice loaded with sarcasm.

'You're not. I'm just a little pushed for

406

manpower, that's all. I've got a team looking for Mubarak Al-Massad and another shadowing Ahmed Zia.'

'Who's he?'

'The manager of the Finsbury Park branch of Go Easy Go Getaway travel agency.'

'What else do you know about him, Richard?'

The answer was quite a lot. He had been known to Special Branch before Landon had suggested MI5 might like to have a look at the travel agency. Ahmed Zia was a devoted Muslim and attended the mosque in Finsbury Park at least twice a day whenever work permitted. He had been granted asylum in 1996 and had never had anything to do with Ali Mohammed Khalef. A hard-working man, Ahmed Zia had gone into business on his own account, buying Kamal Allam, Printing and Stationery from a distant relative.

'Zia has just taken on an assistant,' Neagle continued. 'Holding down two jobs was getting too much for him.'

'Where does he live?'

'Above the travel agency.'

'And the man Ahmed Zia has just taken on?'

'We're still looking at him, but Zia you can forget. He's clean.'

★ ★ ★

It was the first time Alvin Dombas had been present in the room while Ensley Holsinger was being questioned and Jill Sheridan didn't like it one bit. She couldn't help feeling his presence

407

indicated a lack of confidence in her ability to break little miss smart-arse. The bone of contention was Holsinger's totally inadequate description of the Gartenfelds. If the two geniuses in the cellar had shown the photofits to her before they rushed them to the CIA Headquarters at Langley she would have told them they had been hoodwinked by this chit of a girl. If Alvin Dombas had seen the photofits beforehand he would surely have stopped them; so would Miles Delacombe had he been at his desk instead of glad-handing it at some official reception in furtherance of Anglo-American relations. Now guess who had egg on their face? Not the geniuses in the cellar, not Alvin Dombas, not Miles Delacombe, but good old Jill Sheridan.

'Close family friends,' Jill snarled, and shoved the photofits at Ensley Holsinger. 'What are you suffering from? Memory loss? Look at Carl Gartenfeld. According to you he's Mr Anybody. His wife is something else. What movie star were you lusting after when you described her?'

'Here we go again,' Ensley said wearily. 'How many times do I have to tell you? Describing the Gartenfelds as close family friends was just an excuse to get the police off my back.'

'Have you ever met them?'

'No.'

'So the descriptions you gave us were conjured up out of your head?'

'Only for Carl. I'd seen his wife from a distance.'

'OK. What's her first name?'

'Seeing is not meeting.'

'Don't get smart with me, lady,' Jill said, and almost struck her.

'A word with you,' Dombas said, and jerked his head to indicate that Jill should follow him out of the room. 'I'm going to turn Holsinger loose tomorrow,' he added quietly when she joined him in the hall.

'What?'

'I want to see where she will go, who she contacts.'

'You are going to keep her under surveillance?'

'That's the general idea.'

'Well, let's hope you don't lose her like you did Abbas Sayed Alijani,' Jill said acidly.

* * *

Organised by Dilys Crowther at the last minute, the farewell party for Victor Hazelwood had taken place after all and a very intimate affair it had been too. The fact that it had been held in the conference room at lunchtime had been a godsend for Winston Reid and those assistant directors who had never liked Victor. They had taken their cue from the DG designate, who had made a speech praising his predecessor while everyone present was still on their first glass of champagne. Winston Reid had then departed, followed at staggered intervals by his acolytes intent on acquiring a few Brownie points. Ashton had been the only senior officer to be there at the beginning and remain to the end, as had Ralph Meacher, the acting Head of the Mid-East

409

Department. The other stalwarts had consisted of staff members who rarely had occasion to visit the top floor. They had included Brian Thomas, the Head of the Positive Vetting and Technical Services Division, Terry Hicks, the electronics whizzkid, the chief archivist, and sundry Grade II intelligence officers.

Will Landon returned from Gower Street just as the party was breaking up. A glass of champagne, a couple of bite-size sausage rolls and a cheese straw later, he left the conference room with Ashton to have a word in private. As succinctly as he knew how, Landon told him about the location of Montpelier House, its proximity to the All England Lawn Tennis Club and its potential as a launch pad for a terrorist attack on the grounds.

'And Neagle wasn't impressed?' Ashton said when he'd finished.

'He said there wasn't enough hard evidence to justify a surveillance operation, that my principle source was Ensley Holsinger and we both knew how unreliable she was. In any event, Special Branch was already overstretched.'

'What do you want to do, Will?'

'I need to verify Ensley's story and get the hard evidence Neagle wants to make him change his mind.'

'All right, find out what you can about the Gartenfelds; put some flesh on their bones.'

To do this Ashton suggested he should get in touch with Land Registry to find out who was currently the owner of Montpelier House. If they couldn't help, he should go to the public library in Wimbledon and ask to see the electoral roll. As a final resort the local council tax office would know who was paying for council services.

'Does that give you enough to go on?' Ashton asked.

'More than enough.'

'OK, Will, come back to me when you have something and I will lean on Neagle.'

25

They were there in the flat above the Blockbuster Video shop directly across the street from the Go Easy Go Getaway travel agency. While Ahmed Zia couldn't see the Peeping Toms he could sense their presence and was pretty sure he knew why they were so interested in the travel agency. On Saturday he'd walked past the police station in Blackstock Road where a large poster on the notice board outside had caught his eye. The heading asked 'Have You Seen This Man?' Below it, placed side by side, was an artist's impression of the subject and a blurred photograph, supposedly of the same man, that showed only the left side of his face. The artist's impression didn't strike a chord with Zia but he had no difficulty in recognising Mubarak Al-Massad from the blurred photograph. Whether anybody who hadn't come across the Palestinian before would make the connection was a different matter.

He had discussed the situation with Mubarak later that day. Aware that for many years now he had been number one on the Israeli hit list, he had acquired a sixth sense that enabled him to keep one jump ahead of Shin Beth. It had, therefore, been no idle boast when Mubarak claimed he would have noticed had anybody so much had glanced at him sideways since his arrival in the UK. That comforting thought had lasted until late yesterday afternoon, when his employer had visited the travel agency. Simmonds had jokingly asked him if he was thinking of making a bid for Go Easy Go Getaway since his printing and stationery business was obviously doing well. Zia had laughed it off, even though it was evident somebody had told Simmonds he was no longer living alone in the flat upstairs. Whether the informant had been a member of the office staff, or whether the police had observed Mubarak coming and going was immaterial. Sooner or later the police were bound to take an unhealthy interest in the shed down by the railway line. To ignore the threat was unacceptable. Leaving the dining room overlooking the street, he tapped on the door of the smaller of the two bedrooms at the back, and walked in on Mubarak.

'There has to be a change of plan,' Zia announced without any kind of preamble.

'A change of plan?' Mubarak echoed.

'Too many people know you are living here in the flat. The police know me of old but they lost interest once they were satisfied I had nothing to do with Ali Mohammed Khalef. Now they are back, looking at me again and this time they will show more than a passing interest in Kamal Allam Printing and Stationery.'

'We have to move then,' Mubarak said calmly.

'Yes, tonight when it is dark.'

'You realise my work is only half completed?'

'I do. You will have to finish it at the new site. I want the shed put back as it was, which means everything must be loaded into the Transit

413

van — explosives, tubular steel pipes, hacksaw, oxyacetylene torch, oxygen cylinders. Start on it as soon as you arrive.'

'I shall need help.'

'That has been arranged. The man I have chosen answers to the name of Walid. You will recognise him because he could be mistaken for me. When you challenge him he will reply 'The Wrath of God' in English.'

'Can he be trusted?' Mubarak asked.

'Walid has chosen martyrdom,' Ahmed Zia told him, 'and he will find it.'

★ ★ ★

Even before Richard Neagle welcomed the other members of CATO to the meeting Landon had known that this was going to be one Tuesday morning the MI5 officer was unlikely to forget for a very long time. Intuition had nothing to do with it. He had been present when Ashton had telephoned Neagle to inform him that the Security Service had better act on the information he was about to receive or he could look for another job. That wouldn't be the only sword hanging over Neagle's head by a thread. For the second time in a little over a month MI5 had managed to lose Ali Mohammed Khalef. Exactly a week ago Neagle had confidently predicted that there was no way the cleric could slip out of Bahrain without being noticed and intercepted. Now he had to admit Khalef had simply paid his hotel bill at the Tyhos, taken a cab to Muharraq and boarded a Middle East Airlines flight to

414

Kuwait. There had been no cloak-and-dagger stuff; he had done it quite openly.

'When did this happen?' Defence Intelligence asked.

'Sunday,' Neagle said, colouring.

'And when did you discover Khalef had gone?'

'We were informed yesterday afternoon by Police Headquarters, Manama. To be accurate the inspector in charge of the surveillance detail contacted our Head of Security at the Embassy.' Neagle allowed himself a small, bleak smile. 'I'm afraid we have no extraterritorial rights in Bahrain. We have to work through the local police and, no doubt, money changed hands.'

'I bet it did.'

The half colonel who was representing Defence Intelligence that morning had a reputation for being abrasive and was said not to suffer fools gladly. It wasn't necessary to be a mind reader to know what he was thinking. Neagle had sat back and allowed the local police to run the show supervised by the MI5 officer at the Embassy, who was simply a glorified paper keeper and office snooper. In his blinkered eyes that made Neagle a fool.

'We have, of course, alerted our people in Kuwait city,' Neagle said.

'Bit late for that, isn't it? The bugger will be in Iraq by now.'

The half colonel was right in that respect, Landon thought, but if you didn't advise Kuwait, how would you pick up Khalef's trail again?

'Have you anything for us, GCHQ?' Neagle

415

asked, deflecting the spotlight from himself as he began to go round the table.

The eavesdroppers of GCHQ had been doing rather well lately, particularly 9 Signal Regiment in Cyprus, which had set up a listening post on Mount Troodos. For some time now everything in and out of Belgrade had been an open book despite being encrypted. Serb police and paramilitaries in Kosovo had finally cottoned on to this and had begun to rely on mobile phones under the mistaken impression their communication would be much more secure. Nothing could be further from the truth, as Defence Intelligence had confirmed, citing the number of targets the allied air force had been able to intercept.

When it came to his turn, Landon informed the committee that the Russian Intelligence Service had come out of their shells and had furnished photographs of Lev Muskhadov and Boris Zakayev. By prior agreement with Neagle he said nothing about the Gartenfelds and Montpelier House. That subject became the agenda once the representatives from GCHQ and Defence Intelligence had departed.

'Now tell me why your boss is so excited about the place,' Neagle said when they were alone.

'OK. First of all the Gartenfelds don't own the house, the people who do are a Mr and Mrs Philip d'Avigdor. He was sales director of Unilever before the FCO borrowed him. For the past fifteen months he has been the Minister Economics, at the British Embassy, Washington. The Gartenfelds rent the property. They signed a two-year lease at the beginning of April last year for one thousand pounds a week.'

'What!' Neagles voice registered amazement.

'Yes. At today's prices Montpelier is worth three million plus. It has seven bedrooms including four en-suite, dining room, snug, drawing room, study, kitchen, utility room, garage space for two cars, indoor swimming pool and a one-acre garden with tennis court.'

'Where did you get all this information?'

'From various sources,' Landon told him.

Between two thirty and five o'clock on Friday he had telephoned Land Registry and visited both the library and council tax office in Wimbledon. Land Registry had politely declined to help him because they wouldn't deal with queries over the telephone unless Landon could quote the reference and date of the last letter he had received from them. At the library he had obtained the electoral roll for the appropriate ward and had discovered the d'Avigdors were still registered voters. A helpful librarian who knew the couple well had then told him they were currently living in Washington where he was on the staff of the British Embassy. While perusing the electoral roll he had also ascertained the names and addresses of the people living immediately above and directly opposite Montpelier House. The council tax office hadn't been quite such a rich vein of information. He did, however, find that the council tax rate for Montpelier House was in Band H, the top rate, which didn't surprise him.

'What did surprise me,' Landon continued,

417

'was the fact that the Gartenfelds are responsible for the council tax. They pay it through a standing order with their bank.'

'You were lucky,' Neagle told him. 'Whoever you dealt with must have been born yesterday. A person could lose their job if it became known they had disclosed personal and confidential information to a third party.'

The section head had thought he was dealing with a Special Branch officer on a matter of national security because Landon had flashed a fake warrant card in his face and pitched him a convincing story. There was, however, no reason for Neagle to know that.

'It occurred to me that d'Avigdor wouldn't have put his house in the hands of a local estate agent, he would have gone to one of the big firms in London, the kind that advertises in the *Field, Country Life, Tatler* and *Harpers and Queen*. So on my way back from Wimbledon I rang Nancy Wilkins, my clerical officer, and asked her to ring the key estate agents at the top end of the market. It turns out d'Avigdor chose Paul, Franks and Parker of Knightsbridge to be his agents. In July 1996 Carl Gartenfeld had written to Paul, Franks and Parker of Knights-bridge stating he had been commissioned to produce a catalogue about the UK and Europe and wished to base himself in London. He was looking for a large house to rent for a minimum of eighteen months and stipulated it should be in Wimbledon because he was a tennis fan.'

Gartenfeld had given Paul, Franks and Parker a smart address on East 60th Street between

Madison and Park Avenue. As further proof of his bona fide intentions he'd had his bank in the Caymans send the estate agents a cheque for one thousand pounds to defray expenses. My guess is he wrote to more than one estate agent,' Landon said.

'What's the name of his bank in the Caymans?'

'The Standard.'

'It's not on our list of banks Talal Asir was known to be using.'

'Couldn't this be one that hasn't come to our notice until now?'

'Let's not rush to judgement, Will.'

'Look, here's a man who wants to rent a large house specifically in Wimbledon because he is a tennis fan and then disappears before the championships even begin. We should put Montpelier House under surveillance and have an assault team ready to go in at three minutes notice.'

'That's not on,' Neagle said. 'The assault team will be held back until it's clear negotiations have failed. The police always try to end a siege situation peacefully.'

'Have you listened to yourself?' Landon said aggressively. 'The terrorists we will be pitted against are not interested in talking to or negotiating with anybody. They want to become martyrs and are ready for death. In fact they will embrace it with open arms. Try to establish contact with them and the balloon'll go up.'

'You're advocating that we send in an assault team the moment we're satisfied Montpelier

419

House is in the hands of the terrorists?'

'Damned right I am,' Landon told him.

Furthermore, he was arguing that the operation should be conducted by the SAS with the police in a purely supporting role. Of the neighbouring houses on Arthur Road only the one directly opposite Montpelier was of any use as an observation post. He had no idea whether the occupants would agree to his proposal but should they refuse there was an alternative.

'We borrow a couple of vans from Transco,' Landon continued, 'and dig up the road. Nothing unusual about that; they are forever doing it all over the country.'

The excavation site would be just down the hill from Montpelier where they could look straight into the drive. They would only be able to deploy four men without arousing suspicion and they would have to do both tasks, observe and assault. They would have two Transit vans on site all day, one of which would be the armoury. The four-man team would erect a canvas shelter, which would serve as an observation post should it rain on and off, as had been the case for much of the first week of the lawn tennis championships.

'It's not a bad idea,' Neagle conceded, 'but the SAS team can hardly stay on site all night.'

'Of course they can't. They'll leave the site at the end of a normal working day — say about six p.m.'

'And who will be keeping Montpelier House under observation then?'

'Nobody, unless for your own peace of mind

420

you decide to put someone in the house opposite, but it's not strictly necessary.'

'You can't be serious, Will.'

'Well, think about it. These people mean to inflict hundreds of casualties, and Wimbledon is made for it. They are not going to waste their resources on a piddling little target. That is especially true if Mubarak Al-Massad is making them the mother and father of a bomb.'

''If' is the biggest word in the English language,' Neagle said.

'The fact is, Mubarak surfaced, we lost him and he's possibly in this country right now. You said it yourself, Richard, the enemy is amongst us.'

'Yours is a high-risk operation, Will.'

'To do nothing is much more risky.'

Neagle fell silent. It seemed to Landon that having raised one objection after another, the chairman of CATO now realised he had exhausted every argument he could think of.

'I suppose we could have a team in place by Thursday,' Neagle said eventually.

'What's wrong with tomorrow?'

There were a dozen reasons in Neagle's opinion. Transco, the gas and electricity companies would have to be briefed to ensure they all spoke with one voice in case anybody in Arthur Road phoned in to find out what repairs the workers were doing. Temporary traffic lights would have to be installed and the police informed. He was still in full spate when Landon interrupted him.

'It's not eleven a.m. yet, Richard,' he said.

'Why not give it your best shot and see if we can't get the assault team on site by nine o'clock tomorrow morning?'

Neagle gave it some thought, then said, 'You're right, we can but try.'

★   ★   ★

The man who called himself Abbas Sayed Alijani arrived Heathrow Terminal 4 at 15.00 hours on British Airways flight BA307 from Paris. From Chicago he had flown United Airlines to Detroit and then to Montreal to board an Air France plane to Paris, the penultimate leg of his long journey. Exactly twenty-five days had passed since that hard-faced whore had called at his house on West Hollander to inform him he had just won twenty-five thousand dollars in a competition he hadn't even entered. Then before he could get a close look at the cheque she was waving in his face, the whore had asked him to confirm he was Mr Leon Abbot. Six whole days after she had visited him he had figured it was safe to move and his long journey had begun. Full of confidence he followed the directional signs for Arrivals and joined what looked to be the shortest queue for non-European Union nationals at immigration.

The Immigration officer who examined the passport of Abbas Sayed Alijani was an old hand and had acquired a nose for sniffing out the bogus tourist. There was nothing on the landing card Alijani had completed to arouse his suspicion, but the passport was something else.

It had been issued four years ago and still looked brand spanking new. Furthermore, Montreal and Paris were the only two immigration stamps within the covers, both in the last six days. That in itself was suspicious; when the photograph and personal details of Abbas Sayed Alijani appeared on the VDU it was evident that something was very wrong. The Iranian who had walked into the British Embassy, Bonn, fourteen years ago to ask for political asylum and had subsequently disappeared in 1993 would now be forty-six years old. The man standing in front of him was in his late twenties, early thirties. Confronted with this obvious discrepancy the Immigration officer decided he had no alternative but to have the impostor detained.

It was done in a typically quiet, typically English fashion. Reaching under the desk he pressed a button to summon two plainclothes security officers. When they appeared on the scene moments later, he politely invited the bogus Abbas Sayed Alijani to accompany them.

★   ★   ★

It had been the hardest day Neagle could remember and it wasn't over yet. His first task had been to sell Landon's concept to his own Director General, and even though he had the support of Colin Wales, the Deputy DG, he'd still had to contend with a barrage of questions, many of them virtually unanswerable. He didn't need to be told Wimbledon was a high-risk

423

operation when he'd made that very same point to Landon himself. But how could you possibly guarantee there would be no innocent casualties, that nobody would blunder into a firefight? It was all very well for the Director to say that the area should be cordoned off but the terrorists weren't stupid. They would know something was up if there was no movement of any kind on Arthur Road and they would then seize the initiative. The argument had raged back and forth, after going over the same ground again, until finally he and Colin Wales had won the day. By that time it was gone one o'clock and the pressure was really on.

The afternoon had been one long round of meetings starting with Transco, and the provision of vehicles and equipment from their depot at Merton near Wimbledon. He had then liaised with the gas and electricity companies serving that part of London before moving on to V District headquarters at Kingston-upon-Thames, where he had conferred with the commander, detective chief superintendent and the district chief superintendent. In retrospect, leaving these senior officers until the last had been a mistake. V District included Wimbledon, and many of their officers were already deployed on crowd control at the All England Lawn Tennis Club. Worse still, outline details of the forthcoming operation had already filtered down from above. Although aware that his DG intended to brief the Commissioner of Police, Neagle hadn't allowed for it happening quite so quickly. Putting that right had required tact, time, diplomacy and a certain amount of socialising.

Neagle had been on his way back to Gower Street to look in at the office before calling it a day when he learned that Abbas Sayed Alijani had been arrested at Heathrow. The Iranian was now being held at Paddington Green and his presence was required, Colin Wales had left him in no doubt about that. There was, Neagle thought, no peace for the wicked.

Paddington Green on Harrow Road was unlike any other police station in the Metropolitan area. Built like a fortress, it was used as an interrogation centre for known or suspected terrorists. When Neagle arrived he found Ralph Meacher, the acting Head of the Mid-East Department, waiting for him with a large brown envelope in his hand.

'These photographs are from our library,' Meacher said, and extracted them from the envelope. 'They were taken over a ten-year period from the time he asked for political asylum until shortly before he disappeared in 1993.'

Meacher jerked his thumb in the direction of number 3 Interview Room. 'The Abbas Sayed Alijani in there is an impostor. The entries in his US passport may show the same date and place of birth but he's at least twelve years too young. Anyway, these photos are yours to keep.'

'Thanks, they will be very useful. Has the impostor been confronted with them?'

'Not yet. I thought you'd want to produce them when the time was ripe. Right now he's saying nothing and would like us to believe he can't speak English.'

'That's an old trick and we know how to deal with it.'

'I'll be on my way then,' Meacher said, then snapped his fingers. 'Nearly forgot, a detective superintendent from Special Branch named Mal something or other would like to see you. Says it's urgent.'

'Where do I find him?'

'Upstairs in the detective chief superintendent's office.'

The *Oxford Dictionary* defined urgent as requiring immediate attention, or importunate, earnest or persistent in demand. What Mal had to tell him didn't equate with either definition. An anonymous informer had phoned Hackney police station to say that two Chechens, whose photographs were on the wanted poster, were living in one of the flats at 31 Elm Street. If the informant had come forward three days earlier they might have apprehended Maskhadov and Zakayev.

The other point of interest concerned the surveillance detail that had been keeping the Go Easy Go Getaway travel agency in Finsbury Park under observation. Special Branch had looked at Ahmed Zia before and had pronounced him clean, and from his standpoint Mal saw no reason to change the previous assessment. They had taken photographs of the man Zia had engaged to help run his own business and, while none was particularly good, the employee bore no resemblance to any of the suspected terrorists

426

on the wanted list. Mal wanted Neagle to know that before standing down the Special Branch team, he had tried repeatedly to seek his agreement but had been unable to contact him. Had Neagle not had quite so many other things on his mind, he might have asked the detective superintendent if he was equally certain the premises of Kamal Allam, Printers and Stationery, was equally clean.

* * *

Landon walked out of the Gloucester Road tube station and made his way to Stanhope Gardens. Headquarters, Special Forces had arranged for the four-man SAS assault team and two reserves to be quartered at Hyde Park barracks where he had met them when they had arrived shortly after 6 p.m. He had then spent two uncomfortable hours briefing them. Landon had had no photographs to show the team, no scale model of the immediate neighbourhood, and, as yet, no secure base on the ground from which he could point out the target. The news that the assault team would not have an opportunity to see Montpelier House before they arrived on site at eight thirty tomorrow morning had not gone down well with the brigadier, Special Forces.

At the very least he expected the assault team to be supplied with detailed drawings of the house so that his men knew exactly how many rooms they would have to clear on the ground floor and upstairs. It was all very well for Landon to inform them there were seven bedrooms including four en-suite but how big were these rooms? Were there any communicating doors upstairs? Question after question had followed, swamping him like a rolling barrage until in the end Landon suggested that maybe he should find some dog-foot infantry unit to do the job if the brigadier wasn't happy about it? Commander, Special Forces had then told him he respected a man who could stand up to him and this time when his eyes had crinkled at the corners a smile had actually touched his lips. Thereafter things had gone smoothly. No plan was ever perfect at its conception. Some honing was always required and Landon had assured the Brigadier he intended to do just that in the light of what happened tomorrow.

Landon suddenly realised he had walked past 62 Stanhope Gardens while he was deep in thought. Retracing his steps he let himself into the house and went on up the staircase to his flat on the second floor. Ensley Holsinger was the last person he expected to find waiting on the doorstep, nursing a gift-wrapped box.

'What are you doing here?' he asked.

'One thing I like about you, Landon, you know how to make a girl feel welcome.'

'How did you get in?'

'Which question would you like me to answer first?'

'The one that doesn't involve making a speech,' Landon said, and opened the door to his flat.

'OK. I got lucky and pressed the right button on the intercom and the charming old man who lives across the landing from you answered. I told him I was your fiancée and he let me come in.'

'My fiancée?'

'I figured he wouldn't understand if I said we were an item.'

'Yeah, he's old-fashioned. It's the fiancée bit that got you past the front door.' Landon stepped aside. 'Go ahead,' he said, 'you know where the living room is.'

'And the bedroom too,' she said archly.

'You're a fantasist.'

'Think again. The night you brought me here I looked the flat over while you were collecting your car.'

Same old Ensley, he thought, poised, very sure of herself and radiating confidence. Determined was another label to pin on her; furthermore she was too damned attractive by half, and knew it.

'Now tell me why you're here.'

Ensley placed the gift-wrapped box on the low table in the sitting room, then turned about to face him. 'I want my life back,' she said simply.

'Your life?'

'Yes. You did a hell of a paint job on me. I'm unreliable, dishonest, economical with the truth and never disclose more than I have to. That's what you told Mr Dombas and it got me arrested and taken to Annapolis where I was interrogated. OK, so they let me go in the end, but my phone will be tapped, my mail intercepted and I can forget about applying for a job in any capacity which is funded by the Federal government.'

429

'And I'm to blame for this?' Landon said.

'You're the only man who can put things right.'

'And you are going to bribe me with a gift-wrapped box of chocolates,' he said smiling.

'It's the last photocopy of the first fifteen chapters. It has been lodged with a safe deposit company in Chicago since the eleventh of May and, yes, I lied to you again when I told — '

Landon didn't allow her to finish. Taking Ensley in his arms he kissed her long and hard on the mouth.

'What was that for?' she asked when he finally released her.

'I'm damned if I know. It certainly had nothing to do with the typescript.'

'Then we had better find out, Landon.'

She came to him, wrapped both arms around his neck and rammed her body against him, her tongue seeking his.

★   ★   ★

There was never a time in London when the traffic stopped and the city was still. The only tricky part of the journey came at the very beginning when they had to back the Ford Transit out of the shed and drive up to the lane to join Blackstock Road without being seen. Once they had left Finsbury Park behind them, Mubarak breathed a little easier and was content to leave things to Walid, who, it transpired, knew the route to Wimbledon like the back of his hand. Never once exceeding the speed limit,

Walid headed due south, to reach the Thames at Blackfriars where he turned right on to the Victoria Embankment, then made his way round to Wandsworth Bridge where he crossed the river. Tension gripped them again when they turned into Arthur Road and drove up the hill. Luck favoured them: no pedestrians were about and they didn't meet another vehicle. Tyres crunching on the gravel, they entered the drive and motored straight into the garage.

26

The alarm clock was merely a backup. Landon surfaced and was immediately wide awake at 5 a.m., fifteen minutes before the appointed time. Reaching out with his right hand he switched off the alarm before it started ringing. The luxury of snatching those few extra minutes in bed was a no-no for him; taking care not to disturb Ensley he slipped out of bed, padded into the bathroom and took a cold shower before shaving. This was the third day of the counter-terrorist operation and he was beginning to wonder if his threat assessment had been wrong. Rumours of an imminent major terrorist attack on the UK had been rife in the Lebanon, Jordan and Egypt, and the movements of certain known terrorists like Mubarak Al-Massad had provided some evidence of this. But Landon could not forget he was the man who had divined that the aim of such an attack would be to inflict the maximum number of fatal casualties on the civilian population. He was the one who had plumped for Wimbledon and had convinced the unbelievers.

The fact was, there had been no signs of activity within Montpelier House on Wednesday or Thursday and the rain-affected Wimbledon was drawing to a close. Today's semi-final between Richard Krajicek and Goran Ivanisevic should be a crowd-puller but would the numbers fall away if the inclement weather conditions continued? Landon looked at his reflection in the shaving mirror and told himself to stop worrying about imponderables and get on with the job.

Landon finished shaving, rinsed his face again, then returned to the bedroom to pull on a light grey sweatshirt, fawn-coloured slacks and a pair of moccasins. Ensley Holsinger appeared to be still asleep, curled up in a foetal position on her right side, knees bent and drawn up to her stomach. With her urchin-cut dark brown hair she looked the picture of innocence but she was never that. Much as Landon wanted to trust Ensley he doubted if her reformation was so complete that she wouldn't stretch the truth when it suited. When she had delivered the last typescript gift-wrapped in a box, a small insistent voice inside his head had suggested that if Ensley had made one copy back in May, what was to stop her from making two?

'You're not going to leave without saying goodbye, are you, Landon?' Ensley said as he moved silently towards the open door.

'Of course not.' Landon turned about to face Ensley, who was now sitting bolt upright in the double bed, the top two buttons of her pyjama jacket undone. 'Tempting,' he said, 'very tempting but I have to go.'

'What time will you be back?' she asked.

'Same as yesterday and the day before, nearer eight than seven.'

'You work funny hours, Landon.'

'It's a funny old job.'

He went out into the hall, grabbed the dark

433

blue hip-length anorak from the clothes rack and checked to make sure the Haydn transceiver was in the right-hand pocket before leaving the flat.

The Volkswagen Polo, which the Motor Transport Section had signed out to him was a souped-up version of the standard model. It had a 2-litre engine instead of the normal top-of-the-range 1.6, twin carburettors, an aluminium cylinder head and broader tyres. Although not as fast as his Aston Martin, the Polo was a damned sight more manoeuvrable in heavy traffic.

The assault team and reserves were no longer quartered at Hyde Park barracks where the sight of two Transco vehicles was bound to cause speculation. To avoid this they had moved on Wednesday night to the disused Fighting Vehicle Research Establishment at Chobham, sixteen and a half miles south-west of Wimbledon. Yesterday was the first time they'd had to contend with the morning rush hour converging on London and the journey had taken seventy minutes.

Nobody had been happy about that and the search was on for a base closer in. Landon had also heard that Winston Reid was concerned about the school just down the hill from Montpelier House and wanted marksmen in place in case staff and pupils were the alternative target. The chain of command was also bothering him, which Landon thought was another way of saying someone a lot more senior than him should decide when to send the assault team in.

Leaving Stanhope Gardens, Landon turned left on Gloucester Road and headed west as far as Hammersmith where he crossed the river. He skirted Barnes and continued on the same road through Roehampton to join the A3 trunk road short of Kingston-upon-Thames. From there it was a straight run to Chobham. At twenty past six, forty-two minutes after leaving 62 Stanhope Gardens, Landon drove through the gates and entered the old Fighting Vehicles Research Establishment.

He parked the Volkswagen Polo outside the concrete hut the SAS were using as a billet. As he got out of the car, the smell of bacon sizzling in the pan assailed his nostrils and made his stomach rumble. Members of the assault team were known to him simply as Soldier A, Soldier B, Soldier C, Soldier D, the reserves were Soldiers E and F. Landon was never sure how much of this was basic security or part of the mystique enjoyed by Special Forces. He had no idea of their respective ranks or who was in charge. For their part the SAS addressed him as 'Boss' without actually meaning it, or so Landon believed.

'You want some breakfast, Boss?' Soldier D asked.

'Yes, that would be nice.'

Breakfast was served in a mess tin, was eaten with a spoon and consisted of two small slices of fried bread, three rashers of bacon, a fried egg sunny side up and the inevitable baked beans. It was accompanied by a mug of instant Maxwell House and a packet of Coffee Mate.

435

'Did we pick up anything during the night?' Soldier B asked.

'Not a thing,' Landon told him. 'They're as quiet as church mice.'

Although a phone tap had been placed on the BT line since Wednesday morning there had been no outgoing calls from Montpelier House up to 23.59 hours yesterday. Had there been any since then, one of the duty officers at Vauxhall Cross would have phoned Landon over the Mozart secure-speech facility installed in the Volkswagen.

'Maybe they have been communicating with mobiles?'

'We would still have intercepted any calls made from the house.'

GCHQ, the eavesdroppers, had called on the army's Communications and Security Group in Leicestershire to position an intercept station on Wimbledon Park between the All England Lawn Tennis Club and the cricket ground. The station operated from a small cargo truck with a one-ton capacity. Stencilled on both sides of the vehicle was the legend 'BBC Outside Broadcasts'.

'Same routine as yesterday then,' Soldier A observed.

'That's right,' Landon said. 'I'll be monitoring the situation from the Wimbledon police station on Queens Road. Soldiers E and F will be with me.'

So would an explosives ordnance disposal team who were on hand in case there was a bomb to be disarmed.

436

★ ★ ★

Mubarak went into the utility room, opened the communicating door and entered the garage. At his own trade he was a master craftsman and there was no one to touch him in Hamas, Hezbollah or Islamic Jihad. He took pride in his work and hated to be rushed because the end result was invariably slipshod and did not measure up to the high standard he set himself. The bomb he was making for Islamic Jihad was a case in point. He had told Ahmed Zia that it would take him eight days to construct a weapon of mass destruction and the whole of Tuesday had been lost removing everything from the shed that would identify it as a bomb-making factory. Montpelier House was an indifferent substitute. He couldn't use either the hacksaw or the oxyacetylene torch for fear the people next door might hear the noise and become suspicious. As a result, just over two-thirds of the tubular steel pipes had been cut up and turned into metal barbs. Worse still, there had been no time in which to weld the angled blast walls in place before leaving Finsbury Park. The blast wall was intended to retain the energy created on detonation that split second longer to ensure the blast wave travelled horizontally.

'Is it finished?' Abu Nidal asked softly.

Mubarak flinched as if he had been struck. After allowing himself time to recover his composure, he turned slowly about to confront the younger man. Abu Nidal was only a few months off thirty but the structure of his face resembled a woman's, which even his beard could not disguise, so that he looked no more than twenty. Despite appearances he was a committed warrior, ready to die for the faith and he knew how to handle the Kalashnikov AK47 assault rifle that had never left his side since Mubarak had arrived at the house.

'I'm about to connect the circuit to the firing button,' Mubarak told him. 'Then it will be ready.'

'And there is no chance the bomb will misfire?'

'None whatever,' Mubarak said tersely. The bomb would not be as effective as he had hoped because much of the blast would travel upwards. The Ford Transit would be reduced to pieces of scrap metal no bigger than a man's hand. There would be absolutely no trace of Abu Nidal and Walib.

'Then you had better show me how it works, Mubarak Al-Massad.'

'You can watch me complete the firing circuit but put the gun down first.' Mubarak opened the near-side door. 'I don't want the barrel poking me in the eye.'

The firing mechanism was housed in a small oblong metal box mounted on the transmission tunnel near the gear shift. An electric detonator and primer had been plugged into each bank of Semtex explosive and the insulated cable laid from the detonators to the cab, where they had been taped together. Mubarak picked up the roll of adhesive tape and the pair of scissors he'd left in the cab yesterday evening. Methodically, he cut the adhesive binding into eight-inch strips and bonded the insulating cable with the transmission tunnel. That done, he bared the cables and slotted the exposed wires into the twin sockets at the back of the metal box, then tightened the retaining screws.

'The bomb is now fused.' Mubarak pointed to a handle on the left side of the box that was only big enough to be gripped between finger and thumb. 'To detonate it you first crank that handle until five amps is showing on the ammeter gauge, then flip open the cover and depress the red button inside.'

'And that's it?'

'Yes. Just make sure the cover is closed when you are generating the electrical charge. You don't want an accidental detonation.'

'I'm not a fool, Mubarak Al-Massad.'

There was a threatening edge to Abu Nidal's voice that promised trouble if he didn't smooth things over. 'No one said you were.'

'Good. What will you do when this day is over?'

Mubarak thought it a stupid question. Abu Nidal and Walid would only have minutes to live after they had backed the van out of the garage and turned it around in the drive before setting off up the hill. And Ali Jaffar, the houseman, would not live to see tomorrow either. Minutes after the explosion he would open fire on any pedestrians who happened to be in the street at the time. He would lure the police into an ambush as well as those ambulance men, paramedics, doctors, nurses and firemen using

Arthur Road to reach the All England Lawn Tennis Club. Ali Jaffar would continue his lonely battle until he was killed but Mubarak would not be there to see it. People like Ahmed Zia, Ali Mohammed Khalef and himself were too valuable to squander their lives.

'Did you not hear my question?' Abu Nidal asked.

'What will I do?' Mubarak stared at the younger man through narrowed eyes. 'I will make another bomb for someone like you.'

★　★　★

It was the second time since morning prayers that Winston Reid had summoned Ashton to his office. The only difference on this occasion was the presence of Rowan Garfield in his capacity as Deputy DG. The subject matter was unchanged. Yesterday Reid had wondered if Landon was up to the job he'd been given; today he was voicing his doubts in a positive manner. At the request of Winston Reid, who had wanted to pick his brains, the finance people at the FCO had agreed that Hazelwood could stay on until this Friday. However, following the successful deployment of the SAS assault team on Wednesday, Reid had decided he had no further need of Hazelwood's advice and Victor had departed for good. It was evident to Ashton that the new incumbent was beginning to wish he hadn't been quite so precipitate.

'Sit down, Peter,' he said, waving him to a chair. 'I'm sure you can guess what Rowan and I have been discussing.'

'I imagine it's the same topic as yesterday and earlier this morning.'

'Quite.' Reid cleared his throat. 'We both feel Will Landon doesn't have the necessary experience to run this operation if force has to be applied. By rights, MI5 should be handling this situation . . .'

'Richard Neagle has rather a lot on his plate at the moment,' Ashton said, and ticked off the list of names on the fingers of his left hand. 'Talal Asir, Ali Mohammed Khalef, Lev Maskhadov, Boris Zakayev, Mubarak Al-Massad and Abbas Sayed Alijani, who is proving a tough nut to crack.'

'I'm aware of his difficulties, Peter, and putting Will Landon in the hot seat is not the answer. I want you to relieve him forthwith. You are made for the job. You did a nine-month tour of duty with the army's Special Patrol Unit in Northern Ireland and fought with the SAS in the Falklands.'

'And where do you want Landon to go?'

'Gower Street. Colin Wales has asked for a liaison officer.'

Ashton wondered how he was going to sell it to Will. For the past sixty hours the SIS had left him in charge. Now the DG had lost confidence in him and he was being shunted off as a liaison officer, a job a Grade III intelligence officer straight from the Training School could do with consummate ease.

'Any questions, Peter?' Reid asked.

'The PIO,' Garfield murmured.

'Thank you, Rowan.' Reid turned to Ashton again. 'In case there is an incident the Home Office has agreed that one of their principal information officers will deal with the media. He is on his way to Queens Road police station now.'

'Has anyone told Will to expect him?'

It seemed nobody had but Garfield was eager to correct this oversight. He would advise Landon and also warn him to be ready to leave the moment Ashton arrived.

'That's the last thing you will do,' Ashton told him bluntly. 'Will doesn't go anywhere until he has introduced me to the assault team over the Haydn link.'

★ ★ ★

Hazelwood decided life wasn't worth living and said so out loud, then corrected himself. As a retired DG life was not worth living. This was only his second day away from the office and if this was foretaste of what was to come he would die of boredom before he was in receipt of an old-age pension or whatever fancy name Social Security liked to call it.

He looked at the ornately carved cigar box bought in India a lifetime ago and the cut-down brass shellcase that served as an ashtray, both of which he had brought home from the office in a Tesco plastic bag. He supposed he ought to consign both items to the dustbin because they replicated the ones in his study and Alice wouldn't allow him to smoke elsewhere in the house, except perhaps the garage? He considered the possibility briefly then dismissed it out of hand. There was no central heating out there and it would be bitterly cold in winter. All the same, he wasn't prepared to ditch the contents of the Tesco plastic bag just yet.

In a disgruntled frame of mind he left the house, went into the garden shed and brought out a deck chair, which, with some difficulty, he erected on the strip of lawn by the study. He went back into the house, collected the Viking hardback edition of Anthony Beevor's *Stalingrad* and returned to the garden. He was totally unprepared for this new way of life. Alice had her Bridge Club, was a member of the Townswomen's Guild, attended a keep-fit club, worked in a charity shop for two days a week and was the secretary of the Hampstead Horticulture Society. But he had nothing to fill his days and, except for the SAS bodyguard, the trappings of power had been stripped from him. That he was reading history now instead of helping to make it was the really sad thing about old age.

★ ★ ★

The day duty detective sergeant at Blackstock Road police station had first met Ahmed Zia on Wednesday morning when he had called at the station to report the theft of a blue Ford Transit van from his workshop. Zia had been upset because technically the van would not be his until 1 January 2002. He had entered into a five-year rental agreement with a Mr Baloch

443

Rahman, at the end of which the vehicle would be his. As part of the contract Rahman was responsible for taxing and insurance, the cost of which was passed on to Ahmed Zia.

To support his story, Zia had produced a photocopy of the contract, which showed the Ford Transit was already four years old when he'd bought it. By the time Zia finished paying for it the vehicle would have cost him over three times as much as if he had bought it brand new. In the event that the van was written off in a traffic accident, vandalised beyond economical repair or stolen, Zia had to make up the difference between the sum received from the insurance company and the cost of a brand-new one. The detective sergeant thought it was the worst contract he had ever seen.

Ahmed was angry because he had considered Omar Ibrahim, the man who had stolen the Ford Transit, to be a friend. He had given Omar Ibrahim a job and had allowed him to stay in his flat until he could find a place of his own. Omar Ibrahim had proved himself to be a good worker and a model house guest. Consequently Zia had thought nothing of it when Ibrahim had failed to appear at breakfast on Wednesday morning. He had only begun to suspect something was wrong when there was no answer after he had knocked on Ibrahim's door. Thinking he might be unwell, Zia had entered the room and discovered that Ibrahim had packed his things and had left some time during the night. Thoroughly alarmed by now, Zia had gone straight to his printing and stationery business; half an hour later he had walked into Blackstock Road police station to report the theft of his Ford Transit. He had visited the station yesterday to see if there was any news of his van and now here he was yet again on Friday afternoon asking the same question.

'I can appreciate your concern,' the detective sergeant told him, 'but take it from me, everything that can be done to recover your property has been done. The description and registration number of your Ford Transit is on the data base of stolen vehicles.'

'I don't know what Mr Baloch Rahman is going to say about this.'

'Haven't you been in touch with him?'

'He's away on holiday,' Ahmed Zia told him.

'Holidays don't last for ever, Mr Zia.' The detective sergeant flipped through the case file he had opened, then said, 'We have circulated the description of Omar Ibrahim you gave us.'

'That is good news.'

'He reminds me of somebody, Mr Zia.'

'As he does me. In fact he is a little like the man shown on your wanted notice.'

'There are two wanted posters on the notice board outside. Which one do you mean?'

'I think his family name is Al-Massad.'

'Could it be Mubarak Al-Massad you were thinking of?'

'Yes, that's the name.'

The detective sergeant gazed at Ahmed Zia and wondered if he wasn't just a shade too clever for his own good.

★ ★ ★

BIKINI was a state of alert that had been introduced in the early seventies when the Provisional IRA had extended their bombing campaign to the United Kingdom. The alert state never fell below BIKINI BLACK, which simply recognised a threat existed and that any government building in England, Wales and Scotland was a potential target. It was, in fact, a permanent reminder to civil servants to be vigilant and on the lookout for any object that had been left unattended. At the top end of the scale BIKINI SCARLET meant reliable information had been received indicating an attack on a target in a specific city or town was imminent. BIKINI AMBER and BIKINI RED fell within these two parameters. In the temporary absence of the Director General of MI5, who was attending a NATO meeting in Brussels, Colin Wales had issued BIKINI RED at 14.20 hours. The news had not come as a complete surprise to Winston Reid. He and Colin Wales had discussed the situation over the Mozart secure-speech facility no less than four times, and to all intents and purposes the decision to raise the alert level had been a joint one. It had been taken on the flimsiest of evidence, the one solid fact being the disappearance of two Chechens from their flat in Hackney.

The action to be taken at each alert state had been laid down in Standing Orders, a confidential document issued by Roy Kelso. Aware that the current alert state was to be significantly

446

uprated, Winston Reid studied the document to refresh his memory, then summoned all heads of departments to give them advance warning. Consequently all non-essential staff began to leave the building at 15.00 hours, the security officers on duty in the entrance hall and underground garage were armed and two bodyguards from the Ministry of Defence police were detailed to look after the DG and his deputy.

★   ★   ★

Although the garden in Red Lion Square was strictly for residents only, Ensley Holsinger assumed the staff of Warwick Thompson Associates were permitted to use it. The fact was that she had arrived fifteen minutes early for an appointment with Eve Mullins, who had succeeded George Ventris, and she wasn't about to walk round and round the square simply to kill time. Since the gate happened to be open, Ensley chose to ignore the notice attached to the iron railings and, without a moment's hesitation, she entered the garden and sat down on the nearest park bench.

Warwick Thompson was her very last hope. In the last three days she had tried every publishing house and literary agency and had been turned down flat by all of them. Their reasons had varied from a lack of experience on her part to the difficulties of obtaining a work permit, and culminating with the stark truth that publishing houses were shedding staff rather than taking

447

people on because the trade was going through such a bad patch.

What if there was no opening for her at Warwick Thompson? Did she admit defeat and crawl back home? That was too unpalatable to think about. And where did Will Landon fit into the equation? Good question. Why had she sought him out when she hardly knew him and they usually circled one another like cat and dog? An even better question. Maybe it was the classic attraction of opposites. She was sure of one thing: Landon was one of those Englishmen you couldn't mould. You took him for what he was and hoped for the best. Except she wasn't into hoping for the best. Then what was she doing sitting in this park if she wasn't hoping against hope Warwick Thompson would give her a chance? A rueful smile touched her lips. She would have stood a better chance if she had held on to that last copy of the Ross Frazer memoirs instead of giving it to Landon as a peace offering. Then suddenly it occurred to Ensley that the script was superfluous. From the moment Amelia Cazelet had thrust the memoirs into her hands, she had been at the centre of things. In fact she was the only outsider who could write the whole story. Something very big was about to go down and somehow the Gartenfelds were involved. But what if they were still vacationing in Europe? A phone call to them would settle the issue one way or another. Ensley asked herself what she was waiting for.

From the middle bedroom of seven, Mubarak Al-Massad enjoyed an uninterrupted view of the mixed school nestling in the shallow valley lower down the hill from Montpelier House. The time was twenty-eight minutes past three and any moment now the exodus would begin, offering him just the sort of cover he needed.

The exodus began as a trickle, then rapidly became a flood. Mubarak backed away from the window and went downstairs into the kitchen to say goodbye to the others. He clasped hands with each man in turn and prayed for their success in battle, then opened the back door and left the house. He cut across the lawn, skirted the tennis court and vaulted the fence at the bottom of the garden. He crouched down and scanned the ground from left to right until his eyes were drawn to a large wooden hut on the boundary of the school playing fields and the shallow drainage ditch that ran behind it. The grass had not been cut in the immediate area and there was a lot of dead bracken on the far bank that put the bottom of the ditch in shade. Nevertheless Mubarak was sure he had seen movement there.

He straightened up, turned about and walked slowly back to the house. To have hurried would have confirmed whatever suspicions the observer might have had.

'What are you doing back here?' Abu Nidal demanded when he entered the kitchen.

449

'The house is under observation,' Mubarak told him.

Then suddenly the telephone out in the hall started ringing.

★   ★   ★

By the time Ashton arrived in Wimbledon the police station in Queens Road was bursting at the seams with additional uniformed officers. Of necessity the Rover 600 he'd drawn from the MT Section had had to become his command post, which he shared with the district superintendent.

Ashton knew who was calling him on the Mozart link before he lifted the transceiver. Ever since BIKINI RED had been issued, Reid had been constantly on the phone, wanting to know what was happening. It was the same again this time.

'Nothing is happening up at the house,' Ashton told him.

'When did you last speak to the assault team?'

'Less than five minutes ago.'

'Maybe we're barking up the wrong tree,' Reid said hesitantly.

'So what do you suggest we — ' Aston heard his call sign transmitted over the Haydn communications net and told Reid to hang on. Answering, he found himself talking to Soldier F, whom Landon had deployed in the school grounds. The exchange lasted a matter of seconds. After checking to make sure the assault team had heard the transmission, he called Reid

450

on the Mozart link. 'Looks like we're in business,' he continued. 'One man attempted to leave the area via the school grounds. Then something happened to make him change his mind and he returned to the house.'

'What are you going to do?'

Ashton didn't get a chance to tell Reid. The intercept station behind the All England Lawn Tennis Club reported they had just monitored an incoming call to Montpelier House from a woman who asked to speak to Mrs Gartenfeld.

'Does she have any noticeable accent?' Ashton asked on a hunch.

'She sounded like an American to me,' the operator told him.

A radio net that up till then had only been spasmodically active suddenly became frenetic. Soldier A reported that the garage doors had just been opened from inside the structure and believed he could hear an engine ticking over. Concern was expressed by Soldier D for the safety of the schoolchildren, who were now spilling out on to the pavement. Furthermore, several mothers had arrived to collect their children and had parked their cars outside the entrance. Reid's plaintive voice kept asking what he was going to do but the time for debating the pros and cons had passed. Unhesitatingly Ashton ordered the assault team to go in.

'We're going to need your people to quarantine Arthur Road,' he told the district superintendent, then started the Rover and pulled away from the kerb.

* * *

Each member of the assault team was armed with a 9mm MP5 SD, the silenced version of the Heckler and Koch sub-machine gun with a 30-round curved box magazine. The weapon was also fitted with a retractable butt stock and a 3-round burst facility. Their tactics were based on the simple house-clearing drills employed in a built-up area. Soldiers A and C worked the left side of the street and headed straight for the driveway. They were covered by Soldiers B and D on the other side of the road, who watched the upstairs windows.

* * *

Ali Jaffar had been about to open fire on the schoolchildren emerging on to the pavement when he spotted two armed men moving up the hill on the far side of the road. Swinging round to face them, he brought the Kalashnikov AK47 up into his shoulder and ripped off a long burst of automatic fire, shattering the windowpane in front of him. As the shards of glass tumbled on to the floor he took three sledgehammer blows in the chest that sent him reeling across the landing. His back slammed against the bedroom door and he slid down on to his buttocks, legs splayed apart. Jaffar bowed his head, contemplated his bloody shirtfront, then slowly toppled over sideways and lay still.

* * *

Abu Nidal was engaged in a firefight with two gunmen who had adopted the prone position and were working in tandem at the far end of the drive. Whenever he attempted to deal with one man the other put down prophylactic fire, forcing him to use the Ford Transit for cover as Walib manoeuvred the vehicle back and forth to turn it through ninety degrees in the narrow width of the drive. Abu Nidal heard Walib call out and assumed he was now ready to move off. He worked his way down the nearside of the Ford Transit, his chest pressed against the bodywork, the Kalashnikov in his left hand, the arm fully extended like a signpost as he fired blindly at the enemy. When he opened the door he found Walib lying across the passenger seat with half his skull blown away.

It had been their intention to detonate the bomb where it would kill and maim hundreds but now he would settle for something approaching twenty fatalities. But first he had to move the dead man out of the way in order to generate the electrical charge and press the firing button. Abu Nidal screamed in pain and dropped the Kalashnikov as a bullet smashed his left ankle, a second round took away most of his calf muscle, a third did his hip in and somehow spun him round to present a frontal target that invited a three-round burst from both men. At a range of twelve to fifteen yards, they could hardly miss. Consequently Abu Nidal was dead before he hit the ground.

★ ★ ★

Ashton rounded the bend before Montpelier House, cut across on to the wrong side of the road and pulled up behind one of the Transco vans. Clutching the Haydn, he got out of the Rover and helped the district superintendent to shepherd parents and schoolchildren to safety. The gun battle could not have happened at a worse time, and the fact that no innocent bystanders had been cut down was nothing short of a miracle. He looked back over his shoulder in time to see soldiers A and C enter the garage, moving alternately so that they were able to cover each other. Ashton planned to call in the explosive ordnance disposal team to render the bomb harmless as soon as the SAS reported that the house had been cleared.

★ ★ ★

Mubarak Al-Massad could hear the enemy coming — stealthy footsteps followed by a sudden burst of activity as they kicked in the communicating door between the garage and utility room and then moved into the house. There was nowhere for him to go. He was unarmed, the enemy was to his front and they had at least one man in the school grounds watching the back of the house. In a blind panic he backed out of the kitchen into the hall, then went up the stairs taking two at a time. He turned his back on Ali Jaffar's dead body and chose to enter the bedroom at the far end of the landing simply because it was the room furthest from the kitchen. It was physically impossible to

454

conceal himself under the divan bed and the only hiding place was a fitted wardrobe. Even that was next to useless, since it was impossible to close the second door fully when standing inside the wardrobe. He just hoped the enemy would not be quite so thorough when they came to clear the last room in the house.

The hollow cough, cough, cough of an automatic weapon fitted with a silencer told him the intruders didn't believe in taking chances. They were shooting first before looking inside a cupboard or under a bed. His mouth dry with apprehension, Mubarak listened to them coming nearer and nearer. To his intense shame he was unable to control his bladder and the urine ran down the inside of his trouser leg and formed a small puddle that seeped under the wardrobe door. It was the last thing he did. Moments later his hiding place was reduced to matchwood.

★　★　★

A small green flag hanging out of the upstairs window signalled the end of the firefight. From the moment Ashton had shouted, 'Go, Go, Go,' the operation had lasted less than four minutes, which he thought was pretty remarkable considering the assault team had had to fight an encounter battle with no idea how many terrorists they were up against. Now came the tricky part. He had to get the SAS out of the way before some enterprising onlooker with a camera took a picture of them and sold it on. Ashton called up Soldier A on the Haydn and discussed what they should do about the problem, then asked him for a brief sitrep. The pager linked to the Mozart secure-speech facility was bleeping furiously but he decided Reid could wait, and switched it off while he had a word with the district superintendent. Only then did he return to the Rover and pick up the transceiver.

'I've been listening to the BBC,' Reid told him, 'and there has just been a flash report of a terrorist incident in Wimbledon. I shouldn't have to rely on Radio Two — '

'It's over,' Ashton said, interrupting him. 'There were four terrorists but they've all been accounted for. We were lucky, there were a lot of frightened people around here but there are no friendly casualties.'

'What are you going to do about our friends from Hereford?'

The Mozart was the best secure facility bar none, but Reid couldn't bring himself to talk about the SAS in clear speech and had felt obliged to refer to their base in the west.

'There's a large bomb in the Ford Transit. The police are about to evacuate everybody within a radius of two hundred yards of Montpelier House. Once that's been done, the SAS will pile into the Transco vehicles and drive back to Chobham. When they're out of it, the explosive ordnance disposal team will move in and deal with the bomb.'

'That would seem a satisfactory arrangement.' Reid cleared his throat. 'What is your assessment of the situation now?' he asked.

'In what respect?'

'Well, obviously we have no intention of degrading the current alert state but would you say the major terrorist attack we've been expecting has come and gone?'

'That's an impossible question to answer. But for what it is worth, I believe those terrorists were spooked by a telephone call and they started to launch the attack ahead of schedule.' Ashton paused, then said, 'Of course, it's just a guess.'

'Quite.'

Reid sounded disappointed. With BIKINI RED still in place the evacuation of Vauxhall Cross would continue. Will Landon was to remain at Gower Street to answer any questions the Home Office might have before briefing the press. He also wanted Ashton to be on call at Vauxhall Cross for the same reason.

'One question. Does Victor Hazelwood know we're at BIKINI RED?'

'MI5 will have warned him. They're responsible for safe-guarding VIPs,' Reid said and hung up.

Ashton decided to make sure. Using his mobile he called Victor Hazelwood and learned that Nancy Wilkins had warned him.

'I said you wouldn't regret taking her back. Remember?'

* * *

The motorcyclist and pillion rider were dressed in black leathers and wore crash helmets with tinted visors which made it impossible for

457

anyone to see their faces as they came up the King's Road. Weaving in and out of the traffic at a steady thirty miles an hour, they went round Sloane Square and entered Cliveden Place. Long familiar with the route he was taking, the motorcyclist then turned into Eaton Terrace and cut across to the wrong side of the road. He changed down into first gear and approached number 33 at little more than a fast walking pace. As he did so the pillion rider reached into the pannier, took out a 9mm Mini-Uzi and emptied the 32-round magazine into the target house shattering the large sash-cord window on the ground floor and chipping lumps out of the front door. When the last empty cartridge case hit the pavement, the motorcyclist opened the throttle, shot across the left side of the road, forcing a taxi driver to brake violently. He was doing a touch under seventy when he rammed into a Royal Mail delivery van at the junction with Ebury Street. The time was nine minutes after 5 p.m.

Approximately eight miles to the north of Eaton Terrace a similarly dressed motorcyclist and pillion rider turned off Hampstead High Street into Gayton Road, then made a right into Willow Walk. The large Edwardian residence at the bottom of the road overlooking Hampstead Heath had been subdivided into three properties, the largest of which was called Willow Dene and belonged to Victor Hazelwoood. There was no question of effecting a drive-by shooting: the house was screened by a tall hedge and was invisible from the road.

458

The motorcyclist stopped by the wrought-iron gate set in the hedge and kept the 600cc engine ticking over while the pillion rider dismounted and made his way to the front entrance on the left side of the house. He was carrying what appeared to be a small canvas mailbag with the web strap over his left shoulder. The mailbag had been left unbuckled so that he could slip his right hand inside and pull out the 9mm Mini-Uzi sub-machine gun or if necessary, aim and fire the weapon from inside the canvas bag. Full of confidence, he reached out with his left hand and rang the doorbell. It was answered a lot quicker than he had anticipated; furthermore the man who opened the door was a strange face to him.

'I have a small parcel for Sir Victor Hazelwood,' he said, and began to reach inside for the Uzi.

'I don't think so,' the SAS bodyguard said, and shot him twice in the chest with a .357 revolver he had been holding behind his back.

★ ★ ★

The vending machine by the bank of lifts on the top floor was notorious for producing tea that tasted vaguely like coffee and coffee that tasted like nothing on earth. All Ashton wanted was something to quench his thirst and tea was the least offensive drink on offer. He carried the polystyrene cup back to his office and sat down. The public information officer from the Home Office hadn't rung him and Will Landon had also been shunned.

When they had spoken on the phone he had told Will that a voice print from the intercept station would show that Ensley had called Montpelier House and how she had damned nearly imperilled the whole operation. 'She's your friend, Will,' he'd told him, 'so you sort her out.' And Landon had heaved a sigh of relief, which only went to prove Harriet had been right when she said he was besotted with the American girl.

The Mozart rang and he figured it was probably the Home Office man. When he lifted the transceiver Landon said, 'We've just heard there has been a terrorist incident in Eaton Terrace.'

'When did this happen, Will?'

'Nine minutes past five. Two men on a motorbike tried to hit the Minister of State for Foreign and Commonwealth Affairs. Fortunately he'd already left to visit his constituency in Derbyshire when they shot up his house. Both terrorists are now dead. They had an argument with a van when they were doing seventy.'

'They wouldn't have been carrying any means of identification on them?'

'You're right, they weren't. All we know at present is that they are Caucasian.'

'Thanks, Will. Keep me posted.'

'I'll let you know soon as we have anything,' Landon said, and hung up.

As soon as Ashton put the phone down it started ringing again. When he answered it, Victor Hazelwood began by asking him if he was

460

the only officer left in the building which, except for the night duty staff, was true enough.

'I'm afraid so,' Ashton said. 'What can I do for you, Victor?'

'You can make a note in the operations log that two nasty men paid me a visit at fourteen minutes past five this evening. My bodyguard shot the would-be assassin dead, the other rode off on his motorbike.'

The alarm bells started ringing in Ashton's head and he recalled that Thursday night at the beginning of June when he had tried to contact Victor at home and the SAS corporal had told him the DG was conferring with the Minister of State and Winston Reid. The Provisional IRA would have targeted Victor light years ago and had probably sold the information on to Islamic Jihad. But one of the bikers had almost certainly followed the other two home when they left Willow Dene.

'I'm sorry, Victor, but I've got to go.'

Reid had left the office a good half-hour ago and ought to be home by now. There was, however, no reply when he rang the DG's ex-directory number. Ashton called the transport supervisor, who was still on duty, and learned that Reid's driver had followed him to the office that morning because he had taken his Jaguar into Hammonds of Baker Street for servicing. Worse still, when he had left the office to go home his bodyguard had escorted him only as far as Vauxhall Station.

'Why did he leave him?' Ashton demanded.

'Because the DG said he was going by the

461

underground to collect his car from Hammonds and he therefore didn't need him.'

Ashton hung up, contacted directory enquiries on the British Telecom phone and obtained the number of the Jaguar agency. It was a pretty forlorn hope but he got through to Hammonds anyway. As he feared, Reid had collected his car a few minutes ago. Now he was on his way home, no radio, no bodyguard, the perfect sitting duck. In mounting desperation he raised Landon on the Mozart and told him what had happened.

'I've no way of contacting Reid,' Ashton said. 'You'll have to get yourself to his place in Dolphin Square as quickly as possible. Whatever you do, don't let him get out of his car. Meantime, I'll call the police and ask for an armed response vehicle.'

'You haven't said what sort of car he has?'

'A metallic blue Jaguar XJ6.' He gave him the registration number.

'OK, I'm on my way,' Landon said and put the phone down.

★ ★ ★

Lev Maskhadov and Boris Zakayev had spent the last three days at a safe house in Shirland Road, West Kilburn, to which they planned to return when the job was done. At a quarter to five they left the safe house and made their way to Dolphin Square. Although they knew the target would use Vauxhall Bridge to cross the river and would then turn left into Grosvenor Road they

462

had no idea what time he would leave his office. They did, however, know his exact address. Approximately half an hour after leaving West Kilburn they arrived in Dolphin Square and, without the proprietor's knowledge, began to deliver leaflets advertising Wheeler's Fish Restaurant to every house in the neighbourhood, a ploy to allay any suspicion an onlooker might have about their behaviour.

★ ★ ★

There was no easy way to get from Gower Street to Dolphin Square at the best of times, never mind in the rush hour on a Friday evening. From the moment he filtered into New Oxford Street, Landon realised his chances of arriving before Reid did were about zero. He could only hope the police armed response vehicle that Ashton had summoned would have better luck. What he needed to combat the heavy traffic and what the terrorists undoubtedly did have was a motorbike.

★ ★ ★

Reid too had had his problems. From the moment he had left Hammonds of Baker Street he had been caught at every traffic light to Oxford Street, where he had turned right. There had been the usual stop-go routine to Marble Arch, but the worst hazard was in Park Lane where an accident had restricted traffic to one lane approaching Hyde Park Corner. By the time he had turned into Claverton Street on the west side of Dolphin Square, Landon was approaching Reid's address from the direction of Belgrave Road.

★ ★ ★

Maskhadov had expected the target to arrive in an official limousine, and the Jaguar that stopped outside Reid's address momentarily threw him. He did, however, immediately recognise the man who got out of the car. Yelling at Zakayev to follow him, he raced across the road and grabbed the 9mm Mini-Uzi hidden in the pannier of the motorbike.

★ ★ ★

From a hundred yards away Landon saw it all. As if in slow motion Reid turned about to face the gunman and then just stood there passively. Whipping the gear down into second to give the Volkswagen better acceleration, Landon aimed the car at the terrorists and floored the accelerator. Above the noise of the engine, he heard a prolonged burst of automatic fire that lifted the Director General off his feet and hurled him backwards across the pavement. In the same instant a biker cut across in front of him to pick up the gunman.

Landon was doing approximately forty when he slammed into the biker and ran down the gunman. Unable to stop in time he hit the

464

parked Jaguar head on. The seat belt gave way under the impact and he collapsed over the steering wheel. The last thing Landon heard before passing out was the discordant warble of a police siren.

27

Not for the first time in his life Hazelwood wondered how other people would expect him to behave in a given circumstance. On Friday evening he had been deeply shocked to hear that Winston Reid had been assassinated outside his home. Forty-eight hours later the Cabinet Secretary had telephoned, to ask if he would return to the fold as DG for at least the next two years, and he had found it hard to maintain a suitable gravitas. Had they been face to face when the Cabinet Secretary had issued his invitation, Hazelwood would have found it impossible to conceal the smile that had touched his lips on hearing the news.

Somehow he had managed to suppress the note of excitement that had threatened his voice when he had asked the senior duty officer at Vauxhall Cross if he would arrange for a car to pick him up from Willow Dene at seven thirty on Monday morning. He had then spent the rest of the evening making a list of things that needed to be done. Against Rowan Garfield's name he had placed a question mark. He didn't believe Rowan had it in him to be a successful Deputy DG but at the same time he could not bring himself to have him removed. He also put a question mark against Ralph Meacher, but only because he wanted to promote him to Assistant Director and expected some difficulty from the

FCO. There was, in addition, the question of what he should do about Jill Sheridan but that was something he could think about later. No such indecision applied to Talal Asir, Ali Mohammed Khalef and the Gartenfelds; Hazelwood knew exactly what he proposed to do about them.

Ahmed Zia, the manager of the Go Easy Go Getaway travel agency in Finsbury Park, was MI5's problem. It was ironic that Nancy Wilkins should have been instrumental in refocussing attention on the travel agency after MI5 had given the manager a clean bill of health. What was even more ironic was the fact that Simmonds had absolutely no connection with Islamic Jihad.

There was one reminder. Although Ashton had kept him posted about Landon, who had suffered serious chest injuries, he should visit him in hospital, preferably when the American girl wasn't there at the bedside holding his hand.

It was Eric Daniels, the former military policeman, who picked him up on Monday morning, having volunteered for the job, along with half a dozen other drivers, which Hazelwood found rather touching. It was also Eric Daniels who insisted on carrying the Tesco bag containing the ornate cigar box and cut-down brass shellcase up to the office because he thought it would be undignified for Hazelwood to do so.

Hazelwood was still arranging his desk when Dilys Crowther brought him a strong cup of Columbian coffee and asked if there was anything she could do for him.

'As a matter of fact there is,' he told her. 'Would you please phone that idiot in the Property Services Agency and tell him I want my pictures back.'

We do hope that you have enjoyed reading this large print book.

Did you know that all of our titles are available for purchase?

We publish a wide range of high quality large print books including:
Romances, Mysteries, Classics
General Fiction
Non Fiction and Westerns

Special interest titles available in large print are:
The Little Oxford Dictionary
Music Book
Song Book
Hymn Book
Service Book

Also available from us courtesy of Oxford University Press:
Young Readers' Dictionary
(large print edition)
Young Readers' Thesaurus
(large print edition)

For further information or a free brochure, please contact us at:
Ulverscroft Large Print Books Ltd.,
The Green, Bradgate Road, Anstey,
Leicester, LE7 7FU, England.
Tel: (00 44) 0116 236 4325
Fax: (00 44) 0116 234 0205

CRY HAVOC

Clive Egleton

Will Landon is a junior SIS officer, just important enough to represent the Service at the funeral of the head of the Asian department, who has committed suicide. Landon's job is damage limitation, and the first surprise is that the dead spy had a publicity agent of the Palestine Liberation Organization in the family. The second one is that SIS didn't know his sister-in-law even existed. So when she publicly accuses the Service of killing him, Landon braces himself for trouble — and soon finds it . . . In Florida, meanwhile, ruthlessly ambitious Jill Sheridan — the woman who means to head the Service one day — is engaged in some damage limitation of her own . . .

ONE MAN RUNNING

Clive Egleton

Trying to live as a civilian with his wife and young children in hiding, former SIS agent Peter Ashton finds himself once again thrown into the front line when his old home is blown up. Threatened by his past, Ashton determines that the safest guard for his family is himself. Meanwhile, an assassination in Russia leaves an old friend running from the Mafiozniki. With a price on her head and nowhere to go, she is desperate for Ashton's help. With no protection from SIS and all his contacts denying they've ever heard of him, Ashton is only one step ahead of the IRA terrorists who are out to retire him for good. A Peter Ashton thriller.

THE HONEY TRAP

Clive Egleton

A Queen's Messenger is tortured to death in Latin America — and Peter Ashton is once again in the front line . . . Adam Zawadzki's brutal murder shocks everyone at SIS. When Ashton starts to probe deeper into the Messenger's background and what he was carrying, he comes up against nods and winks urging him not to look too closely. Then an innocent London housewife dies during a botched burglary and the case becomes urgent. Soon, Ashton has teased out most of the actors in a baffling chain of intimidation and bribery. But can he find out how they are connected before more innocents die?